Iphigenia

THE TEXAS PAN AMERICAN SERIES

IPHIGENIA

(The diary of a young lady who
wrote because she was bored)

Teresa de la Parra

TRANSLATION BY BERTIE ACKER

INTRODUCTION BY NAOMI LINDSTROM

 University of Texas Press, Austin

Copyright © 1993 by the University of Texas Press
All rights reserved
Printed in the United States of America

First edition, 1993

Requests for permission to reproduce material from this work
should be sent to Permissions, University of Texas Press,
Box 7819, Austin, TX 78713-7819.

∞ The paper used in this publication meets the minimum
requirements of American National Standard for Information
Sciences—Permanence of Paper for Printed Library Materials,
ANSI Z39.48-1984.

LIBRARY OF CONGRESS CATALOGING-IN-PUBLICATION DATA
Parra, Teresa de la, 1895–1936.
    (Ifigenia. English)
    Iphigenia : the diary of a young lady who wrote because
she was bored / Teresa de la Parra ; translation by Bertie
Acker ; introduction by Naomi Lindstrom. — 1st ed.
        p.   cm. — (The Texas Pan American series)
    ISBN 0-292-71570-6 (alk. paper). —
    ISBN 0-292-71571-4 (pbk. : alk. paper)
    I. Title.   II. Series.
PQ8549.P35I413 1993   93-17895
863—dc20

This English version of Iphigenia *is dedicated with gratitude to all those who have offered me their help and encouragement: Naomi Lindstrom, at the University of Texas at Austin, and Theresa J. May, my editor at the University of Texas Press, who together gave me the opportunity to work with a novel I have long admired, and whose faith and patience have been unfailing; Imajean Gray and Patricia McKinney, who made corrections and suggestions; Joan McInerney, who gave me good advice; my daughter Ruth Bilbo, who also proofed parts of the novel and at whose dining room table the first hesitant passages of this long adventure were transcribed; my daughters Barbara and Phyllis and to everyone who has shown me such trust and patience during the four-year gestation of* Iphigenia.

Contents

Introduction

BY NAOMI LINDSTROM

 The novel *Iphigenia* by Teresa de la Parra (Venezuela, 1889–1936; real name, Ana Teresa Parra Sanojo), popular with readers since its first appearance, scandalous in its day, has increasingly won the respect and attention of literary critics.

Its author was a well-read, socially prominent young woman whose wit, winning presence, elegance, and above all her powers of verbal expression had placed her in demand on the Caracas scene as a speaker at social, diplomatic, and cultural events. She possessed a talent for writing pieces on demand for notable occasions. As was typical for a woman of her time, place, and social class, she had had to pursue on her own the extensive literary learning that she later put to good use in her celebrated novels.

From the outset of her career, the public was very insistent in attributing special qualities of femininity to de la Parra and her speech and writing. At the same time, the author often appeared to invite such an attribution by employing a type of writing that her public would tag as feminine. She exhibited in her work a preference for intimate and domestic subject matter, a mannered style of somewhat whimsical, teasing humor, and, broadly, a chatty, gossipy mode. Her first publications, the journalistic pieces she began publishing in 1915, were certainly in this vein. A critic dubbed her "Miss Frivolity" and her choice of a pseudonym, Fru-Fru, is a good clue that she had reached a similar judgment about her own work.[1] The issue of a discourse certain to be perceived as feminine is an important one in her first full-length novel, *Iphigenia*. (Between her early journalism and her famous novel, de la Parra had pseudonymously published two short narratives with Oriental themes and backdrops.) *Iphigenia* makes a more purposeful use of a hyper-feminine discourse. The heroine, María Eugenia, is given to gushing, and her themes frequently run to personal adornment, household decor and entertainment, domestic intrigues and politics, and amorous involvements. This time, though, there is an important shift: the heroine's speech is utilized to make a critical examination of women, their role, and their ability to speak of important issues. The author had witnessed the spread of feminism in European intellectual circles and had considered how this movement might apply to the Spanish American context, particularly among women who had little if any chance to study progressive social thought. She found especially worrisome the case of young women who had, through travel or hearsay, glimpsed the possibility of greater freedom for women, but remained in a cloistered, sheltered environment. These concerns appear in *Iphigenia (The diary of a young lady who wrote because she was bored)*, a novel whose five hundred manuscript pages were begun in 1922 and completed in less than a year. As de la Parra finished chapters, they appeared serialized in both Spanish- and French-language literary magazines. *Iphigenia* appeared in its entirety as a book in 1924. When the first completed chapter appeared in the Caracas *La Lectura Semanal* (Weekly Reading), the magazine sold out its print run of six thousand on the day of publication,[2] and *Iphigenia* has often been reprinted in book form.

Encouraged by the book's first-person form (the early pages are an immensely lengthy, soul-baring letter to an intimate friend; those that follow are a diary), the public tended to view *Iphigenia* as the direct, confessional outpourings of its author, unmediated by artistry or by critical, satirical awareness. Many readers of the novel without hesitation identified the author with her excitable, daydreaming heroine, María Eugenia Alonso. The linkage of the two is not entirely rational, since the author, who was much in the public eye, was known as an accomplished literary intellectual who could find the right words for any occasion. Her heroine, in contrast, is a half-educated young woman, confused by personal vanity and romantic fantasies, often floundering in her efforts to express a critical outlook on society and personal relations. De la Parra was well aware of the widespread perception of her work as a "confession" and complained that her readership was insensitive to its strong ironic component.[3]

María Eugenia is a young woman of the upper class, though she has been despoiled of her fortune and now is seen as needing a wealthy match. She inhabits almost exclusively the personal and private sphere and has only the most tenuous notions of the feminism developing in the world at large. When, in her long letter, María Eugenia reminisces to a schoolmate about her education, *Iphigenia* offers a sharply satirical look at the options for learning open to the daughters of good families of Caracas. Despite her sketchy intellectual background, María Eugenia is intelligent and independent-minded enough, and eager enough to attain pleasure in life, to begin to develop her own version of feminism based on her experiences and observations. She can draw upon these insights to analyze, sometimes rather ingenuously and sometimes with surprising sophistication and humor, the situations in which she finds herself. María Eugenia's ability to set her new insights down in effective words fluctuates widely throughout the novel. In some passages she melodramatizes her own plight and falls into a self-indulgent lyricism; in others, she is a sharp observer of individual and collective behavior, as able to mock herself as to satirize those around her. From time to time she bursts into a stiffly didactic speech on society and morals; the reader must sympathize with her ardor even while cringing at the awkwardness of her expression.

For all María Eugenia's intelligence, it is a difficult task for her to generate a critical feminist analysis out of the scanty materials she has at hand. One of the fascinating aspects of the novel is that the reader frequently observes María Eugenia faltering and blundering in her efforts to think and act with a new freedom. In her mind, liberation is often confused with simply getting her own way. At various times in the course of the novel, the heroine appears to associate personal liberation with the wearing of low-necked gowns, dancing "American dances" in public, associating with worldly friends, and coming and going at less restricted hours and unchaperoned. María Eugenia persists in her reading despite the disapproval it raises in her household; yet, she reads only for pleasure and it never occurs to her to undertake a program of study.

The limited range of María Eugenia's aspirations not only has made this heroine seem frivolous to readers, as indeed she often is, but has at times brought the same judgment down on the entire book. Amaya Llebot, for instance, complains in 1974: "What's regrettable is that Teresa de la Parra, an intelligent and well-educated woman, raised in Europe, should limit herself to showing that oppression and only fight it in the name of banal and superficial motives."[4] To state a perhaps self-evident point, readers of *Iphigenia* need to keep in mind that the heroine's thoughts and writing, which range from romantic effusion to petty gossip to stilted attempts at serious analysis, are all intended as the expression of a very young woman not well prepared to understand and comment upon the events surrounding her.

María Eugenia is partially successful in learning to articulate her concerns, but she finds no opportunity to create change. By the end of the novel, she faces only a choice between marriage to a family-approved candidate certain to make his spouse unhappy and life as the mistress of an appealingly imaginative and romantic, but married, man. In the sacrifice prefigured in the title, she must weigh her aspirations for freedom and personal pleasure against her need for security. Readers who have built up their hopes that María Eugenia will break free of her constricting environment will be especially horrified by those pages in which the heroine expresses satisfaction over her own domination by her stodgy fiancé, although María Eugenia quickly recovers from this paroxysm of submission. In the final passages, de la Parra has no scruples about resorting to melodramatic twists and turns as the heroine swings back and forth between her alternatives.

The link between the Greek myth of Iphigenia, particularly as Euripides elaborated it in his *Iphigenia in Aulis*, and the story of María Eugenia is charged with more of de la Parra's ironies. In an obvious contrast, Iphigenia's sacrifice gives her heroic stature, while María Eugenia's turns her into a figure of capitulation. Iphigenia offers herself to be sacrificed in order to bring justice and glory to Greece, while María Eugenia's motive is a desire for comfort and security. But even so, parallelisms emerge: in both Iphigenia's story and María Eugenia's, there is a comment on a society's willingness to sacrifice the well-being of its daughters. María Eugenia is a disappointing Iphigenia, but the reader is supposed to experience disillusionment over the outcome of the heroine's conflict. The important point is that the disappointment be aimed, not at the protagonist who was struggling spiritedly in an unsupportive environment, but at the society that headed her toward surrender.

While de la Parra was the object of a widespread public fascination during the time she was writing and serializing *Iphigenia*, she became the target of negative criticism after the book was published. While the complaints were many and varied—some local readers felt that Caracas was not described in its proper beauty—the dominant objection was that the novel was immoral and might harm young female readers. A number of readers were offended that the heroine considered her respectable marriage a defeat in life and criticized her as a light-minded creature obsessed with showing off her beauty and seeking pleasure. De la Parra vigorously defended her book; among other arguments, she stated that the book's detractors were men, while women readers recognized the accuracy of *Iphigenia*'s vision of society.

Teresa de la Parra has been coming in for a rediscovery in recent years, principally for *Iphigenia* but also for her 1929 *Las memorias de Mamá Blanca*. Translated into English as *Mama Blanca's Souvenirs* (1959), the later novel offers a more lyrical and celebratory treatment of the culture of traditional upper-class women. Here a household full of women, with their feminine occupations and their intimate conversations, is nostalgically recalled by a narrator now well into adulthood.

Perhaps because of its genteel setting, upper-class heroine, and the subtly ironic way it presents ideas, *Iphigenia* was not fully perceived as a work of social criticism until after the 1960s–1970s resurgence of feminism, which affected the reading of many existing literary texts. The novel is now especially prized for its early recognition that Latin American women living in conservative environments, while no less in need of change than their counterparts in fast-moving European and U.S. cities, would necessarily approach the issues of women's role and status from a different background and perspective and face a different set of obstacles.

NOTES

1. The source of this information is Louis Antoine Lemaître's biography *Between Flight and Longing: The Journey of Teresa de la Parra* (New York: Vantage Press, 1986), p. 60.

2. Ibid., p. 65.

3. Laura M. Febres, *Cinco perspectivas críticas sobre la obra de Teresa de la Parra* (Caracas: Editorial Arte, 1984), p. 14.

4. Amaya Llebot, cited in Febres, *Cinco perspectivas*, p. 15.

Translator's
Note

 *Girls are not meant to know*
about such things . . .
It's better for young girls
not to be seen . . .
— EURIPIDES, *Iphigenia at Aulis*

Iphigenia takes the form of a long letter and a journal written by an adolescent girl, María Eugenia Alonso, born in Venezuela but reared by her father in France. When her father suddenly dies, María Eugenia returns to Caracas to live with her grandmother and aunt, and there she is plunged into a culture that is totally foreign to her. She must observe years of strict mourning and suffer isolation and loneliness locked up in her grandmother's home. The novel is a tender and sensitive account of a girl growing up in the austere seclusion demanded by the moral code in South America during the first quarter of the twentieth century.

The novel created a sensation. The author, Teresa de la Parra, became the darling of the so-called Generation of '98 in Spain, and her work was especially praised by the great author and philosopher Miguel de Unamuno. The book won the annual prize of ten thousand francs given by the Casa Editora Franco-Ibero-Americana in Paris in 1924 and two translations in French appeared very soon thereafter. Because of the book's instant popularity, dealers had difficulty obtaining enough copies for their customers. But the general reaction in Spanish America was public outrage because of *Iphigenia*'s stinging feminist viewpoint. It had the effect of a bomb hurled by a revolutionary and created shock waves in patriarchal Venezuelan society. The author was accused of undermining the morals of young women, and the majority of critics dismissed this important novel as "strident." However, the reading public has kept *Iphigenia* alive over seven decades. New editions have appeared regularly, some perhaps pirated. One book copies another, following even the typographical errors, scrambled lines of text, and omissions. The novel's continued popularity tells us that María Eugenia has lost none of her appeal for readers today.

Although María Eugenia claimed to be bored, we will never find her story dull. Her intimate confessions follow the inner drama of an immature child with no experience of the world as she gradually discovers herself and forges her own identity, coming to terms with the injustices that confront her. She is an inimitable character, in her own way as unique as Madame Bovary or Don Quixote, with whom some critics have compared her. Not only is the novel a psychological study of great depth and universality, it is often funny, frivolous, and philosophical. Yet it is above all a powerful tragedy. Despite feeling alone, the heroine is very much a part of a society that determines the course of her life, and *Iphigenia*, like Euripides's classic play, paints a world that makes women its sacrificial victims.

We know from her correspondence that Teresa de la Parra was eager to have *Iphigenia* translated into English. She discussed its publication with several people, expressing her concern that the novel was too long or might need revision, and she gave her translators and publishers broad discretion to cut and adapt both her novels. Unfortunately, the original manuscript of *Iphigenia* was lost in Paris during the occupation, according to information which Teresa's niece, Elia Pérez Luna, very kindly offered me. In the second edition Teresa de la Parra made corrections, additions, and deletions, and this version was made available by Velia Bosch in 1982, when Biblioteca Ayacucho published her collection of Parra's works. (Biblioteca Ayacucho will soon republish *Teresa de la Parra, Obra*.) Unaware of this version, I compared six editions of the novel in making this translation and found that in some, passages appear that do not exist in others. I also found some strange discrepancies whose origin can only be surmised. At first, every effort was made to include everything, even when the material seemed out of character. Finally, I have opted to omit a few lines that seem foreign to the text as a whole, especially if they were not a part of the second edition. There was also the problem of how to deal with the discrepancies. In one text, for example, a lady wears a diamond solitaire ring, in another she wears an opal, and in another she wears no ring at all. I tried to choose the most logical alternative wherever such differences appear.

The Caracas of 1924 has vanished and society everywhere has undergone radical changes, but we can enter that lost time and place where María Eugenia, in the pages of *Iphigenia*, is still young, vibrant, and rebellious. I find it an honor to introduce her and her world to English readers. In spite of the inevitable shortcomings of this translation, María Eugenia is sure to win the hearts of those who peek into her diary!

BERTIE ACKER

Iphigenia

*To you, dear absent one, in whose
shadow this book flowered little by
little. To that clear light from your
eyes that always lit the writing
with hope, and also, to the white,
cold peace of your two crossed
hands that will never turn its
pages, I dedicate this book.*

Mother,

*To you I dedicate this book which belongs to you,
since it was from you that I learned to admire the
spirit of sacrifice above all things. In its pages you
will see yourself, Grandmother, Old Aunty, and Don
Ramón himself, with all the attendant discussions
against rebellious speech.*

*Learn from it how great a distance lies between what is
said and what is done, so that you may never fear the
arguments of revolutionaries, if they bear within their
souls the mirror of example and the roots of tradition.*

*Close your eyes to one or another case of nudity;
remember that you gave birth to all of us with very
little clothing; you dressed us. Dress these pages too
with white skirts of indulgence.*

I embrace you with all my heart,

ANA TERESA

Paris, July, 1925

(Dedication Teresa de la Parra wrote in the copy of the
first edition of *Iphigenia* that she gave to her mother.)

 *A Very Long Letter
Wherein Things Are Told
As They Are in Novels*

From María Eugenia Alonso
to Cristina de Iturbe

 At last I'm writing to you, dear Cristina! I don't know what you must have thought of me. When we said goodbye on the station platform in Biarritz, I remember that I, full of sorrow, sighs, and packages, told you while I hugged you, "I'll write soon, soon, very soon!"

I was planning to write you a long letter from Paris and I had already started drafting it in my mind. However, since that memorable day, more than four months have gone by and except for postcards I haven't written you a word. Have you at least received my last postcards? I ask because I didn't mail them personally and I don't know if the people I sent really mailed them.

Actually, I can't tell you why I didn't write from Paris, and much less why I didn't write you later, when, radiant with optimism and looking like a very elegant Parisian, I was sailing for Venezuela on the transatlantic steamer *Manuel Arnús*. But, I will confess, because I know it all too well, that if I still haven't written you from here, from Caracas, the city where I was born, even when time has weighed on me horribly, it was a pure and simple question of hurt and pride. I know how to lie very well when I talk, but I don't know how to lie when I write, and since I didn't want to tell you the truth for anything in the world, because it seemed very humiliating to me, I had decided to say nothing. But now I've decided that the truth to which I refer is not humiliating, but instead is picturesque, interesting, and somewhat medieval. Therefore, I have resolved to confess everything openly, trusting you are capable of hearing the pain that cries out in my words.

Oh, Cristina, Cristina, how bored I am! Look, no matter how you try you can't imagine how bored I've been this past month, locked up in this house of Grandmother's, which smells of jasmine, damp earth, wax candles, and Elliman's Embrocation. The smell of wax comes from two candles, that Aunt Clara has burning continuously before a Jesus of Nazareth dressed in purple velvet, about a foot-and-a-half high, which since the remote days of my great-grandmother has been walking, carrying his cross, under a sort of glass dome or bell jar. The smell of Elliman's Embrocation is due to Grandmother's rheumatism, for she rubs it on every night before going to bed. As for the smell of jasmine and wet earth, which are the most pleasant of all, they come from the entrance patio, which is wide, square, and full of roses, palm trees, ferns, geraniums, and a huge jasmine vine that spreads out green and very thick on its wire arbor where it grows like a heaven full of jasmine stars. But oh! How bored I am breathing these odors singly or combined, while I watch Grandmother and Aunt Clara sew or I listen to them talk. It's beyond explanation. Out of delicacy and tact, when I am with them I hide my boredom and then I chat; I laugh; and I show off the tricks of Chispita, the woolly lapdog, who has now learned to sit up with her two front paws bent very gracefully, and who, from what I have observed, in this system of imprisonment in which they are holding us both, constantly dreams of liberty and is as bored as I or even more so.

Naturally, Grandmother and Aunt Clara, who know how to distinguish very well the woven threads of fine drawnwork or lace, but who absolutely can't see the things that are hidden behind appearances, have no idea of the cruel and stoic magnitude of my boredom.

Grandmother has this very false and out-of-date principle deeply rooted in her mind, "If people get bored it's because they're not intelligent." And of course, as my intelligence constantly shines forth and it's impossible to doubt it, Grandmother consequently deduces that I am amusing myself at all times in relation to my intellectual capacity, that is to say, very much. And I let her believe it for the sake of delicacy.

Oh! How many times I have thought in an acute crisis of boredom, "If I told Cristina this, it would relieve me so much." But, for a whole month I have lived a prisoner to my pride as well as a prisoner within the four old walls of this house. I wanted you to imagine wonders about my present life, and, a recluse in my double prison, I was silent.

Today setting aside all pretense of pride, I'm writing to you because I can't keep quiet any longer, and because, as I have told you, I have recently discovered that this situation of living walled in, as pretty as I am, far from being humiliating and vulgar, on the contrary, is like a tale of chivalry or the legend of a captive princess. And see, sitting now in front of this white sheet of paper, I feel so delighted with my decision, and my desire to write you is so, so great, that I could wish as the poem says "that the sea were ink and the beaches paper."

But my immense need to write you has other causes also. One of them is, of course, my great affection for you; another is the dreadfully sad conviction that I will never see you again. As for the third, much more complicated than the other two, I will explain to you in words that will serve as an exordium or introduction to what I plan to write, because I don't want this letter where I will pour out my heart to ever seem impromptu or ridiculous to you.

As you know, Cristina, I have always been quite fond of novels. You are, too, and I now believe that without a doubt it was our common interest in the theater and novels that caused us to become such close friends during the vacation months, just as during the school year a common interest in our studies drew us together.

You and I were obviously intellectual and romantic little girls, but we were also abnormally timid. Sometimes I've reflected on this feeling of timidity, and I now believe we must have acquired it by seeing our reflections in the glass of the windows and doors at school, with our wide foreheads, bare and framed by the black semicircle of our poor straight hair pulled back so tightly. As you will recall, this last requirement was indispensable, in the opinion of the Mothers, to the good name of the girls, who, besides being very tidy, were intelligent and studious as we two were. I became convinced that straight hair really constituted a great moral superiority, and yet, I always looked with great admiration at the other girls whose heads, "empty inside," as the Mothers said, had on the outside that attractive appearance that came from the curls and waves they used in defiance of all the rules. In spite of our mental superiority, I remember that I always basically felt very inferior to the ones with loose hair. Heroines in novels also were placed in this group of girls with their temples covered, which clearly constituted what the Mothers called with great disdain "the world." We, together with the Mothers, the chaplain, the twelve daughters of Mary, the saints of the Christian year, incense, chasubles, and prayer benches, belonged to the other group. In reality I never had true partisan enthusiasm. That wicked "world" so abhorred and despised by the Mothers, in spite of its vile inferiority, always appeared dazzling and full of prestige in my eyes. Our moral superiority was a kind of burden to me, and I recall that I always bore it filled with resignation; thinking sadly that, thanks to it, I would never perform anything except obscure and secondary roles in life.

What I want to explain to you is that in these four months I have completely altered my ideas. I think I have switched bag and baggage to the abominable band of the world and I feel that I have acquired an elevated rank in it. I no longer consider myself a secondary character at all. I am quite satisfied with myself, and I have declared myself on strike against shyness and humility; I have, moreover, the presumption to believe that I am worth a million times more than all the heroines in the novels we used to read in the summer—novels which, by the way, must have been very poorly written.

In these four months, Cristina, I have lived through many periods of sadness, I have had some disagreeable impressions, some revelations that caused despair, and, nonetheless, in spite of everything, I feel an immense joy because I have seen a new personality emerging in myself that I didn't suspect and that fills me with satisfaction. You and I—all of us who, moving through the world, have some talents and some sorrows—are heroes and heroines in the novels of our own lives, which is nicer and a thousand times better than written novels.

It is this thesis that I am going to develop before your eyes, relating to you in minute detail and as they do in authentic novels, everything that has happened to me since you disappeared from view in Biarritz. I'm sure that my story will interest you greatly. Besides, I have lately discovered that I have a gift for observation and great ease in expressing myself. Unfortunately these gifts have been worthless to me up to the present. Sometimes I have tried to demonstrate them to Aunt Clara and Grandmother, but they can't appreciate them. Aunt Clara hasn't even taken the trouble to notice them. As for Grandmother, since she's very old she has some terribly old-fashioned ideas; and yes, she has noticed my abilities, because twice she's told me that my head is full of bugs. As you can understand, this is one of the reasons why I'm bored in this big, dreary house, where no one admires or understands me, and it is my need to feel understood that decidedly has spurred me to write you.

I know very well that you will understand me. I feel no reserve or embarrassment at all in sharing my most intimate confidences with you. In my eyes you have the sweet prestige of a past that will never return. Any secrets I may tell you can have no disagreeable consequences in my future life and, therefore, I already know that I'll never repent having told them to you. Yes, in our future they will be like the secrets that are buried with the dead. As for the very great affection that it takes to write you my secrets, I think that it is rather like the tardy flowering of tenderness, when we think about those who have gone, "never to return."

🙠   🙠   🙠

I'm writing in my room whose double doors I've locked. My room is big and bright, its wallpaper is sky blue, and it has a window with bars that faces the second patio of the house. Outside the window, right up against the bars, there is an orange tree, and beyond, at each corner of the patio, there are other orange trees. Since I have placed my desk and my chair very close to the window, while I think with my head reclining against the back of the chair, or leaning my elbows on the white surface of the desk, I am always looking at my patio with the orange trees. And I have thought so much, gazing up, that I now know even the tiniest detail of the green filigree against the blue sky.

Now, before starting my story, without looking at orange trees, or sky, or anything, I've closed my eyes for an instant, I have locked my hands over them, and very clearly, for a few seconds, I've seen you again, just as you were when you faded in the distance there, on the station platform in Biarritz: first walking, then running beside the window of my coach as it moved away, and then your hand, and finally your handkerchief, which was waving to me: Goodbye! . . . Goodbye! . . .

Oh, that handkerchief that waved goodbye, Cristina! Its whiteness has remained eternally imprinted in our minds, as if to help us weep for these painful and definitive separations! . . .

I remember very well that when I could no longer see you, I moved back from the window, and that way, at a distance, I stood still awhile watching the accelerated racing of the houses and posts, which I finally turned my back on; I then sat down on the seat, and I saw a mirror in front of me in the coach, and I saw my poor little face so sad, so pale, swathed in the black of mourning, so that I was intensely conscious for the first time of how alone I was. I remembered girls in orphanages and I seemed to see myself as a symbol of the orphan. Then I had a moment of anguish, a kind of horrible choking, feeling that I wanted to burst out in sobs and pour a torrent of tears from my eyes. But suddenly I looked at Madame Jourdan—do you remember Madame Jourdan? She was that distinguished lady, with gray hair, who at the hotel had the table next to ours and who then took charge of accompanying me to Paris. Well, I looked at Madame Jourdan out of the corner of my eye. She was sitting at the far end of the coach, and I saw that she was studying me with curiosity and pity. As I realized this I suddenly reacted and the storm dissipated. And at that moment, as now, as always, I am more or less the same as when you knew me. I never cry in spite of having every reason to cry oceans. Maybe because sorrow always hovers over me, I have learned to hide it from everyone, with an instinctive reaction, as some poor children hide their worn shoes from people who are rich and well dressed.

Fortunately, Madame Jourdan, who turned out to be a charming person, managed, little by little, to distract my sadness with her conversation. She began by asking me about you. At first, seeing us always together and speaking Spanish, she had taken us for sisters. Then when they told her about Papa's sudden death and asked her if she would like to chaperone me to Paris, she began to take a very lively interest in me. She had lost a little girl, her only daughter, and the child, then five years old, would now have been about our age. She asked me how old I was. When I told her that I had just turned eighteen, she answered, breaking her phrases with heartfelt sighs, "The world is a puzzle with no solution! . . . The pieces are scattered and no one can fit them together! . . . I am entering the desert of my old age so alone, because I lost my daughter, and you are marching into that great battle of youth without the support and shelter of your Mother! . . ."

That part about the "desert of her old age" and about "the great battle of youth" she said in such a beautiful way and with such a soft and harmonious voice, that I suddenly started feeling great admiration for her. I remembered the actresses who filled both you and me with an almost frenetic enthusiasm because of their commanding voices and the grace of their movements. I thought Madame Jourdan must be like them, that without a doubt she was very intelligent, that perhaps she might be an artist, one of those novelists who write under a pseudonym. Abandoning my seat and my window, impelled by the most lively and reverent admiration, I went to sit next to her.

At first and in view of her superiority, I felt somewhat timid, somewhat inhibited, but I began to talk to her, and then I told her that I was going on a long trip, that I was coming to America where I had my maternal grandmother and some aunts and uncles and cousins who loved me very much. Then we chatted about travel, about different climates, about the beauty of nature in the tropics, about the gaiety of life aboard a transatlantic steamer, and within two hours, my earlier timidity now forgotten, Madame Jourdan and I were such friends and we got along so well, that it seemed to me I had fitted together some of my personal puzzle. Believe me, Cristina, and this, of course, I wouldn't want Grandmother to know, I would willingly have stayed there to live forever with that delightful Madame Jourdan!

But unfortunately the trip ended, the time came when we reached Paris and then she had to deposit me with my new chaperons, Mr. and Mrs. Ramírez, who were a Venezuelan couple and close friends of my family; definitively checked into their hands, I was left in their care as far as La Guaira.

I immediately liked the Ramírezes because they were happy, obliging, kind, and because they had the admirable custom of never giving me any kind of advice. This latter is quite a rare thing, since generally, as you, too, must have noticed, it is through this system of advice that those superior in age, dignity, or government are in the habit of venting their bad temper, telling us, poor inferiors, the harshest and most unpleasant things in the world.

Mr. and Mrs. Ramírez lived in a very elegant hotel. When I arrived in the company of Madame Jourdan, they came out to receive me affectionately and attentively. After the prescribed introductions, they started out by expressing their sympathy for my situation, something which apparently is *de rigueur* when dealing with me. Then they talked to me about Caracas, about my family, about our coming trip, and they ended by turning over to me about twenty thousand francs, sent by my uncle and guardian to cover expenses of my toilette and pocket money, they supposed, since the money for the travel expenses had already been sent.

Well, you may call me mercenary if you like, but I can't deny that with that unexpected twenty thousand francs, the gloomy thoughts I'd had on the train went flying away like a flock of swallows, because I judged myself fortunate and independent.

Moreover, Mr. Ramírez, who had lived in New York for many years, told me that during the time we were to remain in Paris, he saw no reason why I shouldn't go out alone, unless, of course, his wife and I happened to be going the same way.

Naturally I decided right then not ever to be going the same way as Mrs. Ramírez, and here, as you will see, my experiences, impressions, and adventures begin.

You don't know how interesting it is to travel, Cristina! Not short trips on the train, like those you and I used to take in the summer during the vacation months; no, I mean long trips, like this one of mine, when you can go out alone in Paris, and you meet a lot of people, and you cross the ocean, and you stop at different ports. The only bad part about these trips is that, as with all trips, one must arrive eventually, and when you arrive—oh, Cristina, when you arrive it is like when the coach you were riding in stops or when the music that was lulling you to sleep fades into silence. How sad it is to arrive anywhere forever! . . . I think it must be for that reason that death frightens us, don't you agree?

Going back to my first meeting with Mr. and Mrs. Ramírez, I must tell you that since the day Papa died it hadn't occurred to me that I was what might be called an independent person, more or less mistress of myself and of my actions. Up until then I had considered myself something like an object that people pass about, lend or sell to each other. That is what we young ladies of "proper upbringing" generally and sadly are! And that is what I have become again here in Caracas.

It was Mr. Ramírez with the twenty thousand francs, and the permission to go out alone, who suddenly revealed to me that delicious sensation of liberty. I recall that the very night of my arrival in Paris, I was sitting alone in the hotel lobby, facing a group of people who, at a distance from me, were talking among themselves. Overflowing with optimism and with a certain prophetic spirit, I began to fully savor my future liberty. Isolated as I was before the happy and animated scene, I gazed at myself for a long time in a mirror, as I often do, and I suddenly observed that, without your support and without your company, my schoolgirl simplicity or air of a timid miss looked horribly conspicuous, awkward, and ridiculous. I said to myself that with twenty thousand francs and a little ingenuity it was possible to do a lot. Then I thought that I might well leave my whole family in Caracas *épaté* with my Parisian elegance. I finally deduced that in order to do so it was indispensable to wear more form-fitting dresses and to cut my hair *a la garçonne*, just like a certain lady who at that moment stood out in the group in front of me because of her very lovely figure.

And without further hesitation, my mind was made up.

The following day, very early in the morning, I went to buy some flowers and with them in my hand I went to the home of my dear friend from the train, Madame Jourdan. She received me warmly, as if we had known each other all our lives and as if it had been a century since we'd seen each other. She had an adorable house, decorated with exquisite taste, which contributed to the fact that my admiration and appreciation continued growing *en crescendo*. I explained to her that I had decided to cut my hair, because I intended to return to my country as a truly chic and stylish person. She was very amiable and helpful, and started giving me advice about my toilette and about tasteful style. She recommended dressmakers, milliners, hairdressers, manicurists, and a multitude of other things. She offered to help me in all kinds of ways in the future, too, and under her direction I began my campaign that very afternoon.

Then I wish you could have seen what excitement—all the coming and going—what days I spent! And above all, what a change! I no longer had that droopy schoolgirl air, like a *chien fouetté*, don't you know? I looked wonderful with short hair. The dressmakers thought I had a marvelous figure, very willowy, and as I tried on clothes, they constantly said, "Comme Mademoiselle est bien faite!"

That was something I verified instantly, turning in every direction in front of the three-way mirrors, causing me an infinitely greater satisfaction than the cross for the week, the ribbon or the first place in composition, and all of that great reputation for intelligence which you and I shared in our classes.

Once I fell in love with a black toque that the milliner told me was only worn by widows, and that seemed charming to me. Within a few days, I was going about wearing my toque with its long black veil. They called me "Madame" in the stores, and one day when I went to a shoe store with the youngest of the Ramírezes' children, a darling three-year-old, someone said I must have married very young to have that adorable child who looked just like me. If that were true, I began figuring that given Luisito Ramírez's age he would have been born when you and I were in the tenth grade. Imagine how the nuns would have been scandalized and how much fun we would have had with a little tot then. Surely we would have been forced to hide him in our desks as we used to do with boxes of candy.

But certainly then, with my toque and my assumed widowhood, Paris seemed something new and unknown to me. It was no longer that foggy, cold city where, on Christmas vacations, you and I would trudge, holding hands and followed by our English governess while we trotted to matinees at the Opera or the French Theater. Everything used to intimidate me then. Elegant ladies gave me a feeling of fear and I felt so little, so mousey, beside such beauty and such luxury. Now I didn't; now I had been touched by the magic wand; I moved easily, surely, and very gracefully, because I knew all too well that that "Comme Mademoiselle est bien faite!" was being expressed loudly and with exclamation marks by the eyes of everyone who looked at me. It was such a general phenomenon that I was enchanted. Everybody admired me. My friends Mr. and Mrs. Ramírez admired me; their children admired me; some very nice Spaniards who had the table facing ours in the dining room admired me. Others who admired me were the hotel manager, the waiter at our table, the elevator boy, the manicurist's husband, the clerks at the hairdressing salon, and a very elegant gentleman I saw one morning on the street who said to his companion as he saw me approach, "Regardez donc, quelle jolie fille!"

Decidedly, in those glorious days, Paris suddenly opened her arms and received me as her daughter, just like that, all at once, just because. Oh! It was unquestionable! I now formed a part of that troop of women whom Papa used to evoke, half-closing his eyes with a strange expression which I couldn't quite understand then, because it was as if he were talking about some very rich sweet, as he said, "What women!!"

Nothing like that had ever happened to me, Cristina. I felt a wild joy within myself. It seemed to me that my soul had burst into bloom like those trees in the school park in the months of April and May. It was as if I had suddenly discovered a mine in myself, a spring bubbling with optimism and I lived only to drink from it and to see my reflection in it. I believe that it was because of that selfish satisfaction that I never wrote to you, except for laconic postcards that you answered with inexpressive, sad letters. Today, as I reread them, they seem to communicate all your bitter disillusionment and I am contrite. But I think by now you must have understood the reason for my indifference, which was as fleeting as my joy and I think that you generously must have forgiven me for both.

Sometimes, too, I would think that the optimism and joy of life that made me so happy were improper so soon after a recent bereavement like mine. Then I would suffer periods of sharp remorse, and to quiet my guilt and apologize to Papa's spirit, I would give a few francs to some ragged child or go in and leave an offering in the charity box of a church . . .

Oh, Papa! Poor Papa! There, in the gentle visions of my mind, I see your indulgent face, beautified by the approving indulgence of your smile. How well I recognize it! . . . Yes, how could my happiness anger you! Those brief days, when your prodigal and jovial spirit seemed to be reborn for a moment in my soul, were the only inheritance that you were to bequeath me! . . .

❧　　　　　　❧　　　　　　❧

We stayed in Paris for almost three months, due to a delay in funds and a change of the Ramírezes' plans. The days, which individually raced by with dizzying speed, put together, seemed many and very long. I felt that they were slipping through my fingers and I had the feeling that I was running after them to hold them back. I was very preoccupied by the idea of leaving; I thought sadly that some day it would be necessary to abandon the Paris which was showing itself so kind to me, so affectionate, just as I had to abandon you, Madame Jourdan, everything I have loved and that has loved me in this life. "What a calamity! What a great misfortune!" I thought continually. And this prospect was the only thing that embittered my happy life, free as a bird whose wings have feathered at last.

But as everything comes to pass in this world, a sad day came when Mr. and Mrs. Ramírez and I finally had to pack our trunks. I put on the new travel dress I had chosen with the utmost care for the best possible cut and the greatest elegance. Holding my *nécessaire* in my hand, I strolled awhile in front of the biggest mirror in the hotel and thus verified that I looked like a very chic traveler. Then, with Mr. and Mrs. Ramírez, I took the train to Barcelona, where the transatlantic steamer *Manuel Arnús* was to take us to La Guaira.

I remember that before embarking I sent a goodbye hug to you on a postcard. I didn't write more than that because I was overwhelmed with melancholy and because I had to go buy a bottle of Guerlain liquid rouge, which they had just recommended to me highly for its ability to withstand the violent sea air that erases all powdered rouge from your skin.

Then we sailed.

Oh! My ears still seem to hear that shrill siren as the ship moved out and I get so sad when I evoke the memory that I prefer not to talk about this.

Fortunately life on board soon distracted me. It's a delicious sensation to be on the high seas, surrounded on all sides by the heavens and on your way to America. One thinks of Christopher Columbus, the novels of Jules Verne, desert islands, and mountains beneath the sea; it makes you want to be shipwrecked and to have adventures. But this geographical part is soon forgotten when you begin to enter fully into the very interesting social atmosphere on board. Well, as you know, I am not in the habit of praising myself because it seems in bad taste to me, but notwithstanding, I can't deny that from the time I boarded the ship I was aware that I was causing a great sensation among my traveling companions. Nearly all the ladies lay seasick on their deck chairs or locked in their cabins. I, who had not been seasick for a second, did nothing except parade my repertory of wraps, dresses, and gauzy shawls that I learned to tie very gracefully around my head, under the pretext of protecting it from the wind. They were my specialty: I wore a black and white one in the morning, a lilac one at noon, a gray one at night, and I strolled up and down with a book or a bottle of salts in my hand, with all the poise, grace, and distinction acquired during the days of my Parisian life and which you still have not seen me exhibit.

The men, sitting on deck, with wool berets pulled down to their ears and a cigar or cigarette in their mouths, would instantly lift their eyes from the book or magazine they were absorbed in as they saw me go by, and they would follow me awhile with a long stare full of interest. The women on the other hand admired my chic clothes and looked at them with some curiosity, I think also with some envy and as if they would like to copy them. I can't conceal from you that all this interest flattered me greatly. Didn't it represent charming *succès*, something that until then had been as distant, fabulous, and dazzling as a sun? I felt, therefore, extremely happy to confirm that I possessed such a treasure, and I confess this to you without any sort of hesitation or modesty, because I know very well that you, sooner or later—when you give up long hair, begin wearing Louis XV heels, use rouge and, above all, lipstick—will experience this, too, and therefore you aren't going to listen to me with the profound scorn of people incapable of understanding these things, such as Grandmother, the Mothers at school, and Saint Jerome, who, apparently, wrote horrors about the chic woman of his day.

After the first few hours of the crossing, I soon began to find friends besides my escorts, Mr. and Mrs. Ramírez. They were an Andalusian couple with a darling little boy who adored me; a Peruvian family; the Captain, who was very nice; the Doctor; the Purser; and naturally the small group of Venezuelans who along with us were going to La Guaira.

But the most interesting of my friends turned out to be a Colombian poet, a former diplomat, a widower, a bit old, who, full of gallantry, courtesy, and enthusiasm, accompanied me continually. At night, when they were playing or singing in the ballroom, I, considering my mourning, would avoid the merriment and would seek out some solitary spot on deck, and there, lulled by the music and with my elbows on the rail, would contemplate the fantastic reflection of the moon on the tranquil sea and the white wake we were marking on the dark blue waters. My friend, who was sensitive enough to always notice my absence, would appear beside me in a few minutes, rest his elbows too on the rail, and then softly, with a monotonous hissing of *s*'s, would recite his verses to me. This delighted me. Not because his verses were so pretty, since to tell the truth I never paid the least attention to them, but because, being free from all conversation while he recited, I could fully yield to my own thoughts and I would say to myself, "There is no doubt that he is very much in love with me." And since it was the first time this had happened to me and since the beauty of the night lent itself so well to this, I gave free rein to my memories of those novels from *La Mode Illustrée* that you and I used to read on vacation. I immediately compared myself to the novels' most interesting heroines; I considered myself on the same level with them or perhaps even higher; and naturally, I was so satisfied with such a vision that, when my friend would finish the last line of his poem, I would praise it passionately with the most enthusiastic and sincere admiration.

If the relationship between my friend and me had never gone beyond that, everything would have been fine. He would have acquired everlasting prestige in my eyes, and after we parted, I would have seen him forever in the mist of my memories, fading there, in the distance, beside the sea and the moon like a sweet dream of romance and melancholy. But, unfortunately, Cristina, men have no tact. Even if they are wiser than Solomon and older than Methuselah, they never learn that simple, easy, and elementary thing called "tact." I learned this dealing with my friend the poet/ex-diplomat on the ship, who, apparently, was very well educated, intelligent, and discreet in any subject except this matter of tact, or knowing what is fitting. But I will relate the incident from which this judgment or experience arises so that you may form your own opinion.

Imagine, one night when some national holiday or other was celebrated on board, all the passengers had drunk champagne and were therefore feeling quite happy. On the contrary, I was in a bad mood, because as I was pinning on a brooch I had torn a long scratch on my left hand, leaving it quite disfigured. Consequently, that night, with more justification than usual, while the others were amusing themselves in the ballroom, I went to lean against the rail at my solitary place on deck, and also, as usual, my friend soon came to join me. Due to my bad mood, contemplating the ocean lit by the moon, I was angrily calculating the number of days the scratch would remain on my hand and I didn't say a word. My friend, then, showing a certain delicacy, instead of throwing himself into a recitation of his poetry, questioned me gently, "What's the matter with you tonight, María Eugenia? You seem so sad."

"It's just that I scratched my left hand, and it hurts me a lot."

And since it has always seemed best to me frankly to show those physical defects which, because they are visible, cannot be hidden, I showed him my left hand with a very long red line crossing it diagonally.

He, in order to examine the scratch up close, took my hand between his hands and after saying that the wound was slight and almost imperceptible he continued gazing at the hand and added softly with the voice he used to recite, "Oh! What a divine hand! Like an Italian madonna! It might be carved in ivory by the zeal of some great Renaissance artist to awaken the faith of unbelievers. If, when I visited the Carthusian convent in Florence a year ago, I had seen a virgin with hands like these, I would have taken my vows!"

As you know, Cristina, my hands, really, aren't bad; and as you also will recall, I have always been very proud of them. The change of temperature had given them a pale tone, so that at that moment, ennobled by the moon, polished and groomed, in spite of the scratch on the left one, in truth, they deserved that praise, which, besides seeming precise, also seemed to me delicate, well chosen, and in very good taste. And in order to show off my hands even better, my vexation partly gone, I propped my elbows back on the rail, joined my hands in a languid posture, gently rested my chin on them, and continued gazing at the ocean.

"Now they look like two lilies holding a rose," my friend recited again. "Tell me, María Eugenia, haven't your cheeks ever been jealous of your hands?"

"No," I responded. "Everyone here lives in perfect harmony."

And because it seemed appropriate to give such a brief phrase some expression, without changing my pose, I half closed my eyes. With my eyes slightly narrowed, I gave my friend a long look and I smiled.

But, unluckily, as our amicable dialogue reached this point, Cristina, guess what suddenly occurred to my friend the poet! Well, it occurred to him that his ugly, ugly mouth, with his gray mustache, smelling of tobacco and champagne, might kiss mine, which at that moment was smiling, fresh, and just painted with Guerlain lipstick. Oh! But, happily, as you know, I am agile and quick to react, and thanks to that such a disagreeable plan could not be carried out; because when I suddenly felt myself imprisoned in his arms, I was overcome by fear produced by the surprise itself, and nervously moving my head in every direction, I managed to slip to one side and hurriedly escaped. Once at a distance, out of curiosity, I turned to see how this singular scene had ended, and I realized that the violent movement of my head combined with my brusque escape, had knocked the glasses off my friend's nose. He was very myopic, and therefore at that critical moment, to the pain of defeat and the pain of scorn was added the dark pain of blindness.

Oh! Cristina, no matter how long I may live, I'll never forget that short figure, in confusion, unseeing, bending over toward the deck, hopelessly searching for his lost glasses, which, from a distance, I could see gleaming quite near his feet.

From that night on I didn't speak to my great admirer and friend the Colombian poet. Not because I really felt very offended, but because after what had happened it seemed mandatory to adopt a suitable, silent, and enigmatic attitude. Certainly, locked up in my distinction and rancor, life on board ship was much less fun for me. I no longer had anyone to show his admiration for me in a gallant whisper; nor to laugh at my wit; nor to recite poetry to me in the moonlight; nor to shower me with kind attention. When I went on deck with my filmy scarf tied on my head, I sought solitude, and I stayed a long time on a high bridge sitting, facing the sea, contemplating with melancholy the persevering progress of the ship and thinking from time to time that my friend had committed that great gaffe because he had a somewhat mistaken idea about his personal appeal. I told myself that, without a doubt, he had never realized that I found his nose too big, that I thought him poorly proportioned, too old, too thin, and that relative to his poetry, the only thing I had ever appreciated about it was its monotonous rhythm that allowed my own thoughts to flow.

From that, Cristina, I deduced that men, in general, although they may appear to know a lot, it is as if they knew nothing, because, since they do not have the ability to see their own image reflected in someone's spirit, they are as totally ignorant of themselves as if they had never looked in a mirror. For that reason, when Grandmother, at the table, speaks indignantly of men today and warns me against them, calling them boastful and liars, I, far from sharing her indignation, recall my friend the poet at the moment he lost his glasses, and I smile. Yes, Cristina, no matter what Grandmother says, I think men lie in good faith, that they are braggarts because they honestly don't know themselves, and that they go through life happy and surrounded by a pious halo of error, while ridicule escorts them in silence like a faithful and invisible dog.

🐌   🐌   🐌

After sailing for eighteen days, one calm evening, at nightfall, under the half-light of the most unbelievable sunset, we entered Venezuelan waters at last.

Feeling sentimental and emotional when I heard the news, I went off to sit on my solitary bridge so that I could feel and see from above the triumphant spectacle of reaching land while hidden from everyone.

I will always remember that evening.

There are instants in life, Cristina, when our being seems to completely dematerialize, and we feel it rise exalted and sublime within us, like a visionary who speaks to us of unknown things. Then we experience a holy resignation in the face of future grief, and we also feel in our souls the flowering of past joys, much sadder than our sorrows, because in our memory they are like dead bodies that we can never decide to give up. Surely you, too, have experienced this sometimes? Haven't you ever felt this when listening to music, or looking at a landscape in the infinite tenderness of twilight? That evening, sitting on the bridge, my eyes lost on the horizon and the clouds, it seemed to me that from a tower I was watching my entire life, past and future, and I don't know why I had a dreadful presentiment of sadness.

The ship sailed slowly toward some lights that, beneath the tenuous film of clouds, were confused in the distance with the stars barely shining in the sky. Little by little the lights began to multiply and grow, as if Venus that night had wished to generously lavish herself over the sea. Then, imprecisely, hazy in the half-light and the distant fog, the dark blocks of the mountains began to separate from the sky. The happy, brilliant lights twinkled above, below, scattered across that deep sky of mountains that looked more and more familiar, more hospitable, with arms open to the ship, until suddenly, on the left side, like a fantastic illumination of fireworks, the whole sea lit up at the foot of the mountain. The passengers, leaning against the rail on deck, just under my observation point, with the joy that inspires sailors as they near a hospitable port, began to stir with an immense happiness full of voices and laughter. The lights of Macuto created that illumination, Cristina. It is our elegant beach, our fashionable watering place, the Venezuelan equivalent of Deauville or San Sebastian.

The ship, all lighted up, too, just like a lover pacing the street where his beloved lives, moved sideways, drawing closer and closer to the lights. They, with the gaiety of a celebration, sparkled and were like a thousand friendly voices that were shouting at us from the land.

The Venezuelans then, full of enthusiasm, started to surmise, "Surely from there they can see us too!"

I sank into the darkness on the bridge, silent, alone, observant, squeezed into the angle formed by two lifeboats. From my high position, watching the spectacle, I thought about a morning that I could only vaguely remember when I was very little, with curls down my back and wearing little white socks. With Papa I had boarded the ship that took us to Europe. At sight of the ocean, I had suddenly felt terror of the unknown, and when I embarked, I had grabbed my nurse's hand in fright. She was an indolent, dreamy mulatta who always took care of me with maternal affection from the day I was born, and she even took care of you sometimes, too. She died in Paris, you remember. A victim of the harsh winter.

With my eyes fixed on the multiplying lights of Macuto, I tried hard to recall Uncle Pancho's long, thin face. He was Papa's older brother, who had gone to the boat to say goodbye to us. I remembered how before it sailed he caught me in his arms and he took me all over the ship; he had told me that the furnace was a hell where the stokers, really demons, threw disobedient children who climbed on the deck railings. I remember how then he had kissed me many times, and how at last, without another word, he put me down, gave me a package of candy and a cardboard box where a golden-haired doll dressed in blue was sleeping! It had been twelve years since all that. Oh! Twelve years! Of the three travelers who departed that morning, I alone was returning. Would Uncle Pancho be there tomorrow to meet me? Maybe not. However, I had cabled my arrival, and someone surely would be waiting for me. But who? Who would it be?

Macuto was hidden again, just as it had appeared, behind a sharp bend in the coastline and soon the ship began to slow in front of the bay that forms the La Guaira port. Before dropping anchor, the boat bobbed back and forth a few minutes, stopped lazily, sheltered by the immense mountains studded with constellations of light; in the warm atmosphere it seemed to rest at last from its incessant running.

As I was saying, Cristina, there is always a sad mystery about arrivals. When a boat stops after having run for a long time, it seems that all our dreams stop too, and all our ideals fall silent. Smoothly sliding along on a vehicle is very conducive to spiritual enrichment. Why? Maybe it's because your soul, as it feels you racing without moving your feet, dreams it's flying far from the earth, completely detached from all matter. I don't know; but I remember that night well. The ship was standing still before La Guaira and I fell asleep imprisoned and sad as if they had cut down a harvest of wings in my soul.

I woke up next morning when the boat began moving in to dock. The joy of the morning seemed to pour in with a ray of sunshine that broke against the porthole window and flooded my cabin with scintillating light. As soon as I opened my eyes I looked about an instant, and as if the dazzling light and sunny brightness of the morning had evaporated all of last night's melancholy, feeling happy and curious to see new places, I ran to peek through the porthole. As the boat sailed slowly, a panorama slipped gently past. I had often heard people ponder the ugliness of the town of La Guaira. Given this preconception, the view surprised me agreeably that morning, like a smiling face we thought unknown that turns out to be the face of a childhood friend. Before my eyes, Cristina, right on the ocean's edge, a great yellow, barren mountain rose abruptly. It was flowered with little houses of every color, which seemed to clamber up and form stepping stones along the sloping bank and cliffs with the daring of a flock of goats. Vegetation sprang up at times, whimsically, among the tiny houses that hung so rashly at the edge of ravines and that had the ingeniousness and the unreal quality of those little cardboard houses that the Mothers at the college used to strew about the nativity scene at Christmas. The sight of them aroused in my heart the innocent rejoicing of the *villancicos* that every year announced the song-filled excitement of Christmas vacation. I thought with great pleasure that now I was going to abandon the monotony on board ship for the cool shade of trees and for the freedom to walk about on solid ground. I suddenly felt the immense and happy curiosity of someone awaiting great surprises, and while outside, amid the squealing of cranes and pulleys, the noisy work of disembarking began, I, in my cabin, avid to be on deck, began to dress feverishly.

I remember that I had just put my things together and was picking up my hat, when I heard Mrs. Ramírez's voice, speaking with her indolent and musical *criolla* inflections, "This way, this way! She must be dressed by now! María Eugenia! María Eugenia! Your uncle!"

When I heard these magic words I flung myself hurriedly out of the cabin, and in the narrow passageway I could see, with his back to the light, the tall and slightly stooped figure of a gentleman dressed in white linen who was advancing toward me. I was shaken again by last night's intense emotion; I thought about Papa; I felt my early childhood reborn suddenly; and emotional, weeping, I ran toward the approaching man, holding out my arms and calling to him with a cry of joy:

"Oh! Uncle Pancho! Uncle Panchito!"

He hugged me affectionately against his white shirt bosom while he answered in a slow, nasal voice, "I'm not Pancho. I'm Eduardo, your uncle Eduardo, don't you remember me?"

And taking me gently by the arm he led me out of the passageway toward the clear light on deck.

My first emotion had dissipated instantly when I realized that disagreeable quid pro quo. The impression produced by my uncle's figure in the clear light of day completed my disenchantment. That impression, Cristina, speaking quite frankly, was the most disastrous that anybody has ever produced in the eyes of another.

In the first place I must tell you that the features of my uncle and guardian Eduardo Aguirre were absolutely unknown to me. In my infancy this brother of Mama used to live with his family in a place somewhat distant from Caracas, and if I ever saw him, he made no impression on me, since I never catalogued his features in that distant collection of faces that I had always preserved in my mind, though confused and unclear, rather like portraits that have been exposed too long to bright sunshine.

Nonetheless, without knowing Uncle Eduardo by sight, I knew him very well by reference; certainly, Papa named him frequently. Every month letters arrived from Uncle Eduardo. I can still see Papa when he used to receive them. Before opening them, he would turn the envelope over and over in his slender hands, with an elegant and disapproving gesture. Those letters must have always worried him, because after reading them he would say nothing for a long time, and he was dejected and pensive. Sometimes before he could make up his mind to slit the envelope, he would look at me, and as if he wanted to relieve himself with a semiconfidence, he would softly muse, "From that imbecile Eduardo!"

Other times, he would throw the unopened letter on a table as one throws down cards after losing a game, and then, probably to vary his vocabulary—expressing the same idea nevertheless—he would ask himself this question: "What will that fool Eduardo tell me today?"

I had always attributed the depression that the letters produced in Papa to money troubles. And I attributed the names he called Uncle Eduardo, who administered his estates, to the same cause. However, the morning of my arrival, I had no sooner gone on deck, where in full light I could cast a critical eye on my uncle's person, than I immediately acquired the certainty that Papa was profoundly right when he pronounced those brief and decisive judgments every month.

But since it seems to me of interest for the future to describe Uncle Eduardo in detail, that is to say, this Uncle Eduardo of my first impression, I'm going to sketch him briefly just as I saw him that morning on board the *Arnús*.

Picture that at the short distance with which one usually chats on board ship, next to a patch of sunlight and a coil of rope, he was facing me, leaning against a rail, thin, jaundiced, stooped, very pale, with a limp mustache and with the look of someone ill and sad. I later learned that during his youth malaria had undermined his health and that now he suffers from some liver disease or other. His white linen suit hung on his skinny, ungainly body as if it had not been made for him, which gave him a very definite look of carelessness and neglect. He was talking, and as he talked he kept gesturing toward himself, in a horribly awkward way that had no rhythm nor relation whatever to what his voice was saying. His voice, Cristina, besides being nasal, was singsong, monotonous, and very peevish. I looked at him, wondering, and while I was mentally shouting, "Oh! How ugly!" I attempted, behind a friendly smile, to hide my critical appraisal, so little flattering to the one producing this bad impression. And with the objective of dissimulating even better, I began to inform myself about the whole family. I asked him about Grandmother, Aunt Clara, his wife, and his children. But it was useless. My affable interrogation was purely mechanical. My thoughts followed my eyes, and my insatiable eyes never tired of scrutinizing him from top to toe, while in my ears, full of truth and life now, I seemed to hear echoing anew Papa's words: "That imbecile Eduardo," "That fool Eduardo."

Conversing gracelessly and lifelessly, his back leaning against the rail, and with the coil of rope at his feet, he told me that everyone in the family wanted very much to see me; that with the sole objective of meeting me he had come from Caracas yesterday morning because they had announced the ship's arrival for that afternoon; that for that reason, he had spent last night in Macuto; that he had seen the ship go by around seven o'clock; that at any minute his wife and four children should show up on the dock for they had left Caracas by auto more than an hour ago; that probably Uncle Pancho Alonso would come, too, on his own because he'd heard him say something to that effect; that having certain urgent business to dispatch in La Guaira, it seemed best to him for us all to have lunch together in Macuto; that as I would see, Macuto was cool, bright, and very pretty; and that, finally, as soon as we ate we would drive up to Caracas where Grandmother and Aunt Clara were waiting for me consumed with impatience.

And while he was saying this I was looking at him with that amiable smile, judging him ugly, awkward, and poorly dressed. However, in spite of the great lying smile, my countenance must have reflected something because suddenly he said, "I came to meet you like this, you see, because here you can't wear anything but white, it's so hot! And right now I warn you that La Guaira will make a bad impression on you. It's horrible: extremely narrow streets, poorly paved, blistering sun, very hot, and," he added, lowering his voice mysteriously, "many blacks! Oh! It's horrible."

I answered with the amiable smile petrified on my lips, "It doesn't matter, Uncle, it doesn't matter. Since we'll only be passing through, it's not important!"

But I assure you, Cristina, that if we had been in the Palace of Truth, where according to legend the most intimate thoughts may be expressed without taking into consideration this exaggerated respect that we profess for the self-esteem of others, I would have replied, "Very probably La Guaira is as ugly as you say, Uncle Eduardo, and yet I am certain that its ugliness is nothing compared to yours. Yes, La Guaira must have the venerable and discreet ugliness of immobile things; and it is most certain that it doesn't gesticulate, nor dress in clothes too big, nor have a stringy mustache, nor talk through its nose. While you do, Uncle Eduardo. Unfortunately you gesture, talk, dress, and consequently, your active ugliness spreads and multiplies infinitely in each one of your movements."

But naturally, instead of this string of inadvisable opinions, I said that the plan of going to eat in Macuto seemed admirable to me; that I hoped very much they would let us disembark soon; that we had had a magnificent voyage; that moonlit nights on the high seas were a marvel; that apparently the winter in Europe would be very cold; and that in Paris skirts were getting shorter and shorter.

Eager to please me in the matter of disembarking, Uncle Eduardo went off to expedite the procedures. While I was waiting, solitary and secluded in a corner on deck, like last night, again I was absorbed in contemplating the grandiose panorama of the mountain, the sea, the scudding chalupas, the distant sails, and very near me on one side of the ship, the human activity in port.

Another boat had arrived with us and it had the whole dock busy with its loading and unloading. Because of that the bales and sacks were coming and going, noisily crossing high in the air above the narrow levee. Absentmindedly, I watched them move back and forth like strange passersby with a life of their own. Then, little by little, watching the fictitious animation of the inanimate bales and sacks, I started noticing the real force that moved them; it was the port's stevedores, nearly all half-nude mestizos or mulattos who walked slowly, bent beneath the weight of their loads. They were not really blacks as Uncle Eduardo had just said; no, none of them had the unity of characteristics or the uniformity of appearance that I had seen in pure blacks. Rather, each one individually and all as a group constituted a variegated mixture of races, where white prevailed, but distorted, as in caricatures the likeness prevails in spite of distortions. They were crossing at my feet under their burdens, stooping, sweaty, and the weariness that oppressed them didn't seem to come so much from the weight they carried on their shoulders as from an invisible weight, hidden in their own existence. It was as if, besides the bales, life itself weighed upon them. As they returned from depositing a sack, they walked indolently, with their arms drooping, in attitudes of abandonment that contained much of that somber mystery that also weighed on Uncle Eduardo's movements . . . Oh! . . . What caused such languid sorrow? . . . Could it be the influence of the heat? . . . Could it be the result of some illness? . . . Were they weary of life? . . . What was it? . . . And observing curiously, I went on looking at the scurrying humans, now wondering fearfully if the whole family, all the friends, all the relatives in Caracas would also be like Uncle Eduardo and the stevedores on the dock.

But suddenly, when I was most absorbed with the sacks, my observations, the stevedores, and my recent worry, I heard several happy clear voices calling me. I turned my head to respond to the call and I saw that the voices came from a collection of faces, fresh, pretty, and smiling, that were coming toward me preceded by Uncle Eduardo. Grateful for the happy greeting, I ran toward the group to respond to the lively voices with some lively hugs. But Uncle Eduardo judged it proper to give the meeting a certain touch of ceremony, and restraining my impulse, with a very clumsy gesture of his left hand, he said, "Wait, I'll introduce you." And he pointed out, in the order of their age:
"María Antonia,
Genaro Eduardo,
Manuel Ramón,
Cecilia Margarita,
Pedro José . . .
and . . . María Eugenia," he added pointing to me.

I then hugged them in order, wondering if that obsession or mania for double names pertained just to my family, or if it extended throughout the whole of Venezuela, or if, crossing the boundaries, it invaded all of the American continent; thanks to which for a second, between kisses and hugs, I very clearly pictured the map of South America with its shape like an elongated ham.

Since Papa never mentioned Uncle Eduardo's family, and I had never seen pictures of him, no sooner had I given out the orderly hugs than I felt that a confusion of faces and names was forming in my head, which would be impossible to sort out. They were as mixed up in my mind as a salad. However, to tell the truth, Cristina, I must confess that Uncle Eduardo's salad wasn't bad at all. The ages of my four cousins are eighteen, sixteen, fourteen, and thirteen, respectively. At that instant, animated and talkative, they were all talking to me at the same time, and, since as they talked they smiled happily with very white teeth and very black eyes, I was in a good humor and I, too, brought out all my collection of smiles and charm.

But I should clarify, to avoid confusion, that the fresh, pleasant, and well-seasoned salad only applies to my cousins, that is, the four final combinations on the list that I took the precaution of writing for you. Because at the head of the list, the combination "María Antonia" refers to my aunt by marriage, "the honorable matron" as the newspapers will call her the day of her death, the wife of Uncle Eduardo, and mother or cook-author of the salad, who, like her husband, imperiously demands the honors of a sketch, which I forthwith draw for you as well and as briefly as possible.

My aunt, María Antonia Fernández de Aguirre, is rather small, and her figure would be completely trivial and insignificant were it not for her eyes. But María Antonia, Cristina, has immense, round, very black and shiny eyes that are ringed by circles that are also immense, round, and very black, but opaque. This consortium of the enormous eyes with the enormous circles is not at all banal as I said; on the contrary, so much shiny blackness staring out of so much opaque blackness becomes something of a frightful tragedy, like those tragedies that happen in a movie when apaches armed with daggers fight in a dark room. And naturally the intense tragedy of her eyes has a direct influence on María Antonia's whole physique and personality. For example, her closed mouth is always twisting in her face, no one knows why, and the observer, seeing it like this, closed and twisted, instinctively looks for her eyes and the phenomenon is explained as he thinks: "It is the effect of tragedy." He would think the same when considering the dark shadow that like some mysterious ink seems to filter from her pupils to run softly under her skin, and he would suspect some tragedy seeing her very black hair, hearing her voice, and her words, and the sense of her words, and noting the violent and somewhat boring colors she wears. Morally María Antonia is irreproachable. I know, because Grandmother says so often, imperceptibly separating the syllables, while at the same time separating five threads of her needle work: "Ir-re-proach-a-ble." And truly, I think Grandmother is perfectly right about that. A palpable proof is the impassioned and fervent cult María Antonia professes for morality. Not her own morality, which would be horribly egotistical, but morality in general, and above all the delicate and subtle morality which is always exposed and in danger pertaining to the behavior of beautiful women. In order to preserve the integrity of this concrete aspect of morality, María Antonia possesses activity, zeal, acute vision, and a missionary ardor that is truly admirable. And here you have a synthesis of my general impression of María Antonia, her psychology and her eyes, just as they were revealed to me for the first time that morning and just as I have continued observing them since then. Uncle Pancho Alonso, who can say highly absurd things, refers to her qualities this way,

"María Antonia's eyes are fine. They remind you a lot of a pair of brand new patent leather boots, and they seem to be made from some inflammable material, burning and dangerous, something that oscillates between dynamite and what the general public calls black envy. Oh, yes indeed, very black, very clean, very brilliant, very well polished!"

Of course, Cristina, I don't accept these shoemaker's terms when talking about eyes, and I beg you not to take it into consideration either. It's Uncle Pancho's nonsense that, along with his barbed witticisms, mixes and confuses everything.

When my cousins and I ended our mutual greetings and courtesies, we went to see the ship. We covered it several times in different directions and when we felt tired, overheated, and very good friends, we disembarked. While we were still standing outside the doors of Customs, waiting for who knows what, suddenly, like a bolt from the blue, enveloped in a cloud of dust, a worn old car went by and when my cousins saw it they all shouted at the same time, "It's Don Pancho Alonso! Don Pancho! Don Pancho!"

And they began waving their arms at the car, which stopped and backed up.

At last Uncle Panchito was here!

And while they went on waving and shouting, I ran as fast as I could toward the backing auto. I reached it; I nimbly opened the door; and then, slender, gray-haired, paternal, smiling, clean-shaven, smelling of brandy, warmly affectionate, dressed in a new suit, and very different from the way I remembered him, as was the dusty old automobile, with his arms and all his heart, Uncle Pancho Alonso hugged and held me close for a long time.

As soon as we two had embraced each other to our heart's content, and as soon as he, happy and very surprised to find me so pretty, had complimented my good looks with unerring accuracy and charm, he went to say hello to the others. While they were greeting each other, a strange little incident occurred that cast a shadow on the rest of the day.

The thing is, Cristina, that my four cousins, besides having double names, which alone causes confusion, also enjoy the most absolute uniformity in other respects. They all resemble each other. Not only physically, but also in their identical points of view, in the focus of their imaginations, and in the vocabulary used to express their ideas. So when they talk they always coincide with each other as much in substance as in the form of their opinions, but in such an exact way that if this coincidence, instead of being simultaneous, is successive, the result is a kind of litany with the most irritating effect.

It happened, then, that after our effusive meeting, while Uncle Pancho and I were walking together the short distance that separated the car from Customs, my cousins, one after the other, came to meet us and each of them before or after saying hello made the following observation more or less with very slight modifications, "Caramba! How Don Pancho dressed up to meet his niece! He's wearing a new silk suit! . . ."

That's what the first one said, the second one said, the third one said; but when the fourth said it, Uncle Pancho, who really was dressed with unaccustomed elegance in my honor, completely lost control of his nerves in the face of such great insistence. With a rapid movement that is very characteristic, he put his hands on his hips, and as if the others, preceded solemnly by Uncle Eduardo and María Antonia, were all deaf, he asked me very seriously as he looked me up and down, "Tell me, have you ever seen a herd of donkeys that all go by braying at the same time?"

I looked at Uncle Pancho's new suit, his expression, his hands on his hips, my aunt and uncle's faces, my cousins' faces, and it all seemed so comical to me that without saying yes or no, I burst out laughing. One of the members of the herd, very offended, protested when he heard me laugh, "How rude you are, Don Pancho!"

María Antonia, with the fearful tragedy of her eyes, said to Uncle Eduardo, "You see? . . . Such insulting remarks are intolerable!"

And instant discord was established.

However, my cousins don't hold a grudge and they soon forgot the offense. Uncle Pancho drove us around Macuto and its outskirts, bought us cocktails and olives several times, gave us candy, and meanwhile told us the most amusing stories about everything we saw. By lunchtime he and my cousins were friends again.

But the same did not seem to occur with María Antonia. When we sat down for lunch, she took the floor, and, with a guttural and solemn voice that sounded very impressive and very Ciceronian, in the almost empty hotel she held forth before her vast audience of glasses, plates, jars, bottles, and knives and forks, severely reprimanding her children for having cocktails. She related horrors about alcohol in general, giving particular attention to brandy and whiskey, drinks that, as I have since seen, are Uncle Pancho's favorite friends.

This anti-alcohol lecture would have prejudiced me strongly against cocktails were it not for the skeptical and rather irreverent answers Uncle

Pancho gave as he sipped an enormous glass of iced beer. Yes, Cristina, Uncle Pancho is insensible to the magnetic fire of eloquence; I discovered it that day, and since then I have confirmed that he is completely immovable. Yes, I firmly believe that Uncle Pancho never, ever, would have formed a part of those glorious devotees, the pride of humanity, who, fired with enthusiasm, through the centuries have followed Demosthenes, Peter the Hermit, Saint Francis, Luther, Mirabeau, and Gabriel d'Annunzio . . .

After discussing cocktails and alcohol, the subject of Paris came up and María Antonia said, "It impresses me as one huge house of corruption let loose on the streets. An honorable woman with any self respect can't walk alone in Paris, because you see horrors! Horrors!"

And as a sign of horror she covered her eyes with her right hand.

Intrigued and filled with curiosity, I sat for a long time with my eyes fixed on a bread roll, evoking the boulevards of Paris one after another, in order to contemplate those horrors in my imagination, since I couldn't see them with my eyes. But unfortunately, I didn't manage to remember a one and finally Uncle Pancho roused me from my reverie with this original and somewhat paradoxical discussion: "Curses on all transatlantic steamers that establish communication with Europe! I think that like Hernando Cortez, all the conquistadors should have taken the precaution of burning their ships immediately after landing, so as to prevent any attempt to return. That way we would live here contentedly like frogs in a puddle, which are never troubled because they lack the concept of 'worse' and above all the concept of 'better,' the source of almost all human misfortunes. Yes, established beneath the tropic sun after having robbed and murdered all the Indians in patriarchal fashion, we should prudently avoid ominous European influences. Thus we should enjoy one of the most benign climates in the world, we would eat with delight the fruits of our land that are so juicy and fragrant, we would adorn ourselves with the marvelous feathers of our birds, and we would sleep in hammocks, which are without doubt the coolest and softest of beds. As a result of such a wise policy there would have been no War of Independence; Bolívar would have had no occasion to distinguish himself as the Liberator; and at the present time newspapers would not torment us daily lauding our national glory with their profuse hyperboles, redundancies, and adjectives in the worst possible taste; perhaps, perhaps, the newspapers themselves would not exist either, which would be the height of good fortune. As for me, I would not have had the opportunity to install myself in Paris some thirty years ago, and I would not have thrown away my fortune down to the last centime on pearl necklaces, expensive hats, and Japanese lapdogs, things that now seem completely superficial to me. Oh, yes, say what you will, I detest the ancient sailing ships, and still more do I detest modern transatlantic ships. I consider them the origin of our misfortunes. But maybe after all, I can accept the sailing ships. I wish I had been born in the happy epoch of the Colonial days, when our great-grandmothers and great-great-grandmothers traveled the stone-paved streets of Caracas in sedan chairs carried by two slaves who were always faithful, very black and robust, because they hadn't been contaminated yet with the vices and pretensions of the white race."

"Really," said the youngest of my cousins, "I think it must be very nice to ride in a sedan chair. It would be something like walking on air without touching the ground! The bad thing is that you must go very slow. Oh! How different now with the automobile!"

"Don't you believe it, my boy," said Uncle Pancho. "The sedan chair was a much better system. In the first place you saved the expense of tires and gasoline; then there were fewer collisions, and in respect to the time spent en route, that hadn't the least importance back then. For our great-grandparents, arriving early or late was all the same, or even never arriving. Our mania of getting places fast is relatively modern and the most terrible affliction that civilization continually mortifies us with."

María Antonia, whose modesty had been dreadfully wounded by the cynicism demonstrated by the necklaces, hats, and Japanese lapdogs, assumed her Ciceronian voice again and returned to the image of the frogs. "I don't understand why we shouldn't go to Europe. I, thank God, don't consider myself a frog, nor do I think Venezuela is a puddle. We have our faults, true, as they also have theirs, but everywhere, even in Paris itself, there are people who are very honorable and very good that you can associate with. But people who go from here only associate with the dregs of society and they think that is elegant and as it should be. When I went to Europe as a newlywed, I had a very good time, the way decent people amuse themselves! Eduardo took very good care of me! Eduardo didn't ever take me to certain theaters where many South American girls go now; Eduardo didn't permit me to dance under any circumstances; nor to make close friends with anyone; nor to wear makeup; nor to wear indecent dresses, although they were much in style! Nor to . . ."

And while the enumeration went on, I tilted my head slightly, because in the center of the table the compote bowl, heaped with fruit and flowers, hid "Eduardo" from me and I urgently wanted to study the bust of that Othello seated across from me. But, to my disappointment, beyond the fruit bowl, Othello didn't seem to be in character, a circumstance that took away some excitement from the enumeration. At that psychological moment he was sitting tranquilly with a fork in his right hand, a piece of bread in his left hand, and his eyes glued on his plate, very busy picking bones out of his portion of fish. And when he finished that delicate operation, he lifted his fork, balancing the very white pulp, to his mouth, he savored the bite, swallowed it, waited patiently for María Antonia to sum up her lecture, and then said, with a thin thread of mayonnaise imprisoned in his mustache, "Well, I must say the fish is really fresh! I think it is delicious, very well prepared, and I don't understand why we shouldn't be able to get some just as good in Caracas. María Antonia, unquestionably the cook is stealing from us; you can be sure of it. In order to rob us, she always buys the worst fish, the fish nobody wants! Well now, when we go back through La Guaira I'm going to talk to the head of the fishery, and if they'll sell me fish at cost in Caracas I'll give them an order for three times a week. If you agree, the cook herself can pick it up on her way back from the market using the same streetcar that she always takes to get to our house."

María Antonia, whose mental plane was at the moment far from fish, cooks, and streetcars, answered indignantly, "Julia from Martinique absolutely is not robbing us! I know for certain that she is totally honest! And I think this fish is awful! The mayonnaise is made with an abominable oil! How different from the mayonnaise we eat at home!"

"Well, I agree with Papa. I think the fish is very good," said my cousin Cecilia Margarita with a certain melancholy, "but I'm not eating it, because I held my fork up to the light and it leaves a lot to be desired . . . and there's no use asking for another one . . . silverware in a hotel is always dirty! . . . Because they don't wash them, they just wipe them with a cloth. I saw just now as I walked by!"

"Let me give you some advice, my dear," said Uncle Panchito very sympathetically. "Never look at silverware or anything else against the light. With food, as with everything, being anxious to investigate only leads us to unpleasant discoveries and horrible certainties. The happiest people will always be those who have discovered the fewest things during their lives. I speak from experience. Look, since my eyesight has failed enough for me to confuse a fly with a speck of black pepper, I am more contented and have much better digestion."

"Oh! Gross! To confuse a fly with pepper! Eat a fly! Gross!" all my cousins said at the same time.

But Uncle Pancho, in a new and very thoroughly documented lecture, also somewhat paradoxical, demonstrated to us that obviously the greatest damage has been occasioned to humanity by the microscope, hygiene, vaccines, surgery, and medical schools—all things that according to him usually finish off the most robust people, preserving instead the sickly, the poor, the bored, and the unhappy, all wretches who are wronged arbitrarily by being deprived of death, which is something so natural and inoffensive.

María Antonia, who always boils the filtered water, and sleeps every night under a mosquito net, was naturally scandalized hearing such dreadful nonsense. We argued over this; then we talked without arguing; we drank coffee; we argued some more; lunch was declared over; we walked along the beach; we took snapshots under some trees; and then, the heat of the day having abated now, we distributed ourselves in the two autos and started on the way to Caracas.

Before getting in the car I had declared, "I want to sit up front with the driver to see everything better."

And once more, following the flight of the auto along the white ribbon of the highway, over abysses and mountains, in silence, from the temple of my inner feelings, I gave myself up to contemplation, to an intimate communion with nature, to nostalgia, and to the voluptuous fear of arriving . . .

🐌   🐌   🐌

The trip from Macuto to Caracas, Cristina, is a daring excursion over the mountain that lasts almost two hours. To make this excursion possible, both the highway and the train, in rivalry, scale the mountain. The train, very small and narrow, runs on rails that are very close together, and as it races along them, it slithers like an undulating serpent and other times it is as daring as an eagle. There are times when it slips into the darkest and greenest part of the mountain, and when you think it is still hidden in the thickets and rocks at the base of the mountain, it suddenly appears on a peak, hardy and brave, with its plume of smoke. Before it takes flight it first runs near the sea very close to the waves. It enters the outskirts of La Guaira and of the nearby village of Maiquetía; it makes a few indecisive circles and that's when it throws itself forward to conquer the mountain.

The highway, which is freer and less daring than the train, also follows the sea and the railroad tracks for awhile. It passes through the two towns, then moves away from everything and alone, with white spirals, it wraps the mountain with a ribbon of dust.

When we began the ascent Uncle Pancho advised me that the mountain we were going to climb was an offshoot of the Andes, and immediately the landscape acquired immense prestige in my eyes. And actually the mountain is so grandiose that it is worthy of its relationship. It is arrogant, mysterious, and very tall. Its peaks overlook Caracas and separate the city from the sea. Seen from the city it changes color several times a day, condescending to the whims of the surrounding atmosphere. These changes and whims have given it a unique character and all the painters lovingly copy and interpret it; with even more love all the poets sing of it and it is named "El Avila" in memory of the conquistador who took it away from the Indians on some date or another.

From the time we left Macuto, with the breeze whipping my face, I felt a strong curiosity about the spirit of the American land and I gave myself fully and affectionately to seeking it in all the details along our path.

After traveling near the sea and crossing through La Guaira and the outskirts of the town of Maiquetía, we passed by some plantations of coconut palms that stretch along the beach, and from that instant the coconut trees drew my eyes and held my attention.

There is no question. For me, Cristina, all the charm, all the sweet, languid soul of the tropics is personified in the swaying coconut trees. When there are lots of them and you pass near them, they swing like hammocks, evoking the laziness of siestas and the rustling of fans. The sea always glitters there in the background, and through the many trunks that twist and bend in attitudes of human pain, in that landscape that is at once populated and deserted like an empty church, there is an intense peace in which only the blue note of the sea vibrates, softly, far away like a dream. When one climbs a mountain and the coconut trees are seen from above, their disheveled heads on the slender stems look like pins stuck in a pincushion, which is the beach. If the tree stands alone and is seen from a distance, completely isolated, standing straight facing the sea, then it has the melancholy air of a recluse who is meditating and the wariness of a sentinel scrutinizing the horizon; its leaves outlined at such a great distance from the earth look like cut flowers placed in a very tall vase. If seen from so far away that the ethereal trunk is lost from view, those leaves floating in air are then as mysterious as a wisp of incense rising, and they seem to evoke the mystic symbol of prayers offering their treasures to the heavens.

While we were driving up the mountain I lost myself in these thoughts without remembering the La Guaira that we had left behind, when suddenly, on an abrupt curve in the road, there beneath our feet, at the bottom of the abyss, it appeared, but so tiny, so tiny, that with all its houses, its ships, its little boats and launches, it just looked like a child's toy. There, in that diminutive world was our steamship, the *Arnús*, which was going to sail at sunset. From my height it looked elegant and fine like a swallow ready to fly, and for a while I felt infinite jealousy for its adventurous life . . . Oh! It would leave now for port after port, always spirited and active, and it would never ever feel, as I, the barrenness of final, definitive repose!

These were my last "maritime" meditations, because after another abrupt turn of the highway, La Guaira was lost again as suddenly as it had appeared; then a little farther on the narrow blue ribbon of sea was blotted out, and amid abysses and boulders we decidedly entered the heart of the mountain. There we drove a space going up and down, until little by little the abysses flattened, the road smoothed, the valley appeared, and we entered the outskirts of Caracas.

I had just applied my powder and lipstick and in general repaired the imperfections in my face and hat caused by the trip. I was pulling on my gloves again, and while doing so I was watching the succession of streets and wondering, "When will we finally get into the city?" Behind me, Uncle Pancho guessed my question instantly, because he realized on his own without my having said anything: "This is the center of Caracas, María Eugenia."

The center of Caracas? . . . The center of Caracas! . . . then what had become of the streets of my infancy, those wide, long, elegant streets, laid out so straight? . . . Oh! Cristina, how intact they had always lived in my memory and how cruelly black-hearted, infamous reality was disfiguring them!

One-story houses, flat, squeezed under their eaves, painted with vivid colors, the façades decorated with grillwork on the projecting windows, stretched along both sides of the deserted streets, narrow and very long. The city seemed bowed down by the mountain, by the eaves, by the telephone lines whose endless fibers, strung low, innumerable, sketched streaks across the bright blue of the sky and the undefined gray of some distant hills that peeked over a few roofs and between all the street intersections. And as if the lines were not enough, the intruding telephone posts opened their arms and, feigning crosses in a lengthy Calvary, stretched one after another, until they were lost in the remote confines of the horizon . . . Oh! yes . . . Caracas, of the delightful climate, of gentle memories, the familiar city, the intimate and distant city, turned out to be this flat town . . . a kind of Andalusian city, like a melancholy Andalusia, without a shawl or castanets, without guitars or music, without flower-pots and flowers on the balconies . . . a drowsy Andalusia that had dropped off to sleep in the sultry heat of the tropics!

But, however, while I was dejectedly making these judgments, as we raced down the streets, I saw flashes here and there, like sparks of unexpected light, where the marvel of an open window appeared, and in the window, beyond the broad, open grillwork, there were faces, eyes, mirrors, sparkling chandeliers, palm trees, flowers—an intense indoor happiness offering itself generously to the sadness of the street.

Oh! Fraternity and affection and welcome and the familiar embrace of open windows! . . . But which one was it? . . . Which was it? . . . Which one was Grandmother's house?

And suddenly, in front of a wide house, painted green, with three big windows, closed and severe, the cars stopped. My cousins got out in a rush, ran to the entrance, pushed through the half-closed door at the back, and that was when I saw the bright, green, flower-filled patio of Grandmother's house.

It was the first dazzling impression I received after my arrival in Venezuela. Because the patio of this house, Cristina, is Aunt Clara's son, lover, and brother. She cares for it with so much love that it has the soothing atmosphere of a convent, a hospitable tranquillity offered by the open arms of the wicker chairs. In the fresh earth all year round roses, palms, geraniums, heliotropes, and jasmine grow. There is a great lovely jasmine vine that, clinging to the kiosk, presides over everything and always greets visitors with its insistent and obliging perfume. Near the entrance door, at the left, along the wide corridor, the green foam of the ferns and the erect, half-opened arrows of palm sprouts are scattered freely over tables and columns. When I entered that afternoon and looked at the patio I searched everywhere, and it was through this green little forest, there, at the end of the corridor, framed by the back of her wicker armchair, where I finally recognized Grandmother's white head.

Seeing my cousins come in, she had instantly leapt to her feet and when she picked me out in the distance among the advancing group, she cried out to me maternally with her open arms trembling, "My daughter, my daughter, my little daughter!"

I don't want to describe in detail, Cristina, how many hugs and kisses Grandmother and Aunt Clara tearfully gave me then, because that description would be long, monotonous, and repetitive. I will only say that there were tears, memories of the past, minute observations of my face, body, movements; more kisses, more tears, and Mama's dear name always repeated, covering me like a veil and transforming me into her in the torrential, effusive, and indescribable affection of Grandmother and Aunt Clara. I also felt surprised, very emotional, and, to be brief, holding back my tears, with my eyes clouded, I began to inspect everything, up, down, and as, little by little, I recognized old familiar things, I started asking smilingly about the favorite things from my childhood, "And the canaries, Grandmother? . . . And the black cat . . . that one . . . that one with the red bow? . . . And the little fish in the pool? . . . Why! . . . There isn't any pool now and there aren't any orange trees in the patio. I hadn't noticed!"

"Everything is different. The house was remodeled seven years ago before Enrique's death. See, the pool was taken out, mosaic tile was put down, the house was painted, it was redecorated, the dividing wall at the back was changed; but the orange trees," she added smiling, "were never here, they were in the other patio . . . and they're still there!"

I turned my head to look at the new wall screening the back of the patio, and at the door I saw a group of black, woolly heads belonging to the four retainers who constitute Grandmother's domestic service. Their eyes, full of curiosity, were studying me avidly. I took them all in with a quick, indifferent glance. But as I felt in that rapid glance the attraction of a pair of eyes, I looked again and then, illuminated by a spark of memory, just as Grandmother had done a moment before, I too opened my arms effusively and ran toward the door exclaiming joyfully, "Oh! . . . Gregoria! Gregoria! . . . It's really you, you pretty old dear!"

And with a long, fraternal hug of kindred spirits, Gregoria and I sealed our interrupted friendship anew.

For you must know, Cristina, that Gregoria, the old black laundress at this house, contrary to what Grandmother and Aunt Clara may think, is now my friend, my confidant, and my mentor, because even if she doesn't know how to read or write I consider her indisputably one of the most intelligent and wisest people I have known in my life. She was mother's nurse and she has stayed since then in this house where she has the double role of laundress and historian, given her admirable memory and her exquisite artistry in ironing lace and bleaching tablecloths. When I was very little and I would come to spend the day here at Grandmother's house, it was Gregoria who would always feed me, who would tell me stories, and who, when no one was looking, would let me go barefoot or play in the water, in this way taking care of my physical and spiritual well-being. Because her poetic soul, which scorns human prejudices with the elegant harshness of a cynical philosopher, has for all creatures the brotherly charity of Saint Francis of Assisi. This free partnership has made her soul generous, indulgent, and immoral. Her disdain for conventions always preserved her from any science not taught by nature herself. For this reason, besides not knowing how to read or write, Gregoria doesn't know her age either, which is an enigma to me, to her, and to anyone who sees her. Bleaching tablecloths and ironing shirts, she watches the passing of time with the serene indifference with which one watches a fountain flow, because in her Franciscan eyes, the hours, like the drops of their sister water, together form a great clean fresh stream, where beautiful death comes swimming. As I told you, when I was little, she always took care of me with the poetic tenderness with which one cares for flowers and animals. Because of that, that afternoon, when I recognized her standing at the door of the back wall, I ran to her, moved by the same impulse that makes a dog's grateful tail wag with joy and faithfulness.

When I felt myself in her arms, Gregoria, whose sentiments always burst forth linked to the resounding or very delicate shadings of her special laugh, surprised and happy, sprinkled her long laughter, intense with emotion, with these few words, "God keep you! . . . God protect you! . . . You remembered your black nurse! . . . Your ugly nurse! . . . Your old black nurse! . . ."

And we hugged each other so long, and Gregoria laughed so much, and the scene was so prolonged, that Grandmother finally had to intervene. "All right, Gregoria, that's enough, that's enough; how long will you go on! You get started laughing and laughing, and you never stop!"

And then affectionately, Grandmother added, speaking to me, "Come, daughter, come take off your hat and freshen up a bit. Come on, let's go see your room."

With her leaning on my arm and with everyone following, we crossed a part of the patio, we crossed the dining room, and we reached the second patio, this one, the patio with the orange trees, onto which open the door and window of this silent locked room from which I am now writing to you.

At the threshold we stopped to look at my room.

At first glance it seemed to smile at me with its bright furniture and little white bed. At that gray twilight hour it was invaded more intensely than ever by a certain sad charm that seems to always come from these green branches where the oranges ripen. Floating in the atmosphere was that smell of paste and fresh paint that recently wallpapered rooms have. Standing at the threshold, Grandmother, leaning on my arm, began to explain.

"This was Clara's room. Many years ago I furnished it for her just as it is now . . . when María, your mother, got married. Before that the two girls slept together in a bigger room that is near mine. Clara now wants to give it all to you. Since the furniture is white and cheery, it's more natural for you to have it . . ."

"Well," interrupted Cecilia Margarita, "it's a miracle that Aunt Clara has agreed to give you her room and her furniture. She was terribly strict with us! She wouldn't even let us in, because she said we ruined the furniture and that with all our going in and out the room was filled with flies."

Aunt Clara made no reply and Grandmother continued, "Yes, Clara has given up her room to you and she's moving close to me to the room that belonged to her father, your grandfather. His furniture is still there, very comfortable mahogany furniture, and more serious than this . . . Of course everything was painted and papered for your arrival. Look, we put the pictures of your Papa and your Mama at either side of your bed so they will always be with you. This dressing table belonged to Clara too; she made a new skirt for it. You don't know how hard she has worked to finish the embroidery before you got here! Last night at midnight she was still sewing!"

The dresser; the pictures; the resplendent paper on the walls; the white furniture; Aunt Clara; my cousin's observation; all had been producing a tender emotion in me. In the arrangement of the room there was a profusion of details that demonstrated a precise planning, a very marked eagerness to make everything happy, elegant, stylish. This effort, made in such an out-of-date ambience, one so old-fashioned, touched me; and it touched me above all as I realized how little it had achieved the desired effect on me. Those tall, symmetrical pictures, the glaring colors in the embroidery on the dressing table, the overstated appearance, the curtains on the bed, the placement of the furniture, everything, absolutely everything, was contrary to my taste and my sentiments. It made me want to entirely dismantle the room, to redo it according to my taste, and thinking about how this sort of vandalism would have hurt poor Aunt Clara, I looked deeply at her for an instant, with pity, with intense affection . . .

During Grandmother's explanation, Aunt Clara had not spoken a single word. Standing, near the door, keeping silent, she had the hushed and humble desolation of lives that slip by monotonously, without a future, without a goal . . . And yet, under her gray hair, with her long, aging face and her very pale skin, Aunt Clara was pretty; and in spite of her black satin dress, recently made but not in style, she was also distinguished, with that rather ridiculous distinction that old photographs in an album some-times have.

Looking at her this way with gratitude and tenderness, in a fleeting second I remembered how, back in the days of my infancy, when I would come to stay at Grandmother's, she, Aunt Clara, used to sit on the sofa in the living room in the afternoons and talk hour after hour with a gentle-man who would give me candies and make dolls and chickens for me with pieces of paper. I used to play with those paper chickens sitting quietly on the floor, on the rug, while the two of them, on the sofa, continued their conversation, which I found mysterious in view of how prolonged and monotonous it was. Now, for the first time, after so many years, seeing her as she stood beside the door, I remembered the daily and forgotten scene, and remembering it I thought: "If that gentleman was Aunt Clara's sweetheart, as he must have been, what had become of him? . . . Why didn't they get married?" And to show my interest and the faithfulness with which I had conserved his image through time, I was on the verge of describing the scene to her just as I recalled it and then to ask her the question. But fortunately with the words already on my lips I stopped in time. I understood that there might be some secret pain in it; that perhaps the pain was still alive in the romantic ruins of her gray head and that I would surely wound her with such an indiscreet question. Then, in order to express my fondness in another way, I abruptly changed the subject and I said smilingly that everything, everything in the room was adorable and that with love and great delight I accepted those things that had been with her for such a long time.

But that wasn't true, Cristina. No! . . . While I was saying this, looking first at the gray head near the door, and then looking at the white cutwork curtain on the bed, my soul was oppressed with anguish, cold, fear; I don't know what! For the fact is that lucidly, on the surface of the furniture I felt a stirring of the spirit of that inheritance that Aunt Clara was leaving me . . . Oh! Cristina . . . Aunt Clara's legacy! . . . It was a countless throng of long, black nights, invariable, that went by slowly holding hands be-neath the snowy lace of the white curtain! . . .

And for the first time, at that prophetic moment, still feeling the gentle pressure of Grandmother's arm on my arm, I saw clearly, in all its ugliness, the open claw of this monster that now delights in locking all the doors to my future; this monster that one after the other has blinded the blue eyes of my dreams; this hideous monster that sits at night on my bed and clutches my head with its icy hands; this one that during the day walks constantly behind me, treading on my heels; this one that spreads out like

a thick smoke when I look up through my window at the green blissful-
ness of the orange trees on the patio; this one that has forced me to pick
up my pen and to open my heart with the pen, and to squeeze from the
bottom of my heart, to extract the words I'm sending you, many things
about myself that I was ignorant of; this one that permanently installed
here in the house is like a son to Grandmother and like an older brother to
Aunt Clara; yes, this monster—Boredom, Cristina! . . . cruel, persistent,
fiendish, murderous Boredom! . . .

❧   ❧   ❧

But this cruel boredom that I forebodingly felt
for the first time on the afternoon of my arrival, this boredom that has
made me expansive, an analyst and a writer, has a very deep root, and the
deep root has its origin in the following revealing scene that I am going to
relate and that happened one morning, two or three days after I came to
Caracas.

It was about eleven-thirty. Grandmother, Uncle Pancho, Aunt Clara,
and I were installed at the back of the entrance corridor, just there in that
little green forest that I have already described to you, where several
wicker armchairs are scattered around a table, where the day I arrived I
saw Grandmother's white head, and where she sits every day with her
cutwork, her scissors, and her sewing basket. That morning we had finally
reached a normal state. Or rather I, after spending two days as a kind of
exhibit before Grandmother's Gothic friends, that is to say, before a small
number of people of both sexes more or less uniform as far as their ideas,
dress, and age, who flocked to meet me and to congratulate Grandmother
on my safe arrival, and who during their long visits, with slight variations
gave me the same compliments and asked me the same questions, that
morning the parade having finished, I had at last been able to do what I
wished and turn to my personal occupations. The morning, spent entirely
in arranging my room, had been put to good use. When the clock struck
eleven I was tired and satisfied, because joining a spirit of conquest with a
spirit of conciliation, I had managed to impose my modern and rather
daring taste on the routine, symmetrical, and very cowardly taste of Aunt
Clara. Without hurting any feelings the original decoration was now re-
formed. And presided over by two Parisian dolls, blond, very petulant,
and dressed in silk that fluffed out like an "*abat-jour*," their two crinoline
skirts, one pink, and the other green, on my bedside table and on my desk,

the room now looked quite contemporary and quite nice. A little after eleven, they came to let me know that Uncle Pancho had come by to say hello as he often does when he returns at that time from the Ministry of Foreign Relations where he has a job. As soon as I heard he was here, I instantly stopped admiring my work, and it was then that among ferns and palms, at the back of the entrance corridor, I sat down to chat with him, with Grandmother, and with Aunt Clara.

Since it was Saturday, the day for mending, Aunt Clara was sitting before a basket full of stockings and clothes, darning a linen napkin that was very old and worn; Grandmother, bent over her knees, was stitching one of those silk handkerchiefs that, folded in fourths, tied with a little bow, and placed in a cardboard box, she distributes to her grandchildren on their saint's days; Uncle Pancho, sitting in a rocking chair, smoking a cigar, was telling a very interesting story that made Grandmother suddenly stop her sewing and Aunt Clara her darning and which didn't interest me at all because it dealt with people totally unknown to me. Looking at the plants on the patio I was resting pleasantly from the double fatigue, spiritual and physical, occasioned by rearranging my room, reflecting at the same time on what would be the best way to change the course of that conversation that was boring me. Suddenly I said, resolutely violating the interesting story, "Listen, Uncle Pancho, I want to tell you about my plan. Let's go for a ride to Los Mecedores, the two of us, today, tomorrow, the day after, whenever it suits you! I'm feeling romantic. I have a tremendous urge to watch the sunset, lying on the grass, in the fresh air, looking up through the branches of the trees to the sky above them; I want to see Los Mecedores again so much! I remember that when I was little you used to take me there to run and play and I liked it a lot. We used to take the streetcar and we would get off near a church that was called . . . what was it?"

"La Pastora."

"That's right. Well, let's go someday to Los Mecedores, the two of us! Oh! And by the way, Grandmother, when are we going to Papa's hacienda, to San Nicolás? . . . Uncle Eduardo is still the administrator for it, isn't he?"

That question, which had been asked with all naturalness and light-heartedness, was left awhile as if suspended in space, and there was a silence, Cristina, an intense and tragic silence during which Grandmother and Aunt Clara, without lifting their heads from their sewing, looked up at each other for a second over the round frames of their respective glasses. Then, they went back to their sewing, and that was when Grandmother, stitching away and without looking at me decided to speak in a very sweet and sad way, "San Nicolás belongs to Eduardo, daughter."

And she said this with the same compassion with which one talks to very poor children when they want to buy an expensive toy in a shop. After the compassionate and brief statement, there was another much longer silence, more intense and more tragic than the earlier one. It was the horrible silence of revelation. Wrapped in Grandmother's voice, the truth had been presented to me so clearly and finally that I didn't ask for any explanation, nor make any comment. I understood that it must be irreversible and I decided to accept it from the beginning with courage and conviction. However, Cristina, the throng of consequences that sprang from the revelation were so enormous that I could see them at once. And the sight of those consequences unleashed a horrible inner storm in my soul. San Nicolás belonged to Uncle Eduardo! I didn't know how, or why, but it belonged to Uncle Eduardo! Therefore I, who believed myself wealthy, I who had learned to spend with the same naturalness with which one breathes or walks, had nothing in the world, nothing save the severe protection of Grandmother, who was leaning over now drawing out her needle from among the threads of the silk handkerchief, and save the jovial affection of Uncle Pancho, who was also enigmatically silent, leaning back in the rocking chair, holding the burning and fragrant cigar between his teeth . . . With my frightened eyes I looked at the two of them and I went on inwardly contemplating the horrible news that suddenly was opening before my future, like a window on a lugubrious night: poverty! . . . Do you really understand, Cristina, everything that this meant? . . . It was complete dependency with all its attending humiliations and pains. It was a definitive goodbye to travel, to comfort, to success, to luxury, to elegance, to all the charm of that life I had barely glimpsed during my last stay in Paris and to which I aspired vehemently, madly. It was also a definitive goodbye to you and to so many other things and people that I had never known and whose presence I felt, glorious, waiting for me in the world . . . the world! . . . Do you know? . . . The whole torrent of happiness and gaiety that lives beyond the four iron walls of this house of Grandmother's! . . . Oh! Joy, freedom, success would no longer be mine! . . . And faced with such an idea, I felt that a knot was squeezing my throat frightfully and that a tumult of tears besieged me, impetuous and terrible.

In order to hide my emotion and hold back the tears I began by lowering my eyes and fixing them on the ground. There, I started looking at Grandmother's, Aunt Clara's, and Uncle Pancho's shoes positioned on the mosaic floor. I don't know why it seemed to me that those shoes had faces and that they were looking at me. It's very strange to observe, Cristina, how at moments of great crisis the objects that surround us seem to become imbued with life. Sometimes they seem to become accomplices in the evil that tortures us; other times, on the contrary, they look at us with a sad, affectionate intent as if they want to console us. At that instant it seemed to me that those six shoes in their different aspects or attitudes, all had the uniform expression that hypocrites wear. And I don't know if it was an expression of mockery or of pity. Both are equally displeasing to me; but since I wanted to conquer my emotion I told myself that they were making fun of me. I decided that my situation was ridiculous. I recalled the knowing look that Grandmother and Aunt Clara had exchanged over the rims of their glasses. I reflected that if I had an attack of weeping they doubtless would tell Uncle Eduardo about it. I imagined Uncle Eduardo afterwards, in his turn commenting on it to his wife and their children; and, my pride terribly inflamed by this last image, I managed to overcome my great emotion. Then, in order to immediately assume some attitude or other, I lifted my head, looked at the group around me, breathed deeply, and exclaimed, "Oh! How hot it is!"

And getting up from the chair that I was occupying, I very agilely leapt up to sit on a little table or column used for one of the big potted palms that at that time were on the patio to get fresh air and sunshine. Once there, I put my left hand on my waist and began to swing my right foot with a rhythmic movement like a pendulum, whose maximum upward stroke rose till the tip of my shoe struck against the edge of the wicker table around which Grandmother, Aunt Clara, and Uncle Pancho were sitting. I felt that such an attitude must give me a look of absolute freedom from care and I went on stoically swinging my foot, with pride and with conviction.

But all this, which set out in detail here seems very long, had happened in the brief space of a minute. Beneath the rhythmic swinging of my foot the three people present still continued to sit in complete silence and immobility. Only Grandmother, suddenly opting to lift her eyes from her sewing, observed me for a few seconds and since my attitude seemed to convince her fully, she lowered her eyes again and went on stitching the silk handkerchief with great tranquillity. She innocently imagined that the news pronounced by her like a bomb meant nothing to me. That was what I wanted, and therefore I felt satisfied. But I assure you, Cristina, that from that moment, Grandmother began to lose much of my high opinion. I understood that she had very little psychological penetration and that she was utterly lacking in subtlety. Deep down I am glad that she is this way. It is very uncomfortable to live with people endowed with psychological penetration and subtlety. You totally lose your independence and it's never possible to deceive them because they see everything. Nonetheless, Grandmother has a reputation among her friends for great intelligence. Oh! But from that day whenever they talk to me about "Your Grandmother's talent," I immediately exclaim to myself: "It's not true, she has none!"

As I was telling you, Grandmother, after observing me without comment, went back to her sewing. She threaded her needle that had lost its thread, she made a few stitches, she lifted her head again, she observed me once more, and then she said, "María Eugenia, my dear, listen. You are distinguished, you have good manners, you are quite well educated, you have poise, and still sometimes you assume the manners of a street urchin. Look, instead of sitting in a chair like other people, you're perched up there, level with my head on that column that could collapse from your weight. You can see your legs up to your knees, you have one hand on your waist like the servants, and you're swinging your leg with a most vulgar movement . . . Besides, imagine, look, as you hit the table with the point of your shoe you're ruining both things at once: the table and the tip of your new shoe . . . ."

After this exhortation I stopped swinging my foot and I took my hand off my waist, but since I felt a violent need to destroy something, without getting down off the column, a thing that would have shown too much obedience, with my fingernail I began to tear a palm leaf which, to its misfortune, was within my reach. Grandmother meanwhile had submerged herself again in her cutwork and was quiet. Her mind must have traveled now along the terrain of economic affairs because in a little while she said quite naturally, "I'm always forgetting to ask you, María Eugenia, did you bring the two thousand pesos that Eduardo wired to you in Paris by way of Antonio Ramírez? . . . At the rate of exchange I imagine it came to some twenty thousand francs . . . ."

"Yes, as a matter of fact, twenty thousand francs, of which, Grandmother, I changed the last gold coin in Havana. Certainly if Uncle Eduardo had not met me on board, I must say that my own funds would not have paid even for someone to carry a suitcase for me," and swinging my foot again, but so violently that I was on the point of falling over backwards and knocking the column down also, I added, "I didn't have a centime left, not even half a centime, not even a quarter of a centime! Nothing, nothing, nothing!!"

Grandmother dropped the handkerchief, her thimble, her needle, and took off her glasses in fright: "You spent the whole eight thousand bolívares? . . . Did you throw them in the street? . . . Ave María! How insane! . . . Why I told Eduardo, 'Don't send that money without first advising Ramírez,' but he insisted on wiring it and this is the result! . . . So you spent the eight thousand bolívares! . . . But two thousand pesos drawing nine percent would have brought you about fifteen pesos a month, my daughter; maybe they could have been invested at ten percent, even twelve and then it would have been seventy or eighty bolívares a month . . . Think . . . you would have had something, very little, a paltry amount, but something after all, something to buy yourself clothes at least! . . . That money was sent to Paris only for an emergency, in case of an accident, or an illness. A month before, a letter of credit had been sent to the consulate for your trip, to pay any out-of-the-ordinary expense that the death of your father might have occasioned and to buy you some black dresses. It was more than enough!"

Oh! Grandmother's extreme devotion to those two thousand pesos, the last shred of my patrimony, was grating horribly on my nerves, now that the many thousands that San Nicolás represented had just disappeared before my eyes. While she was talking excitedly, I, who now found myself upon the column as immobile and heroic as a stylite, had a firm presentiment that Uncle Eduardo had rendered false accounts concerning my inheritance, and I felt a fearful fury. This fury reached an icy stage when Grandmother said: "You would have had very little, a paltry amount, but after all, something, something . . ." and as I then imagined Uncle Eduardo's hateful face, I hurried to insult it with all my heart, addressing him in my thoughts mechanically with the following apostrophes: "Old, miser, stingy, thief, scoundrel, common, snuffling, broomstick dressed like a man," and unjustly, I made Grandmother an accomplice of my misfortune. Then, with the object of upsetting her somehow, when she finished talking, pretending to be in a good mood, I exclaimed very happily, "Oh! Grandmother, Grandmother, how obvious it is that you have never been in Paris! I had my black clothes made in Biarritz, of course! But it always happens—you have a new dress made, you get to Paris and it looks old . . . See, in Paris, Grandmother, I never once wore the dresses from Biarritz; I didn't even try them on, nor did I even bother to keep them, because the sight of them at a distance, hanging in my closet repelled me. They had an air of the schoolgirl, the ingenue, of the bourgeoisie, how awful! . . . Oh! It was in Paris, Grandmother, where I learned how to dress, where I totally felt this revelation of what is chic! . . . The ten or twelve dresses from Biarritz . . . pss! . . . , I gave them all to the maid at the hotel. Since they were black, they were just right for the maid, with her batiste cap and those little white aprons . . ."

Grandmother interrupted me, desperate, and with her glasses tremulous, held on high in her right hand, she exclaimed several times, in that tragic tone in which one laments hopeless catastrophes, "What madness, Lord, what foolishness, twenty thousand francs on rags when you were already outfitted for the trip!"

"But yesterday didn't you see my dresses, my hats, my stockings, and my silk lingerie, or do you perhaps believe, Grandmother, that they give them away in Paris? . . . Why I bought everything quite cheap! That represents at least . . . at least thirty thousand francs! . . . Let's see, you, you, Uncle Pancho, who say you've bought many hats in Paris, tell me: Did I pay too much for my hats? Are they too expensive? . . ."

And this last question I asked with so much vehemence that once more I was on the point of toppling off the column, but this time nose first and in Uncle Pancho's direction. He looked at me an instant and responded evasively, wrapping his reply in a puff of smoke, "Remember that you still haven't shown me your hats, María Eugenia."

"Well, you'll see the most elegant, the prettiest, the most *dernier cri* that you've seen in your life. Just imagine, I attracted attention in Paris! . . . And since with my hats I had so much personality, so much *allure*, they always called me "Madame" . . . Yes . . . "Madame Alonso.""

"Oh! María Eugenia," said Grandmother in dismay, the hand that held the glasses lying limp on her skirt, "Who knows, my dear, who knows what they took you for!"

But I continued enumerating my expenses. "Well, besides the hats, my shoes were all Louis XV style; add the *déshabillés*; add the lace *liseuse*; add the black kimono . . . oh! and above all, the gifts! . . . I was forgetting, the gifts cost me a fortune. Look, Grandmother, look at the name of the shops on the boxes, all fine things from the Rue de la Paix . . . Oh! My gifts are not just junk!"

"Oh! No, your gifts aren't junk," repeated Grandmother fuming, waving her glasses on high again. "Why, it seems to me that I'm listening to your father! What wasteful characters! But do you imagine, my daughter, that the brooch you brought me can cause me any pleasure now that I know where it came from and what it must have cost you?"

"But I took pleasure in giving it to you and that's enough for me! . . . Oh! If you knew how much I enjoyed my money! If you knew how much it delighted me to try on dress after dress! . . . Look, I would go to the house of Lanvin, I would stand in front of the mirror and start trying on clothes! . . . I would say, I'll take this one, and this one too; that one fits me like a dream; this other one looks even better on me; and the attendant was saying in amazement: 'In this dress you look like a queen! . . . but I must tell you that it is the most expensive of all . . .' and I, who answered with this gesture like an elegant millionaire: 'The price is not important!' and on to see more styles, and shops, and to walk the boulevards, up, down, alone, alone, all by myself, on my own . . . Do you think, do you think, Grandmother, that I would trade those days of freedom just to have twenty wretched pesos a month? . . . Oh! No, no, no! . . ."

"Yes, I already knew from Eduardo, who heard it in La Guaira, that you went around by yourself on the streets of Paris, and that upset me greatly. I don't understand how Ramírez, a sensible man, could ever authorize such a crazy thing. An eighteen-year-old girl, alone, on her own, in a big city like that! How foolish! How dangerous! . . . When I think of it! . . . And don't imagine that here in Caracas you can do the same thing . . ."

"Oh! So that was the 'business' that Uncle Eduardo had in La Guaira? To go around checking up on what I did in Paris so he could come tell you about it. That means he is also a spy and a gossip. With his innocent face!"

"That isn't gossip! It was his duty to advise me, just as it is also my duty to counsel you not to ever commit such an imprudent thing again."

Uncle Pancho and Aunt Clara, with that subtle and refined tact that very good people have, must have felt the subterranean storm that was growing in my soul, underneath that trivial discussion with Grandmother. Both respected my sorrow with their silence; she concentrating hard on passing her needle through the cloth she was darning; he, withdrawn, leaning back, his head on the back of the rocking chair, following with an absent gaze the elongated and tenuous figures that the tobacco smoke was tracing in the air. Suddenly he got up; he threw the cigar stub among the plants on the patio, he stood awhile pensively, then he came toward me, he planted himself before the column with his feet apart, his two hands in his pants pockets, his jacket pulled back behind his arms, and thus, between ironic and festive, he finally intervened, "Did you have fun with your twenty thousand francs? . . . You did? . . . A lot? . . . Well then, they were very well spent! . . . Oh, Niece, you don't know the number of twenty thousand franc checks that I spent in Paris, and like you, I'm not sorry! Better to spend the money having a good time than to spend it on bad business ventures from which a third person infallibly profits. At least amusing yourself with it you don't run the risk of playing the role of an imbecile . . ."

But Grandmother and Aunt Clara, with great vehemence, cut into Uncle Panchito's talk, with two different objections. Aunt Clara said, "But how can you dream that María Eugenia could amuse herself in Paris, when her father's body was still warm, as they say! . . . I don't believe she is that heartless!"

And Grandmother for her part, drowning out Aunt Clara's voice, began to say excitedly, "That's the last straw, Pancho, that's all we needed, for you to come here to preach your corrupt doctrines to this child! Why don't you advise her to drink, too, or to inject morphine or cocaine now that she has no way to spend money?"

Uncle Pancho, without changing his position, turned slightly toward Grandmother and said very calmly, "Let's suppose, Eugenia, that this girl, moved by a spirit of frugality and prudence, arrives in Caracas with her twenty thousand franc check untouched . . . What would have happened? You, in your just desire to increase the sum, get enthusiastic about such and such an enterprise that Eduardo has at San Nicolás. Planting cotton, tobacco, or potatoes, a safe, extra-safe affair . . . Eduardo generously yields a few rows of the crop; the seeds are planted, but a bad winter comes along, worms or locusts; it is María Eugenia's part, precisely, that the plague takes a fancy to and '*De profundis clamavi ad te Domine . . .*' not even ashes are left of it! . . . Isn't it a thousand times better then that she has used her money having some fun? . . . Oh! In agriculture, which is what we in this family have always engaged in up to now, it turns out that the calamities and the poor prices always work against those who are absent, against women and minors, who lose inevitably . . . The natural thing happens! . . . The same thing that happened in the story of the lunch enjoyed by the husband and his wife. The serving that belonged to the absent person is always the one that the cat eats!"

That was a perfectly clear explanation of what I wanted to know and since it turned out to be just what I had suspected, I smiled, gratified, exclaiming inwardly, "Didn't I say so!"

And I think without any doubt, that I would have gotten down from the column to hug Uncle Pancho for his brave accusation, if it hadn't been that Grandmother, infuriated perhaps by my presence and my smile, had straightened against the back of her wicker armchair, and thus, sitting tall, terrible, her mother's love wounded to the quick, she burst out with the arrogance of a lioness, "I can't tolerate this, Pancho, that here, in my house, in my presence, in front of me, you dare to express yourself about Eduardo in that way, and much less still for you to belittle him in front of this child with whom he has been, as you know all too well, as good and as generous as if he were her own father! . . . Just to say things that you suppose are funny, you don't respect anything, not even the most holy nor the most sacred! I think that Eduardo in his life has given sufficient proof of being an upright and honorable man! . . . He has raised an honorable family, he has spent his life working, he has never mixed in politics, nor, as other people do, has he ever shamed his family by indulging in drink and gambling! . . ."

And as she talked this way Grandmother was imposing and haughty.

Because it happens, Cristina, that Grandmother, who never goes out, surrounded as she always is by the Old World atmosphere of this house, bound up in her ideas of honor, with the prestige of her years and her austere virtue, really has the grandeur of a great lady who inspires a profound respect in everyone around her. From her contact with my grandfather, her husband, who was a poet, a historian, a minister in the government, and a professor, she acquired a distinguished grace in her speech and ease and elegance in all her words, circumstances that won her no doubt her great reputation for intelligence. At that instant, defending her son from the suspicions that Uncle Pancho's words might have awakened in my mind, she was, as I say, superbly proud. Her eyes, usually quiet, flashed now, burning with the fire of holy indignation, and under her severe brows, set off by her majestic white hair, they instilled fear.

I can't deny that for an instant I forgot my own ill fortune to admire Grandmother; I admired her with surprise, with veneration, and with pride, for the majesty and elegance she showed when indignant.

But on the other hand, Uncle Pancho remained impassive, for, as I have told you, he is unaffected by eloquence or the sublime oratory in which anger, enthusiasm, or disapproval usually display themselves. When Grandmother ended her brilliant apologetic of Uncle Eduardo with that wounding allusion: "He has never shamed his family by indulging in drink and gambling," Uncle Pancho, this Uncle Pancho who is unmovable, without speaking a word, went on standing still before Grandmother, with his two hands in his pockets, indifferent, placid, silent, contemplating the immensity of space over the patio, like a boulder standing before a stormy sea. I'm sure he was thinking, "And why answer? . . . What use are words? . . . They too are screens, lies, false coins! . . ."

But he didn't say this although he must have been reflecting on it while he stood quietly, during the long pause that followed Grandmother's indignation like a calm follows a tempest. Then, in the same thoughtful and silent attitude, he took a few steps down the corridor; little by little he halted; he took the watch out of his vest pocket; he looked at it, and exclaimed, "The Devil! It's almost twelve o'clock!"

And very calmly, as if nothing had happened, he took his walking stick and his hat from the wardrobe rack; he put on his hat; he gazed a second in the narrow mirror of the wardrobe; he smilingly said goodbye, "Until tomorrow!"

We heard the street door that closed after him, and his steps, which were fading down the entrance hall and the sidewalk.

In fact, shortly after Uncle Pancho departed, leaving us in a sort of suspended animation, the Cathedral clock, a philharmonic clock, Cristina, a chiming clock, which, with a face on each of the four sides of the tower, spends the day chiming the hours, the half hours, and the quarter hours with a monotonous song that is heard all over the city, and which at night recalls the fraternal and egalitarian "we must die" of the Carthusians—this clock began to strike earnestly and with great philosophy, "Tin, tan; tin, tan; . . ."

Well, a kind of song that in musical notes would be, "Mi, do, re, so! . . . (a quarter hour) So, re, mi, do! (another quarter hour) Do, si, la, mi!" . . . etc., etc.

Aunt Clara said at once, "It's twelve o'clock!"

And on her feet, as if moved by a spring, she crossed herself and intoned the Angelus aloud.

In view of my bad mood, I resolved not to answer in chorus with Grandmother, neither to the salutation nor to the Ave Marías. Because of that Aunt Clara gave me a look of disapproval while she was saying, "The Word was made flesh . . ."

But I remained quiet, and as soon as she finished, she crossed herself again, and saying nothing more, she gathered the clothes and the stockings; she folded them; she put them in the basket; she left with her heels clicking; and when the rhythmic beat was lost beyond the dining room and the second patio, between Grandmother and me a painful silence settled definitively. I jumped down from the column instantly with the object of leaving in my turn, but Grandmother motioned for me to come sit in Aunt Clara's little low chair, which was by her side, and then placing her hand on my shoulder, and with a very soft, very affectionate, very persuasive voice, setting her sewing completely aside, she began to talk to me.

"My daughter, you are not a thoughtless child any more. You are old enough to understand everything. You have a very clear intelligence, a very good heart, and with them you must judge things just as they are, without ever nursing hatred or resentment for anyone. We women, my dear, were born to forgive. The treasure of our indulgence should never run out, not even in the midst of the most cruel thorns of sacrifice. It is even more reasonable for that treasure of indulgence to be lavished on beings as beloved as our Parents are! Pancho's imprudent words oblige me to make some explanations to you which, up to a certain point, I would have preferred you to remain ignorant of forever; but given the circumstances, it is my moral duty to defend Eduardo from charges unjustly imputed to him. Listen to me carefully, my dear, because I love you as no one else does, and I'm speaking to you with complete impartiality. If today you own no part of the San Nicolás hacienda, and not even a cent of the inheritance your Mother left you, either, it is only and exclusively your Father's fault. He lived for the day, in the grand manner of a man who lives on his interest income, in absolute idleness, without ever thinking of tomorrow or of death. Oh! And this fatal evil, the same one that infects Pancho, is an evil that comes from their upbringing, an evil that had its origin way back, and therefore neither of them can be reproached for it."

She was silent a second as if to put her thoughts in order, and she continued, "The guilty one, the one really guilty of all this, was none other than your grandfather. Yes, your Grandfather Martín Alonso who was certainly very likeable, very gallant, very gentlemanly, very artful! Oh! And don't think I didn't know him, for as you know, Martín was a first cousin of mine!"

And then, in a tale that was going to be very long, in order to better explain the process of my ruin, Grandmother climbed up several branches in my genealogical tree and began to describe, in detail, the person and the household of my grandfather Martín Alonso, but back, in the most remote times when my adolescent grandfather still had no plans for marriage. According to her, nothing and no one in Caracas would ever again equal the splendor of that house and of those dances, attended by the most select society, brimming with elegance and distinction, sumptuous. (Oh! I have to laugh at the elegance and luxury of those days, Cristina, without electric lights, women without makeup, and couples who must have danced some waltz like "Over the Waves" a yard and a half apart! But don't forget it is Grandmother speaking.) The house of my great-grandparents Alonso was then very luxurious, because the Alonsos were so rich, so very rich, that they were perhaps the foremost capitalists in Venezuela. They had a fortune in jewelry, tapestries, pictures, rugs, and china, and blah, blah! Grandmother, who, as I have told you, has a great way with words, set out, with such enthusiasm and with such detail, to describe the magnificence of that house and of those fiestas where her husband, my grandfather, Don Manuel Aguirre, met her and courted her, that I, in spite of my horrible bad humor, for an instant saw her blossom triumphantly in the Alonso salons, with her wide crinoline pompadour, her black curls falling down the back of her neck, her mother-of-pearl fan in one hand, bent, smiling, fainting with ingeniousness, beside the future professor Don Manuel—well, something of the sort, which vacillated between a portrait of the Empress Eugenia, and that pair of dolls that I had left an hour ago fluffed out in my room.

Having finished the description or apologetic for the early Alonso family, their home, and their dances, Grandmother focused on my Grandfather Martín, principal heir of all that splendor. According to her, my brilliant and seductive Grandfather married very young, married very well, and his life would have been as pleasant and happy as that of his parents if he had not had the misfortune of becoming a widower a few years after his marriage.

"The same thing, the very same thing that was to happen later to your Father!" Grandmother commented with a deep sigh as she reached here. After this comment she paused and went on with her story.

"From a marriage as ephemeral as it was happy, my Grandfather Martín had two sons: Uncle Pancho and Papa. He went to Europe with them while they were still babies, only a trip for his health, planning to return just a few months later. But once in Europe, he lost all judgment! It went to his head, he suffered a delirium of grandeur, he quickly settled in Paris, he gave himself over entirely to diversion, and since a life of dissipation and luxury is a cliff that leads to a bottomless abyss, day by day growing more fond of such a frivolous existence, he never returned to Venezuela. His two sons grew up there; and those children, reared in an atmosphere of idleness and waste, with no habit of working whatever, when they grew up, followed their father's example. Then, together, like three companions of the same age, they gave themselves to dissipation, to squandering money, to pleasures, to the most blameworthy indolence and irresponsibility. Oh! The fruits of bad training! Oh! The dangers of luxury!"

And while Grandmother, with these and other similar words, deeply lamented such a disordered existence, I, truly, just as I had imagined her a little while before, in her ballooning crinoline, now imagined my Grandfather and his two sons, dressed in tails, white tie, a flower in each lapel, and silk hats at a rakish angle; that is to say, something like three jovial characters from a Viennese Operetta, the kind that walk jauntily into some cabaret accompanied by Frou-Frous and Mimis, who stand in a row one after the other, with a glass of champagne in their hands, who lift the same foot in time, while they sing in chorus, first to the right and then to the left, that song of "Viva, viva la alegría" or some other suggestive song of that style. Oh! Cristina, how much fun this Holy Family must have had and what a pleasure it must be to have money and to be a man!

A few years later, when my grandfather died still young, Papa and Uncle Pancho went on spending madly, now without stint or moderation. This, added to a very bad administration, revolutions, crises, price declines, etc., caused their immense fortune to finally crumble in a short time. When Papa at last returned to Venezuela, he was thirty years old and he was now almost ruined. As for Uncle Pancho, he didn't come back; rather, in accord with his theories about the proper use for money, he resolved to stay in Paris indefinitely as long as the mail brought him the celebrated twenty thousand–franc checks.

Fortunately Papa, once here, pressed by necessity, which according to Grandmother is the best of mothers, dedicated himself to recouping his fortune. There was still time to save himself from poverty! And thus regenerated by work he became a different person. What activity, what intelligence, what astuteness he showed in rebuilding his finances!

Within a few years of having arrived in Caracas he had already married and, once married, he met success in his work and stabilized his life. Because he, who had liquidated all of his diminished fortune in order to concentrate it and to redeem the San Nicolás hacienda, a magnificent hacienda, a true "gold mine," which had been in the family many years and was now exhausted, abandoned, loaded with debt; when he got married, he added Mama's little assets to the liquidation of his own assets, and he dedicated himself fully to his project: to redeem San Nicolás. And he became so enthusiastic, so very enthusiastic about agriculture and making the hacienda productive, that he settled at San Nicolás after he got married. There he plunged into work, there I was born; there he spent his very happy years of marriage, and finally there, no one knows how, Mama caught that terrible typhus that killed her in a few days. A short time after this catastrophe, Papa got sick, sad, neurasthenic, the same as my grandfather thirty years before, and he also resolved to go to Europe on a trip for recreation and health. And it was then that, obstinately, against the wishes of Grandmother, who offered to take care of me during his absence, paying no heed to her advice, breaking her heart by tearing me away from her side, never to return, he embarked at La Guaira with my nurse and me, that long-ago morning that I still remember.

Up to here, Cristina, I agree with Grandmother's story. In it the truth appears, pure and clear, as pebbles appear at the bottom of very clean water. But as you will see, from here on the water is muddied, thanks to the handwashing of Uncle Eduardo, and now, under the words sincerely spoken, the truth no longer appears before my eyes with that sharp clarity it had at the start.

It seems, before his tragedy, Papa had become enthused about some industrial enterprise having to do with a textile mill and, in combination with that, he had planted a large amount of cotton at San Nicolás, which by then was completely free of debt and flourishing. When Mama died and Papa got sick, he decided on his trip, drew Uncle Eduardo into the cotton operation, into the industrial enterprise, gave him a full power of attorney, and named him administrator of the hacienda.

Then he left.

"What happened then?" Grandmother continued saying, with her affirmative voice tremulous with conviction. "What I had warned him of so often happened, what I foresaw! Once there, he remained in Paris indefinitely, he went back to his life of dissipation as a bachelor, he flung himself into idleness and spending hand over fist, little by little he was losing his fortune and with it he also lost what belonged to you alone: the small inheritance that your Mother had left you! Eduardo, on the contrary, worked assiduously, never leaving the hacienda, almost without coming into Caracas; you can say his children grew up there; naturally he was economical, and while your father was spending madly, Eduardo was acquiring more and more. As Eduardo has told me, a very short time before the almost sudden death of your Papa, he had called him for the purpose of agreeing on a liquidation. This was done after the tragedy. The result of it was that Antonio left nothing but debts . . . and just think! Eduardo not only covered them, but also, with great generosity, paid for the extra expenses of the clinic and the funeral; he gave the money for your trip, for you to live three months in Europe, and finally, as a gift to you, he also sacrificed those ten thousand bolívares that you so thoughtlessly threw away in Paris. Do you understand now why I was angry about Pancho's terribly unjust allusions? Eduardo has been very generous with you: it is necessary for you to know it and to appreciate it! He has been very generous . . . very generous . . . almost as much as he is nowadays with me! . . ."

These last words of Grandmother had been falling in my soul like a rain of molten lead might have fallen on my head. I felt . . . I don't know what I felt! The tone of conviction, roundly affirmative, with which she was talking had conquered my spirit to such a point that now in my soul the indignation of the bereft victim and the humiliating perplexity of doubt were mixing with desperate effervescence.

So not only did I have nothing, nothing in the world, but besides, I was supposed to be eternally grateful to Uncle Eduardo for his kindnesses! . . . I thought about the air of superiority with which María Antonia had treated me the day of my arrival and it made me want to burn, one after another, all the objects acquired by means of those ten thousand bolívares. Oh! . . . What humiliation! . . . What anger! . . .

But suddenly my first suspicion overcame me again. No! . . . No! . . . Grandmother, who was speaking in good faith, must be deceived by Uncle Eduardo . . . Yes . . . no doubt. Uncle Pancho had said so quite clearly! Besides, that face! Not in vain had he seemed so ugly to me, so horrible, when I saw him for the first time aboard the ship!

After praising the infinite generosity of Uncle Eduardo a multitude of times, Grandmother's voice at last fell silent. Then I, with my teeth clenched, sat reflecting an instant on all that I've told you. While a great confusion of perplexities and doubts was still churning inside me, I, trying to feign indifference, replied with the same firm tone with which she had spoken, "But Grandmother, I never saw that Papa lived in the midst of such wastefulness as you say, and always, always, he used to talk about San Nicolás as if he were the only, exclusive owner. How is it possible that he had never realized his absolute ruin?" "Your Father, my daughter," continued Grandmother with her convinced and magnetic tone, "Your Father, in Europe, never took any notice again of the state of his business. He was absorbed by a book of historical criticism that it seems he was writing, and . . . by other distractions!"

She was quiet an instant, and then she added more energetically, sowing her words with pauses and mysterious reticence, "Oh! . . . Men! . . . Men, my dear, spend a lot sometimes . . . a lot . . . that Paris! . . . Oh! That Paris! . . . It is the tomb of all our great fortunes, and often, it is also the tomb of honorable and tranquil happiness . . ."

She went on talking and the mysterious tone continued to undermine my earlier certainty; because now, mute, with my eyes open, fixed on the plants in the patio, submerged entirely in doubt, I only had strength to comment inwardly, "And who knows! . . . Who knows!"

Yes! The only thing I really knew is that that morning, in that dark hour I had just spent, there had been revealed before my eyes a clear, inevitable, and frightful fact: my absolute poverty, without any remission or hope other than the support of the same ones who perhaps had robbed me!

Grandmother, touched no doubt by my approving silence, softening her voice more and more, went on torturing me as she tried to console me, "I understand my dearest, that this news disappoints you, but think . . . just think, you're not alone in this world! How many other girls are more unfortunate than you, because they live in utter poverty and moreover they have to work in order to eat! They are surrounded by so many dangers! You will never lack anything as long as I live. Unfortunately, I'm not rich, I have nothing save what is indispensable; but I know that Eduardo will always look after me, and I, in turn, will work to fill all your needs. Furthermore you are pretty, distinguished, you are well educated, you belong to the best society in Caracas. You are sure to make a good marriage! Don't look at your situation from the European point of view. There, a young girl's poverty generally spells the complete failure of her life. Not here . . . There they tell a woman: 'You have so much money, you're worth so much.' Not so here. Here the only thing that counts is being pretty and above all, virtuous! . . . In our society, so failing in other respects, there still exists a certain delicacy in men. Our men truly worship virtuous women, and when they are going to marry they never look for a wealthy companion, but rather for an irreproachable companion. Because of that, because of that, my dear, I want to see you always without the slightest shadow of frivolity. I want you to be extremely severe with yourself, María Eugenia. Listen carefully: everywhere, and here more than anywhere else, the virtue of a woman who is beyond reproach is worth a great deal more than her money . . . Look, I was poor when your Grandfather fell in love with me and . . . I was happy . . . oh, so happy! . . . Your paternal grandmother, Julia Alonso, married Martín, a millionaire, when she and her family were living in utter poverty. They had to work just to be able to eat! . . . Rosita Aristeigueta, a relative of none other than Bolívar and of the Marquis del Toro . . . the Urdaneta girls . . . the Soublettes . . . the Mendozas . . . María Isabel Tovar, my cousin . . ."

And going back again seventy years in time, Grandmother, with her very soft, caressing voice, began to weave, one after another, simple chronicles of love, in which, without monetary interest, marriages of idyllic, patriarchal happiness appeared.

Sitting next to her, staring at the plants on the patio, motionless, petrified, in my disaster, I submitted in silence, listening to the old stories of Grandmother's old lady friends; then I listened to the stories of their daughters, and last I listened to the stories of their granddaughters. I heard them all with resignation and with melancholy. For, to my ears, those names were sweetly evocative. I had heard them many times, pronounced by Papa's lips, when he, too, with a very different object from Grandmother's, referred to the same process of Caracas's aristocracy, that is to say, the painful history of almost all those *criollos*, descendants of the conquistadors, who called themselves "Mantuans" in Colonial times, who founded and ruled the cities; who engraved their coats of arms on the doors of the old mansions; who, with their blood, forged the independence of half of the American continent; who declined afterwards, oppressed by persecutions and party hatreds; and whose granddaughters or great-granddaughters, today forgotten or poor as I am now, awaited with resignation the hour of marriage or the hour of death, making sweets for dances, or weaving floral wreaths for funerals.

And since the tone, and the names, and the stories, were in harmony with my state of mind, as I listened to Grandmother's voice, I let myself drift gently on the wings of conformity; my nerves began to calm, irritating ideas died out one after another; the lulling and maternal tone insinuated itself like a lullaby in my spirit and the monotonous words ended by echoing in my ears without meaning . . . Contemplating the green foliage of the rosebushes on the patio, I surrendered to a consideration of the eternal greening of plants under the light of the sun . . . Yes . . . Life had a mysterious force that conquered everything . . . maybe I might yet be reborn to happiness . . . as Grandmother rightly said, marriage, that is, love, that distant love of youth, was still waiting for me in life. Perhaps with it might come the realization of so many impossible longings that now tortured my existence! My soul, like the smallest rosebushes on the patio, had not yet flowered!

And while sweet, benign resignation was spreading languidly over my tormented spirit, looking steadily at the patio plants and with the lulling voice always in my ears, I asked myself for the first time with anxiety and curiosity what love really was, that love that Grandmother was showing me as the only door through which I could now enter life, that love that, having always been familiar to my ears, now seemed to enclose a strange and unknown sense, that love that was now the only possible redemption for my existence. Oh! Love! What miraculous secret was locked in the most intimate part of its essence? And moreover, what do you suppose Grandmother understood by "happiness"?

Suddenly it seemed to me that what Grandmother called "happiness" must be something very sad, very boring, something that, like this house, must also smell of jasmine, candle wax, or rubs with Elliman's Embrocation. And as low as I was, Cristina, faced with such a deduction, I felt an immense desire to burst into tears. But I didn't cry. My eyes just got moist and with my moist eyes I continued to reflect avidly on the same theme, that is to say, on the true meaning of the word "love" and of the word "happiness," because it was as if at that moment I had just heard them for the first time.

After that, without quite knowing why, I began to think about my friend, the Colombian poet that I met on board ship. For a long time I pictured him very clearly in my imagination and strangely, in spite of time and distance, in a mental vision that was very clear, I was little by little discovering in my friend a multitude of charming qualities that I earlier, given my great bewilderment, looking at him up close, had never noticed. I remembered, for example, the exquisite perfume that scented his handkerchief; the perfect tailoring of his clothes; his impeccable grooming; his refined manners; his elegant Bourbon nose; his good conversation; his indisputable talent for making verses; and his surname that was a very illustrious name in the high society of Bogotá.

And suddenly, when Grandmother's voice paused in the long sentimental chronicle, I took advantage of the juncture and instantly asked, "Tell me, Grandmother, do the people who live in Bogotá come to Caracas very often? Is it true that the trip is a very long trip that takes many days?"

And she, abandoning her prior theme completely, very kindly and complacently engulfed herself in a lengthy explanation.

"Well I have always heard that if the Magdalena River is low, the trip is so slow that it becomes almost, almost, like going from here to Europe. You see the problem! In spite of the fact that the distance is relatively very short, it seems when they set up the aerial service that the newspapers talk about now . . ."

⠑⠄   ⠑⠄   ⠑⠄

But that same afternoon, after lunch, around three o'clock, the holy spirit of conformity had fled from me totally. Locked here in my room, stretched out on the bed, barefoot, in a kimono, with my hands crossed behind my head, I successively studied the ceiling, the lurid wallpaper, the little doll lamp on the desk, the half-open shutter on the window, and thought with desperation about the horrible future that awaited me. The only course open to me was the one that Grandmother had set forth for this morning, "Try to be the most irreproachable girl possible," in other words, try to be the biggest zero in the world, to the end that some man, seduced by my nullity, might do me the immense favor of placing himself beside me as a whole number, elevating me by act and benefaction of his presence to a round and respectable sum that would thus acquire a certain real value before society and the world. Meanwhile imprisonment, severity, ennui, and gratitude to Uncle Eduardo . . .

"Oh, oh, oh, what a way to live! What a horror! I wish I were a dog! Yes! I wish I were a bird, a tree, a stone, anything except myself!"

And thinking this, I thrashed in desperation on the bed, like a fish they've just pulled out of the water.

Confess, Cristina, that my situation deserved no less.

Happily, in a moment of calm my eyes fell by chance on the heap of books and notebooks that constitute my small musical library, which, at that historical moment were open and in disarray on a chair, for I had not yet assigned them an appropriate place in the wardrobe. The sight of a page where ordered groups of eighth notes and demisemiquavers peeked, very vaguely brought me the idea of music, then it brought me the idea of the piano, and finally it brought me the idea of study. I remembered that back at school, the professor who came to give us classes often praised my good ear saying, besides, that my hand was the long, firm hand that good pianists have. The word "pianist" made me think immediately about my compatriot Teresa Carreño, who, as you know, became a musical star applauded and celebrated the world over. Thinking about Teresa Carreño, I remembered Papa telling me she was a great artist who owed her glory to the obstinacy and perseverance with which she had dedicated herself to her studies from her youth. Then I again remembered the opinion of our school professor about my musical aptitude, and suddenly, Eureka! A hope lit up the darkness of my future like a match that had unexpectedly been struck in the depths of a cave.

"I will give myself to art!" I exclaimed. "Oh! Yes, I will study the piano eight, nine, or ten hours a day. Thanks to my natural aptitude, developed by patient and methodical study, in a few years I can become a real pianist; I will apply to the conservatory, perhaps I'll get a prize; once the prize is obtained I will give concerts; my concerts will make me famous; my fame may become universal; and then . . . Why not? . . . Just like Teresa Carreño I too will experience triumph, applause, and glory! . . . That's right! . . . And to do this, I will set to work without delay next Monday . . . No! Tomorrow! . . . No! . . . Now!"

And immediately I got up from the bed; I put on my shoes; I wrapped myself in my kimono; I tied the sash tightly around my hips; I took the notebooks from the chair and, having tucked them under my arm, I headed for the parlor.

As I reached the end of the entrance corridor I met Aunt Clara and Grandmother, who had again settled down with their respective glasses on their noses, and their respective sewing implements on their laps. Seeing them so absorbed, I halted and went to them to explain, "I'm going to play the piano if it won't bother you."

And I continued walking calmly toward the parlor door. It was only a few seconds later, when I heard Aunt Clara's highly alarmed voice, that I could appreciate the horror that my announcement had produced in her.

"But, María Eugenia, for Heaven's sake, child, come here," she said with a tremulous voice that oscillated between amazement and reproach, "how can you sit down to play the piano, when your Father hasn't even been dead five months?"

"And what has that to do with it!" I answered after stopping and planting myself insolently in front of her, as she stared at me in astonishment over her glasses. "I'll play studies, melodies, nocturnes . . . well, indifferent things or sad things."

"But since the day we learned of your Father's death, the windows here have been closed, María Eugenia, and no one has touched the piano since. How could it possibly be you, his daughter, who as soon as you arrive plays it again? Think. What would the neighbors say?"

"The neighbors? I have nothing but laughter and scorn for the neighbors, Aunt Clara, I despise them altogether, and what I would like is for all of them to go to hell!"

"And why are you going to scorn and laugh at the neighbors, María

Eugenia, or send them to hell? Why, they are all very decent people, they belong to the best of Caracas! I must inform you that this street has admirably good residents! Doesn't it, Mama?"

"Oh! So, because the neighborhood is very distinguished I am going to live under the control of the neighbors too!"

"But come here, María Eugenia, my dear, come, think," intervened Grandmother with the same persuasive voice she used this morning, "Clara is right! . . . Consider what she is telling you. A father is something very great, very sacred, who only dies one time in this life. You should have feelings . . . You need to educate your heart . . . What can be expected of a woman who is incapable of sacrificing herself a little, just a little . . . no more than what is generally required to observe the sacred mourning for her Father with decorum? . . ."

"But what does the piano have to do with my heart! Darn it! It's not as if . . ."

"Don't use interjections, María Eugenia, my dear, this is the third time I've had to tell you! It isn't proper for a young lady! And furthermore, I'm taking advantage of this opportunity to tell you something. Look at how you are dressed; against the light with that Japanese robe you're wearing you look most indecent. You're completely naked! Why must you run around without a slip, María Eugenia?"

"All right, but let's first settle this matter about the mourning," I demanded, immobile and furious with my books under my arm, "I don't understand at all what logical relationship can exist between Papa's death and the piano in this house! 'Feelings!' Feelings, indeed! Why, music was invented precisely for that—to express feelings! Tell me if it isn't so, Grandmother, tell me. For example, what is an elegy or a funeral march except a refined, artistic, and genial system for condolence, as you might say?"

But Grandmother, who had taken off her glasses now, sketched a gesture in the air with them that seemed to anathematize all reasoning, and shaking her head negatively from right to left and left to right, she said in that peremptory tone that conviction is in the habit of using when it doesn't deign to come down to the despicable and irreverent terrain of argument, "No, no, no, my daughter, you don't convince me! I think if you don't have a good enough heart to spontaneously observe the rigorous mourning demanded by the death of your father, you should pretend that you do. Otherwise you would make a very bad impression on me and on all sensible people who learned of it, I assure you!"

"Well . . . so, without any possible appeal, the piano must not be played! Fine, fine, fine, then not another word. I won't play!"

And making a military style half-turn, I indignantly returned with my music notebooks under my arm, along the same path I had come. When I got to this room, I threw all the music books furiously on the same chair, where they once more acquired their former scrambled appearance. Then I put my hands on my hips and exclaimed out loud, which under the circumstances echoed in the room in a truly sublime way, "In the morning they take away my fortune; now in the afternoon they snatch away my Glory!"

And I stood a few seconds with my hands on my hips and my eyes fixed on the floor.

But, happily, as you must recall, Cristina, my imagination, which is fertile in times of calm, at moments of indignation is even more fertile. After ten seconds of staring at the floor, thanks to this great imaginative fertility, I had already found an immediate plan that was going to serve me at the same time as explanatory, as reprisal, and as entertainment. It was to go out with Uncle Pancho, anywhere, as soon as possible.

"Oh!" I said to myself, "I'll talk to him alone and that way I'll find out the truth concerning Uncle Eduardo's generosity."

And immediately I phoned Uncle Pancho. He agreed to come by for me at four-thirty exactly. Then, very satisfied with my project, having nearly an hour's time to dress, I started grooming myself as I like to, that is to say, slowly, with much calm, tranquillity and detail. At last, my toilette complete, perfumed, my hat on, dressed for a casual outing, you know, simple, sober, very elegant, I spent at least ten minutes walking, smiling, and posing in front of my wardrobe mirror, because if truth be told, Cristina, the fury that had made my eyes very bright since this morning, added to the V-neck cut of my dress, the small hat, the long crêpe Georgette veil, and the Guerlain lipstick, I looked . . . well . . . I looked better than ever! And left to myself I would have stayed longer posing and smiling before the mirror, had not the Cathedral clock with its song like a Carthusian baritone begun to inform me, "Mi, do, re, so! . . . So, re, mi, do! . . ."

Or, that is to say, that it was now four-thirty.

So I wouldn't make Uncle Pancho wait, I went hurrying toward the entrance corridor, where I appeared triumphantly, my head held high, the veil pulled back "a lo manto real," and buttoning my gloves.

As could be anticipated, seeing me appear like this, so unexpectedly, in hat and gloves, shock again took hold of Grandmother and Aunt Clara.

"Where are you going at this time of day and with whom?" Grandmother interrogated me instantly in a deeply aggrieved tone, and taking off her glasses, which, as you must have seen already, is an indisputable storm warning.

Besides being very delighted with myself, I came prepared for the attack. I responded smilingly, very graciously, putting my left hand, chest high, along the line of buttons down my dress, an attitude that must have lent me a certain Napoleonic arrogance, "Well I'm going for a ride to Los Mecedores with Uncle Pancho! I believe it is a very solitary place appropriate for my rigorous mourning!"

And having made this declaration, I opened my purse, I took out my little mirror and began to look at myself under the outdoor light of the patio, because it was very urgent that I know if the rebellious tip of my nose was well powdered. But as I noticed it was still a little shiny, I took the puff out of my enameled vanity, I shook it and began to powder my nose, stretching my mouth with concentrated attention. In the meantime, Grandmother continued, with her glasses held high in her hand, and with the complaining voice, "You're going out just like that, for an excursion with Pancho, without consulting me, without telling me . . . Oh! I see that you are very independent!"

She exhaled a deep sigh, paused, and went on saying with the complaining voice now turned into an emotional lament, "It will be utterly rude for you not to be here, María Eugenia, when this evening guests who already have notified us are coming, and coming just to see you, to say hello to you, to meet you. To slight them in that way! Why, it is a discourtesy without precedent! For politeness' sake you ought to wait at least until those visitors arrive."

"Oh! The visitors, Grandmother! It's too much!" I exclaimed tragically with my vanity case in one hand and the puff in the other. "They all ask me the same stupid things, 'If I miss Paris and if I like Caracas!' I've had enough of that eternal litany! And they're all, all, all just alike! Grandmother, would you like for me to tell you the effect your friends have on me? Well, the truth is, I can't tell them apart! I don't know if the lady who came yesterday is the same one who was here day before yesterday, or the one who will come back day after tomorrow! They are like those volumes of books that you see sometimes in libraries, you know, all exactly alike, all together, all bound in parchment, and if by chance you pick them up and you open them you find that inside they are written in Latin or in Old Spanish. Well, you can't even understand it!"

"You're mistaken, María Eugenia, the people who have come to see you are all very cultured, very respectable, relatives or friends of mine, among the best in Caracas, to whom you should be grateful."

"Oh, Grandmother, for Heaven's sake, let me go out! Look, if I don't go out, I'll smother, yes, I'll die, and tonight what the visitors will see will be my dead body lying in state surrounded by four candles! Oh! Tell them that my head was hurting, my teeth, anything, that I had to go to the dentist's and for them to wait for me. I won't stay out late, you'll see, I won't stay out late!"

"Do what you like, María Eugenia! I can't spend the whole day arguing with you nor do I want you to be miserable because you're in my home. Go on, go out with Pancho if you want to so much!"

And putting her glasses on again, Grandmother went back to her sewing after exhaling another sigh in which complete disapproval was mingled with the most profound discouragement.

And at that precise instant, the door to the entrance hall opened and Uncle Pancho's jovial head, happy, smiling, expressive, appeared in the corridor. After saying hello to Grandmother and to Aunt Clara very affectionately and as if nothing had happened this morning, he found me in the middle of the patio with my mouth still open between the mirror, the powder puff, and the vanity case. When he saw me he came to me, and while he examined me on all sides, he proclaimed with great amazement, "Oh! Niece, Niece, how pretty you are, and what a breath of youth you bring me with that dress and that bewitching hat! How much you benefited from your last little stay in Paris! Eh? . . . In the pictures that you used to send earlier you were not the same girl that you are today, no, no, no! See, now, at this moment you are Paris, pure Paris, from that faint little scent of your black veil, to the tip of your patent leather shoes. And they pretend that here women dress well! Really! How absurd! This! Paris, this is chic! . . . Well, and the fact that you look so pretty, besides! Walk around so I can look at you. Adorable! Perfect! Now, when they see us together in the carriage they'll watch us drive by thunderstruck, and tomorrow they'll drive me crazy at the club asking about the beautiful and elegant stranger, 'the lady in mourning.' They might even believe you are some recently arrived artist whose affections I have won, and since they are so envious . . ."

"Oh! How funny!" I exclaimed, full of laughter and satisfaction. "Suppose I were really an artist, Uncle Pancho! But a good artist! Eh? A celebrity. And suppose instead of being your niece I were your mistress!"

The sound of the front door as it was closing behind us prevented my hearing the energetic protests that Grandmother and Aunt Clara must have voiced, given such suppositions, as nonsensical as they were offensive to my dignity and my virtue. But I, who was charmed by Uncle Pancho's exuberant compliments, once inside the carriage, began to explain in great detail where I had bought my hat, which as he could well see was a very elegant model. Oh! Very, very elegant!

❧   ❧   ❧

But suddenly, soon after the carriage pulled away, I became very serious, and completely forgetting my apparel and myself, I started observing the street, interrogating Uncle Pancho, and communicating my personal observations to him.

It was the first time that I had seen the city since the afternoon of my arrival.

Now familiarized with the inner life of Caracas, initiated into the secrets of its spirit, I was seeing everything from a new perspective. I watched the long rows of houses struck by the afternoon sun, I evoked Grandmother's stories, her lady friends, their romantic histories, and I seemed to be discovering very clearly, beneath the maternal shade of the eaves, those invisible relationships that objects have with their owners, animate mortals before the eternal inanimate world, traces of the past and of the dead, all of that which is like the soul and like the aristocracy of things.

Uncle Pancho commented as he pointed out the wide grillwork bars that were lined up at each side on the walks, "Do you see the windows? Do you see nearly all of them closed? Well, barely ten years ago, at this time of the day, they were already beginning to open, and from five to seven, the street turned into a garden full of inner life. That was traditional, it was classical, and it was very picturesque. But cinematography has come and has done away with the window. Yes, the bored lady who used to spend the whole afternoon sitting at the window for entertainment, and the young girl in love who used to chat with her sweetheart, and the girl who used to stand at the window so the suitor who hovered about her house could see her from afar, well, now they all go to the evening show at the theaters and while the movie houses fill up, the street is deserted! See, see how few of the windows are open."

As a matter of fact, almost all were closed, and thus, closed and all alike, listening to Uncle Pancho's observation, I watched them in succession with melancholy.

Oh! Windows, windows bedecked with flowers from Grandmother's days! Crude altars of love, where the old bars, in the shape of a cross, are the only things that eternally continue kissing! . . . And how strongly I felt that for the first time I was seeing, in its quietude, the very ancestral enigma of my boredom, sitting behind the bars, knitting cobwebs of illusions in the mortal silence of the street!

And meanwhile, Cristina, the carriage, between the double row of crowded bars, was climbing, climbing, up through the city.

After having gone uphill a good while, we reached the highest neighborhood in Caracas, which is the one called La Pastora. We climbed still more and then came to the outskirts of the city.

Uncle Pancho continued satisfying my questions and clarifying my memories.

These suburbs of La Pastora, which are the highest and the most backward in Caracas, are also the most characteristic. The streets there are paved with stones, the sidewalks are made of flagstone, green patches of grass grow wherever a bit of earth appears, and it is the neighborhood where generally brown-skinned inhabitants live, shamefaced poor, and sick people who seek the hilltop breezes. I wanted to see the painful, colorful destitution and, forgetting the country excursion, I first wanted to explore the neighborhood.

"Take me down the oldest streets, Uncle Pancho, take me down the poorest, the ugliest, the dirtiest, the saddest, because I want to see them all, all of them!"

And under Uncle Pancho's guidance, behind the horses' deliberate walk, we began to thread our way through narrow streets—streets, Cristina, that rose steeply or dropped away in an improbable manner. Sometimes, the paving suddenly stopped and the street was a dirt road without sidewalks. Then the street ended, the carriage stopped, and in front of the carriage was a ravine, a deep ditch, with scandalously exuberant vegetation that flung itself downward toward the city, flooding the jumble of rooftops like a great green overflow.

Along these rough and picturesque streets, the inner life of the homes was shown frankly with all the immodesty of its ugliness and poverty. On the sidewalks, beside closed doors, blocking the way, crawled the little naked children of the neighborhood, little blacks or little mulattos who barely knew how to walk, whose deformed bodies, from time to time, showed white smudges of dust picked up as the dark epidermis rubbed against the ground, while above, looking out from behind the shutters or sitting at the wide-open, barred windows, were the brightly decorated heads of the mulattas, petulant, wearing ribbons of violently brilliant colors, whose eyes, as they caught sight of us in the distance, fixed on our carriage ardent and luminous pupils that seemed to be lit by a thirst to see.

Uncle Pancho commented, "Isn't it true that there is something tortured in the expression of these people? Look. You could say that the profound hatred of the races that were reconciled for an instant to form them is still struggling in their features and in their spirits. And in that painful struggle, look! Only equivocation and the grotesque triumph! Isn't it true that in all of them there is something terribly inharmonious that is much worse than ugliness? That's true of their spirit too; it has no defined personality and they must feel the most terrible disorientation."

Since after this morning my life had abruptly taken a turn toward a new horizon, now from my present point of view, I looked at those deep eyes that were devouring us as we drove by, I responded with a kind, fraternal gaze and I said, softening the harsh opinion Uncle Pancho had expressed, "There may be lack of harmony or ugliness in the mixture of features and in their ambivalent desires that impel them to tie a green bow around their heads or some red braid, but look at their eyes, see how brilliant, and how interesting their eyes are. It seems that looking out on the street they are begging for something impossible that will never be given to them!"

"Yes," said Uncle Pancho becoming excited suddenly, "it is the voice of their aspirations imprisoned in a body that tyrannizes them and binds them with chains as it proclaims aloud the mortifying inferiority of its origin. And this quarrel between the body and the sensitive soul of the mulatto, as you well say, is a very interesting conflict. It is the same tragedy that Cyrano's deformed nose hid, much more cruel and much more beautiful here, because it is more humiliating, and it is irreparable. Yes! The mulatto is the patient melting pot where painfully the heterogeneous elements of so many renegade races are fused. In him is locked the cause of all our anxiety, of all our errors, our absurd democracy, our errant instability. Perhaps in him is also being elaborated some social type, exquisite and complex, that we still do not suspect!"

And after philosophizing in this way, without making any further comments, we remained silent a long time, watching on both sides of the carriage that mystery of humble life that showed itself to the street through open doors, shutters, and windows, until finally, we had seen enough of the suburb, and we went out into the countryside.

When I felt the freshness of the sweet country breeze on my face, immediately, without consulting Uncle Pancho, I ordered the driver to stop the horses, and I proposed that we walk the rest of the way. He got out of the carriage very accommodatingly, and I, getting out after him, with my veil rolled up on my arm, raced happily toward a little hillock along the road, I climbed to the top, and once there I drank in the air eagerly, I filled my lungs, and thus, standing on my pedestal, I stood a few seconds greeting the landscape.

The afternoon was as peaceful as I could have wished. In the distance the sun was seeking the top of a hill. The wonderful valley stretched out below, surrounding the city; the city blooming with vegetation nestled in the center of the valley, with white walls, red-tiled roofs, while at my back presiding over everything, the majesty of the great mountain, Avila, rose up maternally and pensively.

After studying the afternoon from the top of the rise, I went back to the road, and, then, step by step in a slow walk full of stops and conversation, Uncle Pancho and I went off down a path until we reached the jungle of my infancy, whose same trees, under their peaceful shade, still support the looped vines I used to swing on at "Los Mecedores."

Anxious to know Uncle Pancho's concrete opinion about Uncle Eduardo and how he had treated me, while we were walking, I repeated to him literally everything Grandmother had told me this morning about Papa, San Nicolás, and Uncle Eduardo. Given my excitement, I was continually stopping the stroll or the story to ask Uncle Pancho his opinion or to vehemently explain to him the multiple reasons for my distrust and my perplexity. But he, Cristina, as if he were very bored with that theme, just as he had done during the carriage drive, now, too, tried to direct the conversation to any detail or incident along the way. This stubborn reticence finally made me so impatient that at last, sitting now under a tree in Los Mecedores, where the stillness and the shadows made my words more urgent, I demanded imperiously that he tell me whatever he knew for certain about the matter, because I considered I had a right to know. The question thus posed, Uncle Pancho sat thoughtfully an instant and as if indecisive, but then, he made up his mind to speak and said very calmly, "Very well, since you are so determined to know what I think about the matter, I'm going to tell you. But I don't want you to let it poison your existence! Misfortune, María Eugenia, of whatever kind, should be accepted with courage, trying to remedy what can be remedied, of course, but eliminating from our memory everything irreparable, so as not to waste energy on hatreds and sterile vengeance. Oh! It is a very useful wisdom to know how to forget!"

And having pronounced this exordium, he added little by little, lighting a cigarette while I, eager for his words, was devouring him with my eyes, "I think . . . or rather I am most certain, that Antonio, your father, besides spending his income, must have spent perhaps a fourth of the capital that San Nicolás was worth; the rest, that is to say, the remaining three-fourths . . . your Uncle Eduardo stole from you! . . . Oh! Have no doubt! . . . In an orderly way, eh? Certainly, in a very orderly way, very clearly, presenting the most correct accounts and, above all, showing lavish generosity, which as you know . . ."

But I didn't let him conclude. Like this morning when I was perched on the column, now, too, in my imagination I suddenly saw Uncle Eduardo's figure, whose likeness, illustrated by Uncle Pancho's prior words was becoming so abominable that I could only rebuke it with my teeth clenched and in a paroxysm of indignation, "Oh! Herod! Caiaphas! Hypocrite! . . ."

"See what I told you?" questioned Uncle Pancho. "You're going to get excited, and if later you can't show enough prudence . . ."

But the word "prudence," heard in such circumstances, Cristina, irritated me a great deal more even than Uncle Eduardo's image, for which reason I again interrupted Uncle Pancho, exclaiming in the greatest agitation, "Oh! If you think I'm going to be prudent after what you've just told me, it's because you consider me deaf, an imbecile, or a mute! Look, I swear to you, Uncle Pancho, that now, as soon as I get home, I'm going to tell Grandmother everything, absolutely everything I think of Uncle Eduardo. Yes! I'll tell her that he ought to go to prison as a thief with clothes striped white and red, the kind that jailbirds wear; that I detest him with all my heart, and that what I would like is to see his horrible skinny silhouette, like Judas, swinging from the gallows, with a sack of coins at his feet and with his tongue hanging out!"

"Great!!" broke in Uncle Pancho with a loud laugh. "Fine, you do that! Look, with that system of historico-descriptive insults, María Eugenia, you'll get the same result that an atheist would get screaming blasphemies in the middle of a church full of believers. If you speak disrespectfully about Eduardo in that violent way or even in a more restrained way . . . You saw what happened with me this morning! Eugenia would consider you a sacrilegious and impious monster, she would accuse me of being a slanderer, most probably she will be truly angry and as a result of her displeasure I'll never be able to set foot in her house again and all of this will not hurt anyone more than you. Be discreet! Be patient, María

Eugenia! . . . Listen . . ." And here Uncle Pancho set about calming me affectionately and tenderly.

He related to me that when Papa died and he learned about my situation, far from viewing it with indifference, he had taken a great interest in my affairs, investigating the case, trying to find information in letters or documents, talking to the lawyers, etc., etc. But that, unluckily, all his efforts had been fruitless, because Papa, when he became a partner with Uncle Eduardo, twelve years back, had unconditionally turned over to him the general administration of his property but with Papa drawing a certain percentage of the income and the profits. Now he died suddenly without making a will or clarifying the state of his business affairs. Therefore, Uncle Eduardo, who was as rapacious as he was methodical, avaricious, and foresighted, after twelve years with a free hand, had been arranging things in his own favor and naturally, with Papa gone, he presented accounts that, true or imaginary, were the only ones that existed! The negligence of the one was allied to the predatory nature of the other and Uncle Eduardo's explanations, the only arbiter in the affair, were irrefutable. The situation was clear and decisive from the start. Come what might, sooner or later, it must be accepted! And since that's the way it was, why not accept it now, at once, with total resignation?

Uncle Pancho was telling me this in a very soft voice, while I, somewhat pacified, listened to him in silence, staring at the tips of my patent leather shoes. I think I would have gone on paying attention to the narrative without any commotion had it not been for the advice about resignation. But I am firmly convinced, Cristina, that it's a very bad idea to preach resignation or any other virtue by naming it with its own name. It makes you instantly want to practice the opposite vice. I say this because when Uncle Pancho formulated his question-recommendation, "Why not accept it now with total resignation?" I, who as I have told you, was very calm, gave a nervous start, moving with such vehemence that I got tangled in the threads of my veil and broke the nail of my right ring finger, leaving the finger very ugly for several days. I exclaimed desperately, "Oh! Yes! That's right! Resignation! You're being just like Grandmother now, Uncle Pancho! Look, do me the favor of not speaking the words 'resignation,' 'severity,' 'prudence,' and 'irreproachable' because I detest them. Grandmother beat them into me this morning at least twenty times. 'You must be very severe with yourself, María Eugenia . . .' I declaimed, imitating Grandmother's voice while I waved the hand with the broken fingernail, as if the well-known glasses were gleaming in it. 'Oh! Very severe!' as if that were any fun! As if with severity and resignation you could buy clothes! Yes!" I added then in a tone saturated with tears. "Let's just see what I'll wear, when I run out of these dresses from Paris, now that I'm as poor and wretched as a rat!"

But Uncle Pancho, who wanted to console me at all costs, answered this time with tact and really admirable success.

"A woman is never poor when she is as pretty as you, María Eugenia!"

And since he then began to enumerate my personal attractions and to praise them warmly, with the peremptory tone of a knowledgeable and exquisite critic, I was growing calm little by little until, at last, after fixing my lopsided fingernail as well as possible, while he still continued his compliments, now quite cheered, I opened my handbag, and to check the exactness of his praise, as I was hearing it, I began to study myself in the little oval mirror. Unfortunately, given the tiny size of the mirror, I could see my face only in two sections—first the chin, mouth, and nose; then the nose, eyes, and hat—but still, it was enough that the mirror, in conjunction with Uncle Pancho's words, made that tearful dampness evaporate from my voice, and now, with a normal tone, looking at my eyes where an almost imperceptible smile was shining, "Well, I'd like, Uncle Pancho . . . Do you know what I'd like? To have lighter eyes and to be a little taller!"

"Come now! What nonsense! Then you'd be too tall. And if your eyes were light it would spoil the harmony of your looks. Why, your eyes are your best feature, María Eugenia. It's hard to find eyes like that. You know that perfectly well!"

As I expected this answer, when I heard it, I accepted it with a frank smile, while I energetically protested, shaking my head, "I'm not pretty at all, not at all, Uncle Pancho! . . . You just think so. You think I'm pretty because you love me!"

And we were silent a moment.

I had to close my handbag finally; my mirror was hidden in it, and so, with the mirror gone, my own image was also hidden, which, even cut off and in pieces, is the only thing that knows how to give me soothing advice. Yes, the only thing that, without saying a word, preaches resignation to me, good humor, kindness, and happiness. Once my image was buried in the blackness of my purse, there were a few seconds of silence, and immediately, Uncle Eduardo's skinny figure arose in my mind again with all its train of irritating ideas. No sooner did I catch sight of it inwardly, than I again attacked the same theme. "But listen, Uncle Pancho, what I can't understand in this matter of Uncle Eduardo is Grand-mother—this thing of her being so convinced that grotesque old Uncle Eduardo is a superior being, magnanimous, extremely generous! . . ."

"The ineffable mysteries of faith, my dear!" exclaimed Uncle Pancho, and he sighed, and rolled his eyes up, very comically and as if he were praying, an expression that made me really furious, because it didn't seem like a laughing matter to me that overnight I should find myself without a cent of my own. For this reason, seeing Uncle Pancho's mystical expres-sion, I interrogated him, in a very bad mood. "'Mysteries of faith'? What do you mean by that?"

"Look, for Eugenia, and for Clara, like almost all the women in Caracas who call themselves '*de hogar*,' generally a single religion is not enough for them and they have two. One they practice at church, or before some altar prepared for the purpose, like that one of the Nazarene that Eugenia has in her room. The other they practice at all times and in all places, and it is what they call 'having a heart and feelings.' The God of this second reli-gion is one of the men in the family. It may be the father, the brother, the son, the husband, or the sweetheart, it doesn't matter! The essential ele-ment is to feel a masculine superiority to whom they can yield a blind tribute of obedience and subjection. And then, whatever this deity does is well done, whatever he says is a law, whatever exists is placed in his hands, and his anger, no matter how just, arbitrary, or grotesque it may be, whether provoked by a violation of the strict laws of modesty on the part of the woman, or whether it suddenly explodes over a dish of tough meat, or whether it develops imperiously, wearing only his under-pants, over a badly ironed shirt, always, always, such a voice will ring through the whole house, majestic and solemn, as the voice of Jehovah rang from Sinai . . . Today in your house that God is Eduardo, who, to tell the truth, I must say in parenthesis, does not have a bad character—he never shouts!"

"Naturally! With that nasal voice! Can't you just see Uncle Eduardo, screaming furiously in his undershorts! He would look like one of those Judas figures they burn in effigy on Easter Day. Well, what he is . . ."

But Uncle Pancho went on philosophizing. "And I don't know whether this deeply rooted custom of deifying men has its origin in Oriental ata-visms inherited from our Andalusian forebears, or whether it obeys a simple economic problem. For women without a dowry or a fortune of their own, as almost all women are in our society, it is always men who are obliged to totally support them; and tell me, for a sensitive and grateful heart, can there be anything more like omnipotent God in heaven than the one who pays for all our expenses on earth?"

"It depends," I said, considering the case with much gravity, "if the things he pays for are elegant and fine and if you have a good limousine, and you live in a chic house where, for example, there are several bathrooms with hot water, and an Oriental parlor with tapestries, incense burners, and a huge black divan covered with cushions, then yes, I agree. But if on the other hand . . . Do you think, Uncle Pancho, that I would be very grateful if someone bought me a satin dress like that one Aunt Clara was wearing day before yesterday, all greenish and with the waistline up to her nose? Oh, no, no, no! I wouldn't appreciate it at all. To the contrary, if I were forced to wear it, I would curse the person who had bought it for me from the bottom of my heart. And that's because I can't conceive of satin, you know, unless it's charmeuse that costs thirty bolívares or more a yard. And the same for stockings! Look, look at these that I'm wearing! Aren't they pretty? Well, why are they pretty? Because in Paris they cost me sixty francs!"

"Fine!!" said Uncle Pancho, laughing again uproariously. "I see, María Eugenia, from that chilling estimate, that you value yourself most dearly! Oh! You are clearly conscious of your own worth, an indispensable condition for gaining value in the eyes of the world. Yes, yes, you are right. If we want others to give us a little esteem, we must begin by esteeming ourselves a lot. Never forget that. It is a very important principle for a woman, whose worth is generally whatever value a man takes it into his head to place on her!"

"Another thing, Uncle Pancho," I said, going back to my deep-rooted obsession. "Grandmother preaches morality to me with such great interest and such great vehemence, 'a woman's honor' . . . 'a woman's virtue' . . . Well, why doesn't she preach it to that dried-up sardine, Uncle Eduardo, I'd like to know? I'll bet she never has made him sit in a little chair by her side and said to him as she said to me this morning, 'a man's honor.'"

Uncle Pancho put a mystical expression on his face again and said, "Because there's no reason to mention the honor of these men as honorable as Eduardo. Merely bringing it up implies a certain doubt or lack of respect for him, a sin Eugenia would never incur. You see, a man's honor, my child, everywhere in the world is something . . . how can I put it? . . . something indefinite, elastic, conventional. But here, in our culture, it has become so elastic and indefinite that, like sacred things, it is completely invisible because it is so transcendental, like the human soul and angels. It is an attribute that exists on its own, independent of the person, and with whose acts, conduct, or behavior it has no relationship at all. Only the woman or the women of the household, who usually are the ones charged with its care and vigilance, have the power to soil it, wound it, or denigrate it with the slightest carelessness in their conduct. Due to this, a man in our society, as zealous about his honor as he is full of logic and abnegation, instead of occupying himself with his own behavior, can only watch, attend, and scrupulously and constantly oversee the woman's behavior. She is the living tabernacle where the holy majesty of his honor dwells. Very well, a woman's greatest merit lies in watching over it at all times, piously, after having accepted it just as it is, contradictory, incomprehensible, and mysterious, like a dogma of faith."

"Oh! Another thing, something else I want to ask you, Uncle Pancho, before I forget! How is it that Aunt Clara doesn't have a cent left either? Yesterday she told me that to meet her personal expenses she has only a small allowance that Uncle Eduardo sends her monthly. Didn't she, like the other children, get anything from the inheritance that Grandfather Aguirre left?"

To satisfy this question, Uncle Pancho engulfed himself, Cristina, in a very lengthy story, sprinkled with observations and jokes that I won't repeat in detail because as you well know, I find conversations about money matters terribly boring. The same thing happens to me with the subject of money that happens with political conversations; that is, if they don't drive me mad with impatience, they put me to sleep with boredom. But to sum up briefly what Uncle Pancho explained to me, I can tell you that today Aunt Clara has nothing, and Grandmother, who inherited a good income when my Grandfather died, has been reduced to, we can't say to nothing, but to almost nothing.

Their respective inheritances had the following histories: Aunt Clara's money was lost in a more or less jovial and picturesque way; that is to say, it passed bit by bit with great joy and metallic jingling from Aunt Clara's sisterly hands to the prodigal hands of Uncle Enrique, her younger and favorite brother. According to Uncle Pancho, this Uncle Enrique, who has been dead for several years now, was the reverse of Uncle Eduardo— happy, wild, generous, and a ladies' man, he spent his life traveling and showering gifts on everyone. Furthermore, he used to gamble a lot and when he won, he triumphantly squandered fortune's favors; but then, in adversity, Aunt Clara offered him a shoulder to cry on and behind Grandmother's back, she would lend him her money to pay his most pressing debts or to satisfy his most indispensable whims. Uncle Enrique, with a profusion of gifts and affection, then rewarded her spontaneous sacrifices, and that was how the two in mutual and common agreement consumed the last cent of Aunt Clara's patrimony.

As for Grandmother, who would never have consented to pay the unworthy debts of the madcap Uncle Enrique, her much larger fortune suffered a still worse fate than Aunt Clara's, for it was lost without anyone's getting any pleasure from it. Uncle Eduardo, who, because of his methodical and placid character, had gained Grandmother's respect and absolute confidence, undertook many years ago some mining venture or other that was supposed to produce a great deal, and for whose development Grandmother lent him all her capital without reserve. Despite the predictions and the assurances, the business went bankrupt in a few years, in the most deplorable way. Only a small amount of Grandmother's capital was saved, which, placed in bank stock and along with a small widow's pension, is the only thing she has left to live on and to maintain this house in a very measured and economical fashion. After the bankruptcy, Uncle Eduardo, who like a good miser is persistent and long-suffering, went on working, first in the same business, and then later, as Papa's partner. Thanks to his thriftiness and his astuteness, he managed to rebuild his capital and today he is rich, but no one has ever spoken again about the money Grandmother lost on his account in the mining venture. On the other hand, to provide for the household expenses, besides the widow's pension and the tiny dividends that the stocks yield, Uncle Eduardo adds a monthly amount for Grandmother and Aunt Clara, and they talk about this every day. Because of this, Grandmother calls him her providence, and the best, the most unselfish, the most generous of sons.

"This is Eduardo's system, do you understand?" commented Uncle Pancho, closing his version of the events. "He takes a thousand, then he give two, and for those two he must be eternally blessed, for he is the protector!"

Even though I had not heard anything new relative to my own situation, when Uncle Pancho finished those prolix explanations, which he had laced with anecdotes and every sort of comment, I compared his story with Grandmother's tale this morning, which in a flash I relived, and again I sat motionless and terrified for a long time, my eyes staring at my own hands lying inert on my black dress, like living symbols of my submission and my resignation.

Oh! If I lost Grandmother, something that could well happen at any time, what would become of me? My God, what would become of me? The horror of dependency on Uncle Eduardo's hostile house!

And in the august silence of the moment, beneath the intense shadows of the trees and the dusk, beside Uncle Pancho, who now sat quietly, moving the tip of his cane over the grass, for the first time, I felt that my soul was clinging desperately to Grandmother's life, as a child who barely knows how to walk grasps its mother's skirt. Yes, she, she alone, only her maternal love could soothe the humiliation of my poverty and my abandonment . . . But as if all of a sudden, thinking about Grandmother, I noticed that the night was settling on us, I stood up quickly and said as I shook bits of grass off my skirt, "Remember, remember, Uncle Pancho, that Grandmother is waiting for me. I promised to come back early, and there the poor thing is, in the drawing room . . . I can see her now, wearing her taffeta dress and her gold chain, sitting on the sofa, facing the visitors, amiable, smiling and very nervous, continually glancing at the door to see if I'm coming."

"Yes," said Uncle Pancho rising from the ground with great difficulty. "Eugenia is very vain about you. You are her pride now, rather like what a new hat brought from Europe must have been in her youth. She wants to show you off to everyone, as a part of herself, I mean, in her home."

"Poor Grandmother! After all she does love me a lot!"

"Without any comparison she prefers you to all her other grandchildren. And Clara feels the same way. In spite of the years they've spent without you, you see! And this is another precept of 'heart and feelings'—to always prefer the grandchildren and nieces and nephews of the women in the family even if they live in Peking and they have never seen them."

Hearing these words, I felt again even more intensely the maternal warmth that Grandmother's life brought to my life, although her pious hands were going to mutilate me cruelly as they zealously, tenderly, and carefully pruned the impatient wings of my independence. Thinking this, and looking at the panorama of the distant city, which was now beginning to light up, Uncle Pancho and I walked awhile in silence through the twilight that was falling with the speed of twilight in the tropics.

But suddenly, among the twinkling lights that were appearing there below, I evoked the flat city, and then the green house with its three big windows that awaited me like a convent, and again I felt all the horror of my imprisoned and boring life.

"Oh, Uncle Pancho, Uncle Pancho," I said halting my steps with philosophical bitterness. "Why are we born? Life! Look at life! What good is it after all?"

Uncle Pancho, who makes fun of everything and criticizes everything like a Franciscan monk, instead of consoling me, answered my question by fondly disparaging life.

"What good is it? None! It's the same nonsense repeated endlessly; it's a meaningless rosary, mechanically told by the centuries; it's a poor monster, blind and awkward, that, lacking the instinct of preservation is nourished by devouring itself in the most cruel pain . . ."

But, desperate and tearful, disdaining metaphysics and generalities, I focused concretely on my case, "If at least I had been born a man! You'd see, Uncle Pancho, how much fun I'd have and how much attention I'd pay then to Grandmother and Aunt Clara. But I'm a woman, oh, oh, oh! And being a woman is the same as being a canary or a linnet. They lock you up in a cage, they take care of you, they feed you and they don't let you out; meanwhile others are happy and flying everywhere! How dreadful it is to be a woman; how dreadful, how dreadful!"

"You're mistaken, María Eugenia," said Uncle Pancho very seriously, also coming to a halt momentarily. "Look, if I had to be born again I assure you that after having been born a rich man, as I was in my youth, now I would choose to be born a pretty woman. It's true. I speak from experience. The most prevalent type of autocracy or human despotism up to now in the world is the rule of a pretty woman. Oh! What limitless power! What wisdom in governing! What a genial dictatorship, in whose shadow the arts always flourish, and that humble and most beautiful science that consists of revealing to the eyes of us men our innate doggish servility, always ready to lick the hand of the master who punishes it, the only delicate and superior side of our poor nature so corrupted by the abuses and pride of the intelligence!"

But such an opinion, Cristina, seemed so paradoxical to me that, far from calming me, it irritated me more and more.

"That's all romance, poetry, and lies! We unhappy women are no more than victims, pariahs, slaves, disinherited! Oh! What iniquity! I'd like to get into the suffragist movement with that woman Pankhurst to burn down men's houses of congress and to slash the famous pictures in the museums! We'd see if all those abuses ended!"

And after sighing deeply as I walked along the narrow path I cried out again in a complaining voice, "Imagine being forever subject to the will of another! Imagine spending the whole day shut in between four walls without even being able to play the piano! How right the suffragists are! Oh! I didn't know how right! Once I attended a feminist lecture in Paris and I paid no attention at all to what they said. If it were today I wouldn't miss a word. But, well, it was because of those feet and those shoes! Just think, Uncle Pancho, the old lady who was giving the lecture, you could see her two feet crossed, on the floor, of course, under the table and they were, well you can't imagine! How coarse! Hobnailed shoes, and thick stockings, this thick, Uncle Pancho, made of cotton! Oh! Those feet shocked me so much that out of sheer horror I couldn't take my binoculars off them during the entire lecture. No, as far as I'm concerned, not even with the eloquence of Castelar could such a woman convince me."

"Apparently, María Eugenia, you want people to preach feminism to you with their feet. You're right. It seems much more eloquent to me too than what is usually preached with words. That's because there is nothing more convincing than the quiet eloquence of things, and a pair of stockings worth a hundred and twenty francs can masterfully overcome the laws of dialectics and of oratory."

Since I didn't care for the all-too-frivolous slant that Uncle Pancho was giving my words, I answered, very hurt, "No, no, that's not it, Uncle Pancho, don't think I'm so superficial. After all, number 100 stockings and Louis XV heels don't matter to me. The only thing I aspire to nowadays is to enjoy my own personality, that is to say, to be independent like a man and for no one to give me orders. Therefore, from now on my slogan will be, 'Long live women's suffrage!'"

"Don't talk nonsense, María Eugenia. 'Independent like a man'! When the fate of the civilized man is the same as his sweet servant the donkey, to wit, to work patiently at all times, and always obey, always! Not to obey suffragists naturally, but well-shod women, as you are now."

And thus, walking behind me down the narrow path, Uncle Pancho went on obstinately unfolding his absurd thesis about the present sway of women. He developed it in a long speech. But given my bad mood, I only listened to pieces of that sort of peripatetic sermon.

"Equality of the sexes, my child," he was saying while I watched beneath my feet the thousands of twinkling lights of Caracas that were glowing now like hot coals in the darkness. "The equality of the sexes, like any other equality, is absurd, because it is contrary to the law of nature, which detests democracy and abhors justice. Think. Look around us. Everything is made of hierarchies and aristocracies; the strongest beings live at the expense of the weakest, and in all of nature a great harmony reigns based on oppression, crime, and robbery. The total resignation of the victims is the cornerstone upon which that immense peace and harmony is built. The democratic spirit, or the eagerness to do justice and to share rights, is a puerile dream that exists only in theory in the poor human brain. Nature, then, is arranged in hierarchies, the strongest animals devour the weakest; they live at their expense and rule over them. The human being is at the head of all the hierarchies and is the supreme expression of the aristocratic type in nature. Very well, in human societies, the two sexes dispute dominance or control. Man and woman. Following the law of hierarchies, which of the two is destined to rule the other, and consequently rule all of nature? That is the question. To resolve it in her own favor, while always leaving a man his vain appearance of command, is the greatest proof of intelligence that a woman can give, and moreover, for the society in which she moves, it is an evident sign of high civilization and high culture. While on the contrary, societies in which men really and truly rule are always primitive societies, barbaric and uncultured. Why, you may ask? Why, for the simple reason that man, in spite of having decked himself out pompously and theatrically from primitive times, with crowns, scepters, and all the other attributes of power, basically is not constituted to command but rather to obey. That is why when he wants to impose his will he always does it badly, with shouts, grotesque and very vulgar gestures like the ones generally used by all those who, not having been endowed by nature with the most precious gift of command, wish at all costs to rule. That's what usually happens there," he added, pointing at the live coal of Caracas that was shining like a fallen heaven at our feet. "Those poor women don't know their power. Dazzled by the idealistic light of mysticism and virtue they race to spontaneously offer themselves as a sacrifice and they throw away their prestige by being too generous. They live drunken on the voluptuousness of submission. Like martyrs, their love is excited by flagellation, and they bless their lord in the midst of chains and torments. They live the deep inner life of ascetics and idealists, they finally acquire a great refinement of abnegation, which is without doubt the highest human superiority, but with their superiority hidden in their souls, they are sad victims. Because they are ignorant of the conquering force of their attraction, they forget themselves; they disdain their power when they neglect their physical beauty, and of course, seeing them worn out and faded, men turn them into pitiful beasts of burden on whose docile and weary shoulders they load all the weight of their tyranny and their caprices, after giving them the pompous name of 'honor.'"

As he came to this point, we reached the place where we had left the carriage. I climbed in hurriedly, sat catty-cornered on the right side, crossed my legs, and then, as the horses pulled away, I cried out dramatically, lifting my arms toward the heavens, "Just imagine being shut up again in that bo-o-o-ri-i-ing house of Grandmother's! And who knows now how long it will be before I get out of it again!"

Uncle Pancho must have been touched as he saw the dramatic expression of my arms, and he replied, saying something interesting, "Soon, you'll see. I have a marvelous plan for you. You're going to be very happy! You'll see . . . you'll see!"

"I doubt very much that I can be happy again," I said more dramatically still than what I'd said before. "My life is destroyed forever! . . . And what is that plan?"

"Oh! I can't tell you about it yet. Within a week, more or less, because it has . . . the plan has its difficulties."

"Oh! No, tell me now Uncle Pancho! If you were going to stop halfway you shouldn't have started. Now you have no choice but to tell me."

"No, because then, if I tell you, it won't happen."

"Yes, it will happen, it's the other way around, if you tell me it will happen, you'll see! Come on sweet, darling Uncle Pancho. Tell! Tell!"

"No, María Eugenia; you're very indiscreet. If I tell you, you'll let it slip there at your house and they'll ruin everything."

"No, I won't let it out. I won't tell even the wall, I assure you, I swear it, come on, don't make me beg, Uncle Pancho, tell me quick, before we get home; you aren't going to have time! All right, I warn you I won't get out of this carriage without knowing."

And then, Cristina, with all the warnings, great care, and calm that Uncle Pancho habitually employs on such occasions, he said, halting between his words, "Well . . . listen . . . the fact is . . . I have a sweetheart for you, but what a wonderful sweetheart!" and in order to emphasize this, he drew in his breath for a second with his teeth and lips pulled together. "What perfection! Look, searching for another with Diogenes's lantern, you couldn't find a better one in all of Caracas! What am I saying, in Caracas, not in all of South America, nor in Europe, nor anywhere! . . ."

I quickly answered something that seemed very elegant to me and quite necessary, "Pss! And that was it? Well, look, probably your work, your search, and everything, will turn out to be a waste of time! Because I'm very choosey about men, Uncle Pancho, one may displease me for any little thing, even if it's the slightest foolishness, and it's all over, don't even speak his name to me again!"

"Come, María Eugenia, that seems to me like too much scorn and too many airs right now."

Uncle Pancho didn't speak for a while, during which time we listened solemnly to the trotting of the horses. Then he added, "Well, I intended to describe him to you, but since you're so picky, maybe it'll be more sensible not to tell you anything so he can surprise you."

"No, no, describe him, picture him, paint him. That won't hurt anything! Let's see this great marvel!"

And then Uncle Pancho set about describing in detail his unexpected discovery, his rich masculine pearl. According to him, this pearl, or prized treasure whose name I still don't know, is endowed with good looks. He is elegant, slim, distinguished. As to his personality, he is intellectual and refined, that is to say, that having had great success in his studies, he is at the same time a man of the world who knows how to tie his tie and keep his fingernails clean. He was graduated from the University of Caracas in law and medicine. After graduation, he went to Europe and in Europe he spent ten years completing his studies, getting a doctorate in philosophy and political science, traveling, acquiring every sort of knowledge, and giving lectures at several universities in Spain and France.

Finally, after returning to Venezuela, he has written a book on sociology and American history, which, Uncle Pancho says, is admirable. (Oh, Cristina, what a pedantic man he must be! I can picture him now with his "slim" right leg crossed over his left, talking about his book and his lectures. But it's not so bad if he is well dressed and keeps his fingernails well cared for!) At the present time he doesn't have a fortune of his own (a frightful deformity!), but he is counting on acquiring magnificent businesses that will make him very rich. Furthermore, he aspires to take part in politics, or to be sent as a minister to some legation in Europe or America. As for his character, he is good-natured, refined, gallant, full of ideas, and he has charming manners. To sum it up, Cristina, except for the huge and momentary defect of having no money, he is clever, a jewel and a treasure, if I may trust Uncle Pancho's words! If you want me to be sincere, I don't have much faith in his description and praise, because I have noticed that men are absolutely lacking in the critical ability to judge each other. They call a "marvel" what is really something trivial, uninteresting, without originality, without anything. Therefore, wisely, I shall abstain from all judgments, and I say with Saint Thomas, seeing is believing!

That's all concerning my future sweetheart, who although a principal part of the plan or scheme worked out by Uncle Pancho, is only "one" part. I still have to tell you about the second part of the plan, also enunciated that evening in the carriage and which is related to the setting, or society where I must meet that knight in shining armor that Uncle Pancho has discovered for me. As you will see, this second part, in my opinion, is much more interesting than the first and I believe it will have more immediate, practical, and positive results.

It is the following: In Caracas there is a married lady, between thirty and thirty-five years old, lovely, elegant, very distinguished, a distant relative and close friend of Uncle Pancho and Papa, whose name is Mercedes Galindo and who, since the day of my arrival, has ardently wanted to meet me. This lady, who is also a friend of the sweetheart in question, delights in arranging marriages, and therefore, she has agreed with Uncle Pancho to arrange mine by bringing me to her house, continually inviting me to dine there and in general creating a setting or atmosphere for me that will be the most suggestive and appropriate for the case. (Oh, Cristina, what an admirable and blessed chance for me to finally wear all my dresses before they go out of style!) It happens that for the immediate realization of the plan, a great obstacle exists, an immense difficulty that must be overcome at all costs, and it is that Grandmother and Mercedes Galindo are not on good terms at present because of a quarrel that occurred *in illo tempore* between my Grandfather Aguirre and Mr. Galindo, Mercedes's father. Uncle Pancho says that, first of all, it is essential to diplomatically arrange a reconciliation between Grandmother and Mercedes. Mercedes is completely in favor of it. Grandmother must be convinced; therefore, great skill, tact, and prudence must be observed. This was the difficulty Uncle Pancho alluded to before he revealed the plan to me.

I hope that Providence will take pity on me and make Grandmother reconcile with Mercedes Galindo, who, as Uncle Pancho says (and also Papa) is a charming lady, generous, very likeable, completely opposite to the Etruscan or Gothic friends who up to now I have had the pleasure of meeting, here, in the drawing room of this house, presided over by Grandmother from her place on the sofa, with all the pomp of the taffeta dress and the gold chain.

When the carriage arrived at the door, Uncle Pancho, as I predicted, still had not finished explaining the requirements and aims of his extraordinary project. With the carriage stopped we had to stay in it a good while longer, whispering quietly, hurriedly, and discreetly. Until, finally, he repeated for the last time the most interesting information and pressing recommendations, "Mercedes loves you very much, not just because of memories or friendship with our family, it's not that. Rather it's because I've told her how pretty you are and that is enough for her to care for you.

She's madly impatient to meet you. She has already planned the presentation dinner, menu, etc., and she has moreover selected several gifts for you. But be discreet, eh? Very discreet! Here, not a word about anything! Because María Antonia, Eduardo's wife, abhors Mercedes and if she finds out, she'll plot successfully against us and ruin everything. The maneuver must be skillful and very fast. I'll take charge of it."

"Oh, Uncle Pancho," I reproached him, as I said goodbye, "couldn't you have told me all that more than an hour and a half ago when we were driving up to Los Mecedores, instead of getting on my nerves with your philosophical observations?"

Uncle Pancho, who, when he doesn't know what to answer, acts like a fatalist, said, "It was written!"

And thus ended, Cristina, that memorable conference, celebrated in a carriage, the inauspicious day when for the first time I had news of my absolute ruin. Uncle Pancho's unexpected plan, bristling with interest, difficulties, and hopes, like an escape plan for a captive, suddenly set my spirit ablaze with the fire of an impatient joy. And this joy was so great that a few seconds after having said goodbye to Uncle Pancho, when I happily made my way into Grandmother's drawing room, I was very gracious to all the Etruscan visitors, I greeted them with a smile, I said beautiful things about Caracas, and as they were departing I accompanied them to the street door with the greatest cordiality. Then when we were going to the dining room, I rushed to offer my arm to Grandmother to cross the corridor and the patio; once at the table, sitting before the bowl of soup, I answered out loud and clearly to the "blessed and praised . . ." that Aunt Clara murmured; I talked the whole time with tact and liveliness; I ate with a very good appetite, and an hour later, now in bed, radiant and smiling under the sheets, I remember that I fell asleep dreaming of myself as an ambassador to a European court, wearing an admirable pearl necklace around my throat, and making a deep bow of the kind back in school they called a twelve-beat bow, do you remember? Those where you counted, one, two, three, four, five, and six, during the first stage of the bow, and then, seven, eight, nine, ten, eleven, and twelve, during the second stage.

I should let you know that, as is proper for every well-bred person before yielding to sleep, and dreaming of the deep bow with the *sautoir* of pearls around my neck, I expressed my glad gratitude as I exclaimed from the bottom of my soul an intimate, sincere, and spontaneous thanksgiving that went something like this, "Oh! Uncle Pancho, dear Uncle Pancho, fertile Uncle Pancho, may God bless and protect forever and ever those green fields of your brain, fertilized daily with whiskey, brandy, beer, and Jérez wine, wherein are born and ripen the wonderful fruits of projects as perfumed in joy as they are gentle, juicy, and most sweet in nourishing hope!"

❧   ❧   ❧

However, Cristina, since that redeeming night, where I am resolved to end my long story, almost two months have gone by. During these months, my life has continued to slip by, monotonous, dark, and unchanging, with no other light than the light of that plan that still has not been realized. And why, you may ask? Well, for the simple reason that a thousand trivial accidents have flocked to block our way. First, it happened that Mercedes Galindo, my charming future friend, had the flu with a very high fever, a week in bed, etc., etc., and she had to go to the country for a period of rest, which was prolonged for more than twenty days; then it was Grandmother who in turn got sick and once more we had to wait for the time of her illness to pass and the time of her convalescence. Now things are quite normal, and Uncle Pancho is only awaiting an opportune occasion to express to Grandmother, in Mercedes's name, her desire to make peace, forgetting all their old resentment. As you must understand, for this reconciliation in which Uncle Pancho will be the mediator, I must be the pretext, and Mercedes, with her tact, her attractiveness, and her wonderful gift for getting along with people will then take charge of crowning the peace by conquering Grandmother's sympathy without reservations. The reconciliation will be attempted, then, this very week and as is natural, once the pardon is obtained, Mercedes will come immediately to visit Grandmother.

The candidate in question, whose name I didn't know for a long time, is named Gabriel Olmedo and he is more than thirty years old. As I believe I have told you, and as I know I have told Uncle Pancho, I have no faith in the charms and fine qualities of this person. I doubt very much that he will suit me. I foresee him as egotistical, pedantic, and vain, but after all, Cristina, one must test life by always answering any of its calls! The worst thing is prison, immobility, and inertia.

Now, I believe at last the moment has arrived to finish this singular letter full of dialogue where I send you the most intimate details of my present life. This letter, which has been teaching me to probe the deep complexity of insignificant things as I relived them with my pen, is the

result of my great affection for you, and is also a summary of this mysterious anxiety that troubles and oppresses me. Receive it then in that spirit,
read it with indulgence and, if you find it ridiculous, discordant, or absurd, don't make fun of it, Cristina; remember that my affection for you
dictated it to me, in days of vulnerability and boredom.

Oh! If you could see how my locking myself away intrigues Aunt Clara;
because in order to write to you, I've continually shut myself away in my
room. Between my books and my letter, waiting for Uncle Pancho's plan,
almost insensibly, the time has been passing little by little. Besides writing,
locked up and alone, it is also here, in this room, where I isolate myself so
I can read. And in my solitude, like an ascetic in his cell, I have learned to
love the inner and intense life of the spirit. I have discovered that in Caracas
there exists a circulating library, where, by means of a small deposit, you
can borrow every kind of book, and my rabid appetite for reading has
freedom and an open range there to slake its hunger. Hiding it from Aunt
Clara and Grandmother, I send Gregoria, the old laundress of this house,
making her the one responsible for taking the divine contraband from the
library to my room and from my room to the library, under cover of her
big black shawl. Thanks to such liberal and discreet intellectual support, I
read as much as I wish, everything, everything that occurs to me without
prohibitions, bans, or censorship.

Oh! If Aunt Clara knew for example that I'm now reading Voltaire's
Philosophical Dictionary! What scandal and what horror it would cause her!
But my readings have the double delight of the delicious and the prohibited, and the *Philosophical Dictionary* when not in my hands lies buried like
a treasure in the double bottom of my mirrored wardrobe.

Therefore, Cristina, now you know the present emblem of my life is—
to wait! Yes, to wait like Penelope, weaving and unweaving thoughts—
these that I send to you and others that I am unwinding in the hidden skein
of my books.

And since there is nothing left to tell you, I beg you now to write to me
and to tell me everything that has happened in your life these past months,
because I want to compare it with mine. Tell me your plans, talk to me
about your changes, describe your travels to me, and so together, as we
were in other times, we will refresh our old memories. Sometimes, I
worry wondering, if, after being so close and so very fond of each other,
I'll really never see you again . . . Who knows! Fortunately, they invented
writing, and in it something is present of this thing that we love so much
in the people we care for, this thing that is soul and spirit, and that they

say never dies, neither is it completely absent, when because it loves, it does not wish to be absent.

Receive, then, this portion of my spirit, and don't forget that here from my solitude, sunken in the silence of its "closed orchard," it waits in turn for you to come.

MARÍA EUGENIA

SECOND PART

 *Juliet's*
Balcony

Having now sent the interminable letter to her friend Cristina, María Eugenia Alonso resolves to write her diary. As will be seen, in this first chapter, the genteel Mercedes Galindo appears at last.

I consider it awfully foolish, and moreover it strikes me as cheap romanticism, old-fashioned and totally out of style, for a person to pick up a pen and begin to write a diary. Nevertheless, I am going to do it. Yes, I, María Eugenia Alonso, am going to write my diary, or my weekly, my newspaper. I don't know what to call it, but anyway, it will deal with my own life, and will be like what they call a "diary" in novels.

Oh! It's so strange how little influence our convictions have on our behavior! I believe that in general our convictions are made to be applied to the conduct of other people, because that is when they appear in all the splendor of their integrity: solid, well-rooted, and unbreakable. On the other hand, when it has to do with ourselves, as in the present case, our opinions or convictions instantly take on the flexibility of wax, and they accommodate and mold themselves wonderfully to the most capricious accidents of our conduct. The great majority of people, endowed as they are with a certain conciliatory spirit, admirably explain away such mysterious discrepancies, with reasons or excuses. Thus, thanks to eloquence and logic, the two inseparable sisters—conviction and conduct—are held in a perpetual embrace of perfect harmony. Unfortunately, I absolutely lack the imagination to establish these agreements and it frequently happens that I find myself, as I do today, in flagrant contradiction. Yes. My lack of aptitude for excuses was inevitable during my infancy and my days in school, I recall clearly. It is innate and irremediable. Therefore, from now on, I will no longer mortify myself by practicing a science for which I have not the slightest inclination. In view of this, I resolve to confess in the future, before myself and before everyone else, that discord exists between my opinion and my conduct. I will always say, such and such is reprehensible and ridiculous, but I do it just because; such and such is admirable and holy, but I don't do it just because. I believe this kind of frankness or confession is usually called cynicism. Since that word is a little disagreeable, I think it is better not to insist any more on the matter and to go on to another topic.

Just a few days ago I finished my letter to Cristina Iturbe. But the letter was so long and it had taken me such a long time that writing it had become a habit for me. When I had finished it and reread it, it was a mammoth document that, with melancholy, I put in a huge envelope, I literally covered it with stamps and I sent Gregoria to deposit it in the mailbox, after demanding the most absolute secrecy about the matter. Given this warning, Gregoria's eyes shone brightly with complicity, and my letter, like the books from the circulating library, went out to the street, wrapped in the nighttime of Gregoria's shawl. And the truth is that in this life of reclusion that I live, my only entertainment, my only exercise, my only sport consists of doing everything, absolutely everything, behind Grandmother's and Aunt Clara's backs. Gregoria seconds me admirably in it, and this system of eternal conspiracy gives me a certain moral independence, and it produces in me, above all, a multitude of little emotions analogous to those of a game, hunting, or fishing, which are not to be disdained, given the boring and insipid atmosphere in which I live.

Going back to Cristina's letter, when Gregoria came back in from the street she told me with much mystery, "I mailed it," and I felt very sad. I felt that I had lost something very great and very indispensable. Since I couldn't go on writing to Cristina for an indefinite length of time, I said to myself today, "Well, now I'm going to write my diary!"

And here I am.

I greatly fear I'll have to interrupt it any day now for total lack of material—my life is so monotonous! From the morning when I sent the mammoth letter until yesterday afternoon, nothing worthy of mention had happened. The days slip by in my life like the beads of Aunt Clara's mother-of-pearl rosary slip between her gnarled, thin, and mystic fingers—always the same thing with the same beginning and the same end!

But fortunately yesterday something out-of-the-ordinary happened. Continuing the simile of the rosary, I can say that yesterday afternoon I reached a variant of Glory and Our Father, in the person of Mercedes Galindo, whose visit we finally received.

Oh! To me she seemed charming, lovely, so nice. Yes, Uncle Pancho was right! She came to see us around five-thirty, and she stayed an hour more or less. During the hour, Grandmother cloaked herself in lordly dignity and she was at the same time both reserved and gracious, but I understood very well that the famous quarrel of long ago still rankles in them. Neither does Grandmother like Mercedes, nor does Mercedes care for Grandmother. The habit of so many years of enmity dominates them and I believe that they will never be true friends.

As for myself, I was a complete imbecile during the visit, I know. This always happens to me. The most sincere way that I have of showing my admiration for a person consists of clothing myself with the tough bark of a timidity that numbs me and imprisons me like glacial cold. This sentiment of timidity is totally invincible, and I have decided now to meekly submit to it, since it's impossible to overcome. The battle against timidity becomes grotesque. That's the way I understood it yesterday and because of that I spoke very little, yes, I barely answered with short phrases the friendly and affectionate things that Mercedes said to me, which, overwhelming me with pleasure, did nothing but augment more and more my unhappy and silent timidity.

But finally, after all, since as Uncle Pancho says, I have a very clear consciousness of my own beauty, my silence doesn't seem haughty, to the contrary, I think in general that being quiet is an aesthetic complement that lends a certain reserved and classic charm to a person. A stupid phrase from a pretty head casts an ominous shadow upon it and ruins the effect. The same thing happens with movements. That's why I have always believed that the immense prestige of Greek beauty is mainly due to the great discretion and immobility of the statues that seem so intelligent, as they reveal their beauty to our credulous eyes. Given this series of reasons I resolved to imitate insofar as possible the discretion and talent of the Greek statues during yesterday's visit, and I am sure that I must have made a good impression on Mercedes Galindo.

But to detail the visit:

When Mercedes's auto stopped at the doors of this house, Grandmother, as usual, was already waiting, sitting on the sofa, and I, who knew and know very well the enormous importance that this visit will have on my future life, was very excited and dressed with more care than ever. When I heard the auto stop, and then the doorbell, instead of waiting like Grandmother for Mercedes's arrival, I ran quickly to hide in the half-light of the adjoining little sitting room from where, without being seen, I could see the whole drawing room. Once hidden there, hoping to make a more impressive entrance, I decided to let them wait for me a few minutes, and so, while I was standing in the shadows, I was able to observe the details of that interesting meeting.

No sooner did Mercedes appear, with the light falling on her at the threshold of the door, than Grandmother stood up majestically, went to meet her, waited for her a second in the center of the room under the chandelier, and there, beaming, as if nothing had ever occurred between them, she wiped out all the past with one firm stroke, as she embraced her, saying with an elegance worthy of Fray Luis de León, "As pretty as ever, Mercedes!"

And Grandmother was telling the pure truth.

In the shadows, contemplating Mercedes's figure, handsome and radiant, I found myself petrified with admiration. Oh! She was truly elegant! She was wearing a dress of black velvet, surely made in some good Paris shop, and as her only adornment, she was wearing a strand of pearls close about her neck. I observed that her white and well-cared-for hands exhibited a single ring, a solitaire, and they seemed to me (her hands) as pretty as mine when I have my nails well buffed. She wore divine shoes on her long, slender feet, she had an adorable little black hat on her head, worn a little to one side, which framed her classic features in delightful effects of light and shadow, and from under the half-light of that hat, speaking to Grandmother, came forth one of the loveliest and most silvery voices that I have ever heard in my life.

And how right, oh, yes, how right Uncle Pancho was!

At last I emerged from the half-darkness, and went to greet her, bringing a very expressive phrase I had prepared in my mind, with which I planned to show her my high admiration. But as soon as she looked at me with her brilliant, inquiring eyes full of delicate critical appraisal, and as soon as I breathed the subtle perfume that clung to her body like a flower, I felt myself invaded by the total paralysis of timidity. Therefore, after having received and hugged me with that naturalness and ease that are her main attraction, I could only murmur in response a few brief and courteous phrases.

During the course of the visit, Mercedes, with her admirable tact, apparently paying little attention to me, constantly addressed Grandmother. Then, free of conversation, silent and still, I observed her and thus observing, I understood that her charm was even greater than her beauty, that is to say, that she carried the art of interpreting herself to the height of perfection. Because while she was talking, her mouth, hands, eyes, head, voice, smile, everything, everything was subtly and harmoniously completing, with a thousand delightful nuances, the sense that the words were expressing. I noticed further that she laughed from time to time, with a laugh that was as pleasant to the ears as agreeable to the sight, and she continually sprinkled her conversation with French words that, although very well and very naturally pronounced, were completely unnecessary because all of them had a perfect equivalent in Castilian. She said for example: "la nature"; "ma fourrure"; "clair de lune"; and "la beauté physique" needlessly, but as she seemed to illuminate with the light of her eyes and the enchantment of her smile whatever words came from her mouth, I found them all of a profound wisdom.

It was only after rising and saying goodbye to Grandmother, that Mercedes decided to dedicate herself entirely to me. Holding my chin with her fragrant hand, she brought my face close to her own, and gently and affectionately, as if I were some little child, she kissed me twice. Then, with my chin still held in her hand, she said, enveloping the phrases in a long smile, "Goodbye, dear! Frankly, I didn't believe you were so pretty in spite of all that Pancho had told me. I thought he was exaggerating, but I see now that you are lovely beyond exaggeration."

(Oh! The wonder, the delight that it is to hear such a thing from the lips of a person of such evident good taste!)

Without answering anything, I smiled with pleasure, thus showing Mercedes that her appreciation seemed to me perfectly accurate. She instantly understood the happiness in my smile and she answered it with another laugh of satisfaction that sounded like tinkling bells and crystal. Then leading me by the arm as far as the street door, alone with me, she spoke to me of her old friendship with all the Alonso family, about the good times they had spent together in Europe and in Caracas, she said goodbye again with a kiss, and she told me, still smiling, in a very soft, confidential voice, "You know, my house is yours. Come any time without notice, without standing on ceremony, any time you wish and with complete assurance. I have a surprise for you—it's a lovely miniature of your Papa when he was ten years old." And after laughing again, she told me in a much lower voice, almost whispering in my ear, "I have something else for you too!"

As my only reply, I blushed and, rather than speak, I sighed, "Thanks . . . Thanks so much . . ."

Then, looking out from the car door, she smiled again, waved, and the little black hat disappeared at last. By then a thousand opportune and clever answers had occurred to me, but unhappily, it was too late!

Aunt Clara did not deign to receive Mercedes. She said she needed to count the clothes, to whip butter with milk for breakfast, to pray the third part of the rosary, to feed Chispita, and that it was altogether impossible for her to abandon such important occupations. Then she added, "And much less to receive a person as superficial as Mercedes Galindo, who is boring, because it is certain that she will only talk about clothes and nonsense."

After having seen and talked to Mercedes, I understand that Aunt Clara has the same creed as the Mothers at school. Only Aunt Clara calls "superficial people" what the Mothers called "the world." Basically it's the same idea, clothed in different words. Aunt Clara is confined in her faction as the Mothers also were confined, and she wants no contact with the enemy. She does well. She's not like me. I, unluckily, the same as in school, am unable to affiliate myself with my flag. I am a sort of plank that floats to the right and to the left over the waves of a kindly and tranquil sea.

But to resume the account of yesterday's event. No sooner had Mercedes's auto disappeared from view than I went back to the drawing room, where Grandmother was still sitting, and instantly, Aunt Clara, now free of her occupations, also came in to hear about and comment on the recent visit. There was a lot to say. They talked about Mercedes's indisputable beauty, about her courtesy and social grace, and they also commented on her wretched luck. They said that she was in an unhappy marriage, that her husband was a libertine and a gambler who, after having thrown away almost all her fortune, now treated her very badly. Grandmother finished a paragraph by exclaiming, "First her father was a scoundrel! Now her husband! She's a fine person, considering how little orientation she has had in her life!"

By that I understood that if Grandmother judged Mercedes "a fine person" it was precisely because she did not think she was fine enough. Oh! But on the contrary, I think she is incomparable and as long as no one can offer me better evidence, like Gregoria, I exclaim to myself constantly: "May God keep and bless her!"

During the course of the conversation, whenever Grandmother referred to her she said, "that child," just as when she talks about me, something that I found absurd since Mercedes is married and is over thirty years old. I noted too that when it had to do with Mercedes's father, Grandmother always took the precaution of saying, as she pronounced his name, "that scoundrel Galindo." This prefix "scoundrel" Grandmother undoubtedly uses as a faithful homage to the memory of my dead Grandfather Aguirre. That's how I took it, and for that reason, it always echoed in my ears, solemn and grandiose, as this kind of family epithet must sound to every well-bred person.

But despite my good intentions, the comments ended in a little incident.

And it was because, seeing that the conversation always revolved around "that scoundrel Galindo," I felt that it was becoming boring and monotonous and very dangerously heated, and I decided to give it a new slant. Judging from the results, I think, truly, it was the wrong slant.

It so happens that, as a general rule, I like very much to say clever things, but since unfortunately I am not sufficiently witty to make them up on my own, I limit myself to repeating, naturally adapting to the circumstances, the clever things that Papa used to say. I mean things that have remained in my mind because they seemed original or penetrating. Given this inclination of mine, when Grandmother was repeating for the twentieth time "that scoundrel Galindo," and thinking that I might mitigate her animosity by affirming two things together: on the one hand the wrongdoing of the man who was my Grandfather's enemy, and on the other hand my admiration of Mercedes's charm, I spoke, "I agree that Mr. Galindo did wrong when he did wrong to Grandfather, but I recognize on the other hand that he did well when he did Mercedes so well."

I imagined that this demonstration that united wit and harmony was going to be very well received, but it wasn't. Much to my surprise, when Grandmother heard me, instead of laughing, she turned to face me, and said with an immense severity that she had never used in speaking to me before, "That language is not proper for a young lady, María Eugenia. What vulgarity!"

"What? Saying 'he did Mercedes very well' is saying something vulgar? It doesn't seem that way to me, just the opposite . . ."

"Yes, very vulgar, now I've told you, and don't repeat it again!"

"But Papa said that very thing once, in Paris, talking about the father of a very pretty actress who works at the Comédie Française and no one thought it was vulgar! In fact, everyone laughed a lot."

"Well, if you're going to pick up the habit of repeating everything that Antonio said, and everything Pancho says, without knowing what it means, you'll cut a fine figure in society!"

And then with the haughtiness of hurt pride I replied arrogantly, "I am accustomed to knowing the exact meaning of the words I speak, because I am happy to say I'm not a parrot or a phonograph!"

Nonetheless, I sat still for awhile mulling this over. I suddenly felt that the phrase in question was loaded with mysterious meanings and for a moment I stared in silence at Grandmother's silver head, which like the ark of the alliance held the keys to many mysteries, until at last in my tempestuous silence, I emerged from my abstraction thinking, "Bah, what it really is, is that Grandmother, even when it's as plain as the nose on your face, doesn't want to admit that 'that scoundrel Galindo' ever in his life did anything that was well done. That's all it is!"

And now, after having reflected much more carefully about the matter, I have not changed my mind and my opinion is still the same.

Wherein María Eugenia Alonso describes the quiet times spent in the corral at her house and wherein Gabriel Olmedo also appears.

 Our forebears, who founded the city of Caracas, even though it may not seem true at first glance, were very talented. They discovered a way to live in a community without renouncing the rustic and bucolic charms of country life. It's true the streets they laid out were too narrow; that they paved them with sharp pebbles; that they burdened them with eaves, and overloaded them with barred windows, but on the other hand they had the good sense and the great foresight to enclose a generous bit of land inside each house. They were refined and foresighted, our ancestors, the founders of the city of Caracas! It is doubtless thanks to their refinement and vision that I, one of their many descendants, have the soul of a dreamer, rather lazy and much given to the delights of leisure.

That's what I thought yesterday, as I studied the different shades of green in the corral, while I stretched out full length on an enormous trunk covered with old travel stickers of every shape and color, which belonged to my dead Uncle Enrique, and which now is sitting under the broad shed in the corral facing the meditative hens and between the ironing board and the basket of clean clothes. There it sits, a relic, sad and decayed, crying with the weeping of its torn labels; and the poor old thing cries nostalgically, remembering, as I do, past travels and past adventures in distant lands.

It happens that this piece of land enclosed between four walls that they call a corral is a delight to me and it is also the source of all my dreams and musings. Aunt Clara doesn't see it in the same light and she says almost every day, "A young lady's place is not in the corral, nor in the society of servants."

She may be right, but anyway Aunt Clara's sermons on this subject have no effect on me. The chickens fascinate me, the treetops fascinate me as they peep over the walls from the corrals next door like the heads of curious neighbors; the green, curly leaves of the acacia fascinate me; the bright-colored cayenas fascinate me; the big, white-stained stones where the soapy clothes are spread out in the sun fascinate me; a little bit of Avila seen in the distance above the trees and the rooftops fascinates me; Uncle Enrique's nostalgic trunk fascinates me; and above all, Gregoria fascinates me, when, in her element, she chats as she scrubs with her black fists at the little islands of clothes that appear here and there in her immense tub, as if in a very white sea of soapsuds.

Gregoria knows my dreamy tendencies and instead of frustrating them, as Aunt Clara does, no, Gregoria feeds them. When I come to the corral and stretch out on the trunk that doubles as a chaise longue, she, knowing my tastes and whims, showers every kind of attention on me. She covers my feet so the mosquitoes won't bite me; she closes the door to avoid any drafts; she hangs a big sheet on the clothesline to keep the sun out of my eyes, and she also offers me a pillow of some soft package of clean, unironed clothes.

Aunt Clara detests my familiarity with Gregoria, and she detests still more the familiarity of my head with the clean clothes. But Aunt Clara's antidemocratic sentiments don't have any effect on me either.

And it's because, I don't mind saying, the simple environment of the corral is the only place where I can relax and enjoy good conversation. Sometimes we don't say a word, and then, while Gregoria washes, I look at the shifting arabesques woven by the tree branches; I look at the weird forms of the clouds as they move across the sky; I look far away at the veiled mystery of Avila, and little by little I lose myself in a sweet labyrinth of dreams . . . Yes, on Uncle Enrique's hard trunk I have learned to dream, as Jacob dreamed on his hard rock!

At other times we talk.

If I were a poet, I no doubt would have written in praise of soap, multiplying itself in foam and luminous bubbles by means of Gregoria's active knuckles. Because in my opinion there is no poem comparable to that whitest poem of the tub, so well interpreted by her old hands, now rather stiff and trembling. How her agile black hands shine on the immaculate whiteness! Sometimes they seem like two enamored swallows frolicking and chasing each other on the same little cloud . . . And yet, much more sparkling and luminous than the soapsuds are the words that all the while come from her mouth and that are richer in philosophy than the richness of the white foam, that grows, and grows, eternally, with the continual beating and rubbing.

This is what Aunt Clara will never comprehend, and what I discovered a long time ago. Gregoria is simple, uncomplicated wisdom. Under the tangle of her woolly hair is hidden, as in the mystery of a black diamond, the bright spark of her very acute mind. Gregoria also possesses the gift of expressing her thoughts, because she has mastered the very rare art of conversation. She is as sparse in her speech as she is rich in ideas and expressive mimicry. Gregoria's mimicry has subtlety and shadings which words can never achieve. Sometimes it is mysterious, long stares like the deep secrets of nature, other times a sudden flash of her pupils that imitates the amazement of a great surprise; she has epigrammatic winks; closed eyes that are a parenthesis, sudden silences that become very eloquent epilogues; and loud laughs that, like the music of Wagner, describe all the feelings and passions that can move the human soul. At times, in honor of the reserve and discretion that certain delicate subjects demand, what began as a sentence ends in mimicry. Silence then seems to rule the scene; in the tub, momentarily abandoned, the soapsuds sparkle, her expressive hands fly back and forth fast or slowly about her face and the three together achieve great feats of description.

Naturally, after having savored the great range of colors that Gregoria's conversational palette holds, when I hear well-mannered people like Grandmother and Aunt Clara talk, I find it very insipid and drab. And that's because, with an artist's supreme good taste, Gregoria manages the whole series of gestures and expressions that good manners, in their wisdom, have decided to ban and completely prohibit, for a lack of intelligent interpreters.

And this is the way, in my long conversations with Gregoria, that I have come to know two things at once: first, many hidden corners of the human heart, and second, all those intimate details about my family that Grandmother and Aunt Clara are very careful never to mention in front of me, and which, for that reason, are the only ones that interest me.

I've learned a lot of things from Gregoria. I've learned that Uncle Eduardo was always selfish, stingy, and methodical, all at the same time; that when he was little he always used to hide his own toys and play with Enrique's, the same thing he has done now as a mature man with the three-fourths of San Nicolás that belonged to me and that he has appropriated entirely for himself. Through Gregoria I have learned that Uncle Enrique scorned all his toys and that was why he happily left them all to Uncle Eduardo, since he greatly preferred to climb the trees to spy on people and to throw rocks and green fruit at the neighboring corrals. Through Gregoria I have learned, and a lot of mimicry came into play in telling this, that my Grandfather Aguirre, although a man of peaceful and regular habits, "went wild" in his old age over a certain French dancer, the result of which was that his bed, under orders from Grandmother, left his room, was angrily carried across the dining room the way the Israelites crossed the Red Sea, until it was lodged here, in the second patio, where my room is now, and that, while that change or anomaly lasted, she would never deign to answer when he called her or spoke to her. Through Gregoria I have learned that when Uncle Enrique returned from Europe, an adult, he would fall in love with every halfway good-looking maid in the house, a fact that caused Grandmother to choose for her servants only those women whose faces nature had cursed with as many defects and deformities as possible. Through Gregoria I have learned that María Antonia, Uncle Eduardo's disagreeable wife, has a very obscure origin, if not to say a black one, that it was Uncle Pancho Alonso who, one time when he took it into his head to trace genealogy, quickly discovered María Antonia's antecedents, which were so troubled and tortuous that María Antonia has abhorred Uncle Panchito ever since, as the vilest and most intrusive traitor. Through Gregoria I have learned that Mama had a sweet, happy disposition, while Aunt Clara, although outwardly placid, was intensely passionate, which was why her life has been so painful and so sad. And, finally, I learned through Gregoria how Aunt Clara, while very young, fell hopelessly in love with that sweetheart of hers whom I remember hazily when he used to give me candy and make paper roosters for me; how suddenly, after many years of courtship, it was revealed that he was chasing another girl who was much younger and prettier; how a while after that he stopped his daily visits, and how one day, after Aunt Clara's infinite and bitter weeping, he finally married the other girl . . .

"Then," adds Gregoria, taking her black hands out of the white foam, and choosing the most sentimental expressions from her repertory, "that was the end of Miss Clara! She stopped going out, she turned to the church, and she started getting thin and pale, pale like she is now. Instead of the old Miss Clara, the poor thing looks just like a wax candle, like the kind people carry in the processions during Holy Week!"

And with that sentence, Gregoria finished one of her long dissertations about Aunt Clara, yesterday around eleven-thirty in the morning.

Now since I am so fond of metaphors or symbols, and since when it

comes to developing an appropriate theme I have an elegance and creativity that any of the admirable poets they call symbolists might envy, of
course, when I heard Gregoria use the symbol of the candle, I didn't want
to miss the chance to develop such an apt theme, and so, while she went
back to her work in silence, I sank into the realm of psychological analo-
gies, and still lying on the trunk and gazing at the mountain in the distance, I began to comment on the matter as I talked to myself, full of sweet
melancholy, "Yes, poor Aunt Clara. You are a votive candle whose idealistic flame is slowly consuming your own life, and your life is the mystic,
persevering light that, forgotten by all, burns in the shadows, beneath the
silence and the loneliness of the altars. That light of yours never shone on
anyone, and the day your flame is quenched you will leave about you no
darkness, nor the cold of sorrow, because you have only been the lyrical
fire of sacrifice, because in your slow destruction, you were never the fire
on a hearth, nor will you ever light a path . . ."

My poetic thoughts were going more or less that way, and would have
continued much longer along the same line, if it weren't for the fact that
the corral door opened abruptly and as if by magic Aunt Clara's head appeared, but not in the sad, pale attitude proper for candles, no, she was
very agitated, a little irritated, her eyes bright, and facing me she said,
"Well, María Eugenia, if instead of being here in the corral with the door
shut, with your head dirtying the clothes we're going to wear, you were
where you should be, I wouldn't have to call you all over the house, just
like Chispita, when she takes it into her head to hide under the furniture.
I've been hunting you through the whole house for more than half an
hour, without remembering your blessed mania for the corral. You have a
telephone call!"

"Eureka!!" I exclaimed, since this, although a little pretentious, was the
only interjection that Grandmother had left me. "Eureka and eureka! Who
can it be and what do they want me for?"

And leaping from the trunk, I ran like the wind across patios and
through doors, until I reached the phone and pronounced the magic
words, "Who is it?"

And it was the thousand-times-blessed Mercedes Galindo, who was
calling to invite me to dinner with her that night. Uncle Pancho would
serve as my escort or chaperon, he would come pick me up and bring me
back home; it was all arranged. Mercedes added, "And I want you to be
very pretty tonight, that is to say, as pretty as the other day, which is as
pretty as a person can be."

This sentence, which I thought resplendent with truth, just as I think the noonday sun is resplendent, put me in a wonderfully good mood. And since on the telephone I couldn't sense that perturbing perfume that Mercedes wears, nor see the splendid pallor of her pearls, nor the soft lustre of her velvet dress, nor that enchanting smile that is a scandal of red lips and white teeth—since on the phone, I repeat, I was not able to perceive this series of circumstances, which, in addition to her person, contributed to awaken in me the day of her visit that unwelcome feeling of timidity, completely free of that feeling, I could answer her flattery gracefully, saying that if that was her opinion, then I was obliged to believe that her house was like the austere and bare cloisters of convents where the monks finally forget themselves after years of never looking at their own image in a mirror.

I said this to Mercedes, which was a way of saying that her beauty is superior to mine, something that can be accepted as a courtesy, but whose falsity is immediately obvious. Truly Mercedes is very pretty, Mercedes is lovely, but I am much prettier than she. It's beyond question. I am taller, blonder; my hair is silkier; my mouth is better and my fingernails are much better shaped. Mercedes's great advantage over me is her refinement, yes, her incomparable chic . . . of course, when she always orders everything from Paris . . . Oh! If I had money! Oh! If Uncle Eduardo had not taken away the three-fourths of San Nicolás that belonged to me!

But to return to the phone call.

After those mutual compliments, and after very affectionate farewells, we hung up. Then I came here to my room, I double-locked the door, with the object of preventing Aunt Clara from bursting in and breaking my chain of thought for the second time. Having taken this precaution, I began to deliberate. The first thing I did was to open my wardrobe and to stand in front of the right side, where all my dresses hang. I put my hands on my hips, a stance, no matter what Grandmother may say, highly suited for moments of great indecision, and I began going through my clothes. As my eyes went from one dress to another, my lips murmured a sort of litany, "Which shall I wear? Which shall I wear? Which shall I wear?"

And at last I resolved to wear my Persian taffeta dress.

With this first problem solved, I pulled my chair next to the window, I settled into it comfortably, and I started thinking along this line, "Surely tonight the much-heralded and much-praised Gabriel Olmedo will also come to dinner. Of course he will come, and they'll introduce him to me this very day. Very well. I must take into account the draconian laws that Grandmother and Aunt Clara always apply to the question of mourning. An outsider might give a dinner the appearance of a party, and if they think it has a party atmosphere, horrors! Either they will call me a 'heart-less daughter,' which is very unpleasant, or they won't let me go to the dinner, which is much more unpleasant still. What should I do?"

Since in my mental storehouse there are always means of smoothing a conflict, as a measure of precaution, I decided to fabricate the following lie: I would say that Mercedes was alone, very much alone, completely alone, that her husband was away and that was why she was inviting me to keep her company.

Naturally, after having solved this second very interesting problem by eliminating guests at the dinner table, I was as satisfied as a general must be after having mapped out his battle plan.

Now, as a commentary, I note that it is truly stupendous how rapidly and deeply this habit of lying has taken root in me. Since I have been living with Grandmother, I lie all the time, a habit that has served as a gymnasium for my imagination, which has developed mightily, and has acquired amazing agility. I never used to tell lies. I despised lying as one despises all things whose usefulness has not been discovered. Now, let's not say that I respect lying very much, or that I have proclaimed it a goddess and picture it sculpted in marble with a long draped tunic and some allegorical object in its hand, like statues to Faith, Science, or Reason. No, I wouldn't go that far, but I do value it because I believe that in life it plays a rather flexible and conciliatory role worthy of consideration. In contrast, truth, that victorious and shining antipode of the lie, in spite of its great splendor, and in spite of its great beauty, like any strong light, is sometimes rather indiscreet and usually falls upon the person who enunciates it like a dynamite blast. Unquestionably it is also something of a wet blanket, and I consider it, on occasion, as the mother of pessimism and inaction. While the lie, the humble, denigrated lie, despite its universally wretched reputation, on the contrary, often gives wings to the spirit, and serves as the right arm of idealism, lifting the soul above the arid wasteland of reality, as a balloon lifts bodies above the arid deserts, and when we live under oppression then it smiles at us sweetly, presenting us with some shiny sparks of independence. Yes, the lie stretches a protective wing over the oppressed, it discreetly reconciles despotism with liberty, and, if I were an artist, I would already have symbolized it, like its gentle sister Peace, in the figure of a snowy white dove, wings stretched in flight as a sign of independence and displaying an olive branch in its beak.

I know perfectly well that these ideas may be written but not spoken. If I were to enunciate them in front of Grandmother, for example, she would immediately put her hands over her ears and she would cut my speech short saying, "Heavens! What foolishness! What nonsense! What immoral ideas!"

That's because Grandmother, like the majority of people, keeps poor morality bound in chains, and condemned to a kind of frightful "*démodé.*" I don't. I believe morals could change from time to time just like sleeves, hats, and the length of skirts. Forever, forever, the same? No, no, that is horribly monotonous, and a palpable proof of something I have always said, "Humanity lacks imagination!" However, I must record that, in spite of my theories, in practice my habitual moral sense does not yet find itself totally in agreement. I felt it yesterday in a sharp sting of remorse, which in my opinion is the alert sentinel that guards the doors of our sense of morality and announces to us its conquests or defeats.

Because last night, dressed in my Persian taffeta ready to go to the dinner, I appeared before Grandmother. She saw me and smiled, with that smile of hers that, like the smile of the Giaconda, encloses a mystery in its expression that I know very well. That mystery is an immense maternal vanity that flatters and satisfies me greatly because it is as mute and as eloquent as a mirror's praise. Well, when Grandmother saw me come in, she immediately brought her tortoiseshell lorgnette to her eyes and she said, emphasizing the mysterious smile more than ever, "So dressed up, and so prettied up just to go eat alone with Mercedes! What conceit, Lord!"

I thought, "Grandmother thinks I look beautiful but she won't tell me that so as not to make me more vain than I already am." At the same time, in view of her credulity and innocence, I felt the sharpest and most wrenching sting of remorse. It was so strong that I was really tempted to exclaim full of contrition, "Don't believe what I told you, dearest Grandmother! Even if you call me a 'heartless daughter,' I must tell you that I am going to dine with Mercedes, accompanied by an army of people, if she sees fit to invite them."

But since lying does not admit the deserter nor the faint-hearted to its ranks, I had no choice but to say to myself like a heroic soldier, "Onward, ever onward!" and I responded, "I value Mercedes's opinion very much, Grandmother. To me a single person with good taste is worth a crowd of people who don't know how to dress."

In reality, there were no armies nor crowds at last night's dinner. It had been arranged in my honor, and in deference to my mourning, besides Uncle Pancho, Mercedes, and her husband, there was only, as I had already foreseen, the much-heralded Gabriel Olmedo. To tell the truth I think Uncle Pancho exaggerated a lot when he described him, so much, that last night when I saw him enter Mercedes's drawing room, I felt real disillusionment, if the word "disillusionment" can be applied to people toward whom we feel absolute indifference. In the first place, his eyes and hair are as black as coal, something I find detestable; moreover his legs are too long for his torso, he wears low-cut shoes, and as I now recall, his ankles are rather thick, not slender. However, looking at him carefully, he's not bad-looking if you happen to like brunets, but since I don't like jet-black hair except on a cat's back, and on people it irritates and displeases me, Gabriel Olmedo, with his smooth, perfumed head, the color of a crow's wing, made a poor impression on me last night. In personality I thought him very pretentious. I believe Mercedes must have told him about "that plan," because, although apparently amiable and correct, he occasionally adopted the attitude of a crowned king, a confirmed bachelor for whom his government is seeking a bride.

As for myself, I am satisfied and aware that I gave myself a hundred times more tone than he. Was it due to Mercedes's pleasantries and exquisite tact? . . . Was it due to the perfumed cocktail followed by several glasses of champagne? . . . Was it due, rather, to the multitude of mirrors that continually reflected the harmony of my figure? . . . I don't know, but the fact is that last night, far from experiencing any shyness whatever, the whole time I had a wonderful sense of my own importance, which put me at ease with the others and with myself. Today, when I think about it, I notice that my sense of importance has sunk since last night. This causes me to believe that it definitely was due to the cocktail and the champagne, which went to my head a little, raising the thermometer of my vanity a few degrees. I've noticed lately that that thermometer is very sensitive, and much more likely to rise than to sink. Anyway, I'm glad, since it helped me to show to Gabriel Olmedo's black eyes the intense wealth of indifference and disdain in my soul for pretentious men.

Mercedes's house is very elegant and her table as sumptuous and rich as in a palace. Everywhere the finest objects of silver alternate with porcelains from Saxony and Sèvres; the walls have tasteful mirrors, tapestries, and pictures, and plants grow happily throughout the house, in genuine jardinières from China. Best of all she has an Oriental boudoir that is a delight . . . That marvelous low divan, immense and square, covered with dark cushions of every shape and tint, soft, luxurious, and warm as a kiss, situated between a Turkish incense burner, a leopard skin, and an ivory chest carved in Japan! What I wouldn't give to have one like it, so I could sink into it and disappear for days on end, reading towers, mountains, and mountain ranges of books! . . .

"These are remains from the shipwreck!" Mercedes said as she was showing me the house, lighting "the shipwreck" with a smile and alluding to the time she lived in Paris in a beautiful, exclusive hotel, rich and surrounded by influential friends like a princess. It's because of the wastefulness and bad judgment of her husband that the two have lost almost all her fortune, and that's what they call the shipwreck.

Alberto Palacios, Mercedes's husband, is very nice and, like her, he's very sophisticated and charming. I noticed, however, that despite his gallantry and outward amiability, several times he spoke to her in a tone tinged with a certain brusqueness, which made me think, "Grandmother and Aunt Clara must be right when they say he treats her very badly, but how can one behave badly to a creature so full of every charm and attraction?"

Going back to my impressions, I must say that last night I had an enchanting time. Unfortunately, I don't know when it will be repeated. If it were left to me, I would repeat it every night. Yes . . . What a delicious atmosphere one breathes in the home of Alberto and Mercedes! It's as if, along with the pictures, tapestries and Sèvres porcelains, they had also filled their house with that divine atmosphere that I was only allowed to breathe for a few days during my last and all-too-short stay in Paris.

Oh! I was forgetting a very strange detail. As we were about to leave, while Mercedes had gone to look for the miniature she had offered me, Uncle Pancho went up to Gabriel Olmedo, who was standing next to the door rather far from me, and he asked in a low voice, "Well, what do you think of my niece, Gabriel?"

"Your niece, Pancho," he answered, more or less in the same low tone, "is the biblical temptation of Paradise, in the form of the most divine Grecian body. I hope, however, that I will know how to resist temptation's assault, and that I will not incur the sin of falling in love with her. I will not sacrifice my freedom, Pancho, not even at the lovely feet of that doll of a niece of yours. But take her away, anyhow, and do it now, please, and hide her where I'll never see her again, for wise and prudent men avoid temptation."

This dialogue reached my ears perfectly, although at that moment I seemed to be deeply absorbed in the contemplation of an oil painting, a copy of Greuze that shows a girl hugging a small dog. Those words, caught at a distance, are one of the reasons why I think Gabriel Olmedo, besides being brunet and short-waisted, is a pretentious creature, full of himself, who talks about the importance of "his freedom" as if he were some town or nation. Basically he doesn't seem to have any good qualities except that of good taste, and of being able to accurately appraise beauty.

Last night, when, back home, Uncle Pancho said goodbye to me, alone in the quiet house where everything was sleeping, I took off the wrap that I had worn to cross the street, and in the cool of the night, in the middle of the entrance patio, beside palm trees and rosebushes, leaning on one of the pillars, I basked in the infinite serenity of the sky. Looking at the moon and the stars, I longed to fly into heavenly space, to go far away, very far, I don't know where . . . the way messenger pigeons fly! And staring above, I thought about the glorious flight of winged creatures, I thought about the phrase Gabriel Olmedo had uttered about his freedom, and thinking about wings and thinking about adorable freedom, and thinking about Gabriel Olmedo's phrase, without quite knowing what I was saying, I began to say, half irritated and half anxious, "His freedom! . . . His freedom! . . . Do you suppose he thinks I don't value mine! . . . I value it, yes. I value it very much . . . so much, that the next time Uncle Panchito comes to see me, I too will say, 'Uncle Pancho, I'll never sacrifice my freedom at the feet of a man with thick ankles! Because I must tell you, Uncle, that I hate thick ankles, and jet-black hair repels me terribly. Yes, it repels me as much as I love my freedom.' "

Once I had made this firm resolution, facing the rosebushes on the patio, and beneath the immensity of the infinite, I finally decided to go to bed, because it was a very cool night and my Persian taffeta dress is too low-cut to stay out in the night air without a coat.

But this morning, I began to reflect . . . Now I think if I were to make that declaration about my freedom the next time Uncle Pancho comes, it is certain that he will laugh out loud and tell me as he chuckles, "Poor María Eugenia! Your freedom doesn't exist! It doesn't exist now, María Eugenia, nor has it existed in the past, nor will it ever exist! Your freedom is a myth—one of the many fantasies or aberrations that your mind invents. Therefore, I think it best that you not brag about it so."

Naturally, in case I heard something so impertinent, I wouldn't stay quiet; rather, I'd answer with great indignation, "You're wrong, Uncle Pancho, you're wrong! My freedom will exist in the future as surely as the sun shines. Because, tell me, who, just who, can forbid me on my twenty-first birthday to go away from here, if I wish, and get work in Paris, Madrid, or New York as a ballet dancer or a movie actress?"

Then Grandmother, if present, will immediately drop her sewing or whatever she has in her hands, will remove her glasses and exclaim in fright, "For Heaven's sake, María Eugenia, don't talk that way! You shouldn't say that even as a joke!"

And Aunt Clara will also express her opinion, "That is the sort of idea you get from your conversations with Gregoria, and from those highly immoral books you must be reading when you're locked in your room!"

And she may get suspicious and one morning while I'm in a reverie, lying on Uncle Enrique's trunk, Aunt Clara and Grandmother may come to my room, look through everything, and find the immoral novels hidden in the false bottom of my wardrobe, and it might cause a horrible upset.

For that reason, I think it's much more prudent not to mention my freedom in front of Uncle Pancho. For the same reason, I locked myself in my room early this morning and I've been writing . . . and writing . . . and writing. Aunt Clara, that's what you don't suspect! When I'm locked in my room, I'm not reading. I'm writing anything I please, because the paper, this white, shiny paper, lovingly keeps everything I tell it, and never, never is horrified, or fusses at me, or puts its hands over its ears!

Today I'm writing, and while I'm writing, I watch the rain falling outside my shuttered windows, because since quite early it's been raining fearfully. It must have been about this time yesterday when Aunt Clara came to tell me I had a phone call. How fast the hours go! Sitting at my desk I look at the clock, I look at the rain dripping on the shiny leaves of the orange trees, I think about the passing of time, and I don't know why today Grandmother's house seems bigger, more silent, and more boring than ever.

CHAPTER III

How a wandering attention
unleashes a dreadful storm,
which in turn precipitates
great events.

 "Pull your chair closer, María Eugenia, get closer
because no matter how good your eyes are you
can't see the threads clearly from that distance!"
That's what Grandmother said a little impatiently yesterday, weighted down with the tablecloth she is working on at present. Then she re-
sumed her interrupted refrain, "See, you take two threads; you leave two;
next you pick up two more; then you pull the needle through to the right;
then you pick up the two that were left before, being careful not to tangle
the thread; then you start over again . . . Why, it's so easy!"

Since, among the achievements of human ingenuity, cutwork is one of
those that intrigues me least, and even less does it awaken my curiosity or
ambition to learn, I still had not yet mastered the absolute laws that govern
the stitch Grandmother is now working on her tablecloth, even though I'd
been watching her expound those laws for a quarter of an hour in a wise
blend of theory and practice.

Grandmother holds the firm conviction that "an honorable lady"
should master among other accomplishments the science or art of cutwork, in all its different variations. To my ignorance of cutwork Grandmother attributes "that bad habit of sitting on tables"; "my excessive use
of lipstick, which is not proper for a young lady"; my laziness; my long
conversations with Gregoria; and my mania for reading "every book or
novel that falls into my hands"; all things that are very prejudicial, to her
way of thinking.

Grandmother often declares dogmatically, "Cutwork is so interesting
and absorbing that it becomes a vice. And while you're sewing, you're

doing something productive in the first place; it is an entertainment at the same time, and most of all, you're working! Because idleness is the root of all evil, and if it is repulsive in a man, in a woman idleness is much more dangerous still."

It seems that I don't have much experience (a useless and despicable thing compared to intelligence) but nonetheless, in the relative amount I possess, I have discovered, thanks to my wits, that the most effective way of exalting the tyrannical spirit of any faith is to deny it, to argue about it, or to scorn it. Therefore, with the aim of liberating myself a little from the apostolic enthusiasm with which Grandmother tries to inculcate her doctrines in me about the excellent benefits derived from the science of cutwork, I decided yesterday to embrace that science. I firmly believed that it was the best system of freeing myself from it. Homeopathy affirms, "Similia similibus curantur" and I thought the time had come to apply that discreet aphorism.

It was for this simple and homeopathic reason that yesterday I took a seat next to Grandmother, and with my knees sharing the fluffy white waves formed around us by the fabric of the future tablecloth, I began to receive my first notions of the science that, according to Grandmother, unites usefulness and pleasure and, as the fruit of that union, sheds endless moral benefits upon the one who exercises it. But to tell the truth, in spite of my good will, while she was saying, "you take two threads; you leave two; next you pick up two more; then you pull the needle through to the right; then you pick up the two that were left before, being careful not to tangle the thread . . ." I was only looking mechanically at the threads pulled this way and that by the brilliant needle and I was thinking of something else.

I confess I did wrong, but who among us is the absolute monarch of the disorderly republic of our thoughts?

A fatal moment came when my eyes found, no doubt, that the undulating threads interfered with the ideas flowing in my mind, and without my realizing it, my eyes discreetly landed on the restful stillness of a mosaic arabesque. Oh, the unforeseen! . . . There Grandmother's inquiring glance surprised them, and she exploded!

"You're not paying attention, María Eugenia! You're not paying any attention at all, and that is a lack of consideration for me! I'm worn out explaining something that you can learn by just seeing it once! And it's because you think it's an asset not to know how to sew, and that you're lowering yourself to hold a needle in your hand instead of a book. I won't teach you any more, just go, go read your novels, and go on being lazy, you'll see what that leads to!"

This attack, breaking the thread of my wandering thoughts, surprised me and had an effect on me like an alarm clock that rings in the middle of the night. I was totally unprepared for it. Besides, faced with the evidence, no excuse was possible. Therefore, limiting myself to refuting only the final phrases of her angry speech, I said hastily, "Grandmother, reading isn't being idle. Reading is instructive, it teaches, and I consider it more profitable, and much more fun, than this sewing and this cutwork, where you're forever repeating the same thing, as if you were walking in a circle to pump water from a well."

Oh, Holy Heaven! What a poor choice of words! You might say it was "the straw that broke the camel's back," unless under the circumstances it seems too weak and pale a metaphor. Instead it might be a more accurate description to say it was like a careless hand that draws the cork from a bottle of champagne that someone has previously shaken.

Because apparently, for more than a month and a half, without my being aware of it, a thousand irritations had been accumulating in Grandmother's mind, produced by my conduct and manner. I didn't know it, and suddenly two moments of imprudence revealed it to me: first, having fixed my eyes on a mosaic arabesque instead of keeping them on the tablecloth; and second, the luckless idea of a frontal attack on cutwork, and rashly invoking the image of the water well, which brings to even the slowest imagination the humiliating and despised donkey that provides the labor. This is how these two imprudent or careless acts caused Grandmother's impatience to explode violently.

I had no sooner mentioned the rash image of the water well than she, wounded in her deepest convictions, released her needle, took off her glasses, and red, scowling, her eyes flashing, and still weighted down by the tablecloth, she began to tell me with indescribable agitation, "I don't know you, María Eugenia! You're not the same girl who came to this house four months ago! Then you were respectful and you were obedient, and you always listened to my advice, and you were considerate of me. But you're not that way now. You think you're very superior, and even if you don't say so, you imagine that my ideas are backward or ridiculous! You're disdainful about staying here with us, and the only thing you think about is for five o'clock to come so you can go to Mercedes Galindo's house, and that's only if you don't go at four o'clock! They've changed you there . . .! You're not the same, no, you're not the same, books and bad company are ruining you, and with all your good qualities! Your family, your own mother's family, doesn't exist for you, and you like only outsiders! I haven't been able to make you a friend of your cousin, Eduardo's daughter. I know you make fun of her, and according to what Clara has told me, you have even made up a name for her. What a difference when you arrived from Europe just four months ago! I always held you up as a model because you were moderate and gentle, and because, although well educated, you had stayed very innocent. But you've lost that innocence, and everything! It's the atmosphere of Mercedes's home that has transformed you. Yes, every day I deplore having renewed relations with her! They detest all of the Aguirre family, and that antipathy has influenced you a lot! You'll get nothing, absolutely nothing good, out of a close friendship with someone I disapprove of with all my heart! . . . And as for Gabriel Olmedo, that fool, that petulant brat, that nobody that they are showing you off to, and whom you consider so wonderful, he is the lowest of the low because of his ideas, his wasteful habits and pretensions. He'll never marry you. No, he's not the kind who gets married, and much less to a woman as poor as you are . . . Just maybe, after amusing himself for awhile he'll leave you high and dry. You'll see!"

If my phrase about the water well had been a mistake, Grandmother's final words were like a whip lashing me across the face. Anyone can understand why the words "and much less to a woman as poor as you" awoke a frenzy of indignation in my heart, but I only know my lips were trembling, and my hands were icy cold. A million words and images were seething in my mind, they halted a moment on my tongue, which, paralyzed with indecision, did not know which to choose nor where to start. Finally, my voice tremulous, my breathing irregular, with concepts and words tumbling out, and with an insolence that made me quite deserving of Grandmother's reprimand, I proceeded to spill out this enumeration, "Yes, Grandmother, you're right; in fact I am very poor, I'm destitute, because I'm not a pirate; a highwayman; a miser; a usurer; nor a thief like others are; on the contrary, I've been robbed! It's a fact, I have solid facts, I know it! . . . and that's why I have nothing! And if I commit 'the crime' of going to Mercedes's house every afternoon, it's because I have fun there and here I'm bored! And that's not her fault nor my fault! . . . And Mercedes never utters the word 'Aguirre' in praise or criticism; and I've never given any name to my imbecile cousin because I think eight names among the four of them is more than enough to make them look ridiculous forever without adding any more names. Yes, yes, Grandmother, if you want me to tell you the truth, I think the four, along with hateful María Antonia, and headed by Uncle Eduardo, are all swimming together in insignificance like a flock of ducks in a pond! And besides they're envious, yes, very envious, they hate me because they envy me, because of envy! And out of envy they're plotting to make you keep me from going to Mercedes's house! Do you think I didn't hear Uncle Eduardo the other night when he told you . . . (and here, talking through my nose and making a terrible face in honor of Uncle Eduardo, I repeated): 'that friendship is not at all suitable for her' . . . Do you think I didn't hear it? I heard it perfectly! Oh! Envious! Stupid! Fools! Cretins! But I despise them, Grandmother, do you hear? I despise them all because I see them as tiny, like ants, in a pit of inferiority. Yes, they're little, squatty, imperceptible, microscopic, almost nonexistent! They're imbeciles!"

I was a prey to the most terrible fury, my lips were exclaiming, trembling, insatiable, eloquent. Grandmother, beside me, now covered by all the weight of the tablecloth, which in my furor I had thrown off my knees, Grandmother, who had never seen me except in my gentle, normal character, forgetting as if by magic her earlier anger, was now overwhelmed by amazement and fear. Whether it was regret for having hurt me, or whether she was afraid of the consequences of my anger I don't know, but certainly instead of becoming more and more irritated with my great insolence, no, on the contrary, as I talked her gaze had been gradually growing softer, until finally when I finished my reply, heaping countless diatribes on Uncle Eduardo's family, she was in the grip of the greatest anguish, lamenting her rashness, sorry for having roused a demon of discord in me, and since her greatest desire is to see me in harmony with my cousins, she began to say in a gentle, conciliatory tone, "But it's not true, María Eugenia. They've never said anything to me! Don't talk that way about your cousins! Don't say such things about Eduardo! You see, don't you see that it's true you don't love your family? The things I told you are for your own good, you know better than anyone how I love you, how much Clara loves you, how we all love you! Why, I'd give anything, yes, I'd give my very life to see you happy and to see you content. Don't you know I love you doubly? I love you for yourself and I love you for your mother. That's precisely why I'm worried, because it seems to me that all this could harm you or could cause you greater suffering in the future!"

But my anger is not so inconsistent or so easily calmed as Grandmother's. Infrequent, actually, when its fuse is lit, it burns a long time, it's very hard to extinguish it, and if it dies down a little, then, like the Phoenix, it is reborn from its own ashes. That's why, in spite of the affectionate and soothing words with which Grandmother was counseling me, I went on for a long time talking and talking and talking, with infinite eloquence, developing the most unexpected and insulting images of Uncle Eduardo's family, whose collective figure was fixed and immobile in my mind like an obsession. My own words did nothing but excite me more and more, which is why, as I was talking, I understood and forgave the voluptuous anger of the Furies.

"Yes! They're jealous of me, Grandmother, and they detest me even if you won't admit it! But I have nothing but scorn for them, and I can't even stand to look at them! Uncle Eduardo's children put on such airs, but they're dreadfully ignorant. They don't even know how to express themselves; the poverty of their minds makes you pity them! Their vocabulary is as poor as their brains are empty! Every time they open their mouths they use superlatives! It's monotonous! . . . Yes, to them everything pleasant is 'beautiful' or 'divine'; everything unpleasant is 'a disaster,' 'frightful,' or 'a mess' and that's what their vocabulary is reduced to. They have no notion of shades of meaning, of averages or gradations. They have no personality. They are as much alike as grains of corn, because they have the simplemindedness and uniformity of idiots. And as for that ugly and ridiculous old María Antonia, she's a nobody, or to tell the truth, she's a mulatta, an illegitimate child, full of evil and racial hatred; Uncle Eduardo, basically, is no more than her instrument, but he is a stingy, imbecilic, and gossipy instrument, to say the least! . . . This is my sincere opinion about all of them. If I'm offending you, forgive me, or rather, forgive the truth for being cruel and pitiless!"

It is true that from my mouth there issued forth, as if from the crater of an erupting volcano, all the facts and information gathered in my conversations with Uncle Pancho and with Gregoria. Fortunately, Grandmother didn't realize that, and this allowed her to maintain her serenity as she continued saying in the same gentle, conciliatory tone, "But calm yourself, María Eugenia, calm yourself. What have they done to make you hate them this way?"

"Oh, I don't hate them, Grandmother! I see them impartially! I'm quite unbiased! And if this is not so, tell me, answer: what is false, what is inaccurate about what I've said?"

But Grandmother chose not to answer at all, and there was a long pause during which she put her glasses on again and looked for her needle, which had been lost among the folds of the tablecloth. When she found it she stretched the edge she was working on over her skirt, she pulled the rest of the cloth together in a chair, she bent her head, and she continued the interrupted cutwork, the innocent instrument of such terrible discord.

For any other person that calm silence would have been considered the end of hostilities, but as I said, my anger tends to rekindle on its own, a phenomenon for which, up to a certain point, I don't consider myself responsible. Besides, Grandmother's attitude, perhaps adopted as a means of pacification, gave an appearance of profound scorn, very suited to a rebirth of my fury. If Grandmother had continued her defense of Uncle Eduardo and company, I would have become calm, I'm sure. Her silence roused my spirit of aggression. As I have already observed several times, Grandmother may know how to make delicate patterns on tablecloths, but the psychological threads of the human heart always knot and tangle in her fingers because she handles them in the clumsiest way.

Facing the bent, silent, and contemptuous head, I felt a new crisis of verbosity, of greater precision and less explosiveness. Provisionally setting aside the theme of Uncle Eduardo's family, which I considered exhausted, with my voice more tranquil and with immense pedantry, I resolved to attack another theme that seemed to me an efficient way to draw Grandmother out of her muteness.

"In your enumeration of my new defects or reactionary behavior, I believe you mentioned, Grandmother, that I had lost my innocence. In fact, lately I have dedicated myself to bringing a certain order and conciseness to my ideas. I don't wish the least ignorance ever to exist in my mind and therefore I have tried to explain the formation or mysterious origin of life in as much detail or as scientifically as possible. Naturally and logically I speak of it in my conversation, as I might speak of a Latin declension or of an algebra problem: it's common knowledge! Well, if you call this system of scientifically clarifying my doubts or ignorance 'having lost her innocence,' then, yes, I have lost it! I don't mind proclaiming it and I congratulate myself on it. It would be as silly to regret it as to regret, for example, losing a debt. Because innocence, which I never have possessed absolutely, thank God, is the most negative, the most dangerous, and the most foolish of all conditions."

To my great amazement, this statement, as passionate as it was suggestive, the first skirmish of new hostilities, remained unanswered, despite all its importance and magnitude. After listening to me, Grandmother peacefully picked up her scissors, cut her thread with them, took another strand and set about threading her needle, not without some hesitations and awkwardness. But all in the most profound silence. Wasn't this a thousand times more insulting than the most dreadful insults? It is then not strange that, once Grandmother's needle was threaded and I was certain I had regained her full attention, I should continue my theme with even more spirit.

"Yes, the innocence of marriageable young ladies, or rather the despotic desire to keep us ignorant in theory of all that other people know or have known in practice, seems to me one of the greatest abuses ever committed by the strong against the weak. In the first place it sows life with mysteries, which is like digging deep holes in a road, it is horribly disorienting; things are seen from a false point of view; it causes surprises that could be unpleasant; and in general is a trap, a blindfold, and a trick, used by others to make it possible to organize our lives more easily according to their wishes and caprices. Innocence is a blind, deaf, and paralyzed creature, whom human stupidity has crowned with roses. It is the humiliating emblem of submission and slavery in which, Uncle Pancho says, almost all honorable women live after they get married!"

The final phrase made Grandmother lift her head with a nervous jerk. However, repenting this slight reaction, she returned instantly to her work and remained wrapped in an aureole of silence. I continued my monologue with all the calm and sufficiency of a lecturer, certain Grandmother must be thinking, "What frightful pedantry and what a lack of respect."

"I therefore consider innocence a whip, an abuse, and an arbitrary practice. But without enumerating the countless great tragedies it has caused in the world, limiting ourselves just to ordinary daily life, tell me, Grandmother, do you think it's very nice for a sensitive person to constantly hear, 'you can't go out alone because *you don't know* what you are exposing yourself to,' or, 'even though others are talking about that immoral affair, *you shouldn't talk about it,*' or even worse, 'that book is well written, that play is admirable and very witty but *you can't* so much as hold it in your hands,' and always supported by such expressions. The thick wall of the mysterious and the forbidden! Don't you think that finally wounds your self-esteem? Don't you think it is horribly distasteful and humiliating? Do you think it is possible always to live this way, like a pariah, pushed aside from action and from life? No, absolutely not! Luckily, I have torn down all the walls. I'm proud to say it! I have stepped into the light and I think of myself as a spectator, who, with only a confused notion of her native city, climbs a very high tower and is able to see everything from there."

Grandmother obstinately continued her silence and her sewing, but I don't know why it seemed to me now that what her fingers were weaving on the snowy cloth was a white elegy dedicated to my innocence.

Then, at the far end of the patio, the louvered doors from the dining room opened and, very peacefully, Aunt Clara appeared, holding against her waist the basket heaped with clothes to be mended. The presence of a fresh and certain opponent heartened me greatly. So, I waited for Aunt Clara to get closer to keep from wasting my words and I went on talking louder; and lavishing more and more pedantry, "Do you want me to tell you what I think now, Grandmother? Do you want me to admit it? Very well! I think that morality is a farce; that it is full of incongruities and contradictions, and that, thanks to those glaring contradictions, in spite of my intelligence, I had confused and mixed-up ideas about the true origin of life. It is true that in my natural history courses I studied botany, and I studied logic at the same time, but it had never occurred to me to apply the laws that rule the plant world to the human world . . . Yes, I had three years of philosophy in school, and the teachers who graded my homework and compositions used to fill the margins of my papers with praise. Therefore order and method guide my intelligence, and naturally, using premises as false and as contradictory as those preached by modesty, decorum, and decency, I could never reach an exact conclusion. I never dreamed that morality gave rise to that incoherence, but now I know it does, because I have discovered it! . . . At last I understand and I know perfectly well why the nuns at school, for example, appreciated innocence and praised modesty; after all, they were virgins! But to talk about modesty when one is not a virgin, when one has had several children . . . that's absurd! Modesty in wives and mothers is a farce, it's a myth. Modesty doesn't exist! Or rather, modesty has taken refuge only in the shadow of convents! . . ."

Aunt Clara, just as I had foreseen, had not even managed to sit down. Standing, facing me, with her mouth slightly open, and the basket still resting against her waist, she was staring at me, held in the grip of the most profound stupor, until at last, drawing in a huge gulp of air as a sign of shock, she burst out, "Iiiiiiiihhhh!! . . . What a string of nonsense, María Eugenia! . . . Those atrocities are something you've read lately in some novel!"

"Novels! Yes! Carry on about novels! . . . That is another incongruity and another injustice! Novels, Aunt Clara, are full of discretion. The most immoral, do you hear, the most immoral, the worst of all I've ever read, as it came to certain moments, generally ended the chapter or omitted that scene. Yet very severe and very respectable people have put into practice the things never mentioned in words, and I find that unjust toward novels and very, very contradictory in general."

But Aunt Clara, who had still not recovered from her state of surprise, again exclaimed in the same way, that is, with a very long aspiration and with her eyes enormously dilated from shock, "I i i i i i i ! Merciful heaven! What an idea! What wild raving! Hush, María Eugenia, for God's sake be quiet, because you're simply delirious!"

"Oh, are you scandalized, Aunt Clara? Well, I never feel scandalized by anything, because I have a profoundly 'naturist' soul and with it I adore the simple truth of things. But what I will never understand is that accumulation of contradictory ideas that they call 'morality.' In my opinion, all of them together form a kind of blanket, which tries vainly to stretch over the truth of nature, but nature imposes itself, and then the blanket is just like hypocrisy. You are under its influence and for that reason you are scandalized. I'm not, because I have my personal ideas. I believe, for example, with total certainty, that modesty is the only thing responsible for the existence of immodesty. I think it is, we might say, the father of immodesty, and I think that at the same time it is its stepfather, because it has managed to vilify it and denigrate it in everyone's eyes. Tell me, do lilies wear clothes, Aunt Clara? Do they dress? Do doves dress? And you see that without dressing they preach purity and they are the symbol of chastity. Clothing is the cause of immodesty. If doves wore clothes, we'd be scandalized to see them fly, because they'd probably lift their dresses with the movement of their wings, and this from below would make a very indecent impression. But since they never dress, they are always modest; that is to say, they have had the talent of purifying immodesty and they possess this talent simply because rumors still have not reached their ears that morality exists. If we did as doves and lilies do, we would be as pure as they. The logical origin of clothing, its practical reason, is to preserve us from cold or to cover and hide imperfections of the body, something very frequent in the majority of nudes. True, 'The Greeks loved nudity because they were handsome.' This last thought about nudity among the Greeks is not mine, I did read it in a book and I assure you, Aunt Clara, that it will remain etched in memory forever as if etched in bronze, because it gleams with truth and overflows with logic!"

"Oh?" asked Aunt Clara, whose shock had not subsided one whit. "Do you mean, then, that according to those theories, María Eugenia, it would seem fine to you for Mama, you, and me to be here, sewing, totally naked, and then, later, for Pancho to come here naked, too, and in that state to sit down in a chair and start chatting with us? . . . Would that seem fine to you? . . . Very natural? . . . Very nice? . . . Eh? . . ."

The idea of such a social scene made me smile slightly, but, scorning the despicable triviality of comedy, I reassumed my dogmatic tone and continued reasoning, "Well, of course!! Certainly it would seem fine to me! Given the climate in Caracas, at this hour of the day," and I consulted my wristwatch, "ten-thirty A.M., the sun is high and it's rather hot. Therefore, if we wear clothes it's only out of a spirit of imitation, and out of habit. Accept it, Aunt Clara, it's just fawning adulation, copying the cold countries. If we had a well-defined personality and if we obeyed logical conduct in accord with our climate, at this time of day we should all be naked, everyone! . . . Maybe, when we go outside, to protect ourselves from the sun, we might wear a big hat or carry a straw umbrella, but nothing else!"

"Mama," said Aunt Clara turning to Grandmother, "what I find so strange is that you are calmly allowing María Eugenia to say such horrible things in front of you! It's an unparalleled lack of respect! What ideas, for God's sake, what preposterous ideas!"

And Aunt Clara, who had been sitting in her little low chair for some time, had put her basket of sewing on the ground, lifted her two hands to her head, in such a tragic attitude, that I felt truly satisfied seeing that my words at last provoked the sublime horror worthy of them.

"Leave her alone, Clara, leave her alone, don't excite her any more," Grandmother broke in to say then, without abandoning her pacific expression, and without taking off her glasses or lifting her head from her work. "For over fifteen minutes she's been standing here spouting the greatest nonsense! What amazes me, what surprises me, is the ease of expression she has. Yes, it's like a river spewing absurdities! Where does she find so many words? How do so many things occur to her at the same time? . . . Her father was just like that!"

"Yes, thank God, I do have a rich vocabulary! I do know how to express myself elegantly, and even in ordinary, domestic conversation, with good taste and in three languages, I can use images that any good orator would not scorn to use. And this is not common, because I know people whose vocabulary is so poor, so limited, and so pitiful, like the vocabulary that the most primitive savages use to express themselves."

"How vain you are, María Eugenia, how awful!" Aunt Clara said again. "You're like a peacock! You're going to burst, you're so swelled up. Remember that God punishes pride."

"I'm conscious of my qualities and I declare them. Modesty is just another hypocrisy!"

"Yes, apparently, you think everything good is hypocritical!"

And then, as she pulled a hand towel to mend from her basket, she added, making an association of ideas, "Well, if you're so fond of all that is true and natural, then why do you have your mouth as red as a beet so that you stain every napkin you use and every hand towel put in your room? Gregoria herself is the one who says that!"

"Look Aunt Clara, I wear lipstick, and I always will, because our intelligence tells us to correct and perfect the work of nature. But this doesn't mean that my makeup is a lie or a hypocrisy; I'm not trying to fool anyone, quite the opposite, the proof is, as you have just said, even the napkins proclaim the fact! I adore makeup! Yes, I declare, confess, and shout it! I like it so much that I'll wear it now, and later, and I'll wear it when I'm old, I'll wear it when I'm dying, and even after I'm dead, on Judgment Day, when I awake, I think I'll hear my sentence with a lipstick in my hand painting my lips!"

As she heard this last declaration, Aunt Clara, irritated and very annoyed, asked, "Just why, María Eugenia, must you always mix holy things, godly things, with your nonsense? This is the second time now that you've said that foolishness about how you'll be applying lipstick on Judgment Day!"

"I have only adapted an article of faith to the demands of modern life. Basically, there is nothing sincere about it because I no longer believe in the dogma of the Resurrection of the Flesh, nor in hell, nor in any mystery whatever, not even in . . ."

"Stop it!!!" shouted Aunt Clara enraged. And as she said "stop it!!!" her scissors clattered to the floor, and as a result of the unexpected metallic sound, I started, I entirely forgot what I was going to say about the mystery of the Incarnation, and it was she who took the floor, saying, "How nice, yes, how nice for you to talk this way, like an atheist or like a materialist, and all because you're so conceited, María Eugenia! You consider yourself a 'genius'!" And she repeated for the second time in an apocalyptic tone, "God punishes pride . . . and He punishes it in this world! . . ."

"Does he? Well, I can't see at all that God undertakes to hand out punishment in this world, because if he did, Aunt Clara, there are some people—people who come to this house a lot—on whom he would have rained fire from the heavens, as he did on Sodom and Gomorrah."

"Great Heavens!" she exclaimed, filled with curiosity, "and just who are those monsters?"

"For pity's sake, Clara, don't argue with her anymore. Leave her alone, as a favor to me. Let her alone! Let her alone! . . . I know that in her heart she can't believe any of the things she's saying; she's only doing it to mortify me!" And drawing a deep breath for a long sigh, and lifting her eyes to heaven, Grandmother began to say in a pained, low-pitched voice, "This is the reward I reap for loving her!"

And she spoke with such a bitter and such a profound tone of disillusionment that my anger abruptly dissipated, leaving in its stead an unpleasant reaction. After Grandmother's expression of hurt, I suddenly felt that I had wounded her too deeply. Repentant and very disgusted with myself, I resolved not to say any more.

A long general silence followed then, because Aunt Clara, pensive and much intrigued, was silent too. After my insolence, after Grandmother's last words, and above all after that unusual calm, she had sensed no doubt some mystery. Because of that, once in awhile, between stitches, she looked at me curiously as if to understand it, and Grandmother in turn must have longed even more to be able to tell her, so they could comment on it together at length. For that reason alone, I wouldn't leave. Motionless in my chair, staring at the two heads, bending over and absorbed in their sewing, I stayed a long time. Meanwhile in my head, in the peaceful silence, the precise idea began to dawn that everything, absolutely everything I had just said, ruled by my fury, was an imprudent revelation that could have disagreeable consequences. This clear-cut idea, and others as yet indefinite, started to worry me so much, that at last I decided to surrender myself to the judgment of Grandmother and Aunt Clara. Leaving them in complete freedom to comment, without saying a word, I stood up and came here. Once in my room, I locked the door, pulled the little chair up to the desk, and alone with my thoughts, looking at the little doll lamp or the orange trees on the patio, sunk in the arms of this friendly confidant, my chair, I began to reflect . . .

I was still very nervous, my face felt flushed and my hands were cold and shaking slightly . . . Oh! I had been so angry! . . . It was the first time that this had happened to me with Grandmother . . . and in my unbounded fury, without measure or limits, I had wounded her in her love for me and in her mother's love . . . I had hurt and mortified her! And after all, what caused that fury? . . . Why? Why? . . . It was because Grandmother had said, "That fool, that petulant brat, that nobody . . . he's the worst . . . he's not the sort of man who gets married and much less to a woman as poor as you." Yes, and all that came from information received from Uncle Eduardo . . . Uncle Eduardo had told that to Grandmother, urged by María Antonia, and maybe by my cousins . . . Yes, of course. All of them had joined forces to make Grandmother be harsh with me . . . Oh! Jealous, liars, imbeciles! . . . What a pity they couldn't hear all I had said about them just now! . . . But I had hardly warmed up to the subject! I would have said much more to them directly, much more . . . But . . . After all, what did it matter what that herd of cretins might say about Gabriel Olmedo? . . . And what did I care either about Gabriel Olmedo? . . . Yes, Gabriel Olmedo . . . Gabriel . . . Gabriel . . .

                    Even though Grandmother said that morning, "You don't think of anything except for five o'clock to come so you can go to Mercedes Galindo's house, unless you've already left at four o'clock . . .," at four o'clock on the dot, I was entering the elegant hall at Mercedes's house. Among palms and orchids while I was taking off my hat and arranging my hair in front of a mirror, I began to call her as is our established custom, "Mercedes! Mercedes! Where are you?"

"Here I am! Here!" she answered, as she always answers, her silvery voice muffled behind doors and windows, from the soft shadows of her Oriental boudoir.

Mercedes has built an Oriental setting for her Creole indolence, and instead of swinging in a hammock to the whispering breezes and the waving palm trees, as celebrated in the music of the *habaneras*, she rests on her huge, low Turkish divan, pale, stretched out, surrounded by a multitude of pillows, among whose soft mounds, shaded by curtains, she reads, dreams, meditates, sips tea, feels bored, and sometimes, too, she cries. Mercedes is so pretty in the undulating landscape of pillows that she takes on an aura I find very exotic. I always think when I see her there that the famous Oriental queens must have been like this. Since I don't think it would be in good taste to call her Cleopatra, I call her instead "Semiramis," for the queen of Babylon with its hanging gardens.

When I went to her boudoir yesterday afternoon, Mercedes was reading, surrounded by many books. When she saw me she sat up, merrily stretched out her arms to me, and then, after giving me a kiss, she had me sit down beside her on the edge of the divan; she marked the book she was reading with a paper knife, and she said affectionately, with a smile, taking me by the hands, "How early you came today! Well! That's wonderful! . . . I was just thinking about you; I was going to phone you . . . Why didn't you wear your crêpe Georgette dress, the one I like so much?" and she added with a smile and a little wink, "Gabriel is coming to dinner tonight!"

"I can't wear the same crêpe Georgette every night, no matter how much you like it; that's overdoing it!"

"No, no, you're wrong, María Eugenia! When a *toilette* is becoming you should wear it as much as possible. Even more with a little black frock, so simple, so *seyant* . . . But you must be very uncomfortable there, dear, lie on the sofa, relax *à ton aise*. Here! Here!"

Mercedes began to pile cushions on my side of the divan. I made a sort of long nest with the cushions and the wall, I leaned back, and resting one elbow on a small cushion, I leaned my forehead against my closed hand. Settled in comfort I began to tell Mercedes how worried I was, "You can't imagine the terrible scene I had with Grandmother this morning. I got so indignant and furious that I said dreadful things about Uncle Eduardo, María Antonia, and my cousins—I insulted them all. Really, I said the most frightful things about them, everything I could think up, horrors, Semiramis, horrors! . . . Toads and snakes!"

"What a great *maladresse!*" exclaimed Semiramis, who, when she is on her Turkish sofa and under the influence of her books, is more liberal than ever with spontaneous Gallicisms or French expressions. "Why did you commit such a *gaffe*, María Eugenia?"

"Because I can't always control myself! . . . Well, after insulting Uncle Eduardo and his family, I also insulted morality, which is like insulting another of Grandmother's sons."

"Oh! la! la! . . . That's even worse! What did Eugenia say?"

"Absolutely nothing at all! Not then or later. And that's the tragic part, Semiramis, and what has me horribly worried. Grandmother's silence is threatening. Silence usually is very treacherous. I don't know why I believe that Grandmother must be premeditating something awful against me."

"What happened, tell me, what caused that *brouille?*"

"It was because of something silly! You see, Grandmother at all costs wants me to learn to do cutwork, because she says I'm very lazy, and that idleness is the root of all evil—that old saw! Well, to please her I was trying to learn, on a Battenburg tablecloth she's working on now. But to tell the truth, Semiramis, so many threads coming and going make me dizzy and since I wasn't understanding it at all, I got distracted . . . When she saw I wasn't paying attention, Grandmother got very upset, and, using her displeasure as an excuse, she gave me a dreadful lecture about a million things that had nothing to do with the tablecloth or with cutwork. She said I wasn't obedient or respectful like I used to be; that I was disdainful about living in her house and about being a friend to my cousin, that I had given a nickname to my cousin, that I made fun of her, that I only wanted to be with you, that you were the one who had instilled a feeling of aversion in me toward all the Aguirre family, that she disapproved of our friendship, and that Gabriel Olmedo, to whom you were 'showing me off,' was the lowest . . . that he would jilt me . . . and that he would never marry me . . . because I was . . . a very . . . poor . . . woman."

I said these final words hesitantly, with great effort, and repugnance. I would have liked to omit them from the enumeration, but I thought about it too late, because I had already started to say it.

Mercedes didn't fail to notice my vacillation and repugnance. While I was stammering, she started smiling, and when I ended the story, barely letting the last words escape my lips, she was openly laughing with her bright, sonorous laughter. She half-closed her eyes and, mixing her words with laughs and winks, she said, "Oh! María Eugenia, María Eugenia, that was why, it was because of what she said about Gabriel that you got so indignant!"

"No, Mercedes, no, no, don't think that, I assure you; that's not so. What do I care what people may say about Gabriel? What really made me angry was how unjust she was to you, because I clearly saw Uncle Eduardo's hand, and his family, in that. They can't stand our friendship and they're influencing Grandmother to forbid it. Grandmother basically doesn't dislike you. But of course, since she never sets foot in the street, she knows nothing of the world except from the stories that imbecile Uncle Eduardo brings her. It's the only thing she hears and the only thing she believes. The real informant is María Antonia, don't you know? . . . Because she's the one, that devil, that gossip, who fills Uncle Eduardo's head, so Uncle Eduardo will stir up Grandmother."

Mercedes didn't answer. For an instant she was quiet as if reflecting. Then she spoke, "Really, what an injustice! . . . Especially what a *parti-pris!* . . . When have I ever spoken ill of Eugenia, or Eduardo or any of them?"

"That's just what I told Grandmother, and after that I started my string of insults against Uncle Eduardo and company. I called them imbeciles and scoundrels until I was tired. I was simply furious! Imagine, my lips were trembling, my hands were trembling, never had I been in such a state!"

"It doesn't sound like you, María Eugenia, my dear; you are so sweet, so gentle, so discreet. You, infuriated? . . . To be so upset. . . Eventually it causes wrinkles. Yes, naturally, people with a bad temper, by the time they're thirty, *ça y est!* Wrinkles, gray hair, *mauvais teint*, all the calamities put together, everyone knows this!"

I meditated a few seconds and, still thoughtful, softly hemmed about by pessimism and pillows, I began to say with philosophical seriousness,

"But you know, Mercedes, after all, Grandmother is perhaps not so far from the truth? . . . It's true that you have never said anything against anyone in my family, but having me here where I breathe this atmosphere you have created, this divine atmosphere that I adore, because it pampers me and swells my heart, you have kept me from becoming acclimatized in the atmosphere there. . . My rebellion comes from comparing my two worlds! . . . These sudden continual changes prevent custom from growing and taking root . . . custom! You know? For it is like a mother and a consolation to unhappy people! I remember when I arrived in Caracas, just a few months ago, I felt very sad because its narrow, flat streets seemed ugly to me. Now when I walk down them, do you know what I think? I think that Paris streets are the sad ones, because to make them so broad they've had to stack the houses one on top of another like empty boxes that are closed and dark inside, stacked up in an attic. And it's because in my eyes the streets of Caracas have grown pleasing with familiarity . . ."

After I said this we sat silent quite a while.

It seemed as if over the divan, under the shadow of the drapes, the echo of my words continued to float, and if the two of us were so quiet it was because we were still listening to them. At last Mercedes slowly said in a very low voice, for yesterday she was sad, and she said with a sigh, "Maybe that's true about custom, and perhaps, wishing to do you a good turn, I've done you a very great wrong!"

And we fell silent again. I felt now that our thoughts, joined together, were fluttering about the same object, like two butterflies that both flit around a light. This impression was so intense that in the semidarkness and in the silence that surrounded us it seemed that you could almost perceive the steady invisible fluttering of our two thoughts. I felt that under its influence my spirit was slowly being oppressed, and I felt like crying. But Mercedes broke these threads of the abstract or the intangible, as she suddenly said with the rude energy of real things, "No, María Eugenia, no, I haven't done you any wrong, I am sure!" And sitting up, pale and nervous against the black of the divan, with a commanding look, her lovely penetrating eyes stared into mine and she declared with conviction, "Look. You love Gabriel and Gabriel is crazy about you. You know it; he does too. And although you may not have said anything to each other, your flirtation is beginning, because I have seen it. Well, I'll bet that within a month—no, not a month—within a week, Gabriel will decide to marry you."

I felt that an immense light gleaming from Mercedes's eyes was dazzling my soul, and since I couldn't face that glorious brilliance, I lowered my eyes and said nothing. She went on, "Yes. Gabriel is mad about you. No matter how he tries to hide it, he doesn't think of anything but you! And it would be hard for him to ever in his life come across a woman who could charm, and satisfy, and interest him the way you interest him. Believe me, if instead of being thirty, Gabriel were only twenty, he'd be here all day long, here, with us, wanting to be with you every instant, not seeing or hearing or existing for anything except you. But Gabriel has lived a lot, and because he has lived a lot and has experienced a lot of success, he has caught the fever of ambition, of business; he always wants more. Nothing ever seems to be enough. Yes. He's terribly ambitious, he's involved in many projects and he dreams of making millions. Besides, he has political aspirations and it's because he's so ambitious that he's so afraid of marriage! The idea of any *entrave* that might hold him back is terribly frightening to him . . . But, it doesn't matter, love is stronger than all that, and a passion when you're thirty is greater and more enduring, because one still loves with the enthusiasm of youth, but also with anxiety, feeling that divine youth is passing! Well, also what is happening is that Gabriel feels safe about you because you're hidden and locked away in Eugenia's house, never seeing a living soul. If other men were buzzing around you, he'd be jealous, afraid, he'd be afraid of losing you and then, ah, then you'd see that he'd forget his ambition and his business affairs! But say nothing to him. In such matters there is no better ambassador than time and seeing each other often; seeing each other, above all. That is the breeze that fans the flame!"

Until yesterday Mercedes had not ever spoken to me about Gabriel with such precision and clarity. She mentioned him constantly, but always, with insinuations and smiles, in that delightful teasing tone, in a voice both affectionate and flattering, making jokes about love. Her frankness now surprised me and disturbed me so much that it left me paralyzed and wordless for a long time, with my astonished eyes fixed on the sofa. Within myself I felt a strange awakening of a thousand obscure things that, choking me with surprise and pleasure, smothered my voice. Finally, not knowing what to do, nor what to say, I fluffed up some pillows, I changed positions, I smoothed my hair, and randomly I asked, "Why did Grandmother say this morning that Gabriel has bad ideas?"

"Because Gabriel is a *libre-penseur*, he doesn't believe in anything, he has no religious ideas. That, really, *c'est dommage!* Besides Eugenia is scandalized because Gabriel has a reputation of being dissolute. The truth is that since he is so generous, so gallant, and so good-looking, he has always had, here and in Paris, a *succès fou* with the women. Of course, out of envy people exaggerate and gossip about him. But if Gabriel were married to you, he would be a model husband, I am sure. Don't you see that you, along with all his ambitions and ideals, would fill his life completely? Of course! Look, 'your Gabriel' is very ambitious, and he's very intelligent, and above all he has admirable *savoir faire!*" Then she lowered her voice, and, smiling mysteriously, she added confidentially, "Don't ever tell him what I've said, please, but he has been offered a position as ambassador in Europe, and it's amazing, but *il s'en moque.* He didn't accept! Because he's involved in some petroleum deals that might yield millions. His backer in the government is Monasterios, who is considered all-powerful now. Well, people say that Monasterios wants Gabriel to marry his daughter. She's dark, chubby, and short, and she goes around decked out in the most ornate and vulgar way on earth. Gabriel lets the rumor circulate and he laughs about it. Naturally! Because imagine a man so refined, so elegant, you might say a connoisseur, marrying a creature like that!"

Mercedes laughed her happiest, most silvery laugh, a very welcome sound to me. This information about Gabriel, far from frightening me, made me deliriously happy. It seemed to me that the ambition and projects were mine, too, I shared them with great enthusiasm and I saw them rise like a pedestal on which Gabriel grew and grew enormously. If that pedestal put him at a distance from me, so much the better! That was the way I wanted him, as difficult and brilliant as victory! That's why as Mercedes laughed gaily and mockingly, I saw before my eyes, like a sublime apotheosis, the glory of love united with the glory of all my ambitions realized . . . And at that exact moment, without anyone touching the switch, in the darkness that surrounded us, the shaded reddish light that illuminates the boudoir at night turned on. As if a gust of mystery had just passed through the room, I shivered and Mercedes, who is rather superstitious and given to a belief in the occult, sat up on the pillows and asked me fearfully, "Did you turn it on? Then how did the lamp light by itself?"

I smiled, and also sitting up on the divan, I exclaimed mischievously, "A whim of your lamp, Semiramis. Look, look, it's on . . . How red and how pretty it looks today! . . . It's the heart of the boudoir . . . and like yours and mine and everybody's it too suddenly has its whims and its playfulness!"

The lamp's caprice seemed to me as jolly, as well-timed and as good an omen as Mercedes's laugh making fun of Monasterios's daughter!

"Probably last night you left the light turned on and now the electricity has come back on."

"But I turned it off myself before I went to bed, I'm certain!"

And finally, reaching out an arm, bared as her filmy negligee fell back, she turned the light off. We sat in the darkened room, for it was a cloudy afternoon and the two bedroom shutters were barely open behind the curtains. Mercedes pressed the bell next to the light switch and its tinkle echoed in the distance.

"It's tea time. I'll order some!" she told me.

"Yes, yes," I exclaimed, leaping down from the sofa on the wings of joy. "That's a great idea. I'm so hungry! And do you know what I'm going to do while we wait for tea? I'm going to smoke a cigarette in your long ivory holder!"

"But, María Eugenia, you've told me a thousand times that you despise cigarette smoke, and that after the maid has cleaned your room, you fan the air with a cloth to get rid of the tobacco smell she always leaves wherever she goes."

"Because the cigarettes the maid smokes aren't Egyptian!"

And having clarified that point, and lighted the cigarette, thinking voluptuously, "If you could only see me now, Grandmother!" I sat on the big table in the boudoir, and, my profile to the mirror, with my feet crossed in the air, after two or three puffs, I exclaimed happily, "Look, Semiramis! Look, see my profile! I think I look pretty this way. Up high, my head back, my shoulders relaxed, the long cigarette holder, and then the smoke rising . . . rising, in spirals! Oh! I love smoking with your ivory cigarette holder!"

"Well, I'll give you one soon, very soon. It will be to celebrate 'the triumph of love'! I mean, the first kiss! Because you'll tell me about it, won't you? That is, if *ce n'est pas indiscret!*"

"What? What? The first what?"

And since at that very moment, I was trying to inhale the smoke, it went up my nose, bringing tears to my eyes and making me cough terribly. Then I put the cigarette out, pressing it against the ashtray. I left the holder on the table, I jumped down, I went over to sit on a pillow on the floor, quite close to Mercedes's face, and I suggested, "Listen, what you told me about my dress when I came has been worrying me and now I feel so ugly with this old Persian taffeta rag. I detest it! Shall I go home for just a moment to change into the *ourlet à jour* that you like so much?"

"No! Absolutely not! You're not going to leave me alone, this late, to stay until eight o'clock at your house *en train de te disputer* again with Eugenia or Clara. But instead, look, I was studying you when you sat on the table, and I thought you looked lovely. Your eyes are very bright and your skin is clear and rosy. I think today you look beautiful. What I would like to do is change your hairstyle. For days I've been wanting to see you with one that I discovered in *Vogue*. It's parted down the middle, and the hair is pulled back off the forehead. Shall we try it?"

After having seated me before the mirror, Mercedes, standing behind me, rapidly and skillfully created the *Vogue* hairstyle for me. Then she put rouge on my cheeks, lipstick on my lips, some light shadow under my eyes, and stepped back to see me at a distance in the mirror. Smiling and amazed, she exclaimed in excitement, holding her two hands together,

"Oooooh! *Ma chère*! What a difference! You are *épatante*! You shouldn't wear any other hairstyle. Yes, you'll see what a smash you'll be tonight!"

And so, *épatante*, made up, and wild with joy, I went back to the divan with her and we had our tea. I drained my cup in one swallow and I didn't taste any of the pastries or anything, because Mercedes's words had been weaving a sort of intoxicating tightness in my throat, and it was a divine intoxication that made me disdain cigarettes, pastries, tea, and all the marvels that the world might offer me.

And since Mercedes began to talk about indifferent matters, and I wanted her to say more along the lines we had been discussing earlier, things like the cigarette holder, I broke in, "Look, Semiramis, after all, I understand why some men don't want to get married! If I were a man, I wouldn't marry either! Think what a delight and how splendid it must be to be free and roam the world, having adventures and spending thousands and thousands and millions!"

But after setting her empty cup aside on the ebony bench, Mercedes sighed, and adopting the sad, serious tone of a wise counselor, she admonished me, "Don't care so much about wealth, María Eugenia, for wealth promises so much, and basically it gives us very little! It is almost, almost empty inside, the deceitful snob!" And sighing for the second time, she added, "I was rich and I saw it firsthand and it could never give me the only thing I wanted!"

"Poor Semiramis!" I said, very moved. "You must have taken it into your head to ask for something totally impossible! But don't deny that you have been greatly admired, that you have enjoyed amusements galore, and that it was always money that provided the admiration and amusement. I'd like to have some fun too!"

"Admiration! Amusement! They are empty too! Look, María Eugenia, happiness is not in any of these things that dazzle us so much. Do you know where happiness is found? Do you know what it consists of? Well, just having someone you're close to, someone who is a kindred spirit, who is like the water you drink when you're very thirsty, or the bed you sleep in when you come home exhausted. That someone, you know, who is always waiting for us somewhere and whom usually we never find, because, as in the game of blindman's buff, we pass by him many times, and we never see him. I think that like our eyes or like our arms, people are born to be two. Except that eyes come already paired on the same face, and arms are also joined on the same trunk, but people are born separate, and we almost never find our mate in the world. Usually we accept 'one who isn't' and when this happens, no matter how much we may have, we are always like those poor cripples who have a glass eye or a wooden leg. Money may buy them perfect copies, but really they don't help the person who wears them because they don't see and they don't feel like the real things! And other people's happiness is so often just a wooden or glass simulation! I always remember that, many years ago, soon after I got married, I used to love a sculpture of *Paul et Virginie*, an insignificant and poorly done statue that a friend of mine had in the patio fountain at her house, which was an old house. As I said, the sculpture was nothing much, the two little children were barefoot, taking shelter from the rain, nestled with their arms around each other under the leaves of a banana tree, but they were so close and they looked so happy and laughing, in spite of the downpour, that I loved to look at them. I imagined that they were flesh and blood and I felt happy with their happiness, since I could no longer be happy for myself. It's because in life, María Eugenia, never forget this, in life it's always raining! The question is not so much the roof we choose to keep dry, but rather to keep dry with someone who can be very happy and very close to us while the rain lasts. You see, *Paul et Virginie* were laughing under the banana leaves, even though they were getting wet there!"

"Well, I'd like to keep dry with the same joy as *Paul et Virginie*, but under a good roof. I don't care for banana leaves or embraces in rough weather."

"If you marry Gabriel, as I expect and as I wish with all my heart for you, you're certain to realize your dreams, but if you don't marry Gabriel, then, watch out! It's very hard to find everything together, and mistakes like mine that last a lifetime are frightful!"

And in the darkness that now surrounded us, Mercedes's voice quivered with the unmistakable tremor of tears. I was puzzled for a moment and then, affectionately, I asked her in a soft voice, "If you're so miserable, Mercedes, why don't you get a divorce and free yourself of all this distress?"

"Why? Why? Do I myself know? Ask the person with gangrene in his arm why he doesn't cut it off, and you'll see he'll tell you he prefers the pain to the deformity and that he'll stand it as long as he can. Sometimes I think I can't bear any more, but it's something so deeply rooted and in your blood that it's impossible to tear it out! And don't think it's love; it's not. Because it's absurd to imagine that love can exist in your heart together with scorn and hatred itself. No, it's something else that I can't name. I don't know if it's force of habit, as you said before, if it's fear, or weakness, slavish submission, or if it's compassion. I think it must be compassion, but I'm not sure. There is something, María Eugenia, that binds more than love itself, and it's knowing we're indispensable to another person's life, as a mother is indispensable to the life of her unborn child. Knowing we are indispensable leads us heroically to give our entire existence bit by bit, leaving nothing for ourselves. And this is a devotion that no one appreciates and no one understands, not even the one who gives it, as I do, nor the one who receives it, as Alberto does! There are men who, as a horrible torment for women, after imposing all sorts of suffering on us, tie us to them with a chain of compassion which nothing can break, nothing, because it is so like the slavery with which mothers tie themselves to their children!"

"That's love, Mercedes! Tyrannical, eternal, and classic love. Don't make so much of it!"

"What love? Quite the opposite! When we're in love, María Eugenia, if we hear our lover's footsteps, they please us, if he enters and interrupts what we're doing, we greet him with joy, and we happily set aside what we were working on. His voice delights us, and what he says, and everything he thinks, and everything he proposes to us. When he leaves, even for a few hours, we are always a little sad and if, while he is absent, we see a book of his on some table, or a wrinkled handkerchief, or his hat, we touch the object with affection or we look at it with regret and sadness! But this, this that I feel is just the opposite! It is a continual discord in everything, the nerve-wracking note that is forever out of tune in a chord, forever, forever, at every instant, without being able to avoid it for a second, and to increase our martyrdom, having to hide the discord from everyone's eyes, and having to defend against everyone the very thing that torments you, because it is as much yours as your own existence, since he has given you a name and a home, and a second personality that is yours, yours, even if you hate it and it destroys you!"

I felt rebellious at the image of her servitude and, with the fire of one who preaches revolution, I exclaimed, "Well, if that is the case, either I don't understand what you're telling me or if I were in your situation, I'd send Alberto to hell! No matter how much you may deny it, I think all these chains are just romantic and poetic notions very similar to those that Grandmother and Aunt Clara create in their imagination. Actually you could break them very easily. Don't you have money of your own to live on? Don't women in other countries get divorced? Why, you don't even have any children, Mercedes!"

"You don't understand these things, and I hope you'll never understand them. If I had not found myself in this situation, or if I were as selfish as some women, I, too, would find this abnegation of mine foolish, and even unworthy. But I've never known how to refuse anything to someone who asks me, if I have the thing he wants and if the person who begs, begs me anxiously and hungrily because he truly needs it. Alberto, besides tormenting me, needs me morally, materially, and even physically too. And although I know all too well that if he loves me it's only because of this selfish motive of needing me, I cannot, I cannot throw him out on the street no matter how dreadfully he annoys me, as he is annoying me at present and as he always has annoyed me! It is true, very true, if I divorced Alberto, I could live happily and in freedom, but I have seen evidence that he would sink into the most horrible *débauche*. He has often confessed that without me, he would indulge in every vice and that only my presence can protect him from that and save him from destitution and debauchery. Well, what he says is absolutely true, it seems to me that he is always shouting at me to stay and so, *me voilà!* Here I am and I'll go on sharing his burden of ignominy so the burden won't grow too great and crush him. Oh! Pity, compassion, charity—how they shackle our life and how they steal it little by little, distributing it to those we meet along the road! Only selfish and hard-hearted people live their own lives fully!"

Here Mercedes's voice died away, smothered by the tears that, in the intimacy of confidence, began to flow abundantly and ardently from her eyes, while she made no effort to hold them back. From this I gathered that some terrible scene had taken place between her and Alberto, a thing that happened often. Then I got off the divan and while I was thinking, "Apparently it's been storming everywhere," I went back to sit on the pillow on the floor near her head, and stroking her hair I tried to console her, as well as I could, "No, Semiramis, no, you're doing something much better and much more generous than selfish, hard-hearted women do. Now I think you're more beautiful than ever because I seem to see you from the time you were born, always so generous and so good, stripping the leaves from your life, so others could walk on them, like flower petals are strewn on the ground when some procession is going by. With Alberto you do what they say about sandalwood in the Indian proverb, 'let it avenge itself on the woodcutter by perfuming the axe that cuts it down.' You, too. Do you see? You're like the sandalwood and like the flower petals in a procession!"

"Oh! Musset, Chenier, Bécquer, my poetess!" she said patting me and smiling through her tears.

Then, since she now wanted to confide her sorrows, she continued to pour out her feelings.

"Do you think I don't suffer, María Eugenia? Do you think it's not humiliating and degrading to be the wife of a man who defames himself with every vice? Yes, it's humiliating, humiliating and distasteful. And your life together becomes intolerable and hateful. You can't understand it and Alberto himself, however much I tell him, doesn't understand it either, because if he did, he'd be shocked. Women like me who are very weak, very self-sacrificing, or very contemptible . . . whatever it is, stay in this loveless love life, suffering all the anguish and repugnance of women who sell themselves to the first man who goes by on the street. But no one knows about these things because they are hidden and kept quiet by conventions and laws. And the worst thing, María Eugenia (and this is why I'm telling you these things), the worst thing is that I'm not a skeptic. No. I believe that happiness exists, and that it would be easy to find it, if we had someone who generously would help us to look for it. That's why ever since I got married I've tried to make other people happy, to bring together couples who could live happily together, so at least I can rejoice in the happiness of others, as I did in my friend's patio when I looked at *Paul et Virginie,* so close and smiling in the rain! That's the reason I'd like to see you married to Gabriel some day. I'm sure, very sure, that the two of you would make an extremely happy *ménage.*"

Since in the darkness our faces were barely visible, without embarrassment or reservations, I asked her softly with an intensity mixed with my admiration for her and my deep, secret emotion, "Yes? Really? Do you really think so, Semiramis?"

And immediately, to evoke the glorious image of my future happiness, Semiramis's voice revived in her garden of joy, and forgetting her own acute grief, just revealed to me, vibrant with certainty and enthusiasm, she said, "Absolutely! And you are both so good-looking! You know, I'd like to dress you and Gabriel some day as *bergers* and photograph you together, in the style of one of those pastoral idylls by Watteau!"

When I heard this I sighed with pleasure, I hid my head in the soft warmth of a pillow, and in the deep night of my closed eyes, I saw myself beside Gabriel, as if in a pastoral scene painted on a fan. Then I took one of Mercedes's hands and in appreciation for what she had said, still pretending to console her, I kissed her hand with grateful intensity.

Then I waited a few seconds, I lifted my head and I saw that she was trembling with impatience and happiness.

"Look, Semiramis, it's getting late, and if you wait any longer, eight o'clock will find us here still lounging about."

"That's right! Turn on the light!" she said.

And when the red glow of the lamp lit the boudoir again, Mercedes's white hand, adorned with her beautiful solitaire, pressed her handkerchief to her eyes, perhaps because the light bothered her or perhaps because now, in the reddish glare, she felt embarrassed by what her lips had spoken and by the tears her eyes had shed.

Then she rose lightly and quickly off the black divan, she washed her eyes for a long time with verbena and warm water, she sat down at her dressing table with its three mirrors, and lifting her shapely white arms, which were multiplied in infinite repetition, she began to comb her hair.

Since I was ready, I sat on a footstool behind her where I watched and admired her in the mirrors. She chatted with me as she combed her hair, applied her makeup, and while she was still buffing her nails, the lacy white *déshabillé* swinging, the street bell rang in the distance. When she heard the ringing, she smiled, and with the nervous alertness of a stalking cat, she listened and said, lighting the phrases in the splendor of her fresh hairdo and her freshly painted lips, "That is Gabriel! Hurry, you go meet him. I'm going to take my time dressing, then when I'm dressed, I'll walk very slowly to the kitchen to order the cocktails, then I'll arrange for some flowers, and then I'll rush to the drawing room, because as I see it, this flirtation is getting serious, and it might not be wise to leave you two alone!"

Joking this way, Mercedes laughed her silvery laugh again, with so many nuances of meaning, so like her. And while she laughed, I tried to hide my heady emotion with a tremulous smile and I spoke almost without knowing what I was saying, "Oh, how mean you've become, Semiramis! You make fun of me whenever you can! And besides, you spend your time dreaming up the most improbable things!"

But the announcement of Gabriel's arrival and Semiramis's forecasts for my future had shaken me so much that, with my heart pounding and my hands very cold, I left the boudoir, crossed the patio, and reached the entrance hall just as the servant was unbolting the door, and there, against the gray, open door, Gabriel appeared.

When he saw that I was coming to meet him, he stood to one side, under the fanlike leaves of a palm, as if to get a better view. He smiled gallantly and happily as one might smile at glory in person, and then, his hat still in his hand, immobile and ecstatic as he watched my approach, he observed from a distance, "Well, tonight we have an enchanting new hairdo!"

"Just Mercedes's nonsense to style my hair this way today," I answered, holding out my hand in greeting.

"Then, tonight, I affirm with greater conviction than ever what I've always said, long live nonsense!"

And, praising nonsense, with my hand held tightly in his hand, he said sympathetically, "What a cold hand! Great heaven, who has frightened it?"

I was going to say who knows what, and he to make some reply, when the sound of footsteps was heard, the bell rang, a key grated awhile in the lock, the door opened, and Alberto came in, nervous, worried, and agitated, as he always gets after the scenes he so often has with Mercedes.

"Of course he'll go straight to his room to dress for dinner," I thought optimistically.

But Alberto didn't leave. He settled down to chat with us in the hallway, until, when it seemed he was finally going, we again heard steps near the door, the bell rang again, the servant opened, and it was Uncle Pancho who now arrived.

My eyes gazed at him and my hands greeted him as my mind wandered through this soliloquy, "Oh! Semiramis! Semiramis! Good, kind Semiramis! You would not have come walking to the door, you would not have rung the bell, you would never have come!"

And as I thus invoked her while I said hello to Uncle Pancho, she must have recognized at a distance, with her alert intuitiveness, knowing from the doorbell about the comings and goings of everyone, making her kind stratagem useless. She then appeared, pretty, swaying, slender, smiling, in her beautiful black dress that fit her body like a silken glove, the mistress of her castle, among her palm trees on the patio.

When she reached the hall, she greeted Uncle Pancho with great affection; she swept past Alberto as if he didn't exist; and, to greet Gabriel, who was farther away, she gently took my arm, led me with her, and when the two of us were very close to him, as if she were about to confide a great secret to him, her voice like a musical, silky caress, she held my face be-

tween her cool hands, and presenting me very close to Gabriel, like one
who offers a gift, prettily and gracefully, like a generous Wise Man, she
said, "Don't you think she looks much prettier like this?"

Gabriel smiled at me with the same smile he had given me when he
came in, and imitating Mercedes's flippancy, he exclaimed tragically and
sadly, like someone begging for mercy, "For Heaven's sake, Mercedes,
how long can I bear this? Don't keep making her prettier! You've gone far
enough!"

But Uncle Pancho came over to us, with two golden goblets, one in
each hand, and gallantly ruined the present moment with a view to future
animation as he offered, "A cocktail!"

Alberto, who looked absorbed in thought in his chair, roused himself
hurriedly when he saw the amber glasses, and rushed away exclaiming,
"Oh, I must hurry and get dressed. I'm late!"

"Yes! Now you leave, when it's too late."

&.   &.   &.

As usual, during dinner, Mercedes sat between
Uncle Pancho and Gabriel, who were seated at the two ends of the table,
Alberto faced Mercedes, and I sat between Alberto and Gabriel, on the
opposite side of the table from Mercedes.

No doubt due to the mysterious and evident argument that had made
Mercedes cry, she and Alberto weren't speaking. However, the general
conversation, enlivened by the cocktails and the Médoc wine, was gay,
vivacious, and wide-ranging. Uncle Pancho was in good form and since
Mercedes, Gabriel, and I, joined by the delight of our secret, all felt
equally happy, we applauded everything Uncle Pancho said with happy
laughter. Alberto, however, was furious, and his fury made us laugh too.
Besides his quarrel with Mercedes, they had just turned him down, this
very afternoon, for an appointment he had expected from the government
for several months. Therefore, as a reprisal for his defeat, he decided to
say terrible things about the government, reporters, diplomats, police,
businessmen, poets, and the whole country in general.

"What a disgrace! What a country! How horrible! The only recourse
we have is to leave, to emigrate anywhere, as soon as possible, in a row-
boat, in a fishing boat, swimming. It doesn't matter how!"

Uncle Pancho invented atrocious things that could happen if you travel
by swimming. Gabriel laughed, but then, little by little, began to discuss

and closed the argument with a sort of speech that Alberto listened to patiently, Uncle Pancho with a smile, and Mercedes and I with devotion.

"You're wrong, Alberto, you're absolutely wrong about what you're saying! Look, we're well off in Venezuela. It's well organized, progressive, and at peace. What more do you want? Your big mistake is wanting to be equal to the great European nations, countries that have been moving forward for centuries on the formidable foundation laid by their past and their traditions, united like a single entity in the firm character of an established culture. We, on the other hand, are gong through a period of sociological gestation, a period of racial fusion, whose principal manifestation must always be anarchy. Therefore, during this sociological stage, the government that knows how to maintain peace above all, will always be the ideal government for Venezuela. The present government does keep peace. That is the mainstay of its program and consequently I state and I'll always affirm that we're getting along very well! Don't ever think that it's frivolous—this task of eliminating our famous *caudillo* spirit. It is the result of this uneasy fusing of races, and of past triumphs and past grandeur. Our *caudillo* spirit was born from the glorious seeds of Independence, and it is still nourished by it. It is choking us, it annihilates us, it won't let us live, it's a weed that must be cut down. We have paid dearly in Venezuela and we will continue to pay for the luxury and the elegance of having brought independence to half the continent!"

But Alberto suddenly decided not to argue anymore. When Gabriel finished, he looked at him a few moments in total silence and finally said, "You are certainly pro-government! And, Gabriel, that smells like oil to me! Your contracts with Monasterios must be working out very well!"

Gabriel put his hand over his heart, and answered with a tone of deep conviction, "On my word of honor! I'm speaking impartially, in all honesty! I'd say the same thing if I were an enemy instead of being a friend of the government, and if instead of Venezuela we were talking about any other nation in the same circumstances."

Alberto then forgot the government and all its ramifications and began a heated denunciation of reporters, historians, and poets. He reviled them all and ended by saying, "Definitely, they are a flock of cretins and imbeciles!"

Uncle Pancho, who had just finished drinking his second glass of Médoc, answered calmly, "I don't know why you're so indignant about writers, Alberto. To the contrary, I find our literary school very picturesque, very altruistic, and quite good. It's a sort of kindhearted, happy carnival of print. The theme, whatever it may be—a leader of the Independence, a famous artist, or a historical event—will generally be hidden beneath a brightly colored avalanche of praise and of adjectives stuck on at random, here and there, the way confetti falls in the hair of people in a carnival parade. Isn't that pretty? Isn't it jolly? Doesn't it vividly demonstrate our happy, generous character?"

"Oh, yes. That's true!" exclaimed Mercedes with a grimace of disgust. "And that's why I never read that type of article in the newspapers. They seem like a carnival to me, too, Pancho, and for years I've been horribly displeased with the carnival! It's not an amusement for decent people."

Gabriel offered his opinion, "Really, I think that basically our love for the carnival, and our love for adjectives, spring from the same source—exuberance! Our exuberance is authentic and genuinely Creole. It stretches geographically from California to Tierra del Fuego, slightly accentuated in the tropical zone. It's a matter of temperament. It was present in the proclamations of all the leaders of Independence. We have it and our grandchildren will not be able to condemn it because they will have it just as we do or worse. How could it be otherwise, Pancho? In our blood we carry a yearning for the grandiose. It was our legacy from the conquistadors and it is perhaps that same mad, unsatisfied longing for the grandeur of El Dorado. We enjoy extravagance, we are prodigal, generous, vain, and quite ridiculous. That's why the French have taken our well-known slang expression of 'arrasta cueros,' which they first converted to 'rastoqouer,' and which finally became the comical abbreviation 'rasta.' It's like a cocktail where you whip together, with a drop of bitters, all our psychological makeup. Well, they go to the other extreme—that of stinginess and avarice, something much worse, but that will never earn the honor of a national epithet, because they practice it in their own homes, and because it is less ridiculous. But in spite of everything, I'm not ashamed of our excessive prodigality, and I think it's due to the immediate influence of our rich and luxuriant nature. It's the potent sap of a new land; it's the sun; it's the tropics!"

"No. It's the black!" affirmed Uncle Pancho with great certainty.

"Really, Pancho!" Mercedes parried disapprovingly. "You're going to start 'blackening' everybody. Well, right now I warn you that I abhor economy and I love to spend exuberantly, just as Gabriel says. Nevertheless, I consider myself pure white. I'm sure of it. Ah! Ma généalogie, mon cher, c'est quelque chose de très chic!"

"Ta généalogie! Mais la généalogie, ma pauvre Mercedes, c'est tout ce qu'il y a de plus factice et de plus conventionel!" answered Uncle Pancho, and he went on explaining in Spanish in great detail. "Look, Mercedes, so you can see clearly how little credit your certainty or purity of blood deserves, take note of this one detail. During the War for Independence, Bolívar, in his proclamations, for reasons of state, managed to exalt and to make brown-skinned people fashionable. I say no more. You know how women are about fashion!"

But Mercedes noticed the presence of the black servant who was waiting on the table, and out of consideration for him, fearful of what Uncle Pancho might say about the matter, she interrupted him, and indicating the woolly head with her eyes, said, "Mais, parle français, Pancho!"

Uncle Pancho ignored her warning and continued his explanation.

"In that hurly-burly of patriots leaving, of royalists coming in, the earthquake of 1812, the emigration of 1814, women were going one way and their husbands another and there were Mantuan women like the Aristeiguetas who had a lot of fun. I don't criticize them. I think they did right. Yes, poor things! After three centuries of cloistered boredom, why shouldn't they have the right to be a little independent, at least while the war lasted? And that's not counting a classic right, sanctioned by history and by tradition since the war of Troy. Yes, it's a well-known right, it was, is, and always will be forever and forever. While men are realizing great feats, covering themselves with glory, with gold braid, with plumes, and with medals, women, who actually are much less ostentatious and much more moderate, secluded in the shadows, silently cover themselves with the glory of love and of kisses. Then, peace comes and the patriotic ideal is cheered with wild enthusiasm, the heroes are recognized, epic poems written, statues erected, children are born, and everything is back to normal! Therefore, you may be sure, Mercedes, in the War of Independence, as in every truly important war, free trade was established. A proof is that since then the old convents that flourished so in Colonial times began to decline and it was rare indeed for an old maid to survive the Independence without having some mysterious adopted child. Look, as well as I can recall, I can name two or three relatives of yours and mine . . ."

But Mercedes cut Uncle Pancho's oration short and began to say angrily, "Not a bit, not a bit, none of that is true! And above all, any slur about the Aristeiguetas, Pancho, is nothing but a lie! I assure you. I am a descendent of one of them on my mother's side of the family, and I have always heard that the rumors were all false, the love affair with the prince of Braganza, totally false about Piar, and about Segur, and about everybody! The 'nine muses' were very honorable. It was just that since they were beautiful and must have been rather disdainful of the *bourgeois* and the *Tartuffes* of Colonial times, what always happens, happened. People were envious and because of that they lied about them."

"Very well! The only thing I can answer, Mercedes, is that Bolívar, who always distinguished himself as a clairvoyant and as a visionary, and who was their cousin, foresaw all of them in hell. There must have been a reason!"

"To brag, it must have been to brag, because all men, without exception, no matter how decent they may seem, are braggarts!"

"But, Mercedes, Bolívar was much younger than his cousins, the Aristeiguetas, and he never concerned himself about them."

"The Liberator," Gabriel said dogmatically, "put the Aristeiguetas in hell because of his generous eagerness to free hell and make it independent of lugubrious and traditional theological suffering. Doubtless, he must have thought, as I do, that the presence of a pretty woman is more than enough to transform the most horrible sufferings into an abundance of joy and happiness. But unfortunately they are rare, truly pretty women are very rare everyplace! Do you suppose the Aristeigueta girls were in fact pretty? Maybe it's a case of some undeserved and usurped reputation, such as we still see often in Caracas nowadays? It's quite probable! People at the end of the eighteenth century must have had very poor taste!"

I wasn't paying attention any more to the general conversation, because when Gabriel said that truly pretty women were very rare, and that their presence transformed the greatest sufferings into an abundance of joy and happiness, he had slowly moved his hand next to mine where it lay on the white tablecloth, and with his little finger, he very softly stroked it, as if to let me know that he was speaking for me alone. That tenuous contact, so imperceptible, ran over my skin with an unknown shock, which was as mysterious and vibrant as an electric current. Then, almost unconsciously, I lifted my eyes to Gabriel's eyes, which seemed to be expecting them, and our eyes, having met, gazed at each other briefly, and then we both smiled, because without a word, with just our eyes and the light touch of our fingers, it was as if we had spoken volumes. But, perhaps from timidity or a feeling of reserve, I lowered my eyes, remembering that Mercedes had said "this flirtation is getting serious, and it might not be wise to leave you two alone!" Then, still smiling, with my eyes fixed on a white rose that stood before me in the Saxony centerpiece, its head drooping on its stem, I remembered what Mercedes had said when she offered to give me a long ivory cigarette holder. Gabriel continued to talk and, still staring at the rose, I began to think, "Why did Alberto, who arrives so late every day, arrive so early today? Why did Alberto, who always goes straight to his room to get dressed, resolve to stay with us in the entrance hall today? Oh! What bad luck! Well, Alberto stayed in the hall because we were in the hall. If we had been in the drawing room, he would have gone on by. It's stupid to stay in the hall when usually it's so much nicer in the drawing room! How silly! Gabriel was going to say something very interesting when we heard Alberto's footsteps at the door! And there was still time to have gone to the drawing room! Of course! And there he would have said it! But, once there, if, instead of saying something, Gabriel had suddenly kissed me, as Mercedes so greatly fears, and as my friend, the Colombian poet, tried to do that night . . . What would I have done? I don't know. But certainly I would not have told Mercedes about it for anything in the world. No, no, no! Furthermore, if she, who never misses anything, had suspected it, I would have roundly denied it, even at the risk of not getting a cigarette holder. But, anyway, what a vast difference between Gabriel and my shipboard friend! The Colombian made a sort of grimace when he smiled, moving his nose like a rabbit, while Gabriel . . . How different Gabriel is!"

And to verify the difference, I raised my eyes again, and I met Gabriel's eyes, fixed upon my bare forehead and seeming to penetrate it to read all the thoughts that had vaguely crossed my mind as I smilingly contemplated the rose. Seeing that I was looking at him, Gabriel smiled again. And I instantly knew, "What a difference!"

And with a faint voice, he said with the same expression he had worn earlier under the palm tree in the entrance hall, "María Eugenia, I must repeat the same thing I told Mercedes a while ago: You have no right to make yourself so pretty! It's plain abuse!"

"Quite the opposite. Why, this dress looks so ugly on me!" I said, looking away and on the point of bursting into laughter.

Unwittingly, I looked across the Saxony centerpiece at Mercedes's lovely head. Enigmatic and absorbed, paying no attention to anyone, she was tracing the lines of her cut-glass goblet with the tip of her silver knife, but even so, absorbed in the pattern of the crystal glass, she was smiling. Oh! She was smiling so mysteriously that I calmly waited until she looked up, and then, also smiling, I said to her from the distance with my eyes, "You already know everything, Semiramis. You know about the little finger, about the abuse, and everything! Well, then, for your eyes, as for the eyes of God, is there nothing hidden on this earth? What an X-ray mind, and what a genius you would have been as a police investigator!"

Meanwhile Alberto continued to lament his bad luck like a Jeremiah, pondering the enormous disadvantage that it is for everyone not to have enough capital. But Uncle Pancho decided to back the cause of Holy Poverty, and, joining the spirit of Diogenes to the evangelical spirit, he said, "There is no rich man! Nearly all rich men are poor, very poor, and the poverty of the wealthy is the most heart-rending because it is irremediable. Their physical state is such that they can neither eat nor drink, because they usually have dyspepsia and they need to care for themselves a great deal in order to have someone who will take care of their money. Spiritually they can't eat or drink, either, because generally they also have dyspepsia of the intelligence. You see, Alberto, rich men have magnificent galleries of pictures and, basically, they have no feeling for painting. They collect books, and they don't read; they attend concerts and star-studded operas, and they suffer the torments of boredom as they sit in their theater boxes because the music says nothing to them. Well, now, is there anything more terrible and more painful than such eternal fasting in the midst of eternal abundance? The spiritual fasting of the wealthy would be as tragic as the hunger of Tantalus except that it's grotesque instead of tragic. Yes, Tantalus was conscious of his fast, and he felt his denial, he felt the sublime pain of hunger, while these others don't. Although they can chew and swallow they can't savor anything because they completely lack a sense of taste. They are not aware that they have no sense of taste; they haven't the remotest awareness of their eternal fasting, and they are horribly grotesque, because in the midst of surfeit, it's as if they still had not tasted the first bite!"

Gabriel said, "I'll make a note of your thesis, Pancho. 'The Starving Rich.' It sounds like a much newer and more interesting socialist formula than 'The Miserly Rich,' which is so overworked."

"Well, and besides not eating," Uncle Pancho continued, much encouraged, "the wealthy work too much. They are always tired, weak and wasting away from making keys and locks to guard their money, and the alarm with which they watch over it, and the psychology that motivates them is like that of a watchdog that hears thieves around his garden, and instead of sleeping, barks. They also believe themselves deserving of the highest honors, and since their vanity drives them mercilessly to seek honors they are also much like racehorses, when, exhausted and panting, they go by, trying to catch up with the winners."

"In all, Pancho, you're putting wealth in the hands, or better said, under the feet of animals," said Alberto stupefied. "Well, after all, it's one way of consoling me for my poverty!"

"No. It's a sincere and very honest conviction. I firmly believe and I have always believed, that it was not so much through the words of Jesus that God praised poverty and condemned money, but rather that the true scorn, the immense anathema that God daily launches against wealth, as may be seen clearly and palpably, is when you consider the personnel chosen by God Himself to exhibit and to bring said privilege to disrepute at the same time."

Mercedes said, "Look, Pancho, for quite awhile you've been talking like a *sans-culotte* and I don't like your ideas at all because they sound like socialism. I'm not addicted to money, but democracy, bohemian attitudes, and holy poverty repel me. Say what they will, I think all three need lots of soap and water! Remember, too, that we were rich. By insulting rich people, you insult yourself and you insult me in the past."

"Oh, precisely because we didn't deserve to be rich, because it was a mistake and a paradox, is why God decided to erase us forever from the list."

"Well, I side with Mercedes," said Gabriel, "let them put me on that list even if afterwards I grow horse's ears and a dog's tail."

"Oh, yes! I should say so!" said Alberto, giving himself airs. "I volunteer to head the list, not just with horse's ears, which might be hidden to some extent under a cap or under some very curly strands of hair, but frankly and openly with a whole donkey's head!"

"Well, they can put me down," Mercedes said, laughing out loud, "but I promise I'll keep my own head, and I won't sprout any kind of ears or tails!"

I hurried to exclaim, "Let them write my name, too, let them list me, and then let come whatever God decrees!"

And with great naturalness and amusement Gabriel began to say, "Contrary to your opinion, Pancho, I'd a thousand times rather suffer the grotesque surfeit of the rich than the sublime pain of hunger, as you put it. Think a moment what it means to face this horrible martyrdom of having a highly refined sense of taste if we know that it is condemned to never taste anything or almost nothing. Suffering is not just the absence of good, which is the case with your rich men, but in our case, suffering is based on the consciousness of the absence of good. If you suffer without knowing it, you don't have any suffering. It's like a patient undergoing an operation under anesthetic who knows nothing of his pain, because at that time he has lost feeling and consciousness. In order to fully experience the divine intoxication of life, Pancho, money is indispensable as the key to enter all the banquets where life enraptures us, as you well know! In my opinion, there is a supreme trinity without which our joy will be maimed or incomplete. It is composed of, first and above all, divine love, the origin of all happiness and joy, but an absolute love, the heavenly love of a woman who is as beautiful physically as she is select spiritually. Then in second place comes intelligence, that subtle consciousness of all things, that 'spiritual taste,' as you put it, that is always escorted by an endless train of the most delicate nuances, and of exquisite sensations. And finally, in third place, as an attentive servant, as a priest attendant upon those first two deities, and as a provider to the 'spiritual taste,' comes money, which is an essential part of the trio, the tripod without which the building would come crashing down. Let those scorn money who do not aspire to divine, absolute love, and those who don't feel the vibration of intelligence! I seek it ambitiously because it is an indispensable complement to my trinity, it is an ever-generous friend, and it is a faithful and accommodating servant. Money is not despotic and tyrannical except to those who don't know how to treat it, like those rich imbeciles you talk about, but for those of us who will know how to put it in its place and keep it there, for those of us who will always have it at our feet, able to keep it subject to us without being dominated by it, let it come to us, with all its army of coins, and like a servant or a squire, let it accompany us and help us to conquer life!"

"Bravo for Gabriel!" exclaimed Alberto enthusiastically. "You spoke with admirable eloquence! Long live money and down with holy poverty! Let's drink a toast to the intoxication of life and to the divine trinity, 'Gabriel Olmedo' brand."

Again, as he was talking, Gabriel had been making signs to me that his speech was meant for me. When he mentioned "divine love," not only did he give me a quick, bright glance full of meaning, but he also put his hand next to mine as he had before, but in a special way, much more expressive and much more intense. Then, when Alberto said "let's drink a toast to the divine trinity, Gabriel Olmedo brand," he hurried to fill my empty glass with wine, and leaning over as he did so, he said softly in my ear, as if telling me a delightful secret, "Yes, let's drink a toast, because we two almost have that trinity!"

But as I picked up my glass, Mercedes lifted her hand ordering us not to drink and she said, "That's not a toast for wine, that's a toast for champagne!" and turning to the servant, she ordered, "Open a bottle of champagne, quickly, quickly, very quickly!"

And when all the glasses were full to the brim with gold and bubbles, she was the one who lifted her glass first and toasted, "For love, for wealth, and for the happiness of those present!"

And she smiled at Gabriel, who immediately understood who "those present" were.

Uncle Pancho, then, feigning great humility, began to say as he stared at his glass, "You've defeated me, Gabriel! But I consider my defeat a glorious one, since it ends in champagne. I toast also, yes. May that miraculous trinity reign forever, even though unfortunately I no longer believe in it nor expect it!"

And with much joy and laughter we all drank together.

After dinner, we went to the drawing room, where we had coffee. I served the liqueurs, and while everyone was still talking passionately about love, happiness, and money, Mercedes, sipping at the emerald green of her mint liqueur, gazed at me a few seconds and then proposed, "Why don't you play something, María Eugenia? Yes, play that tango for us. What is it called?"

"'Cielito lindo'?"

"Yes, that's it, 'Cielito lindo.'"

"It's not a tango; it's a sort of Cuban tune."

"Yes, really, 'Cielito lindo' is a *contradanza* that has the spirit and the emotion of a tango," said Gabriel, abandoning the discussion. "You must play it tonight, María Eugenia!"

And since the others demanded his attention, he continued discussing.

Docile and obedient, I went to the piano, which is placed in a corner, forming a sort of triangular nook against the wall, very nice and private for the person who plays. Once there, I felt sheltered in its isolation. Under the gentle pressure of my fingers on the keys the sweet rhythm began, and above the rhythm, the flock of notes trotted amiably. Little by little the music was arousing a subtle cloud of mysterious sensations in my soul. Surrounded by the subtle interior cloud, my fingers and arms were moving and my spirit was drifting in the voluptuous charm of "Cielito lindo," when suddenly, Gabriel appeared by my side next to the ebony of the piano. My fingers went on moving tranquilly along the ivory paths, and Gabriel, leaning against the piano and looking at me, began to sing the same thing my fingers were singing.

"Ah-a-a-ah! Cie-li-to-lin-do!"

But soon he gave up singing, because his eyes were no longer enough to express all he wanted to tell me, and he had to say it with a clear fountain of words. Happily, I listened as those words, gallant and clear, like raindrops or flower petals, fell from Gabriel's lips. My mind began to mix his words with the melody and it was a mixture of such intoxicating delights that for a while I firmly believed that they had only written that music for my hands to play and so that Gabriel, next to me, could softly comment on it with such divine lyrics.

Finally, after the last chord, when the music died, I tremblingly got up from the piano and tried to leave, but Gabriel blocked my path and, commanding and strong, took my hands and held me in front of him and said, his words tremulous from the passion in his voice, "No, no, María Eugenia, don't go! Go on playing, please, that song, that same one or anything else, or nothing. No, don't play anything, María Eugenia. Stay here, alone, alone with me, the two of us all alone. Can't you see that I don't want to hear anything or see anything, or know about anything except you? Don't you know that? Don't you understand it?"

And when he said, "Don't you understand it?" Gabriel squeezed my hands and moved his lips so, so close to mine that I suddenly felt a frenzy of fear, of invincible, omnipotent fear, the kind of fear that gives you the strength to break away from anything, and gives you wings to fly from anything. So, mad with happiness and terror, on the wings of my fright, agile and fast, just as I had done on shipboard that distant moonlit night, I wrenched myself free of his hands, I slipped out of the enclosure where he held me imprisoned, escaping rapidly along the length of the piano. I left him behind me still talking, and hardly knowing what I was doing, scared and shaking, I ran to sit at the far end of the room, beside Mercedes, facing Alberto and Uncle Pancho, who were still imperturbably talking and arguing. But Mercedes, without a word, with all her attention fixed on them and her back to the piano, seemed to be listening to them with such close attention that she didn't see me arrive. I still felt dazzled by what I had heard and, mute, blind, and happy, I sat for a long time. Finally, Gabriel, acting very strange and quiet, also came back from the piano and he sat down with the others and he too remained silent for a long time. My poor dazzled eyes didn't even dare to look at him. But later, bit by bit, while I began to feel a vehement and disquieting desire to return to the piano, he was fatally attracted by the conversation and started to enter into it. His attention grew, his replies increased, until he was completely immersed in it like a traveler in a sinister and deadly swamp.

And that horrible conversation turned out to be a most interesting conversation. It dealt with fluctuations in the price of coffee, of its influence on the economic situation of the country, of possible evolutions, combined with Brazilian crops, and that kind of Gregorian chant, that sand pit, that sticky trap where Gabriel had been snared like a bird, that crude web of words that, like old burlap, smelled of warehouses, green coffee, mice, the holds of steamships, that calamity, that disaster, and that horror didn't end all night long!

Oh, what ill fate, what destiny, what bad luck!

Only Mercedes, as curious and as good as ever, seeing me down-hearted, was kind enough to renew somewhat the emotion of the earlier scene by asking me, as she indicated Gabriel with a look, underscored by a smile, "Eh, bien?"

I answered with a vague, indefinite expression, and for a while I was left floating in an ocean of perplexities. Then my eyes happened to fall on my own image, which sitting in its chair appeared in the distance in one of the drawing room mirrors. I stared at it a moment and, contemplating it fixedly, I summed up all the perplexities in this simple word, "Fool!!"

And afterwards I started humming, "A-h-ah! Canta y no llo-res."

But it was useless! My fate was so adverse that Mercedes didn't ask again, "Why don't you play something, María Eugenia?" and meanwhile above my voice, drowning out my Cielo lindo, black coffee, persevering, as horrible as misfortune, went on dripping and dripping ceaselessly.

🐚   🐚   🐚

A little later, beside the street door of this house, I parted from Uncle Pancho. I closed the door myself, I bolted it, and the squeal of the bolts, and then the echoing of my steps in the entrance and in the unlit patio, seemed to me like the great hymn of my soul that was singing its joy through the deserted house.

Against the darkness of the patio, Grandmother's lighted and open room threw a long strip of light over the mosaic, because, as always, she was lying in bed awake, waiting for me to get home. And, as always, I turned off the light in the entrance hall and, guided across the patio by the white strip of light, I reached it, pushed open the door, and went in to say goodnight. When Grandmother saw me beside her bed, she anxiously inquired, her eyes sad and worried, "Why did you come home so late?"

Then, kissing me goodnight, she added, "And why did you come like this, without a wrap, when it's so cold tonight?"

And she touched my arms, which she thought were like ice. Then she halted me with a gesture, and said gravely, like someone preparing to perform a rite, "Don't go. Sit down a minute, María Eugenia. I want to talk to you."

"Oh-oh!" I thought, as I pulled the leather kneeling stool toward the head of the bed and sat down on the low seat, leaving me almost at floor level. I waited obediently, because the joy that had filled me since five that afternoon was so great that it would have been capable not only of moving mountains, like perfect faith, but also of transforming me into a model of all the virtues.

Quite solemnly, Grandmother pulled herself up as high as she could on her pillows until she was almost sitting up in bed. Then, between her neck and the dark walnut bedstead, she propped a little square pillow of ruffled organdy whose lace trim formed a sort of white halo around her hair.

As I squatted on the low stool, I looked up at that white halo and suddenly felt that Grandmother's head had acquired the prestige of absolute authority. Her head seemed the center of authority and the lacy ruffles like visible rays denoting her position of respect. I now believe that without the ruffled pillow, Grandmother would not have dominated me as she did during her admonition, and that her reprimands and recommendations perhaps would have slipped off my spirit as water rolls off oilcloth. But thanks to that detail, apparently so unimportant, I, as I looked up from my abyss on the stool, was able to appreciate the great moral distance that separated me from Grandmother. Her solemn words one after another were engraving themselves on my mind and, despite the immensity of my secret joy, all the while in relation to her, I felt so small, as tiny as an aniseed. Sunk in humility, staring at the lace ruffle, I reflected, "Here without the least doubt is the reason for the adornments that authority has customarily placed upon its head. It is evident that a little physical detail rising from the cranium can exercise a great influence on moral events, and I no longer doubt that it is this that gave rise to crowns, tiaras, miters, grenadier's caps, helmets, plumes, kepis, toques, and cowls!" And while I soliloquized thus, Grandmother was saying, her hands resting on the folded-back sheet, with a voice that remained imposing, quiet, and majestic, "María Eugenia, my dear, you must learn to control yourself! You are so independent that I am truly alarmed. You have independent ideas and independent conduct. But your ideas are a real chaos. You have not digested all your reading, and I wonder with anguish what will become of you with that confusion you have in your head that grows more mixed-up every day. This morning you said the wildest things. Clara is still crossing herself when she thinks of your extravagant ideas and how bold you are. You don't respect anything or anybody, María Eugenia, and I see that you're trying to imitate Pancho, and that's something horrible for a young lady of your age. I excuse you because you're so young. I understand very well that you still cannot judge the importance of certain words, but nevertheless, the ideas that you expressed this morning in the privacy of your home, if you had expressed them before an outsider, I would have been covered with shame! I want you to know that I was really disappointed to hear you talk that way. If I didn't reprimand you severely then, as you deserved, it's because I've always thought it best to make these reflections in moments of calm, and this morning you were in a frenzy of madness and nonsense. That's why I said nothing; it seemed more prudent. But now I am speaking and I tell you, don't ever let such a thing happen again, ever! Do you hear? And another thing, María Eugenia, was the way you talked about Eduardo and his children, and with a tone that hurt me deeply. Not only did you show ingratitude toward Eduardo, to whom we owe everything today, but you also were very inconsiderate and very disrespectful to me. You shouldn't have forgotten that I am Eduardo's mother, and besides being his mother, I love him especially because I appreciate his affection and his behavior as a model son. I'm not ungrateful, I'm not an ingrate! I repeat, María Eugenia, never speak in my presence again as you did this morning!"

As I was very uncomfortable with my knees almost touching my chin, I decided to stretch my legs out under the bed, and I remained silent, my head bowed, my eyes lowered, calm, mute and gentle as a lamb.

Grandmother went on, "Eduardo ate dinner here tonight, and we talked a long time. If you could see what an interest he takes in you! He doesn't know, or even suspect, how you repay him!"

And there was a moment of silence when Grandmother seemed to want me to speak, so that I could take advantage of this juncture to pay the enormous debt on my account with Uncle Eduardo. But I decided not to do so, and I let the silence speak on my behalf, and if Grandmother chose to understand it, fine. But, luckily, Grandmother doesn't have an ear sensitive enough to hear the arguments of silence. Therefore, she didn't seem displeased, but on the contrary, she went on talking, now with less severity.

"I also wanted to tell you that this very week, Eduardo, his family, Clara, you, and I will all go together to San Nicolás . . ."

"Crash, bang!!" I thought with horror. But I hid the exclamation in the stoicism of my meekness and silence.

". . . I think that spending some time in the fresh country air will do you good, and I hope that while you're there you'll lose this unfounded and unjust antipathy that you feel for your cousins. The climate at the hacienda is not good for me because I suffer so much there from rheumatism. It's so damp! But I've never said anything to Eduardo in order to spare his feelings. Yes, a period of two or three months with the two families together at San Nicolás means a great saving for him, since during that time he doesn't need to support us almost totally, as he does when we are here alone. All right, then, María Eugenia, you know what I have told you. We're leaving this week. I hope that you will reflect, that from now on you'll watch what you say, that you'll stop using the insolent tone that you assume sometimes, and that you'll overcome that independent spirit, the fruit of your upbringing and which shows the lack of having a mother to guide you. Moreover, you must learn to respect me, and you must love and respect your whole family. Strangers won't watch out for you if someday you need help! True affection, the only sure and disinterested affection, comes from your family. Don't forget it!"

Through this lecture, as if through a sheet of glass, I had clearly seen Uncle Eduardo's head, with all its contours and details, in his afternoon visit. However, that circumstance did not prevent my lips, full of compunction and respect, from answering at last, "That's fine, Grandmother, that's fine. I'll do just as you say. Good night."

"Good night! May God bless you, and don't ever make me repeat the things I've said to you!"

And I went away, gently, sweetly, filially.

But then, when I was stretched out in bed, I weighed the thousand diverse impressions of the day, and I felt an immense optimism flower in my soul. Everything, everything was smiling at me!

As to the ominous decision to go to San Nicolás, I thought it was as contemptible and vain as the presumption of a dog that howls, trying to bite the moon. I considered that decision a glove that destiny was throwing down, challenging me. But I considered myself a colossus, and destiny I considered an ant. And this consciousness of my strength reached such a point that, a few moments later when sleep was gently spreading its veil over my rejoicing and very tired spirit, it seemed to me I had stood up and, as if in a tournament, I was bending over to pick up a gauntlet from the ground, and that then, with the glove in my hand and for the last time using that insolent tone that a moment ago I had promised Grandmother I'd banish forever and ever from my lips, I was saying, "You want to bury me in San Nicolás, Grandmother, like burying me in the prisons of an inquisition, to convert me to this cult of family, whose only God is Uncle Eduardo; but I will never be converted even if you fry me in an auto-da-fé, because I don't believe in that religion, because I don't like its God, and because, moreover, I've already chosen mine! Yes, I have my God, Grandmother, and no matter how you may resent it, he is a stranger. I adore him with all my heart, and in his doctrine I yield homage to a certain trinity that in my opinion is the most delightful of all the ones that rule over any religion. You may take me to San Nicolás, Grandmother, but you can only imprison my body there; you'll never imprison my spirit, never, because every day it will fly up to the branches, it will perch for hours and hours on the telephone lines, it will fly over the hills, it will dart over ravines and rivers, it will hop across the rooftops, and it will come to sing like a sparrow in the eaves of Mercedes's patio. There, at night, from eight o'clock to eleven, with its invisible eyes, it will see everything it wishes. And perhaps soon, very soon, when you least expect it, those weak sparrow's wings will fly away with my body, too, because I'll get married. Yes, I'll get married to Gabriel, and when this happens, you, Uncle Eduardo, María Antonia, my cousins, and Aunt Clara herself will be terribly surprised and you'll all look amazed and a little ridiculous like hunters with their dogs, shotguns, and all their hunting gear, when their prey escapes them, flying above their heads!"

CHAPTER IV   *In which she waits, and she waits, conversing with an acacia branch and a few flowering vines of bougainvillaea.*

 We have been at San Nicolás for more than a week now.

This house is the old hacienda house of the Alonso family, perhaps built by the family slaves, who would also be called "Alonso" like their masters. This house, with its thick walls and very high ceilings devoid of beams, has received me with great affection and great melancholy. It undoubtedly knows that I am the last child of its ancient owners, and it shelters me with veneration and pity like one of those poor dethroned scions who vegetate sorrowfully in some corner of their lost domain.

Like the dethroned scions, I have my solitary corner in San Nicolás, and it is this room that they have allotted to me alone. Now it's so full, full and overflowing with my own spirit, that I love it very much. I love it besides because it is like my room in Caracas, and because it has wrought iron bars over the window, shaded and covered with blossoms like the one in Caracas. But there, in Caracas, the orange blossoms that bloom on the tree at my window belong to the orange trees. Not so here. The flowers on the acacia branch that shades my window don't belong to the acacia tree. Instead they belong to a bougainvillaea that has grown up the wall just beyond the window. It has trapped the acacia; it has grown into it, and it has the tree bent down and interlaced with vines and flowers. And the acacia, instead of protesting against such an abuse, stretches and spreads with satisfaction, like an immense parasol. It seems quite content to accept all the flowers that the bougainvillaea is putting on it, and on one of its branches it brings and offers them to me here at the barred window.

When I wake up every morning, I say to the branch, "Many, many thanks! If it weren't for you, the bright glare from the sky would shine right in my eyes. You shield me from it; you're very kind; and your make-believe flowers, like the ones I sometimes wear on my hat, are as becoming to you as mine are to me. Don't ever take them off, and don't let it ever occur to you to fight with the bougainvillaea even if it bothers you a little."

Well, dethroned and all, I would be happy in this obscure corner of my domain, I would be happy talking to the flower-covered branch, or rocking in the hammock that hangs across my room from one side to the other, were it not that I too have in my soul a vine like the acacia has. Except that mine oppresses me, chokes me, is killing me, and it still has not given me even one of those millions of flowers that the bougainvillaea has given the acacia.

Oh! My vine is barren and this is why so far it has only oppressed me with its thousand tentacles! Yes, it weighs me down, it crushes me, it squeezes me as if it would like to see me dead in its long fingers, and its name is . . . is . . . the anxiety of waiting!

Since that heavenly night when we toasted love and I played "Cielito lindo," I haven't seen Gabriel. How many times have I thought desperately, "Why didn't I want to stay at the piano as Gabriel asked? Why? Why?" And those interrogations of myself are as sharp and piercing as remorse, and as tenacious and persevering. Because the day after our toast to love, Gabriel was called away urgently on business and he had to leave Caracas. Then we came to the hacienda, and therefore I haven't seen him since or heard anything about him. I mean, yes, I have heard, but only indirectly, through Mercedes.

A few days ago Mercedes called me on the phone and told me, "Gabriel was in Caracas for a few hours. He came to see me and he was very sorry not to find you here. He gave me a package to send to you, some books he had promised you. And he said that when he comes back to Caracas he'll arrange with Pancho to visit you at San Nicolás. He seemed happy to me. I think his business is going well. We were both making plans and, naturally, as we planned, we had to talk a lot, a whole lot, about you."

That day, as soon as I left the phone, with Mercedes's words singing in my heart, I came here, I stretched out in the hammock, and I started swinging gently and dreamily as I am so fond of doing. I remember that then, with the rocking of the hammock, this room of mine, this solitary corner of my lost domain, began little by little to be covered with dreams, to fill with visions, to be populated by white flowery silhouettes. It was like Dante's dream of Beatriz, or rather, as if, capriciously, the bougainvillaea had grown through the bars of the window and had begun to weave and to hang garlands, many garlands, on the walls, across the floor, in the corners, on the ceiling, until it made a river, a lake, and a cataract of tiny pink flowers.

While I savored the words as the hammock swung to and fro, it was as if the magic of Mercedes's words caused this room with its bare walls and ceiling to be adorned from top to bottom as if for an extravagant party!

Still lulled by the soft swaying of the hammock, after staring a long time at that crowd of rosy dreams, I at last began to form some concrete ideas from my sweet visions. More or less, I thought along these lines, "Mercedes says that Gabriel gave her a package of books for her to send me. Well, I must send to get that package, right away, soon, very soon, as soon as I can. When is the soonest? Well, the soonest is tomorrow, very early, with the servant who does the shopping every day in Caracas! So the package will get here tomorrow at ten-thirty, or maybe, maybe, it may not get here until eleven. Well, half an hour more or less is not important. Sometimes it can seem very long. But the time will pass. The half hour will pass; eleven o'clock will get here and by eleven at the latest, the servant will return. I'll go out to wait for him, I'll take the package, with the package in my hands I'll come to my room, I'll lock the door, I'll sit down on the hammock, and then, with my hands shaking and cold, I'll open it bit by bit. I'll open it shaking with emotion because I already know beforehand that without any doubt between the pages of one of the books there will be a surprise. Yes, yes! Between the pages of some book a letter will be waiting for me! I can already see it. I can see it now. It will be a big, snowy white envelope. It will be a big silent envelope and inside it will hold the treasure of a letter. Or maybe not, maybe on the envelope there will be Gabriel's handwriting, which I have seen only once, and which is like little fly's legs linked together.

"Miss María Eugenia Alonso, Hacienda San Nicolás."

Well, whether there is writing on it or whether it's blank, I'll tear it open with difficulty, because my hands will be very clumsy and because they'll be much colder and much shakier than they were when I opened the package. At last, after a little fumbling, I'll finally tear open the envelope, some folded sheets of paper will fall from it, and then . . . Oh! Then I'll feel rich, I'll think I'm a multimillionaire, because my lap will be full, full to overflowing, crowded with armies and legions of fly's feet! Oh! And how those legions will parade before my eyes a thousand, thousand times! Yes, right here, in this very hammock, I'll read the sheets of paper one after the other for the first time, and then one after the other I'll read them again, two, three, and four times to take in all those things that escape us in the excitement of a first reading. Then when I am certain that I have missed nothing, I'll keep reading my letter for the sheer pleasure of reading it, as we read prayers and poetry that we already know by heart. When I'm tired of reading it silently, I'll read it out loud, so the whole room can hear it, and when the room knows it and has listened to it carefully, I'll go out to read it to the whole country. I'll hide it in my bosom where no one can see it, and I'll go read it to the big canal, there, under the ceiba tree, where the water forms that riot of murmurs and foam just because it runs into the sharp pointed rocks that close the floodgate. And when the water in the canal has heard it, I'll go read it to that huge bucare tree that is like a giant held prisoner by little soldiers, the coffee bushes, the loneliest place, where no one ever goes. And when I've finished reading it to the bucare tree, after a cloud of mosquitoes has bitten me, I'll go down to the weeping willows on the pond; I'll read it to the willow trees and the little white stones that lie under the water will hear it; the short grass that grows on the bank will hear it, and the ducks that swim through the silence of the pond will hear it too. Afterwards, late in the afternoon, when twilight comes and the sun has set entirely, I'll walk along the rocky shortcut to the ruined walls of the old sugar mill, and there, sitting on some crumbled ruin, I'll read it loudly so my voice will reach the tops of those two tall chaguaramos trees, which grew so very, very close together that they are like an idyll of pastoral beauty in the melancholy of the old sugar mill. And if by chance night should surprise me sitting under the chaguaramos, I'll open the letter on my knees, I'll sit immobile for a long time, and then the fireflies, who like the wise virgins are the only ones who always carry a lighted lamp for their love at night, will light my letter for an instant, will flood it with bright specks and will read it with their little eyes of light while they fly over my head. Then, only after they have all heard it, the water of the big canal, the bucare among the coffee bushes, the weeping willows, the little rocks at the bottom of the pond, the short grasses, the ducks, and the two tall chaguaramoses by the old sugar mill, and all the fireflies that fly over my head, only then, when I am tired of reading it to the whole country, will I return home. On the way I'll feel burdened by the enormous weight of my happiness, and then, if Grandmother sees me come in weak and exhausted and asks, "What have you done all day, María Eugenia, out in the hot sun?" I'll answer so that Grandmother won't even suspect the existence of my letter, "I've been looking for butterflies to send to one of my old teachers in Paris who has a collection. And don't worry about the sun, Grandmother, because I wore my big rice-straw hat." But then, the next day will be the best, the greatest, the most intense of all, because I'll write my letter of reply. Oh! The reply! Then my soul will become a river running, racing over the immaculate riverbed of the paper! And what a surprise for Gabriel when he reads it. What a surprise and what loving admiration!

That's what I thought more or less the other day while I was swinging in the hammock, and while the words Mercedes had spoken on the phone still seemed to be singing in my heart and my ears. But the next day came; eleven o'clock came; the servant came from Caracas; the package of books came; but the letter I'd foreseen and awaited with such a celebration of love was the only thing that didn't come. In vain I searched each book, in vain I went through them page by page. There was no white envelope; there was no envelope with my name on it; there was nothing, nothing! The books he'd sent were the works of Shakespeare, five volumes, exquisitely bound in moroccan leather with gilt edges. On the first page of each volume, with ruff and pointed beard, in accord with sixteenth-century fashion, there was an engraved portrait of the author. Since the page with the engraving was the thickest one in all the books, and since it was next to the cover, after my volume-by-volume search, it happened that instead of having Gabriel's letter on my knees, as I had dreamed during the slow passage of an entire day, in its place I had only the five resplendent pictures of Shakespeare piled up, to my silent disillusionment. Sad and depressed as I was, I sat staring at the first pages of the books, that thin face that rose elongated and satirical from the ribs of the pleated neck ruff. I looked and looked at it, and because, finally, I decided that it was an inopportune intruder, indiscreetly encroaching on the spectacle of my disappointment, I rebuked it, saying, "And just what do I care about you, Shakespeare? All your works put together, all your glory, and all your immortality, I'd trade them all a thousand times over for just one of those scribblings of Gabriel! Now that no one can hear me, I confess that your plays, instead of amusing me, bore me. They say you were an imposter, that you're not the one who wrote your works, and I believe it, because you've fooled me too. You've tried to take Gabriel's place, and now you seem to be making fun of my sorrow. Well then, along with your detractors, I declare you an imposter, and since your presence doesn't please me, but irritates me, one by one I close your five beautiful gilded books so I won't see you anymore!"

But to tell the truth, this long story about the letter with its disappointing end was from start to finish purely the product of my fantasy. Mercedes never told me that Gabriel would come, nor did Gabriel ever tell me he would. How could he, when that last night at Mercedes's house we never imagined that our goodbye then was to be followed by so many days apart? But there is something that Mercedes roundly affirmed on the phone, something that will happen because it is certain and evident. Mercedes said, "When he returns to Caracas he will arrange with Pancho to visit you at San Nicolás." That is certain, then, positively certain and not a fantasy. Gabriel will come to see me.

I expect him every day, from dawn until night, and this waiting and this hoping is like the water my soul drinks and at the same time it is that vine that, without having flowered, still tortures me, oppresses me, and rends my heart.

But Gabriel will come! Oh, yes, Gabriel will come and then, as I watch his arrival from a distance, the sterile vine that crushes my heart will miraculously be covered with millions of flowers. Will Gabriel come in the morning? Will he come in the afternoon? If he comes in the morning, I'll dress all in white, I'll put on my big straw hat, I'll tie it with tulle under my chin in the *Directoire* style, I'll carelessly hold the flowering branches of some wild shrub and, with my parasol in my hand, I'll go toward him as Flora goes toward her lover in the first act of *La Tosca*. If he comes in the afternoon, I'll wear black. I'll watch his arrival from my window. As I see him cross there near the mango trees, I'll go out to meet him, walking slowly, and when I go down the sunny path I'll open my white lace parasol and the white parasol open above my dark figure will symbolize the flower of my joy.

But will he come? Will Gabriel really come? Oh! Doubt sometimes assaults me like a thief who wants to steal my treasure of dreams!

That doubt has its foundation and origin in the following scene that happened three days ago, a trivial and torturing scene that I constantly try to erase from my memory, and that my memory always retains with the insistence of a lighted lamp that disturbs one's sleep.

It must have been about nine in the evening. We were all together in the dining room. We had already finished dessert and coffee. We could clearly hear the nocturnal sounds of the country—the croaking of frogs, the chirping of crickets. The meal seemed to languish indefinitely in a boring after-dinner conversation. I was lost in my distant preoccupations. My eyes fixed on the open window, I was looking at the black square of majestic night, palpitating with stars, when someone spoke Gabriel's name. I don't know how he came into the conversation, but I remember that María Antonia, as soon as she heard his name, took advantage of the opportunity to be disagreeable to me without any breach of etiquette and, accompanying the words with the blinding brightness of her black eyes, she came out with this piece of news, "They told me today on the phone that in Caracas people are talking a lot about the marriage of Gabriel Olmedo to the eldest daughter of Monasterios. If it's true, he's marrying very well. She's a very wealthy girl, her father is a power in the government, and besides, she's so pretty. She has lovely eyes!"

"Yes, beautiful eyes!" affirmed my cousin, brimming with admiration.

"Yes, beautiful!" repeated, in the same tone, almost all of the herd, as Uncle Pancho would say.

I couldn't restrain myself and I exclaimed, "I don't know what her eyes are like, but I've heard that the rest of her is pathetic." And literally quoting Mercedes's judgment, I added, "She is completely *fagotée*! Gabriel Olmedo, who is so meticulous, so *raffiné*, so *gourmet*, as you might put it, will never marry a creature like that."

María Antonia, who must have guessed the source of my information from the torrent of French adjectives, was about to reply, aggressive and most annoyed, but at that moment someone spilled a cup of wine on the tablecloth. The incident changed the course of conversation and nothing more was said about the matter.

But the words are engraved in my mind, and they torture me night and day. They are the thief that tries to rob me of my treasure of illusions; they are the lighted lamp that disturbs my sleep; they are a dagger that constantly slashes my hope, and it is they that have shown me this horrid demon of jealousy, which my eyes had never looked upon before.

Oh! If I could talk to Mercedes, there in the intimacy of her make-believe Orient, then she, with the penetrating vision of an astute sailor who knows the secrets of all horizons, would tell me . . . would tell me!

But I can't talk to her or to anyone, and this doubt is growing enormously in my secret of love and now it is overwhelming me. Who will help me bear it?

When I finished writing these words, I lifted my eyes and saw the acacia branch that, blown by the breeze, seemed to gesture at me from the window bars. Its leaves open partially and move, like fingers in the greeting of hands we love. It has scattered over the ground its gift of little pink flowers. I looked at it, I looked a long time, my imploring eyes lifted in a deep gaze full of faith and hope as one looks at the venerable and miraculous image of a patron saint, and imploring from the bottom of my heart, I prayed to it, "Oh! Generous old acacia, you that shield me from the sun and that adorn yourself night and day with the flowers the bougainvillaea lends you; you that know the evil of vines that coil around your heart like serpents of regret; you that have borne with the patience of the Nazarene

the cross of so many thorny and sterile embraces; you that are good because you stretch out your compassionate hand to the helpless who implore your help, and like Saint Isabel of Hungary, your charity turns into
flowers in your lap; you that maternally spill your shade on those who love
you and those who hate you; you that know all because you have the
experience of many springtimes; tell me, generous old acacia, will my vine
flower some day as your bougainvillaea has flowered?"

Here, María Eugenia Alonso, sitting on a large rock, confesses to the river; the river gives her advice, and she, obediently and piously, decides to follow the advice exactly.

 Grandmother was right when she foretold that living with my cousins would put an end to that vehement antipathy that I had professed toward them a short time ago. As a matter of fact, after barely a month together at the hacienda, I like the herd! Now I find them quite nice and quite pleasant.

I think that antipathy is an impulsive and superficial feeling that really doesn't exist or have any reason to exist. Actually, almost no one is unlikable. If you evaluate people by getting to know them and if you penetrate the essence of their psychology with kindness, you end by admiring their good qualities and tolerating their defects, as in the physical world we tolerate rain, heat, spots on the wall of the room we live in, or the hard pillow on our bed. It's all a question of time and patience. In my opinion, this is one of the most tangible proofs that man is a social animal, born to live in the company of his own kind. If certain faults we see in others got on our nerves forever as much as they did when we first noticed them, then no doubt we'd finally prefer suicide to the company of those people. But fortunately everything in nature is very well ordered, and custom, which is very conciliatory, acts as a cordial on our nerves and evangelically preaches, "Love one another." Antipathy only lasts really when it is based on envy and fed by close contact and a growing admiration in the mind of the envious. Setting aside all modesty, I admit that this is the situation in which I find myself in respect to my aunt, the honorable, hollow-eyed, moral, and most eloquent María Antonia Fernández de Aguirre, the wife of my uncle Eduardo Aguirre. Just as I have reconciled myself with her children, María Antonia, on the other hand, detests me more with every day that passes. With what a flood of sincerity does she show me her admiration and hatred together, summed up in her envy! And how this envy of hers puts magnifying glasses before her eyes and finds ways to exaggerate my poor merits!

Grandmother and Aunt Clara, who really, as Uncle Pancho rightly says, have a marked preference for me over my cousins, become indignant about María Antonia's feelings, and they take it upon themselves to defend me very heatedly when she directly or indirectly attacks me. Since this happens continually, it gives them a lot of work, and they spend their lives arguing eternally. Deep down, María Antonia's growing antipathy, far from displeasing me, flatters me, because I philosophically consider its origin. Moreover, it gives me some amusement, since I have now found a way to get even. This consists of daily extending the power that I exercise over her children, especially over Pedro José, the youngest, who is thirteen. The four of them, instigated by their mother, no doubt, were hostile to me at first, but as we got to know each other their feelings have changed. We started by being friends, and now they have decided to make me their model and they copy everything about me. María Antonia is exasperated by her children's servility, but her indignation notwithstanding, my laws and my influence rule them with all the despotism and sway of empress fashion. My cousins talk as I do, they copy my expressions, they share my daring ideas, they have adopted my tastes, they hum the songs that I hum, and even at meals they prefer the same dishes that I prefer.

Oh! Dear herd, disciplined army, how well you serve me in my peaceful and terrible tactic, which keeps those two brilliant luminaries, framed by those two darkest circles, forever flashing!

But nothing can compare to the power I hold over Pedro José, and his almost fanatic devotion. To demolish his mother's work as far as possible, and since I couldn't alter the basic essence of his being, I have altered his name, which is the symbol or graphic representation of that essence. Instead of Pedro José, I call him Perucho, and Perucho is my page, my squire, and my troubadour, all at the same time. Never a day passes that he doesn't bring flowers to my room, avocados, mangoes, or some very sweet sugarcane, peeled and cut into tiny segments. Perucho dedicated some poetry to me that earned him a warm hug, and it is he who always accompanies me on the long and silent outings that I take every afternoon.

These daily excursions are my delight and greatest joy, and at the same time they put María Antonia in the worst possible mood. No sooner has the clock struck four than I, in my full-cut riding skirt, my boots, my wide-brimmed hat tied under my chin cowboy-style, and willow switch in my hand, with the sole object of making María Antonia's eyes pop, I begin shouting through the house, "Perucho! Perucho! Have you saddled up yet?"

And Perucho, who is waiting for me under the guayabo trees with the horses ready and tied to the tree trunks, answers me with an ear-splitting whistle like the shrilling of a locomotive. So much absolutely unnecessary noise to announce our departure naturally produces the desired effect. María Antonia in her indignation begins to mutter, "That sort of nickname is so repugnant to me! And how ugly and how dangerous to be so familiar with young boys!"

But I behave as if I'd heard nothing, and I head for the shade of the guayabos where Perucho and the horses are waiting for me. He helps me mount while he explains something that is usually more or less like this, "I gave my horse a lot of corn so he won't be as lazy as yesterday. I saddled yours with the majordomo's mule cinch, the chestnut's bit, the new saddle blanket, and Papa's reins because they're so soft."

His system of selection creates the greatest disorder in the saddle room and it brings down on poor Perucho the most terrible lectures. But with a stoicism worthy of a better cause, he bears the onslaught and the next day he does the same thing over again.

Pleased and smiling at seeing us so close, Grandmother watches us leave and, as the horses start out, she always shows her nose and mouth between two bars of a window to shout these or similar recommendations, "Slowly, children! Don't go so fast! Be careful of tree branches! Don't let the horses stumble! And watch out in case they shy! And Pedro José, you take care of her, ride behind her. Remember, you two, that falling from a horse is very dangerous!"

And trotting away, with the breeze whipping our faces, my squire and I go down the road from the house, walk awhile across the meadow, then we plunge into the craggy terrain of the ravines and we begin to climb up the mountains. Then as I gaze at the landscape or at my horse's white mane, gently blowing in the breeze, I meditate upon the last words of María Antonia and Grandmother.

These little meditations usually awaken philosophical thoughts, if they can be called that when they are only observations or reasoning that I am in the habit of making when I am alone and that I never reveal to anyone for fear they might seem impertinent or ridiculous. So, while my horse runs beside Perucho's horse, and while Perucho, like me, is sunk in profound silence, I make these observations to myself, "It's strange! María Antonia, who detests me, takes the most lively interest in my moral health, and she has discovered that my close relationship with Perucho is ugly and dangerous. On the other hand, Grandmother, who every day declares the importance of moral health and seems to be convinced of its great superiority over physical health, in this case, is worried only about the latter. She sees no other dangers than those I might suffer if the horse trots too fast. She, who loves me so much, seems profoundly indifferent to me in her disdain for my precious and delicate moral health."

And since at such moments everything that surrounds Perucho and me seems to speak a language of grandeur, in spite of my inexperience, I see for an instant with extraordinary lucidity the ineffable mystery of things, I divine the secret equilibrium of life, and I wholeheartedly admire the kindness of Providence, which, with wise economy, has placed the care of our physical health in the hands of those who love us, and the care of our moral health in the hands of those who abhor us. "Thanks to such a wise distribution," I continue in my silent monologue, lulled by the breeze and by the rhythmic trotting of the horses, "hatred becomes as altruistic or more altruistic than affection, which would always be blindfolded like Cupid, if it were not for the discreet warnings of the former on matters of strict morals. Here you have, then, the reason we shouldn't judge things hastily, and why hatred, in spite of its bad reputation, is really the sentinel that guards our virtue, the basis on which our moral sense rests and the seedbed where purity and foresight grow together and are intertwined."

But such soliloquies are immediately paralyzed in my brain when I recall that this unlucky propensity for philosophy is the cause of my misery, the source of my sorrows, and the origin of my reclusion at San Nicolás, something that so far I've borne stoically. For if I hadn't formulated in words my particular impressions about modesty and morals, Aunt Clara wouldn't have been scandalized that day, and Grandmother wouldn't have been alarmed to the point of decreeing my immediate exile from Caracas. And since I have taken that fateful experience to heart, and since I have seen and learned that storing up ideas of your own is as foolish as carrying a dynamite bomb in your pocket, I quickly reject all philosophy and begin to talk to Perucho, who is slowly walking behind me now, along the narrow, long, and very shadowy path that stretches out beside the winding left bank of the river.

When we come to a quiet eddy where the river splits in two and reaches out one arm of water to the mountain, Perucho always consults me.

"Shall we stay here at the pool, or shall we go farther upstream?"

Usually I prefer to stay at the pool because there the river holds a serene and mysterious charm for me. So, no sooner have I answered Perucho's question by saying, "Let's stay here today," than he jumps off his horse, helps me dismount, and, after he ties the horses in the shade of a huge matapalo tree, we start looking for a place to sit, jumping from one to another of the rocks that protrude from the water. After much debate, I always sit down on the large stone that divides and channels the current away from this deep pool. There I settle down to contemplate the river, and I look at it, I stare at it fixedly and closely until gradually my whole world of thoughts grows still. I forget the ideas born a few moments ago as my horse trotted along. One after another the different material images gathered during the day are wiped away. Converted into an unconscious part of nature, I begin to listen to the simple, generous voice of the water. At that moment nothing exists for me—not Grandmother, nor María Antonia, nor the house down below, nor my room, nor my books, nor my grief, not even myself, because from looking so hard at the river I feel that I too have been carried away in its current, and that, with the rocks and sand on the bottom, with the fallen fruits and dry branches that float past, with the lacy trees and bits of blue sky that are reflected from above, the water also carries in its bosom this divine and torturing poem of my love. Seated on the stone, in the silent landscape, I copy the immobile spirit of the stone, and I stay calm and quiet so that the passing river will sing my poem to me in its murmurs and will show it to me in its mirror.

Such a state of rapture lasts barely a few minutes, because it arouses an inexplicable and lively joy in me. Then I begin to talk loquaciously to Perucho. I laugh for no apparent reason, I race over the rocks, I throw pebbles at the trees and at the boulders in the river, and I am subject to the strangest whims. From where he's sitting, Perucho watches my joy with eyes full of shy adoration and, as I invent a thousand fancies, he immediately carries them out to please me. If it's a fruit, he climbs the tree and picks it; if it's one of those big butterflies, he chases it and tries to catch it with his Panama hat lifted in the air; if it's a flower, he cuts it and brings it to me, even if he has had to take off his shoes to climb trees or wade into the water up to his knees.

One day I had an immense longing to experience the fresh, turbulent secrets of my sleeping pool and I wanted to go bathing there. No sooner had I phrased my desire than Perucho had mounted his horse, ridden down to the house, and in less than twenty minutes, sweaty and out of breath, he was back again carrying my towel, soap, and cologne. Alert to prevent anyone from coming there, he quickly went to stand guard beside the horses at the opening to our rocky bower. Alone and nude, feeling that I was the soul of the landscape, I sank into the longed-for coolness of my favorite pool. And I remember that that day, submerged in the pool, I lost, as I never had before, the notion of my own existence, because the flowing water made my skin numb with some mysterious delight, and because my eyes, gazing above, unconsciously had started interpreting the loves of the multitude of branches that embrace and kiss each other above their riverbed.

Only when twilight disappears altogether do Perucho and I return home. The horses, anxious to be back in the stable, gallop as they traverse the little river path and they fly like two birds as soon as they reach the meadow trails. This unbridled race that knocks our hats off and blows our hair also gives wings of mirth to our spirits. With all the fun of the race, on two horses that tear side by side down the road, Perucho and I wave our arms to frighten the oxen that are consuming their stalks of sugarcane in front of the ranch houses; we shout at the white shapes of people in the night; we sing together at the top of our lungs; and, standing up in his stirrups, he answers in the same tone every turkey hen or lizard that calls from its hiding place in the tangle of underbrush. I laugh out loud when I hear him, telling him how good his imitations are and I praise his feats of horsemanship, and when we reach the bottom of the canyon, at the same time we both cry out mournfully, awakening the echo that answers us from the black recesses of the mountain.

These daily rides at nightfall are as much consolation as confession because they free my soul from its sorrow. The river, with the mercy of its plants, its rocks, and its murmurs, is the confessor who absolves me every day from the blackness I take to it; it gives me hopeful advice, and it always leaves the infinite grace of happiness in my spirit. I bless it with all my soul for its gentle advice; I bless the breeze that blows my hair; I bless my horse that runs against the wind; and after blessing all of nature, I also bless Perucho, who is my squire and my acolyte on these joyous pilgrimages.

I now notice that my great intimacy with Perucho deserves a special chapter, because our relationship is at the same time simple and complicated. While it distracts me from my concern over my unhappy love, it also allows me an opportunity for practice.

I began by being a friend of his, in a very careless and childish companionship. He was useful to me for his agility and for his obliging and dreamy nature, always ready to please me, and I tried to take him with me on my solitary strolls, as I might have taken a big, silent dog that would walk beside me without disturbing my daydreams with importunate words. But from the day when María Antonia said for the first time, "How ugly and how dangerous that intimacy with young boys seems to me!" without knowing why, Perucho began to acquire great interest in my eyes. For me, his presence was the living presence of love. Just as children play with trains and dolls, pretending they are real, from then on I started playing with Perucho, as if he were my toy, and in my imagination I turned him into Gabriel. Naturally, given this point of view, Perucho has gained a great importance to me. He truly loves me with a huge, silent, and timid adoration. Out of generosity to him, and in order to act out my love, while I passionately dream of Gabriel, I shower Perucho with looks and smiles. It is a divine way to make ourselves happy, and also to make others happy, a skill not all women possess, and which shallow people scornfully call flirting.

Thanks to my closeness with Perucho, I have discovered that, to a high degree, I possess the gift of flirtation, which, like a fond mother, guides or teaches us to walk along the divine paths of love. Naturally, since, in my deepest convictions, I consider that gift both a source of joy and a proof of generosity, I don't object at all to admitting it, and also recognizing that I'm quite satisfied to possess it. With every day that passes I deplore more and more that I hadn't discovered and exercised it before with Gabriel. Of course! Instead of that stupid timidity that inhibited me and paralyzed me in his presence! But these are the whims of destiny! What a tangle of mysteries and surprises we all bear, Lord, in our hearts!

I'm certain that if Grandmother, Aunt Clara, or any other serious person with solid principles were to read what I have just written, they would find it very wrong and would make some unpleasant, offensive prophesies about my future reputation. But they would be mistaken. Showing off or flirting with Perucho, in my own eyes, is the most palpable and certain proof that I am essentially a faithful woman. In spite of his indifference, and in spite of how he's abandoned me, I love only Gabriel, and it is quite certain that if I had never met Gabriel, Perucho would not have seen any of the charming and insinuating smiles that make him so happy.

My short experience leads me to believe that in the love of women there exists the same invisible and sublime subtlety as in the pure theological love of God. From what I can see, it is not possible for us to love the one we would like to love when he is absent. Of course, unable to love the one we love directly, we can only love him indirectly in one who is available. Very well. In this supreme faithfulness to the absent lover, loved through another object, are there not great points of contact with the pure love of the ascetic, who essentially adores God, by apparently adoring an image of wood or plaster? In my own case, isn't there also the august mystery of intention that purifies everything and transforms crass idolatry into holy and pious veneration? Well, all these delicate shadings also exist in my soul and, thanks to them, in the eyes of my love, Perucho is not Perucho, but instead the live image that at times turns into Gabriel by the grace of the august mystery of intention. Mine is a case of human love that seems to be allied with the sublime theological subtlety of divine love. Nevertheless, I am sure that, elected judge of the question, whether it were Grandmother, Mercedes, or Gabriel himself, all would commit an injustice. It's quite probable that they would designate me with the epithets of fickle, faithless, changeable, or any other disagreeable concept of that sort. But, in a similar case, I would also judge them, as the Church judged those heretics called iconoclasts, who, in their great stupidity, were never able to measure the abyss that separates the material image from the ideal essence, or the visible form from the sublime and invisible substance.

Finally, as a summary or conclusion of all the previous reasoning, I declare that my love for Gabriel is more vehement and greater every day, that my little demonstrations to Perucho are only a way of expressing outwardly the cult of this love that lives and overflows in my soul, that I possess in general a very elevated and somewhat pantheistic concept of love, and that, last, my system of spiritual fidelity, let thoughtless people say what they wish, is a thousand times more pure and meritorious than the external and common fidelity that men, convention, and the law are in the habit of imposing.

And to better show to my own conscience the truth of these statements and the loyalty of my love for Gabriel, I am going to record this little scene that occurred two afternoons ago beside the river.

I was sitting as usual on the large rock that closes off and protects the backwater. My feet were almost touching the water; I had put a sprig of trinitarias on my hat and I was entertaining myself by setting some mamon hulls afloat. Perucho had thrown them down from the top of the tree into my skirt. It was a big green bunch that I was picking slowly. When I pulled off a piece of fruit, I would break the hull in two; I would lay bare the pit with my teeth and, having cleaned it, I would put the pit back in the hull that served as a boat. Careful not to sink it, I would let it float in the water and, as it drifted down river, I imagined I was watching funeral barges in India, each manned only by a corpse, in a solitary descent down the sacred Ganges.

I was absorbed in such gentle and poetic considerations while Perucho tirelessly ran and slid like a lizard in the labyrinth of branches, leaves, and forks in the gigantic genip tree. Suddenly I heard a shrill whistle that made me lift my head. It was Perucho, astride a very high branch with his bare feet hanging in the air and his hands cupped around his mouth to form a megaphone. He was trying to get my attention just as if it were some indispensable and urgent matter.

"Listen, María Eugenia! Do you know who you look like when I see you from up here? Well, with those trinitarias on your hat, you're just like, exactly like the girl in the picture about the Ross pills, that ad on the door of the drugstore, on the corner down from the house in Caracas!"

Since I have seen the picture in question, and the girl is really enchanting, his judgment caught my ego by surprise, made me forget my melancholy task, and suddenly brightened my mind with smiling and pleasant ideas. Perucho's observation struck me as a hundred times more interesting than if he had compared me to the Venus de Milo, which would perhaps have sounded like a cliché incapable of flattering my vanity. This compliment about the Ross pills shouted from the top of the genip tree seemed charming and very sincere.

And to repay Perucho for his timely gallantry, looking up and lifting my head, I gazed at him through the branches and leaves for a length of time, and then, illuminating my expression with a smile that I judged to be the most suggestive in my repertoire, I asked him sweetly, "Yes?"

And there above me, the effect produced by the smile and the tone of my question was so clearly reflected on Perucho's face that I instantly thought, "I'll talk this way and I'll smile like this at Gabriel when I see him!"

Then all at once I threw the green bunch of fruit in the water and the current carried it away. I lay back on the rock, and I started dreaming, watching the river flow.

As if I were under the influence of a hallucinogen or intoxicating drugs, the short dialogue held with Perucho awoke such a lively and powerful memory of Gabriel in my mind that I felt it move in the river, in the trees, in the birds, in Perucho, and in everything that surrounded me. Then I felt it inside myself, and I felt it so deeply that I had the urge to write to him right there, a sincere, wild letter telling him all the joy and all the suffering of my love.

And I lifted my head again; again I looked up; with my hands cupped around my mouth, I called to Perucho, just as he had shouted a few minutes before.

"Listen, Peruchito! Come down for a minute from that jungle, go over to the horses, and on my horse's saddle get a book that has some paper and a pencil, and bring it to me because I want to write a letter."

When he came back with the book and my writing materials I begged him sweetly, "Now stay quiet, and don't call me, because you'd bother me. I can't write when anyone talks to me."

On the rock in the river, I used the book as a writing case and my knees as a desk, from time to time sharpening the point of my pencil on a nearby stone. As long as daylight lasted I wrote. I feverishly wrote this letter, which has the mad sincerity of all ardent and silent love letters that are never sent. In it I depicted the gentle truth of nature that surrounded me, and in the truth of nature I also depicted the truth of my soul, with the pure immodesty with which water reflects our image, and with the fresh nakedness of the rocks bathed by the eternal, murmuring river.

More or less, this is what it says in the letter that I wrote that afternoon while sitting on the rock and using my knees as a desk.

"Gabriel:

"I love you, because one day, you told me in words that you loved me. I love you because, before saying it to me with the clarity of words, you had already told me clearly with your eyes—eyes that are lamps to my soul in the dark of night. I love you because the memory of you is locked within my memory, held in silence with fragrant and mute submission, as a sandalwood case holds a jewel. I love you because you live and move in me, as alive and as handsome as if I were the still mirror and you were the living image that peers into it. I love you because my soul has also looked into your soul, and as it studied itself, it has shivered with surprises like the thirsty little lamb that for the first time sees her fleece gleam white, reflected in the still waters.

"Gabriel, your love has come to me, and in your absence it is a little songbird that travels imprisoned in its cage. It hops merrily about in the narrow space of the cage, and warbles, 'Oh, if someday a strong hand would open my cage!'

"Your love, Gabriel, has come with me; it has brought to my exile all its harvest of roses, with them it has woven a white garland, and it has pinned it to my heart with a thousand sharp thorns. The thorns are dyed in my blood, and my heart blesses them, accepts them in its soft flesh, and under the thousand wounds, in pain and drunk with fragrance, it lies still—it wouldn't want to shatter the roses.

"Gabriel, with the halo of your love on your forehead, walking down my arid road, I saw you come toward me, and since then you have been the Messiah of my soul. The tracks of your sandals in the dust have traced a path of hope for me, and I run after you down the path. I am exhausted and thirsty, but I am in good spirits, because I think of the pleasure of the wine of Canaan and I hope to slake my hunger in the miraculous abundance of the loaves and the fishes.

"You are the sweet Messiah of my soul, Gabriel, and your love is the water of Jordan that has redeemed me forever from the prisons of Limbo. In abstinence and solitude in my desert, I bless your hands, as generous and as good as the hands of Jesus, because they reached out one day and opened my eyes, which were as closed and dark as the eyes of the man who was blind from birth.

"You are the sweet Messiah of my soul, Gabriel, and I bless your feet for bringing you to me. As the anointed feet of Jesus led him to the house of Jairus, your feet brought you into the house of my soul. You found it pale and sleeping in its white shroud of innocence and you said to it 'Arise!' But, Gabriel, you haven't shown the generous mercy of Jesus in your miracle, because you took away the sun that my eyes longed for, and you left my awakened soul alone and locked in its house.

"Gabriel, your love is wed to my soul, they live and move together constantly, locked in my body. When I place my fingers on my temples I hear a tumult of wings as your love flutters within me. And like the captive bird whose cage door was left open, I feel it alight at the open door of my eyes; I hear its wings beating in the air, and a moment later I see it fly, arrogant and happy, to the freedom of the open fields.

"It's true, Gabriel. As I sit on my rock in the river, where I'm writing to you now, your love flutters everywhere around me. It sings the song of water churning against rocks; it runs past holding the river by its hand, in a mad race, bumping into everything; in the water its cool and disturbing lips sometimes splash on the rock to furtively kiss my feet, and at its touch my whole body shivers with surprise and pleasure; it makes itself so handsome and with its straw hat covered with flowers, it appears in the pool, greets me, and imitates me cleverly when, thirsty to see it, I lean over the river searching for it in the water; it climbs the trees, and calls me, nodding at me from the branches above; it sits between the two wings of the breeze to kiss my eyes and caress my hair while I fly joyfully home on my horse at twilight; it hides in the dark to ambush me, and it answers me with echo's voice if I implore it with shouts from the depths of the ravines, and it dresses in black, looks out of my cousin Perucho's eyes, animated and sparkling, it calls and gestures to me, as a mother calls her child, so I will smile at it.

"Gabriel, I'm writing you today because I want to tell you that on the white beauty of my body I have seen the sudden flowering of spring in its great abundance. Heavy with flowers, with the gift of my love held in my arms, I impatiently await you, Gabriel, daily, and my love, when it feels you near, opens its eyes, leaps with joy and tries to escape from my arms to run and meet you, like the willful baby kid that has heard its mother's bell in the distance.

"Gabriel, I'm writing you because I can no longer bear the weight of my secret, and to make you come and share it with me I want to tell you that to me your love is the exquisite song of my Song of Songs. Your mouth is as wise and as glorious as the mouth of Solomon, it almost touches me, it grazes my ears with its breath, and it sings softly to me so only I and no one else can hear it.

"Like the Shulamite, Gabriel, I too have learned the words of the Song, and like her I call you constantly in my solitude and in my song I tell you, 'When the day is cool and the shadows lengthen, come, come my Beloved, my Fair One, like the roes and hinds on Mount Bether' . . . But you don't hear me, Gabriel. The voice that sings my song has often been lost in the darkness of night, and because I want to raise it louder and louder until it reaches the height of your ears, I send it flying to you, held between the wings of this letter.

"Gabriel, in the burning desert of your absence, you are my glorious Solomon, and I am your adoring Shulamite. I am stretched out on the scorching sand and, covered with my jewels and burning with thirst, I vigilantly scan the horizon because I want to be the first to see your palanquin shining in the distance, my triumphant Solomon.

"I am your loving Shulamite, Gabriel, and for the festival of love with which I await you, I have adorned my fair body with all the pomp of the Betrothed in the Palace of the King.

"And I am your sorrowing Shulamite, Gabriel, and for the resigned torture of the wait, I have dressed my mute torment with the painful humility of the grass that my horse tramples as he runs at night.

"Gabriel, with the pomp of the Betrothed and with the humility of the grass, I am your Shulamite and I wait for you night and day, my glorious Solomon. Hear, hear this voice that calls to you from my letter, my Beloved, my Fair One, come down from Mount Bether as fast as the roes and the hinds, and come, let your mouth teach my silent lips the most beautiful song of the Song of your Songs!"

And once this wildly eccentric letter was finished, I remained for a long time motionless. The faded light kept me from reading what I had written, and I began to review it in my memory, while my eyes watched the winking fireflies and from time to time the sparkling of the polished strip of river. Together with my stillness and silence, the darkness gradually was growing denser, until at last, it mixed with the rocks, it fused completely with the water, it squeezed me close, it embraced me, and I felt in my arms a coldness that was like fear or perhaps delicious, shivery fear that seemed like cold. For a moment, I thought I was entirely alone in the darkness, and I was terribly startled when Perucho's voice close to me said, "Can we leave now, María Eugenia?"

When I heard him, fearfully and greedily, I gathered up the three sheets of writing that glowed white in my lap like three bright moons. I hid them in my bosom. Holding hands with Perucho, jumping from one rock to another, I crossed a part of the river, and together, we quickly took our horses, which were stamping impatiently in the deep night under the matapalo tree.

🙼   🙼   🙼

At home, during supper, while everyone was talking, I didn't say a word. With my hand across my chest, I made the three sheets of paper next to my skin rustle in my bosom. Deep in my thoughts, I saw the sheets in my mind's eye and I read them mentally. I felt happy, isolated from everyone, alone in the company of my letter. I was proud of having written it, proud of having dared to write it, and I thought with anxiety and joy about the effect it was going to have.

But a little incident in the conversation, fortunately or not, shattered my lyrical mood, as it suddenly gave me the absolutely opposite point of view from the soaring idealism inspired by my letter.

Perucho, who, contrary to my advice, is in the habit of commenting during dinner on everything we do on our excursions, began to tell what happened that afternoon, and he said with romantic enthusiasm, whose true sense almost no one grasped, "Today María Eugenia stuck on her hat a branch of trinitarias that I cut for her with my machete when we rode past the vine at the old sugar mill. With her hat covered with flowers she sat on a very big rock in the river, above the pool, and she started writing a letter. I was up in the top of the mamon where I could see a lot of the river, and sitting on the rock in the middle of the water, writing, she looked like a picture. If I knew how to paint, María Eugenia, I'd climb up with my brushes and everything to the top of the mamon and I'd make a picture of you like that!"

Perucho's descriptive enthusiasm was so impassioned that María Antonia's eyes, enormous and glittering, looked at him an instant and without the least room for doubt, they indignantly commented on the planned portrait with this brief judgment, "Imbecile!!"

Then, the same eyes, enormous and brilliant, stared at Uncle Eduardo, and they said, aided now by a feigned whisper that was perfectly audible, "I can understand letting them go riding alone even if they wear the horses out and ruin the saddles and bridles, but when they dismount and stay by themselves all afternoon long on the river, it seems highly improper to me and I can't understand how you permit it. What need is there to go write letters at the pool? I think that here at home we have more than enough tables and desks!"

And since Uncle Eduardo couldn't answer because he was eating and had his mouth full, María Antonia spoke impatiently to Perucho, this time in a clear and ringing voice, "I refuse to let you continue being so idle, Pedro José! The only thing you think about is roaming around the country like a bandit. You don't study; you don't do anything! Since you're so crazy about climbing trees, saddling horses, and doing menial jobs, tomorrow afternoon you'll help me put up a new fence around the chicken yard. The one there now is broken and at night the possums get in!"

Aunt Clara objected, "It's not the possums that get the chickens. I'm almost certain that people are coming at night and stealing them. I think it's a waste of money to replace the fence around the chicken yard!"

Meanwhile, at the opposite end of the table, Grandmother, who couldn't hear the conversation at our end, commented on Perucho's description, as she said with alarm, "María Eugenia, my dear, what foolishness! Why must you go to the pool to write letters? Don't you know the river is swarming with dangerous mosquitoes? You might come down with a fever! Don't do that anymore! When you want to write, write here, at home, as we all do."

I didn't answer a single word, but the letter that still rustled beneath my hand, hidden in my bosom, now profaned by the breath of reality, had just expired in my soul. Once the mystery was destroyed, the daring charm of the plan was destroyed, and everything I'd written that afternoon now seemed completely ridiculous to me. Under the spell of the words pronounced by María Antonia, Aunt Clara, and Grandmother, the spirit of Don Quixote had fled from me, leaving only Sancho, sitting in a far corner of my soul, rightly mocking such a nonsensical letter.

In my disillusionment, I looked at Perucho, intending to reproach him, but like me, he wasn't talking either, and he didn't see me. He had understood his indiscretion. He was mortified and, with his head bowed, he was busy making designs on the tablecloth with the four tines of his fork.

As soon as dinner was over, I said goodnight to everyone and retired to my room. Once there, I took the three sheets scribbled in pencil and I opened them in the intimate and familiar circle of light that the table lamp traces every night. I saw that the words of my letter looked indecisive and poorly written on the straight lines of the paper. To me they looked twisted, because they were heaped with absurdities and, considered like this, in the cold, hard light of reason, they seemed a thousand times more ridiculous than they had before, at dinner, seen and judged in the uncertain light of my imagination. With the crumpled papers lying open under my eyes, which no longer were looking at them, I sat reflecting for quite awhile. What could I have been thinking to write such a letter! Oh! What would Gabriel have said if I had been mad enough to send it to him! No doubt it would have seemed to him absurd, forward, "improper," to use María Antonia's classic word. Yes. Especially that pretentious and ridiculous idea of comparing myself to the Shulamite. Probably Gabriel no longer even remembered the *Song of Songs*!

And having formulated these considerations, with my elbows propped on the table, motionless, I again mulled over those scribbled sheets until, finally, as rebels against the laws that rule all letters, as indiscreet, and as nonsense, I sentenced the three of them to be converted into a heap of tiny, illegible pieces to then be burned in a pyre, as a work of insurrection and heresy. But at the very instant of tearing them up, I remembered the love with which they had been written two hours before, and I revoked the sentence. I limited myself to wadding them up in a ball, and, converted into the uncertain symbol of my own destiny, I threw them to the back of the deepest drawer in my table. Then I locked the drawer, and in the secret corner of a shelf, I hid the key.

But not in vain has it been said that the adventurous spirit of Don Quixote is immortal, and that it is as tenacious as the eternal rebirth of life.

An hour later, in bed, with my light out and my eyes closed, I could still hear those telling words, full of positivism, that in such a timely way had awakened me to wholesome reality. "What need is there to go write letters at the pool?" "You'll help me put up a new fence around the chicken yard." "The river is swarming with dangerous mosquitoes." "When you want to write, write here, as we all do." Nonetheless, while my imagination was busy reproducing that sensible and prudent advice, in the upper regions of my soul, somewhat whipped and battered but still courageous, the enterprising spirit of Don Quixote again appeared. And apparently, from this struggle against sensible advice, the following conclusions were reached.

On the one hand, I completely accepted the inarguable principle that a young lady with any self-respect has no right to send letters to a man who is not her father, her brother, her husband, or her sweetheart. That the idea of writing such a letter had not occurred to me while sitting in a chair, in front of a mahogany table and facing a whitewashed wall, but instead had occurred to me at the river, under the trees and the sky, was reason enough for me to have rejected this wild idea immediately, for almost everything suggested to us by nature is profoundly immoral, since it disdains the most elementary conventions and always mocks healthy social principles. Having accepted these wise reasons, my good judgment rejoiced greatly and my conscience breathed a sigh of relief.

However, on the other hand, the adventuresome spirit we all have within our souls arose temptingly and whispered in my ear, "Is it possible you can renounce your love?" "Don't you see that Gabriel, who adores you, when he finds out you love him, will leave everything for you?" "Maybe the river is right! Remember, madness is mother of the sublime!"

Until finally, from this controversy, I was able to clarify that wrong is not in its essence but in its form, and that apparently all sin is an angular, hairy, and deformed body that can turn out to be very handsome and dignified if clothed in the right costume. I resolved then to change the appearance of my plan, which was "improper" and ridiculous in its guise as a letter, and I decided to enclose it in the form of poetry, which I would cause to reach Gabriel's hands indirectly. Therefore, saying in substance the same thing as the letter, my ideas would not run the risk of flouting convention or of looking ridiculous.

It happened that the night before, I had finished reading the works of Shakespeare, and I had decided to return them to Gabriel because I was not certain that he had offered them to me as a gift. Since I believe I have a certain poetic talent, I like to write poems, and once in awhile I do, even though I have never shown them to anybody. Lying in bed, having given up the idea of the letter, and ready to transform it into poetry, I told myself with the enthusiasm of a lover and an artist that by polishing and working hard, I might perhaps describe my love by describing the love of some sad heroine in Shakespeare, and that only in this way, in a pointed comment written in the margin of a play, could I show Gabriel the whole truth in my heart. My enthusiasm for the plan was growing, until I felt perfectly optimistic. I found the idea of returning the book with my verses hidden in it delightful. It was as if I were sending Gabriel the timid gift of myself, veiled and trembling. I planned to let Mercedes in on the secret, so she, with her wise and exquisite tact, could advise Gabriel about the surprise.

And twisting and turning in bed, after much deliberation, I decided to hide myself behind the image of a Juliet on her balcony, waiting endlessly for a Romeo who doesn't appear. In the darkness, I tried to find rhymes for quatrains until, in a fever of inspiration, I got out of bed, wrapped myself in my kimono, turned on my lamp, and after much erasing and changing, in the early hours of the morning, I had written this sonnet:

JULIET'S BALCONY

How long my wait! In the dark night
Of my infinite thirst, I watch the road
To see if, before the new day shines its light,
Your ladder will appear at my balcony, my Romeo.

But no! You do not come, and in my melancholy,
Bleeding in the shadows, it is your shadow that I see.
Theobald has wounded you? Who severed the joy
Of your open wings, my beloved Romeo?

Now the wise moon, with her cold warning,
Has said pityingly to me, "Do not await the dead!"
But I shall not close my balcony until morning.

I'll wait for you until the dawn, and in the light
I'll search for your dead body, and on your still lips,
My lips on yours, I'll bring you back to life!

Having finished the sonnet, I copied it at the end of *Romeo and Juliet*, and I went back to bed.

The next day, early in the morning, I wrapped up the Shakespeare books, putting the volume I was concerned with on top, and I sent the package directly to Gabriel. Then I wrote a confidential letter to Mercedes, explaining my plan, and I insinuated that she should help me with it. No sooner had she received the letter than Mercedes called me on the telephone and in the conversation she said, "Gabriel isn't in Caracas, *ma chérie.* Why did you return those books to him? He sent them to you as a gift. I'm certain, quite certain, because he told me so himself. And tell me, does it really matter to you whether I speak to him about that poem of yours?"

I don't know what I answered, nor what I said after that. I only remember that a little while after leaving the telephone I felt bowed down by a strange affliction, ashamed of having written any verses at all, humiliated, very sad. I remembered that Mercedes, always so ready to tease me, for two or three days now, when we talked on the phone, had avoided mentioning Gabriel. Her silence had irritated me then, but now . . . now. In my horrible pessimism, I seemed to understand.

And so intense was the disillusionment I experienced after talking to Mercedes, I felt so grieved and so alone that, walking haphazardly, not knowing where I was going, I reached the edge of the reservoir, and I lay down on the grass in the shade of the weeping willows. I thought enviously about the eternal silence of cemeteries and, pretending I was dead, lying still under the willows, with kerchiefs of shadow and sun on my eyes, I wept a long time for myself.

CHAPTER VI   *Rain, a letter, and an afternoon*
that, like a road, glides, winds,
and is lost in the past.

Today it rained. It rained with a clattering of
raindrops, a pelting, short summer shower. The
shower has passed now, the thirsty land has
soaked up all the water, and now with its heavy
perfume of wet earth, it seems to give thanks to
heaven, intoning praise to the Lord, in this per-
fume that rises majestically to the clouds, scales the mountains, and dances
joyfully on all the atoms as in one of the exultant psalms of David.

I couldn't get out today because this rain has drenched everything. I'm
alone in my room. Through the open window, through the lace of the
acacia branch, I look at the landscape; I think about the favor of heaven in
the water that fell on the fields; I feel the happiness of the grateful land in
the smell of wet earth. And without envy or hate, from my sorrow, from
this drought in my soul where it still has not rained, I, too, sing the joy of
the water, as in the fiery furnace the three young captives in the Book of
Daniel sang a great hymn of praise.

"All the water that is in the heavens, fountains, seas and rivers, dew and
frost, ice and snow, bless the Lord!"

Oh! But the implacable heaven does not spill that beneficent dew on
my burning spirit. Cooling moisture penetrated to the furnace of the three
captives, but my fiery furnace of doubt will continue to burn me night
and day, without compassion and without respite!

This morning I received a letter from Cristina Iturbe. It's still here on
the table, beside the torn envelope, just as I left it after having read it. It is
her grudging and late reply to my poor mammoth letter. It is written on
gray paper, edged in gold, scented with sandalwood, covered with Cris-

tina's pointed, firm handwriting in lines as straight as a musical staff. All very elegant, very correct, and horribly painful in its casual tone and triviality.

Now, as this morning, looking at the gray sheet of stationery next to the torn envelope, I have once again questioned it with the mute interrogation of my eyes, "Why weren't you lost on the way here? Why couldn't you show me the mercy of silence?" Because of all possible repentance, the most perfect and absolute, the one that incites the greatest desire to reform is this repentance, this great regret for having made a sincere, intimate confession, that was not understood. It is the grief of a beggar's heart who is answered, "Not today; come back some other time!" Oh! What a betrayal of oneself; what an irreparable indiscretion; what a feeling of shame before the nakedness of one's own soul! These confidences and secrets, once spoken, and despised by a friend, cannot be retracted. They fall upon us again, like a rain of disillusionment!

Cristina has barely answered my long letter that was so intimate, that held so much of myself.

She scribbled a few phrases alluding to my conflicts and hurts, joking phrases in the worst possible taste. And finally, in a few short words she ends by telling me of her marriage. She boasts of joy, of happiness, of mutual love, in the braggart tone of a newly rich person trying to dazzle everyone with ostentatious luxury.

"You can't imagine how happy I am. My fiancé is so handsome. He adores me, and we just live for each other. When we get married, the family title of count and countess will be settled on us. In addition, Father is giving me a dowry of two hundred thousand duros. He's also giving us a small hotel in San Sebastian and any automobile we may pick out."

Oh! Cristina, Cristina, that's not the way I answered you when, in the convent, under the elm tree in the garden, with your lunch basket on your arm, you sadly confided in me! How I remember it now, here, before my table, before the funeral for your letter, and before the wet face of this rainy afternoon!

My close friendship with Cristina de Iturbe, that intimate friendship that today lies dead in the form of a gray letter; that great affection, earth and sun of my infancy, had two things as its basis. First, a great admiration, and then a great secret that we shared. On the windowpane, this wet afternoon, I call up a picture of Cristina, as if in a mirror. I remember her voice; I remember her blue eyes; I remember the huge moiré bow that spread out on top of her head. And I seem to relive another cloudy, cold afternoon in the European winter, when, lunching together under the elm in the convent, each with a little lunch basket on our arms, she made me her best friend, as she trusted me with her most intimate secret. The halo of mystery is sacred and aristocratic. How it attracts, how it imposes itself and how it rules eternally if the suggestive half-light that is its empire is never totally dispelled!

Summed up in that long-ago mystery, how clearly I see all my infancy pass before me!

I had just celebrated my eighth birthday when I entered the Sacred Heart School as a boarding student. Up to that time studying had bored me fearfully. During the first two years of our stay in Europe, that is to say, when I was between ages six and eight, Papa was constantly changing my tutors. I had English ones and French ones, tall ones and short ones, pretty and ugly, old and young. To me they all seemed charming and nice as long as we were going walking down the Champs Elysée. But I thought them all importunate, hateful, and cruel when they would sit down in front of me at a study table, and for a space of hours that seemed like years, they would say the most boring things in the world, as, on my poor timid eyes, they would fix the two blinding lanterns of their eyes, which were usually duplicated by the shiny glass of their spectacles. That was horrid. Obsessively, it troubled my sleep, embittered my life, and when I thought about it outdoors, I envied the good luck of the pavement, the trees, and the lamp posts that lived outside, seeing people go by, without having a governess or a study table.

Several times a week Papa was in the habit of making these or similar comments, "María Eugenia, my dear, you are a very ignorant little girl. You still don't know how to read. Just think, Paulina, the gatekeeper's little girl, is the same age as you and she already knows her multiplication tables. But you don't. You don't know anything. Your ignorance is absolute and it embarrasses me."

But nothing embarrassed me. I had become so familiar with Papa's opinion that, when he said, "Your ignorance embarrasses me," to my ears, my understanding, and my self-esteem, he might as well have said, "The franc has gone down," "Mistinguett really has splendid legs," or "Universal disarmament is a Utopian dream." All these phrases that belonged to his repertoire seemed to me equally unimportant and empty of meaning. "Ignorance!" What did it matter if I were ignorant, as long as I had a mouth to eat candy, feet to go walking, and, above all, eyes to watch

Punch and Judy shows on the Champs Elysée, the elephant at the zoo, or to see the shop windows?

When my tutors talked to Papa they always made this critical judgment about me, "Monsieur, elle n'est pas bête, mais il n'y a moyen de la faire étudier."

Others, however, gave up on me entirely as they told him frankly and pityingly, with an exclamation and a sigh, that I lacked any intelligence.

Both opinions left me equally indifferent because the word "ignorance" as well as the word "intelligence" held vague, boring, and useless concepts for me, without the least importance in my mind.

It has truly been said that days follow each other, but they are not alike. And suddenly, to support this aphorism, when I least expected it, a little incident, quite trivial in appearance, was more than enough to change my opinion and my monotonous routine, and to thrust me into a totally new existence.

This is what happened.

It was a very hot noon in summer. I was sitting at the study table with Miss Pitkin, my latest governess. Miss Pitkin was English, and naturally she wore glasses. As usual, at that period of the class, she was facing me and therefore facing the balcony, which was wide open behind me, revealing the green, leafy tops of one of the trees on the street. Depending on the circumstances, the leaves blew lightly in the breeze or the tree swayed majestically beyond the wrought iron railing of our balcony. Unfortunately, that day the tree was still because there was absolutely no wind and Miss Pitkin, who, like myself, was very hot, was impatient and mired in a discussion that was terribly complicated and terribly monotonous. She was trying to explain the hierarchical and inalterable order in which various numbers should be written in vertical rows before drawing a horizontal line, and finally, beneath the line, uniting the various numbers into a single number, thus performing the synthetic and ingenious operation called addition. But, as it seems, heat is not a very good setting for the flowering of science, and Miss Pitkin, red, perspiring, greatly dilating her green, myopic pupils behind her glasses, was obliged to repeat over and over, "The hundreds are written in the column for the hundreds; the tens are written in the column for the tens; ones in the column for ones; and then comes the decimal point in case decimals are to be added. So then, if I have an apple, and they give me ten apples, and then they give me one hundred . . ."

"A hundred apples!" I began to think as I sat before Miss Pitkin, with my two sweaty little hands open on my skirt, "How wonderful to eat a hundred apples, one after another in this scorching weather, right here, on that dreadful table, always boring and bare, where you can't even prop your elbows! Apples! Apples! How delicious! Especially if, instead of the red ones, they were those other green ones that are big, juicy, and a little tart!''

While I was thinking this, I held Miss Pitkin's eyes with my eyes, in order to show her my deep interest in arithmetic. But it happened that when the two of us were most absorbed in the imaginary apples, I discovered that, in Miss Pitkin's shiny left lens, there was a diminutive picture, round, green, and quite still in its nimbus of light, of the treetop that usually rocked rhythmically in the breeze on the street behind my back. The mysterious paths of destiny! The vision of the tree in Miss Pitkin's left lens, and the mental image of the apples suggested by my imagination, were enough to completely switch the monotonous course of my days, to reform my opinion, modify my tastes, and to generally change my whole code of personal principles. Situated as I was in front of Miss Pitkin and the rosy image of the tree and the fruit, I felt a passionate desire for the fresh air, indolence, and freedom of the country, enjoyed in full independence, far away, very far away, where no voice could reach saying, "The hundreds in the hundreds column." My thought, like a poor imprisoned bird, began to flutter, timidly at first, then with greater spirit. Finally, making a determined flight toward the past, it was lost in a forest of vague memories, imprecise, full of Virgilian and bucolic sweetness. Staring at the tree reflected in the left lens, I remembered sweetly, with fruition and great melancholy, those long-ago days in San Nicolás, the hacienda in Venezuela, when I used to sit on the ground under the guayabo trees covered with fruit, my hands free, independent, and altogether my own, and I would play in the dirt for hours and hours, accompanied by my friend María del Carmen, the cook's little daughter. How happy I was then and how happy María del Carmen must still be! Yes, she was probably still sitting on the grass with her ten fingernails black with dirt, cross-legged, and her feet cool and happy in her dark sandals, at the end of which you could see the surprise of the two white tips of her big toes!

Really, after all, it wasn't worthwhile to have been born white, with blonde curls, rosy lips, a rich father, to have embarked one morning in La Guaira, and to have sailed more than two weeks to finally reach this disastrous conclusion—awful, cold weather or asphyxiating heat, the study table, Miss Pitkin, and arithmetic. Why did we have to leave the hacienda in Venezuela? And how happy María del Carmen must still be! And I evoked that friendly head that spent the whole week crisscrossed by an intricate hieroglyphic of tiny braids that linked together and which, on Sundays, after she bathed and put on a clean dress, were transformed into very short, fluffy hair. When María del Carmen sat on the grass on Sunday mornings, without the thousand little braids, her head, seen from a distance, acquired a highly picturesque look. It was like an enormous mushroom that had suddenly popped up in the grass at the foot of the guayabos. And why? Why did María del Carmen's hair fluff up that way when she combed it out loose on Sundays and wore a red ribbon?

As I reached this point in my pleasant ruminations, Miss Pitkin's voice had taken on that aggressive and most disagreeable inflection that a teacher's voice usually acquires when she decides to end a long demonstration with a short question. And just exactly as I was wondering, "Why did María del Carmen's hair fluff out that way?" Miss Pitkin's voice interrupted imperatively, "Let's see, then. If they give me one apple, and then they give me ten, and then a hundred, and then a thousand, how should I write these amounts before I add them together?"

And to facilitate my answer, she handed me a pencil; she also handed me the arithmetic notebook with a piece of scratch paper lying in the middle of it, through her glasses her eyes pinned me down, compelling and terrible as two daggers, and she waited.

I didn't speak for a few seconds, but then, showing evident signs of a keen spirit of observation, great investigative method, logic, experimental genius, originality, and independence of judgment, I said, without touching the notebook or the pencil she was holding out to me, "I think black people's hair curls up because, being in the sun too much, the sun twists it and makes it draw up. Sometimes I've burned a strand of my hair in the Saint Patrick candle, and I saw it twist and coil up like a spring. I'm almost sure of one thing, that if I always went out without a hat, I'd end up with kinky hair too!"

Miss Pitkin, like the great majority of people, had the bad habit of stubbornly judging life from her own point of view. Thus she could not appreciate my investigative talents, and instead of praising them, she unjustly scorned them. She considered my theory of kinky hair in relation to her apples, and naturally she found it so incoherent, so absurd, and so irritating that she opted not even to comment on it. Showing all her disdain in eloquent action, she slammed the arithmetic book shut, she slapped the pencil down on the table, her thin lips, beneath a perspiring fuzz, exhaled noisily, and she said with an English intonation, "Ooooooooooooh!"

Very upset, speechless, she took off her glasses, she took her white batiste handkerchief edged with light blue, she passed it across her closed eyelids two or three times, she wiped the perspiration from her forehead, her mustache, her neck, her chin, and at last, nervously, with the same handkerchief, she began to rub alternately at the twin lenses of her glasses.

As I sat there watching the activity of her fingers on the handkerchief and the glasses, I was puzzled. I wasn't yet familiar enough with the Saxon psychology of Miss Pitkin and I didn't know exactly how to interpret the meaning of her actions. That "Oooooooh!" preceded by her noisy breathing might equally well be a protest against the asphyxiating heat of the day or an outburst of indignation triggered by my neglecting to take the pencil and notebook she had offered me, or perhaps, more probably, it might be a new system of reproving my disobedience in playing with fire, burning strands of my hair in the candle she used to light on Sundays to Saint Patrick, her favorite saint.

However, since this equivocal situation was prolonged, I thought complacently that it must be time to end the class. Miss Pitkin's eyes, bereft of glasses, vague, sad, green, and near-sighted, seemed sad and monotonous to me, and I turned my back and began to look through the wrought iron railing on the balcony at the familiar and pleasant tree, whose leaves, shaking in the breeze, were swaying now in little puffs of wind that were almost imperceptible.

And that was my last class with Miss Pitkin because that night, at dinner time, she made me appear before Papa and after solemnly declaring my incorrigible lack of attention and my disgraceful laziness, she declared her lack of patience or aptitude to correct them and added that, having finished the first part of her contract and having been called to England because of her mother's illness, she had decided to resign her position as my governess.

When Miss Pitkin had finished airing her reasons to Papa, she ceremoniously left the room. I stayed in a corner, close to a table, inhibited, timid, and very frightened, expecting reproofs and reprimands that were sure to come. But Papa, who never fussed at me for anything, was in the habit of expressing out loud, in front of me, all of his personal impressions, without caring whether I understood, approved, or shared them. So, after Miss Pitkin left and the dull clacking of her low heels was lost at the end of the corridor, Papa said, as his only comment, with his eyes fixed on one of the prisms of the lamp, while a vague, mysterious smile seemed to play across his features, "I always thought that Miss Pitkin had an *amant*, but now, I don't know why, I have no doubt, I'd swear she's going away with him to England!"

I didn't know the exact meaning of the word "*amant*," but somehow, it reminded me of the word "*diamant*." Asking nothing, and no longer troubling my head to solve problems, sticking my fingers between the fretwork and moldings of the table, I imagined Miss Pitkin dressed for a trip, with her suitcase in her right hand, and with a gorgeous jewel pinned on her jacket. The jewel, flashing with a rainbow of colors, added to the sparkling of her glasses, enveloped her whole bust in a glorious halo of reflections. Satisfied at seeing her thus, glowing with light, on the way to England, I saluted her departure with a smile of tranquillity and happiness.

But I believe Papa also must have had a lover, and in spite of his goodwill, and his paternal abnegation, my presence, care, education, and tutors were things that continually preoccupied him, hampering his freedom and upsetting his life. Certainly, due to this circumstance, in addition to my stubborn refusal to study, Papa didn't try to replace Miss Pitkin. One morning after breakfast, he called me and told me affectionately, "It hurts me, my dear, for I didn't want to be separated from you, but your ignorance is absolute and it embarrasses me. I feel that I must put you in a school. You can see that you learn nothing with private tutors. I have already spoken to the Mother Superior of the Sacred Heart, and on the first of the month you'll enter as a boarding student."

Really, that news did not distress me. In part, I liked the idea of trying a new way of life. Recreation at the school must be a lot of fun. I had heard other girls tell that at school they played most interesting games called "*la balle oiseau*" and "*la balle empoisonnée*," suggestive names that were engraved in my memory. Moreover, I was very flattered to think that when I drank water or wine at meals, I was going to have a silver goblet, made *ex profeso* for my personal use, with my three initials engraved in the center, under my regulation school number, which, probably, like my name, would have three digits.

Actually, I did become acquainted with the delights of "*la balle oiseau*" and "*la balle empoisonnée*," and I had my silver goblet with my three initials engraved under my school number, because just as Papa had announced, the first day of the following month I entered the convent school of the Dames of the Sacred Heart as a live-in student.

From the time I arrived at the school, the girl with the blue eyes and the black hair absorbed all my attention and kept me from feeling homesick. She sat to the right of the teacher, indicating that the previous semester she had earned the highest grade in composition. A class ribbon and cross adorned her chest and were solemnly conspicuous on the three pleats of her navy blue uniform, which was as clean and crisp as the one that I was wearing for the first time that day. From the neck and cuffs of the dark uniform, her face and hands emerged, all three so white and pale that they seemed to radiate the coldness of marble, and to have the bland inexpressiveness of very white things. As soon as the class started and she stood up and began reciting, her gentle, inexpressive whiteness became radiant with glory in my eyes. Without knowing how, or why, from the depths of her coldness I saw for the first time the dazzling beauty of science—the same science that up until then, voiced by my teachers, had only plunged my spirit into a dark fog of weariness. How could this miracle suddenly take place? I don't know, but the fact is that I was amazed and intimidated as soon as I realized the learning of that white lily, who was the same age and size as I but was also disciplined, sedate, and eloquent. But what truly filled me with wonder was to see such discipline alongside so much wisdom. When a very complicated demonstration of some problem of subtraction with decimals was demanded, or something about the chronological order of the kings of Israel, the teacher would turn to her right and invariably she would say, "Miss Iturbe, please go to the blackboard."

Or, with less ceremony and greater brevity, "To the blackboard, Cristina."

And the snow girl would rise noiselessly. She never stumbled over her bench or her desk, or over the teacher's table. She never dropped her ruler or pencil box, and her books, as wise and quiet as she, lay on the desk top in strict order, lined up by their size, the whiteness of their pages appearing between the navy blue covers, as if they were trying to imitate the superior and discreet personality of their owner. I was all attention, mute and motionless in my chair, my two feet crossed in the air. I didn't know what to admire most, her orderliness, or her knowledge. My wondering eyes went back and forth between the books and the blackboard. Generally it was the blackboard that absorbed my admiration. The white hand had picked up the chalk and had begun to write in very straight lines, with firm, pointed letters or numbers, a thousand things that were profound, incomprehensible, and full of mystery, among which from time to time, there appeared, like a lightning flash, the memory of Miss Pitkin's boring explanations. I can see it. What prestige that hand with the short-cut fingernails held for me! It raced across the blackboard astride the stick of chalk, whose whiteness became one with the whiteness of the hand, and between the two they created from the void a profusion of enigmas in which the mysterious attraction of Science lay hidden!

Strange! Those meaningless enigmas, nonetheless, had a great meaning. Because, while the white hand ran across the blackboard, the four words spoken by Papa flashed into my mind, "Your ignorance embarrasses me," expressive, bright with significance. It was like a neon sign that had suddenly been turned on in the dark. The silent hand, tracing mysteries on the blackboard, was a thousand times more eloquent than all of Papa's eloquence, for he had never managed to illuminate the words "ashamed" and "ignorance." I don't know how this phenomenon happened, but the fact is that the very day I entered school, Papa's negative phrase, which I had considered empty, banal, and to be scorned, "Your ignorance embarrasses me," was full of meaning, and it shone brilliantly beside this corresponding statement that I silently dedicated to the snow girl, "Your wisdom astounds me."

Those two concepts so fired my imagination that, from then on, Cristina, the snow girl, seemed to me the very incarnation of wisdom. I admired her with all my heart, and above all I admired her two blue eyes, in which I saw the graphic representation of science and the wells where the solution to all problems lay. The teacher of our class, coincidentally, had blue eyes, and the Sacred Heart portrait in the study hall also had blue eyes, so that I came to feel a true devotion to blue eyes. I believed in their preponderance, I lived under their influence, and I felt deeply afflicted to think that mine would forever, without hope, be brown. In my first week at school, I would have given a lot of money and many years of my life in exchange for blue eyes. Happily, it was not possible for me to make any transactions in this matter, which, no doubt, would have had a disastrous result on my future.

In view of the fact that I couldn't imitate the snow girl's eyes, I dedicated myself to imitating her in everything else. The day after I met her, I had already sacrificed my fingernails, cutting them very short; I combed my hair straight back, exchanging the black satin ribbon that held it for another made of moiré like the one she tied like a big butterfly on top of her head; when I got to class I stacked my books on the desk in the order of their size, and as she did, while I was reciting my lesson, which consisted of saying by memory the fours and fives of the addition table, I clasped my hands, thumbs locked across them, and held them in front of the buckle of my leather belt.

Thus, bit by bit, imitating the details, I finally imitated everything, and following the form, I reached the essence. After a few months of school all the enigmas had been clarified and all the mysteries dispelled. I, too, sometimes wore the class ribbon and cross on my chest, and I, too, went to the blackboard to make the most difficult demonstrations before the whole class. As they did with Cristina, everyone started consulting me about hard problems, and when I set foot in class, I shared her prestige and superiority. Just as I never envied her, she never rebuked me for having usurped her privileges and prerogatives. We never felt the least rivalry. In our common achievements, the two of us became a single success, and we lived in perfect harmony.

I believe our great harmony was based not so much on a feeling of mutual generosity as on the powerful influence that, from the very beginning, Cristina held over me. I continued imitating her in every way; I always consulted her; I followed her advice; and I firmly shared her opinions. It was a kind of fanatic admiration, the affection of a neophyte for the apostle and of an initiate for the initiator. Perhaps if I had not met her in my class, I would have continued to be as ignorant as I had been until then under the instruction of my tutors. School would have turned into a jail for me, a cavern of desperation, where I would have gone on envying the good fortune of the pavement, the trees, and the lamp posts. But Cristina's influence had redeemed me from ignorance, and I worshipped her as if she were the very light of intelligence.

Besides, Cristina attracted me because she was mysterious, solitary, and unique.

Her father was Spanish; her English mother, whom she did not remember, had died. She always spent the long vacations either with her father, who lived in Madrid, or with an aunt and uncle, who always spent the summers in San Sebastian. But when she came back to school after the vacations she would avoid talking about her family, and she said nothing about her summer entertainment. No one ever came to see her during the school months, and when they ended, when everybody else had already left, poor Cristina, surrounded by her prizes, was left alone for two or three weeks waiting for someone to come from Spain to pick her up.

And although she was very pretty, neat, thoughtful, and orderly, she wasn't vain. She had a monastic disdain of *toilettes*, parties, and worldly amusements, but on the other hand she possessed an overwhelming passion for the theater. She frequently said to me in confidence, "Look, when I grow up, I would stay here as a nun, if it weren't that they, you know, since they never go out, they can't go to the theater!"

Cristina, who had infected me with her love of study, also communicated to me her sovereign disdain for worldly pomp and vanity. I followed her in this as I had followed her in everything else, but, to tell the truth, I followed her without conviction, because, while I left my cheeks unpowdered, wore plain clothes, and put the huge moiré butterfly on my pulled-back hair, at the bottom of my heart, I always felt a nostalgia for mundane vanity! All the aplomb and great prestige the two of us had in class, we immediately lost when we left there, and if, during vacation at a beach or watering place, we ran into elegant and well-dressed people, we were unbelievably awkward and timid. When we initiated a conversation we didn't know what to do with ourselves, what to do with our hands, our feet, our eyes, anything!

I've thought a lot about that bothersome and invincible feeling and now I think that such absurd timidity is a kind of spiritual modesty. Both Cristina and I, upon appearing in public stripped of vanity, were constantly blushing, because, no matter what theologians and moralists may say, vanity clothes us divinely, covering our poor self-esteem, which is chaste and worthy of always being well dressed.

I don't know how Papa would analyze my timidity, but at times, very disheartened, he would just look at me and say, "You finally have learned with the nuns, but you'd think they teach by beating you. You act like a bedraggled chicken, my child!"

By then, Cristina had long ago confided her great mystery to me.

That intimate confidence took place ten or twelve months after I entered the school. I remember that it was a winter afternoon during lunch recess while we were chatting under the elm in the garden as usual. This recess for lunch was the only time conversation was tolerated; it was totally prohibited at any other time. While we ate lunch our hands were busy with the basket that held bread and fruit; we couldn't run or play, and, of course, they had to allow us to talk. For that reason, lunch was the most amusing and interesting recess of all. Cristina and I, who always had vacation plans or class concerns to discuss together, would separate ourselves from the general group, and under the elm that grew at one end of the garden, strictly against the rules, we would always talk Spanish. We felt close in those sweet moments, because we were both of Spanish origin, only children, and both motherless, so that, having lunch, conversing in Castilian, alone and hidden, it seemed that for a brief time, under the shelter of the elm, we orphans were united in the fraternity of our language.

So, one very cold afternoon, speaking Spanish beneath the elm, with our two little baskets on our arms, Cristina opened her silent heart, which until then had been doubly swathed in sadness and mystery. I don't know how the conversation started or how she came to speak of such a confidential matter, but the fact is that between bites of bread and apples, and stopping to throw crumbs to the pigeons that always flocked about at lunchtime to pick up bread at our very feet, Cristina, with the quaint speech of a highly educated little girl, told me her story and her grief. The tale took about three-quarters of an hour, the length of the lunch period.

She began by confessing that her life away from school was a secret ordeal that no one suspected. She had always lived with an uncle, her father's brother, and she now spent her vacations at his house. He was married and had two little girls more or less her own age who were very nice and very pretty. During the winter the family lived in Madrid, and they spent the summers in San Sebastian. Everybody in the family loved her and they were good to her and treated her with affection, but since that was not her house, and the two girls were not her sisters, many strange things happened that worried her and made her sad, although no one knew, or even suspected, how she felt. She had never, ever, spoken of this before, not with her Papa or with the Mothers at school, or with anybody in the world. She was going to tell this for the first time to me alone.

After this prologue, Cristina, assaulted no doubt by her innate English reserve, stopped as if sorry, but then she looked me in the eye and, encouraged by my strong interest, emptied all the crumbs out of her basket for the pigeons and dove into the subject.

"When I was very little and living in Madrid, my two cousins used to go out with the English governess, and a young maid almost always took me out to walk alone. They never took me visiting and no one invited me to the children's parties where my cousins went. But since that had always happened since the three of us were infants, I was used to it, because I'd never seen anything else, you know? Although it seemed strange and it hurt me a little, I explained it to myself, thinking, 'Since they are sisters, they go out together and since I'm just one, I go out alone!' But one day . . . Oh! . . . One day something happened that I'll never forget. Can you believe it, María Eugenia? It's been about two years since it happened and I remember it so clearly and so vividly, as if it were happening right here, at this very moment."

And when she said, "right here," Cristina waved her hand in a circle around us which seemed to take in all of the shadow of the elm. Then she begged me and I solemnly promised to keep the secret eternally. Having taken this precaution, she went on, "It was one evening during Christmas. My two cousins had gone out with the governess, to a Christmas Eve party where they'd been invited. I didn't want to go walking with the maid. I preferred to stay home playing with some new dolls that had been given me. It's true, I always had dolls, and dresses, and sweets, just as now, you see, I have everything I want. Well, it was the same then, they gave me everything they gave my cousins, and sometimes they gave me more and better because my aunt always said that since I didn't have a mother, as the other girls had, it was only right that in compensation I should have all the best . . . Well, that afternoon I was very engrossed in dressing my dolls while my aunt and uncle were talking in the bedroom next to me. Suddenly I heard my name, and listening very hard, I realized that they were discussing me. As the room next door was closed and the rugs and curtains muffled their voices, no matter how close I got to the door I could only hear snatches and phrases here and there. But the little I heard, I heard so well, so clearly, that I'll never forget it! Never! I heard my aunt saying . . ."

Here Cristina's tone of voice changed; she muttered as if trying to imitate some painful, long-ago echo, "It's impossible to go on this way any longer! These conflicts are horrible! I don't have the heart to leave her like some poor Cinderella. When she was younger, it was different. But now, she realizes!"

"Then, María Eugenia, my uncle spoke awhile, but since a man's voice is harder to distinguish, I only caught this bit out of all he said . . ."

Again her voice assumed that tone of a distant echo, saturated with mystery and melancholy, as Cristina repeated the phrases she had heard through the closed door.

"Of course! . . . What do you expect? . . . After all they're right. . . . She's a natural child! . . . We can't force people to accept her if they don't want to . . . Neither can we sacrifice the other two children . . . I'll talk to my brother . . . These are delicate matters that must be arranged at the proper moment."

"And then, María Eugenia, my aunt began to talk again, and she was speaking badly, very badly, of someone. Well, at first I couldn't hear her well, then as she got more excited, you know, her voice began to rise until I heard her very clearly.

"It's a hopeless case! . . . She has no shame; she has no heart; she has no good qualities!"

"When I heard her, I thought it was me she was talking about with such rage. Putting my ear against the frame of the door, I couldn't stop thinking 'My God, what have I done wrong? . . . Why would she say I have no shame and no heart?' But it chanced that when I was straining most to hear, trying to ascertain that, a servant came to announce that visitors had arrived. My aunt and uncle left the room then by the door opposite mine, and they went to the drawing room. But I didn't leave; I didn't move; I stayed right there, sitting on the floor beside the door, with my half-dressed doll in my lap, without even looking at it, and thinking, thinking. Finally, after much thought, I went to hide behind the balcony curtains where no one could see me in case they went by the room, and hidden there, drying my tears on the curtain lining, I started crying. Even though I never cry, that day I cried and cried all afternoon. Don't you see, María Eugenia, I knew the truth now? I knew that I created a horrible conflict for my aunt and uncle; I knew that when I didn't go to parties and out to visit with my cousins, it was because people refused to accept me. And I also knew that my uncle had said that I was a 'natural child.' But what hurt me most of all was that they said I had no shame and no heart. And especially that my aunt, who was always so good to me, had said it . . . And when I was the most desperate, thinking about that, I suddenly stopped crying because it seemed to me that it wasn't about me that my aunt had spoken so badly . . . Now I'm almost certain that it wasn't about me, but . . . You see, María Eugenia? I've always had some doubt about that, because if it wasn't about me, then who could it have been?"

Very intrigued, for the first time taking an active part in the conversation, without knowing what to reply, I answered her question by repeating it.

"That's true . . . Who could it have been about then?"

"Well," Cristina continued, "do you know how everything was finally arranged? The next morning, hidden where my teacher couldn't see it, instead of studying my lesson, I wrote a letter to my Papa. I wrote very poorly then; my handwriting was bad, I made ink blots, and I made many spelling mistakes. It was laughable! I ran words together, I used capital letters . . . once in awhile! . . . But even so, as well as I could, I wrote to Papa to tell him myself, before my uncle told him, that I wanted to go off to a school abroad, because I didn't like Madrid any longer, or the English girl who taught me, or my aunt and uncle's house. That they were all very good, but that I was tired of being with them so much, and since he had said several times that when I was older I'd go off to school, well . . . I preferred to do it now! Shortly after the letter was sent, my Papa, who had been away, came to Madrid, and talked to my aunt and uncle. They fitted me out with school clothes, we came to Paris and since then I've been at the Sacred Heart. Well, I like it here, don't you see? . . . But away from here, during vacations, you can't imagine what I go through. When Papa takes me with him to Madrid, although I'm very bored because I stay alone all day with the maid, I can stand being bored and I'm happy. But it often happens that Papa has to travel almost all summer. He doesn't want to take me on so many trains and staying in hotels, and then, since I can't bring myself to tell him what I overheard, he doesn't know anything, so he leaves me to spend the summers with my aunt and uncle in San Sebastian. Well, my aunt and uncle are always kind, of course. You can't imagine! They give me presents, and there, in San Sebastian, they do let me go out walking with my cousins and the governess. But just the same, in spite of their kindness and gifts, for me, being in their house is like walking on hot coals. It's torture! Do you understand? Because, no matter what I do, I can't forget what they said that Christmas afternoon. That's the way I am. When things offend me, I don't forget them. I remember them all. You see, it's been two years, and I remember it as if it were happening now. Just as if it were happening now."

And repeating "the same, the same," Cristina's voice gradually faded away to a low, soft murmur. There was a long pause, filled by throwing crumbs and watching pigeons hop about the ground. Because I had listened with such immense interest to all the details of the story, but now that it was ended conclusively, I still didn't know what to say. Cristina waited a moment, then seeing that I was volunteering nothing, she decided to condense her doubts into a single question, and raising her cold, blue eyes to mine, and fixing on my eyes an imperious gaze, she said, "Do you, María Eugenia, know what it means to be a natural child?"

Like her, I knew that being a natural child was unusual. I even suspected it might be something bad and disgraceful, but not knowing for sure, and not wanting to wound her in any way, in the face of her commanding inquiry, I feigned great perplexity; I shrugged my shoulders; I pursed my lips, and I answered hypocritically, "Natural . . . natural . . . well, natural is what is right! You say 'it's natural' or 'naturally' to say that something is as it should be. Look, you and I are natural, since we don't have anything wrong with us. But poor Jeanne Meric isn't natural because she's cross-eyed and awfully ugly."

I thought Cristina was going to reply sharply as she often does when I make glaring mistakes in my lessons. "You're speaking without thinking, María Eugenia. Concentrate, for Heaven's sake, and you'll see that what you're saying is nonsense." But she didn't. This time the nonsense was not challenged. Cristina, like the great majority of mortals, despising logic, decided to have faith in order to hold on to hope, and she answered with conviction, "That's exactly what I think! I've looked the word 'natural' up in several dictionaries, and they say more or less what you said." She was quiet a second and then added, sighing, "I've done everything I could to find out for sure. One day, some time ago, before you came here, I was reading a history book, and I found a sentence that said, 'The battle of Lepanto against the Turks was won by don Juan of Austria, the natural son of Charles V.' Taking advantage of this opportunity, as soon as I had walked into class and put my books on my desk, I asked the teacher why don Juan of Austria was the natural son of Charles V. But the teacher answered that there was no reason to concern myself about don Juan of Austria, who is a part of modern history, when I should pay attention to Bible history, which is the history to study for seventh period. And, of course, I didn't find out."

"Oh!" I broke in, "It's a pity don Juan of Austria wasn't the natural son of Solomon, for example. Then, I wonder what Madame Destemps would have said! She'd have been obliged to explain it!"

But this time, hearing such an anachronistic supposition, Cristina protested, shocked, "Really! That's atrocious! Solomon's son! If don Juan of Austria had been Solomon's son, María Eugenia, he would have had a biblical name, and he wouldn't have won a battle against the Turks, but rather against the Moabites, the Philistines, or the Assyrians, who were the enemies of the kingdom of Israel."

As usual, I fell silent respectfully, as I recognized her great erudition, and Cristina, after a short silence, decided to return to her problem, and she said thoughtfully, "Of course! 'Natural,' 'naturally,' 'it's natural,' 'it's unnatural!' I think you must be right about that." But suddenly she shook her head, and said to herself, "But why did my uncle say it with so much scorn that afternoon?" She was quiet again, and finally, turning to me, she said decisively, "Listen, María Eugenia, so we can know for sure, let's do something. I don't want to ask, just because I don't. But you, as if it were your own idea, could ask your papa, without mentioning me. How about it? You could bring up don Juan of Austria or whatever occurs to you, then ask him, and when you know and you thoroughly understand, no matter what it is, you'll tell me, won't you?"

As always, I obediently replied without hesitation, "Fine!"

Since at that instant the bell rang announcing the end of recess, Cristina and I, so they wouldn't notice our breach of the rules, began to run, without another word, toward the general group.

A few moments later, standing in formation and in dead silence, she insisted again whispering and making signs, "Do you promise me?"

"I promise you!"

"Do you swear, María Eugenia?"

"I swear, Cristina!"

"I see two young ladies who are still talking after the bell has rung for silence!" declared the stern voice of the proctor from the draped folds of her wimple. With irony, she added, "You must have something very important to say to each other!"

It was then, under the reign of absolute silence, while I was walking in a very straight line toward the study hall, looking at the big moiré bow on Cristina's head, as I walked three places behind her, that I quixotically resolved to right all the wrongs of that poor, sad, and silent life.

❧   ❧   ❧

As a matter of fact, the following Sunday, no sooner had Papa come to see me than I asked him to agree with Mr. Iturbe, whom we had already met, to let us spend the summers together. That way Cristina would stay with us when her father was traveling and it would no longer be necessary to leave her with the aunt and uncle in San Sebastian, with whom she didn't feel comfortable. Papa, who took a great interest in Cristina, my best friend, assured me that everything would be arranged properly and that, as I wished, we'd spend summers and vacations together. Once I had achieved my main objective, following Cristina's pointers, I spoke of different topics, and it was only a good while later that I made the agreed inquiry, which I phrased in this way: "Tell me, Papa, what, from his father and from his mother, is a natural son?"

Papa, in a quite complex explanation full of pauses and unknown words, explained to me the abnormal situation that natural children occupy in life and in society, since their parents, not being married, generally don't transmit to them either their name or their fortune.

But Papa's explanation was a real hieroglyphic to me. It seemed to me nonsense that people could have children without getting married first; and to condemn these rare children to be eternally nameless and disinherited, besides seeming like nonsense, also seemed unjust and wrong. I was deeply worried as a result of this. I told myself that there was no doubt about the matter, that Cristina, my beloved friend, my model, my nymph Egeria, belonged to a completely abnormal type of being. I must resign myself. I had to accept the truth and I must also take courage in order to notify the interested party, because I had sworn and promised to do so a few days ago.

Again, under the shade of the elm, with our lunch baskets and a white semicircle of pigeons at our feet, Cristina and I celebrated a second conference, during which I transmitted word for word the entire explanation Papa had given me on his Sunday visit.

Cristina listened to me with the same attention she gave in class to the explanations of the teacher. Then, she put the nail tip of her index finger against her white teeth, she stared at the ground, and she spent several seconds without blinking, an attitude that in her case showed the height of concentration.

"Then . . . then . . . it's just what I thought. It's true! My mother isn't dead. She's not dead at all! My mother is alive! She was the one my aunt was speaking of so badly. It was she . . . the one who didn't have a heart . . ."

With this discovery, with this abrupt resurrection of her mother, Cristina's eyes, which had been wide open, blue and immense, looking at me, fixed themselves again on the ground, gazed up in the clouds to follow the flight of a pigeon, swept over the whole landscape, and finally, peacefully, came to rest on a branch of the elm, staring, and so blue, so blue.

Like Jesus, in the presence of Mary and Martha, I had just raised a beloved being from the world of the dead. I, who had performed this miracle, full of curiosity, looked at those two blue eyes, and, as always, they were so inexpressive that I was unable to read in them whether they were happy or sad at seeing the revival of the dead woman, who, as she rose from her sepulchre, was crippled and deformed, because she had no shame and she had no heart.

When Cristina abandoned her meditative attitude, her only comment was, "And be careful not to tell this to your Papa, or to Madame Destemps, or to anyone! You can only talk to me about this!"

From then on, that secret was the center of our conversations and a tie that bound us ever more closely with the great attraction of the mysterious. Cristina worked ceaselessly searching her memory for facts, and then she would tell me the results of her investigations. According to her, her a priori judgment was evidently right. The dead woman had not died! Nevertheless, she remained a sphinx in our eyes, an impenetrable mystery. We knew she was English. Cristina had inherited her blue eyes, her snow-white skin, her reserve, and her spirit of independence. But where was that Englishwoman? What was her story? Why would they have said she was dead? And upon this veil of mystery we wove all kinds of golden, shining legends, in which Cristina's prestige grew as if in a tale of enchantment and magic.

Finally, one morning, on vacation at Biarritz, after having talked at length with a certain Spanish lady who had known the Iturbes well in Madrid, I went running to the garden bench where Cristina was absorbed in reading a book of short stories. Trembling, excited, I gave her the news, "I know now, Cristina, I know! I know! I know! Your Mama is an opera star! Your Mama sings divinely in the theater! Your Mama is beautiful!

Your Mama has many diamonds, she has gorgeous dresses, and she has tiaras like a queen. Luisa, the Spanish girl staying at the hotel across from ours, has seen her. She says that she adopted an Italian stage name that she doesn't recall, and that when she finishes singing anything, they applaud her deliriously!"

An opera star! Oh! Dazzling reality beyond all our fantasies! An opera star! And while my lips announced the good news, Cristina, sitting silently before me on the green garden bench, with her book of stories in her lap, seemed to me to have bluer blood than all the blonde princesses of the ruling houses of Europe.

But, much to my surprise, she didn't seem to share my frenzy or to take pride in her background. As she listened to me she gently closed her book and she only answered dreamily, thoughtfully, with the monosyllable, "Yes?"

I remember that in the blue sky of her eyes I saw something like a cloud of disillusionment and melancholy.

Then days, months, years went by, and Cristina and I separated, without ever, ever, learning the name of that probable star of lyric art. With her phobia about asking anything of the people who knew everything, we never learned anything concrete. However, she had a constant obsession to see the face of that anonymous and glorious Mama. It didn't matter if it was only from a distance, amid a fog of conjecture, without even identifying her!

Her love of the theater was born of that vehement desire. I shared it enthusiastically. The two of us made a sort of fanatical religion of that love and of the secret. From then on, ignoring everything else, our only objective was to attend the opera. We knew the names of all the famous singers, and when we were on vacation, holding hands as we walked down the street, we would stop a long time before the big posters with red letters that announced the program and cast of the performances. We never missed a single matinée, and if some famous soprano was much applauded, Cristina would lose all her phlegmatic English reserve, become as enthused as I, and clap boisterously with outstretched hands, in accordance with a system we had discovered for making the most noise. And when the applause ended, under the conductor's baton the poetic charm was renewed. There on stage, the pale soprano, idealized by success, opened her mouth, stretched out her arms as if she were about to take wing on her lyrical voice, while, leaning back in my velvet seat, I would blow on my burning hands, red from so much clapping, and beside me, Cristina, motionless in her seat, with her eyes fixed on the idealized figure, and her face aglow with the divine expression of glory, would comment, smiling in total ecstasy, "Suppose she were this one!"

Many years later, when Papa died and, finally, in Biarritz one morning, the two of us parted forever, the great mystery of our infancy was now an anguished and transcendental mystery that seemed to bury Cristina's whole life under its weight. Life! What did either she or I know of life then?

In my long story I haven't mentioned yet that Mr. Iturbe was a very rich industrialist. Naturally, Cristina, pretty, distinguished, individual, like an exotic and late-blooming flower, in the fertile warmth of wealth, must have burst into life, as buds open, and as it happened to me too a few months ago, there in Paris, in the warmth of my last twenty thousand francs . . . Cristina is no longer the same little girl who infected me with timidity and misanthropy. No! I read that in her letter! I am certain that, thanks to money, one day, in Paris, in Madrid, in San Sebastian, or wherever it was, she, too, suddenly, miraculously, without knowing why, burst into joyous blossom. In that way, in the full summer of optimism, she learned to dress, she learned to smile, she learned to swoon with happiness before her mirror, she learned to see mirrors in everyone's eyes, she learned at last to be aware of herself, and then, drunk with the divine intoxication of being pretty, she became intoxicated afterwards with the other divine drunkenness of love. Yes, I'm sure. How must it have happened? What voice awoke her? And what has she done today with the tormenting mystery of her infancy?

By now she must be married.

Cristina, the sad child of the past, today is immensely happy, because she is surrounded by beauty, luxury, and love. She is loved and happy, she is pretty, wealthy, a countess. She lives her dream of love in a charming hotel on a beach facing the sea and she parades her happiness through the windows of a luxurious limousine. By now she has become reconciled with her enemy, the world. She will no longer scorn the wonderful *toilettes* of the great designers. She will no longer feel the emptiness hidden in the vanity of social affairs. Dressed in furs and jewels, distinguished, reserved, she moves through the world seeing everything with the blue, cold eyes of an English aristocrat.

How destinies change, and how many mysteries are held in the secret future! Oh! My luck, my life, how different, how dark and sad it will be perhaps, compared to the brilliant existence of Cristina de Iturbe!

But, as I said a little while ago, seeing the rain that fell on the cracked earth, neither do I feel envy now seeing Cristina's torrential joy. I don't feel resentment, nor hatred, nor anything. I want to flower humbly in the holy grace of resignation! These tears that now pour from my eyes, against my will, fall from time to time on the ink; they turn the letters into little red fountains that run across the whiteness of the paper. I don't weep from spite, no. My tears are the gentle dew of my momentary night of sorrow. Tomorrow they will dissipate when the sun of hope rises again. Because I will keep hoping. Yes! In the fiery furnace of my anxiety I will always await my love, with the same miraculous and fertile faith as the three captive youths of the Song of Daniel!

Now, under the acacia tree, dark, perfumed night has crept into my room. For many hours, leaning over my desk, I've been feverishly relating the story of my friendship with Cristina—a story no one will ever read, and a story I did not need to write for myself because it is already written in my memory.

On the bare table, I have turned on my lamp and the light has dressed the table with a big red circle. My hands and the white paper on which I am writing are tinted by the color of the light. Through the open window, moths and insects from the fields come in to greet the bright flame, they dance at their party, and they kiss my poor tired, thirsty hands, which, like two pious pilgrims, are weary from trudging so long across the past. Cristina's letter, the theme of my long dissertation, lies outside the light, in the zone of shadow. Not wishing to touch it again, I look at it with pain and distrust. I mustn't touch it anymore! It doesn't hold anything but old matters, dark illusions, withered feelings that I should not keep among my memories, like sad, dried flowers. I must let them die in the open air! That's why, tomorrow, very early, when I wake up, I'll take the gray sheet, I'll tear it into little pieces, and from my window I'll let the trembling band of torn bits fly into the field. Ashes of my childhood, sick turtledoves, withered petals of my first roses—let them fly above the branches, let them twist in the sun, let them close the little blind eyes of their brief words, and let them die at last, embracing the only eternal affection—the blessed, hospitable affection of our Mother earth!

CHAPTER VII

Supremum Vale!

 For many days I've been waiting for it, this horrible news, and yet, when I heard it, I experienced the strange shock of a vibrant and perennial pain, always new and always sharp. It is plastered on my heart, and it hurts me so much, so very much, that I would like to die at once or I'd like my soul to die in my body, so that it at least could rest in the unconsciousness of idiocy or madness. My pride is the only pillar that sustains me. Sometimes I bless it for being great and strong, and other times I reproach it for insatiably monopolizing all the strength of my body and spirit. At night it leaves me drained. For hours on end I may lie in the hammock without undressing, still and quiet, my eyes open, blurred with tears, staring at the beams on the ceiling.

Thanks to my pride, no one in this house knows of my terrible inner turmoil. When I heard the news, my pride rose, controlled my emotions, and controlled my body until I was able to reach the privacy of my room. Here I cried . . . cried . . . cried, with these deep, infinite tears that seem to wash away pieces of my life and steaming clots of my blood.

It was yesterday, at lunchtime, that I found out.

And naturally, as could be expected, it was María Antonia who told me the news. She has the habit of reading the newspapers around eleven o'clock, but as a refinement of cruelty, in spite of having seen me all morning long, she waited for lunch so she could tell me at the table, in front of everyone, where I couldn't run away without confessing my humiliation and pain. There she thrust home this poisoned dagger that tortures me night and day, without truce, ceaselessly, like the slow agony of those sentenced to the torture of dripping water.

"In the paper today they announced the engagement of Gabriel Olmedo to María Monasterios. It was celebrated yesterday with a formal dinner followed by a dance, at that luxurious country house the Monasterios have just built . . . I'm sure the dance was magnificent, because the house, surrounded by gardens, is a perfect setting, and Monasterios knows how to do things! Apparently they're getting married next month. She will be a beautiful bride because she is really pretty, adorable . . . She's what I call a pretty girl, not like others, so thin that they look like dressed-up strands of wire!"

In spite of the dreadful shock, I recall that I spent the first second after the initial impact of the news verifying how exact my predictions were. I knew it would be María Antonia who would tell me about it, I knew she would tell me at the table, and I knew finally that the news would be followed by a little eulogy concerning the beauty and physical attributes of María Monasterios. My prophetic insight was very useful at that instant, because being fully conscious of things, my pride was prepared beforehand. My pride was instantly alert, and, heroic and strong, it drank my tears, and with its iron fingers it held all the muscles of my body, even the slightest contractions of my face, which remained impassive.

I remember that as soon as I heard the first phrases, while María Antonia was still talking, I picked up my glass of water from the table and drank every drop, thinking, "I'm drinking the poison of these words that kill me." Then I fixed my eyes on the crystal pitcher full of red wine and I thought, "This is like the blood that is dripping from my heart now, but like the pitcher, I'll hold it inside myself, and no one will see its stain spilled anywhere. No one will ever see it!" And I finished lunch unconscious, deaf and mute, lost in my desolation, with no other positive force except the force of my pride, which possessed me wholly, as if it came from some exterior and unknown influence.

Afterwards I cried. I have cried a lot, a great deal in two days. Now I know the voluptuous excess of grief, of this horrible grief that is made of jealousy, humiliation, and the definitive farewell of death!

And as if my troubles were not enough, another still has come to add to their immensity.

Oh! Yesterday was the blackest day of my life!

About four in the afternoon, when I was shut in my room, alone and abandoned to the depths of my despair, they came to tell me that Mercedes was on the phone.

When I heard the news, I washed my eyes, which were red from crying, and I went running to answer Mercedes.

Her voice, slow and rhythmic as a caress, spoke to me of things foreign to my grief, and, although I said nothing to her either, from the first moment, we felt a sympathetic current of emotion because we both knew that the other knew. She expressed her regret in the gentleness of her voice, and after expressing thus her great sympathy, while I was experiencing an earthquake of tears in my whole being, she went on in the same caressing voice, "Listen, María Eugenia, I've called you especially today because I want to tell you some news and let you in on a plan. And I warn you right now that I won't take no for an answer! Next month I sail for Europe. It's definite. Alberto has been named consul in Burdeos, but since he has affairs to conduct in Paris, I will settle permanently in Paris, while he will divide his time between the consulate and business. He has great expectations for that business. He expects to earn a lot of money. Well, you know him . . . but I have become so skeptical that I don't believe in anything, at all."

Here she paused and her voice continued, more gentle, more tender, more maternal.

"Well, this is not just a courtesy offer that I am going to make you. No. It's a deep desire that I want to see fulfilled. I'm going to ask a favor of you, *ma mignonne!* Alberto, as well as I, want you to go with us to Europe, and to stay at our house as if you were our daughter, as long as you wish, whether it is a few months, a year, two years, however long you wish! In view of the relationship and closeness of my family with the Alonso family, this proposal that I'm making is very natural. I loved your father Antonio as if he were my brother, and I look upon you the same as if you were my daughter. Eugenia couldn't object to your staying in my home for awhile. She knows what an interest I take in you! You'll spend a few happy, carefree months. You'll be such company for me, my dearest! I'll take care of you and you'll have a wonderful, wonderful time, you'll see! There with me you'll soon forget *tous ces petits embêtements* that make you so sad now!"

She told me all this bit by bit, in a musical tone and with exquisite delicacy. Her voice, which seemed to implore some favor, in reality, was full of infinite compassion. I felt it vibrate in the most sensitive regions of my heart, but, given the circumstances, her kindness only increased my pain. With my voice trembling, choked by tears, I answered, "Oh! Mercedes, this is all I needed! For you to leave me too! Imagine how much I want to go with you! But I think it's useless even to propose it, and right now I can tell you, don't count on me!''

But Mercedes insisted, and without any hope at all, certain ahead of time of the humiliation of refusal, I offered to speak to Grandmother.

I did it yesterday. Grandmother listened to me affectionately, and with pity she gave me an evasive reply. She gave me to understand that, even though in principle it seemed unacceptable to her, she would nonetheless consider Mercedes's offer calmly.

"Yes. She's going to consult with Uncle Eduardo." I thought. "Tomorrow the definite refusal will come."

But she spoke to me last night. Her previous compassion erased, with the strength of spirit and the unity of feelings that come from a clear conviction of duty, Grandmother delivered a long sermon full of advice in which she showed me the absolute impossibility of accepting Mercedes's invitation. Alberto was a man without a shred of respectability. Mercedes herself had very liberal ideas, a wrong concept of life. I was very impressionable. A child my age was as delicate as glass that is easily stained and easily broken. She could not in any way accept such madness. It was against her principles, against her duty as a mother.

That part about "delicate glass" gave me to understand that in the deliberations about the plan, not only Uncle Eduardo, but also María Antonia, had taken part. Not only is she greatly addicted to that metaphor, she also enjoys respect in Grandmother's eyes in these matters that touch on honor or morals. "María Antonia has very good judgment," Grandmother often says on such occasions, "and that's why I always like to know her opinion."

But my grief is so great that all this phantasmagoria about a trip with Mercedes has passed through my spirit without even making an impression. It was like a mirage that shone for a second before my eyes, which refused to look at it. Through the mirage, from the first, my eyes have only seen the frightful emptiness that Mercedes will leave in my life. And seeing only emptiness constantly, I exclaim through my tears, "When I leave the consoling peace of the country, and I return to Caracas, hurt, humiliated, and without a hope, without the merciful affection of Mercedes, what is to become of me, my God!''

There are times, lying in the hammock, watching the tremulous company of my acacia, when I review in my mind all the events in my life. I remember the dark predictions that a certain famous psychic read in my hand one time in Biarritz. I finally acquire the fearful certainty that my fate is a calamitous fate, and then I think sadly how fortunate it would have been if this body of mine, so pretty and so wretched, had never been born. Wrapped in my black silk kimono, longing for death, I rise from the hammock, and I go to look at myself in the elongated oval of the mirror. I stand there a long time, sunk in the painful pleasure of contemplating my face, so fine, with such pure lines, so harmonious, so sad. So sad, and so lost for the object of its yearning! Yet, there before the mirror, suddenly daring and pagan, I grasp the edges of the kimono and stretch out my arms and the open kimono becomes the wings of a bat stretched out behind the pure miracle of my body. Then, dazzled and happy, I look in my eyes, and my eyes and I smile at each other, full of satisfaction, because we understand that, in spite of all the suffering and all the humiliation, it is I who will triumph forever in this tournament of love before Gabriel. I tell myself that his bride, that María Monasterios, will never compare with me in Gabriel's taste, that he finds me beautiful, divine, because he told me that himself, and I have seen it, and Mercedes, who knows so much about these things, has assured me it's true. So, in front of the mirror, smiling at my beauty, with the delicious sense of my superiority, I temporarily forget my hell of jealousy, I laugh aloud with scornful laughter as I think about the trivial figure of that María Monasterios. I despise Gabriel, who was not able to create an independent and brilliant life for himself without sacrificing the exquisite pleasure I would have been for him, and then, thinking of all the years of youth that lie before me, my hope flowers again, and I tell myself that Gabriel is only one form of the multiple and eternal forms of the divine wine of love that will celebrate the festival of my youth.

Wrapped again in my kimono, and wrapped in the happy conviction of my beauty, I return to the hammock, and rocking, like that first day when I felt crushed by the spectacle of my absolute poverty, I begin to think again, and again I wonder with anxiety and fear what great and terrible thing is this love that always awaits us, and stalks us everywhere with open claws.

Oh! Love! Love! Why ask the swaying of the hammock? I have already felt it! It is this subterranean and silent tragedy that everyone treats with indifference, as one might ignore the macabre torment of someone buried alive. Why deceive myself? I have experienced it! It is a live coal, always sizzling and glowing; it is this painful burn that makes me feel the awful agony of the flesh, and makes me think with anxiety and infinite nostalgia about the sweet silence of the void!

Toward the Port of Aulis

After long months of deep sleep, one morning, from the depths of a wardrobe, lying among ribbons, lace, and old fabric, María Eugenia Alonso's literary verbosity has suddenly awakened. Here it is still rubbing its eyes.

 About two years ago, I was in the habit of writing my impressions. But that habit only lasted a few months, because at a certain moment, without knowing why, I found it stupid, ridiculous, and very boring. I told myself that it was nonsense to write things to oneself, and just like that, one day when I was feeling energetic, I took the written sheets, I made a big package of them, I wrapped it in a newspaper, and after tying it with a white silk ribbon I hid it in the false bottom of my wardrobe where no one could ever find it.

Yesterday, since I was feeling energetic again, I decided to thoroughly rearrange my wardrobe. I spent a long time untangling lace and folding ribbons, I set to one side all the dresses I'm not wearing any longer, and I divided them into piles to give to the maids, and when I was quite surrounded by boxes, ribbons, handkerchiefs, and old clothes, it occurred to me to open the bottom of the wardrobe. I caught a glimpse of the package buried two years ago with its white ribbon, I took it, I opened it, and here and there, at random I started to read the scribbled sheets.

They held my attention so much that I instantly left my work of liquidation and partitioning. I put things back in the same place I'd just taken them from, I took up the autobiographical package, and holding it in my hands, I installed myself as usual facing the orange trees outside the window and, sitting in my little armchair, I began to read.

To tell the truth, that reading gave me a pleasant surprise, so much so that, after reading the first pages, I immediately resolved to renew my forgotten narrative of impressions. For this purpose I am at my desk early today, my pen at the ready, and in a very loquacious mood.

I now think I was judging myself too harshly when I found the custom of writing my impressions ridiculous. To right that wrong, I wish to declare solemnly that the scribbled sheets that were at the bottom of my mirrored wardrobe are not ridiculous. On the contrary, they hold great psychological interest for me. As for the literary form, it has many flaws that I have noted, besides numerous others that I have not noted. It seems flaws belonging to this second category swarm by the millions, hidden before the very eyes of an author, which is why writers, who are very honest about their convictions, are in the habit of considering most delightful all the works that come from their pen. For the same reason, with no less honesty, they are in the habit of condemning as imbeciles and cretins all readers who do not judge their works delightful.

Since I am at one and the same time the author and the only reader of my works I enjoy the immense satisfaction of admiring my literary talent without having any reason to complain about human idiocy, nor to describe my fellow man with insulting words, which, as well as being disagreeable and irritating, is hardly Christian. I believe that if all authors did as I do, they would spare themselves numerous upsets. But as I see it, prudence and foresight do not abound in the writers' guild.

Reading the sheets written and buried two years ago took a large part of the morning and the whole afternoon yesterday. Considered from the literary viewpoint, from my very false perspective as the author, I have found them superior to the chronicles, stories, and prose poems with which many newspapers and magazines are given to embellishing their pages. This is not much praise for my work, nor am I being blatantly immodest, because the majority of the stories, poems, and narratives I am referring to, with apologies to their authors, usually seem pretty bad to me.

This is my sincere opinion concerning the literary form of my old, resuscitated pages. Now, considered psychologically, I repeat that they have been very useful to me, since, thanks to reading them, I have been able to verify the immense progress I have accomplished on the steep and arduous path of virtue. Naturally, such a discovery, besides satisfying me greatly, will now serve as encouragement and spur me to advance further along that steep, arduous path.

Yes! The moral and material progress I have made in these last two years is immense.

Foremost, I should declare that I have completely lost the anarchic, disoriented, and chaotic way of thinking that, as Grandmother quite rightly used to say, constituted a threat and a horrible danger to my future. As a result, or as palpable proof that I have lost such a wrong standard of judgment, is the fact that I no longer paint my lips with *Rouge éclatant de Guerlain*. Instead I paint them with *Rouge vif de Saint-Ange*, whose tone is much softer than that of *Rouge éclatant de Guerlain*. I never sit on a table, but always, always in rocking chairs, on sofas, chairs, or tabourets, depending on the circumstances. It never occurs to me to hum and much less yet to whistle naughty songs, which are indecencies more fitting for café entertainment, unworthy of being intoned by the lips of a young lady. Likewise I very carefully avoid every kind of interjection, even those that seem quite innocent such as the French expression: "sapristi!" and the Castilian ones: "canastos!" "caray!" and "caramba!", for I am convinced that basically they are nothing but hypocritical synonyms for other words that are worse. I never go to the corral to chat with Gregoria while I stretch out on Uncle Enrique's old trunk. Instead I talk to her standing up, for only as long as absolutely necessary to give some order relative to the washing, and this, generally, takes place in the kitchen or second patio. I don't read novels whose heroines have lovers, a word that, by the way, I don't mention nor even deign to hear, except when María Antonia pronounces it between two proper names, duly scandalized because she has discovered or guessed it in real life.

Such an enumeration would suffice by itself to give me an approximate idea of my progress toward a better character, were it not that I have just noticed that this enumeration is formed only of virtues or conditions that we could call "negative" and that I need to add the list of my new "positive" conditions or virtues in order to show how these two past years, although it is true that on the one hand they have been very restrictive, it is no less certain on the other hand that they have also been highly fruitful and profitable.

Yes. In these two years I have learned a great many things.

I have learned to embroider and to sew admirably by hand as well as on the Singer sewing machine; I know three kinds of drawnwork; I know how to make very difficult desserts like chipolata, moka, and gâteau d'Alsace on its platter with caramel syrup and all; at night I water the ferns in the corridor, and they have grown very green and thick; I count the clothes every Monday when I give them to Gregoria for the laundry, and I count them again every Saturday when I receive them clean and ironed; I mas-

sage Grandmother with Elliman's Embrocation when her knees hurt her;
I know how to give injections; I say the rosary with Aunt Clara; and I have
a sweetheart.

Of all the progress and changes in my life, the sweetheart is the most
recent and it's only because of that I have placed it at the end of the list.
Had it not been for that circumstance I would have put it at the head of
my list because I believe that having a sweetheart is an event of great importance for me. Meditating on the subject calmly, I observe that the importance of such an event is not only related to my present life, but that it
will perhaps have a great influence on the future life of coming generations, since a sweetheart leads to marriage, marriage to children, children
to grandchildren and great-grandchildren, a long descent, which can multiply infinitely, infiltrate everywhere and thus notably affect the destiny of
the world. This idea based on geometric progression fills me with satisfaction, because it awakens in me a feeling of my importance as a human
entity, it tells me that I perhaps will be the trunk of a complicated coales-
cence of genealogical branches, and it lets me know that long before my
birth, I was already an indispensable and indestructible link in the very
long human chain whose origin is lost in the darkness of prehistory, according to what some people say, and, according to others, like Aunt
Clara, it isn't lost at all, but shines as bright and clear as the richest brooch
in a golden chain, there, beneath the jungles of Earthly Paradise, in the
Virgilian, patriarchal, and fertile love of Adam and Eve.

But I have just realized that I am philosophizing, and since I don't want
to waste my intelligence saying profound things that no one will ever read,
here I halt as far as philosophy goes and I move ahead to relate to the best
of my ability how and when this great event of the sweetheart happened
to me.

Here is my account.

One day, about five or six months ago, Grandmother, Aunt Clara, and
I found ourselves sitting around the table, and as usual the three of us were
eating lunch in silence. Except that I, just to have something to do and say,
was fanning myself with my napkin from time to time and exclaiming,
"How hot it is!"

Because, although I didn't feel at all hot, it was August and it didn't
seem appropriate to say, for example, "How cold it is!"

María del Carmen, the servant who in earlier times was my favorite
childhood friend because of her undeniable elegance in the art of playing
with dirt, today possesses, under the skillful guidance of Aunt Clara, an
equally undeniable elegance in the art of serving at table. This same María

del Carmen passed a platter on which lay a piece of beef with steamed potatoes. Aunt Clara and I served ourselves and we began very deliberately to cut and eat our respective slices of roast beef. Grandmother, who because of her arthritis is not allowed any red meat, was not eating. She was waiting, with her hands clasped above her empty plate, for Aunt Clara and me to finish our meat, and meanwhile her eyes were observing me very fixedly and obstinately. Suddenly she said, "It seems to me, María Eugenia, my dear, that you have lost a lot of weight lately. You have circles under your eyes and you look pale. I think you should take Robin's Syrup of Glycerusphosphates, Scott's Emulsion, or some other tonic."

There was a long pause, during which the pieces of meat kept traveling from my plate to my mouth, while Grandmother, with her hands folded, continued to observe me as fixedly and as obstinately as before. After looking at me for quite a while to her complete satisfaction, doubtlessly inspired by the same theme, she spoke again and she said, "It's been two years since Antonio died. Today is exactly a week after the mass celebrating the second year of his death . . . how time passes, Lord!"

Here Grandmother sighed. There was a pause permeated by all the sentimentality of the sigh and then she spoke again. "Clara, I don't understand why the windows haven't been opened yet. I want María Eugenia to have some amusement. She needs some fun, to see people and to have friends. Everything has its alloted time! Youth should be enjoyed! It's perfectly lawful and natural! It's time now for María Eugenia to stop wearing black and to sit in the window."

That very afternoon, Aunt Clara, after saying the rosary, told María del Carmen to carefully dust the inside and outside of the two barred windows in the living room and to get down from the top shelf of the linen closet the little rug and the two cushions that are used to lean your elbows on when you are in the window.

And it was about five-fifteen when, for the first time, Aunt Clara and I, very dressed up and with our hair carefully arranged, just as if we were going visiting, sat down facing each other in the two window seats on the right side of the living room. Our four knees were so close that they seemed to silently kiss each other in a mute ritual. Grandmother installed herself near me in her wicker chair and Chispita, Aunt Clara's woolly dog, extremely satisfied finally to be able to renew customs of long ago, which, during the lapse of these past years, must sparkle brilliantly in the monotony of her virginal existence, Miss Chispita, as I was saying, leapt to the window, stretched herself out on the little rug, stuck her little black muzzle through two bars of the grating, and, scorning the noise of the street, gave herself over to her daydreams, rolling up her eyes voluptuously.

And that was how I was solidly established in the practice of that lawful principle enunciated by Grandmother at the table during lunch: "Youth should be enjoyed!"

Until that historic moment of my life I had never "sat" in the window and I was completely ignorant of its psychology. Of course, I was quite used to seeing, through the open windows on both sides of the street, ever so many feminine busts, with heads more or less interesting or trivial, more or less ugly or pretty, more or less indifferent or curious, which, as I went through the city, would watch me go by, following me with their gaze through the bars. And it was true that I had sometimes sat at the windows at Uncle Eduardo's house together with my cousin. But in reality, until that afternoon, I had not experienced the exact sensation and the true sense of that phrase, symbol of joy, "to sit in the window."

Now I remember that at first it seemed somewhat ridiculous to me. It seemed to me that we four, that is, Grandmother, Aunt Clara, Chispita, and I, had adopted, for that species of inaugural ceremony, immobile and solemn attitudes that were horribly false. Faced with such a sensation of falsity I judged myself ridiculous; as a consequence of that ridiculousness I began by being bored, I went on to a feeling of irritation, and I ended by violently missing my afternoons spent alone in my room with my embroidery and my books.

Nevertheless, in spite of being so bored and nervous, at last, unconsciously, I started to enjoy myself. My attention little by little had been meshing with the details of my surroundings and, imperceptibly, once focused on them, it led me down the path of observations. First I noted that as the time approached for the *paseo*, the number of automobiles was increasing until cars filled the whole street with noise and movement. When the bustle was at its height, unexpectedly, from the bottom of my soul the following philosophical exclamation suddenly burst out:

"Oh! The sad fate of those condemned to watch life pass by, seated thus in the guise of a humble spectator! Oh, dear heaven! It would be better to be one of those gray tires, tied by four straps to the back of the cars, which race joyously through the world!"

That desperate hypothesis made me leap up, stung by my impotence. And since it happened that at that very instant the end of the cream-colored silk curtain that adorns the window was caught and wrinkled like a handkerchief between the palm and the fingers of my distraught left hand, as I leapt up, goaded by my sense of impotence, the entire curtain shook. Seeing the commotion, Aunt Clara said, "Sit still, María Eugenia. You're going to tear that curtain."

And she and Grandmother renewed the inexhaustible and terribly interesting comments which had been gushing from their respective mouths for half an hour about the pedestrians, vehicles, and passengers.

Grandmother observed, "I see, Clara, that many fewer people go by on foot than did awhile back. How strange!"

"There's nothing strange about it, it's very natural," answered Aunt Clara. And she explained: "Look, from five o'clock to five-thirty all the people who are going to the movies pass by. Afterwards, the street is empty until seven-thirty, which is when they go by again on their way back."

"Aaah!" said Grandmother, as she grasped the phenomenon. Then she added, "It's amazing how a taste for the movies has spread in Caracas! And they tell me that, in the majority, those films are highly immoral. I think as Eduardo does: the movies and American dances are killing off wholesome customs here and throughout the whole world!"

Meanwhile, I was observing something not at all trivial nor to be despised. And that was that everybody, absolutely all the people who passed by, with very rare exceptions, regardless of whether they were men or women, old or young, walking or in a car or coach, when they saw our window they would stare at me, giving evident signs of curiosity and admiration. This experience began by arousing my interest and finally by flattering me extremely, so much in fact that, in view of the general insistence, I resolved to get up and go to see for myself in front of the living room mirror if that unanimous assertion by the public was true. Standing before the mirror, in the twilight, I studied myself carefully for a good while, and to tell the truth, I found myself so pretty with my white Chinese crêpe dress, my slender bare arms, and my garnet necklace lying against the snowy white of my throat, that I stayed there a long time arranging the two blond, silky curls of hair that clung neatly to each side of my temples. But Aunt Clara's voice at last awoke me from my happy and lively self-absorption, as she called from her place by the window, without turning her head and with her eyes riveted on the street, "Since you're up, María Eugenia, turn on the lights."

I went to the living room door, turned the light switch, the room lit up gaily, and I sat down again in my empty spot facing Aunt Clara, smiling with great satisfaction, telling myself that after all it was a true crime to have let two years go by depriving the pedestrians of the pleasure of admiring my beauty, and depriving my beauty of the immense pleasure of feeling the unanimous admiration of the pedestrians.

And having once made such a judgment, far from being bored, I started enjoying myself greatly. I found that seated like this, in the lighted room, at the window wide open to the bustling street, my person acquired a notable likeness to those luxury items that are exhibited at night in store windows to tempt shoppers. In this case Grandmother was the shopkeeper, Aunt Clara, one of the clerks, and like me, Chispita also was for *réclame* in the showcase. This idea became so fixed in my mind that finally I put it into words. "Yes. I am actually a fine, expensive object for sale in the fair of life."

And since the simile, in the broad sense, was very true, and since moreover I find it tremendously amusing to enter in my imagination into any thing, animal, or person outside myself, I endowed the metaphor with life, and imagining jewels, brocades, and every kind of precious object, I, immobile in my window seat as the people streamed past, began to announce in a very low voice: "I am for sale! . . . Who will buy me? . . . Who will buy me? . . . Who will buy me? . . . I am for sale! . . . Who will buy me? . . . Who will buy me? . . . Who will buy me?"

But Grandmother, who despite her seventy-eight years still has very keen hearing, suddenly interrupted my refrain when she asked impatiently, "What are you saying to yourself, María Eugenia?"

As my only answer I raised my voice and went on chanting my refrain in the same rhythmic style. "I am for sale! . . . Who will buy me? . . . Who will buy me? . . . Who will buy me? . . . I am for sale! . . . Who will?"

"Well, you're talking nonsense! Yes, something very improper that a young lady should never say even jokingly, and much less here in the window where people can hear you and misinterpret! If someone passing by should make an insulting remark you would deserve it and you couldn't complain!"

Grandmother said this very angrily. Then she waited for a few minutes and added in a much gentler voice, "I don't know; I don't know, María Eugenia, my child, when you will learn the importance of watching what you say."

I didn't repeat the refrain in question anymore, but I remember that mentally I kept saying it that afternoon and all the following afternoons as I sat down again in the window, alone, between Aunt Clara and Chispita, because Grandmother, who has a fear of the drafts and the dust from the street, did not keep us company anymore in our habitual afternoon diversion.

It happened, then, that one rainy afternoon when few people were going by due to the bad weather, suddenly the majesty of a Packard automobile invaded the deserted street. The Packard, which was painted red and occupied by a single passenger, would come "Pssssssssssss!" raising a fine subtle mist of water on the drenched asphalt. I distractedly watched it race away, but Aunt Clara who had seen it from the front, turned her head to the left, following it with her eyes between the bars on the window and said, "What a magnificent automobile! It belongs to Dr. César Leal. And he must have just bought it because, just look! It's brand, brand new. Before, César Leal had a coach, not a car. But, apparently, now, everybody prefers to have a car."

After a little while, "Pssssssssss!"

Spraying water the same automobile invaded the street again. Aunt Clara repeated, "César Leal's automobile! . . . He's gone by twice. He must be in love with some girl on this street!"

But this time I had noticed the car, and I had noticed also that its owner, the aforementioned César Leal, as he went by us, reclining on the soft cushions of a chocolate-colored seat, had looked at me with an insistence and with a more intense expression than that usually employed by the majority of my anonymous admirers. Given this circumstance, I instantly thought with great certainty and conviction: "Aunt Clara is right and there is no doubt that girl is me."

But I remember that I expressed just the opposite, because I replied, "I don't think that he is in love with anybody. There are times, Aunt Clara, when circumstances force us to go back and forth down the same street without wanting to. Not only not wanting to, but without the least intention of doing so. Besides, remember that a little way from here there's a service station and cars pass our house on the way to buy gasoline."

However, Dr. Leal's automobile kept on: Pssssss! . . . Up and down, and we only stopped seeing him when it grew dark and we had to close the window because it was time for dinner. I remember very well that every time he had gone past Aunt Clara had repeated her very accurate opinion: "He must be in love with some girl on this street."

And then while the auto sped away zigzagging easily between all the obstacles in its path, as she watched him losing himself in the distance, Aunt Clara, with her head turned completely to the left would add this or some other comment of the same type: "Oh! . . . he's a very good catch! . . . Quite a philanderer, very slippery, certainly. He has already jilted several sweethearts, but he's magnificent in every sense. Oh! The girl who manages to marry him will be getting a real prize."

As for me, I didn't say a word, except that as I heard, "Psssssssssssssss!" I understood that his driving back and forth was all dedicated to me, so for the sake of graciousness, manners, gratitude, etc., I would gaze vaguely toward the chocolate-covered seat and I would smile slightly, very slightly, with an imperceptible smile, which, being more gracious than timid, was more timid than gracious, and which being completely involuntary was at the same time completely voluntary, with just a dash . . . well, to sum it up in a few words, when I heard a Psssssss! I would smile instantly in a way that is very easy to do and very difficult to explain.

But speaking frankly, in spite of the immense success of my smile, which flashed off and on with each up and down, up and down of the resplendent Packard, somewhere in the depths of myself, I was smiling without conviction, since I firmly believed that neither César Leal nor his automobile at all deserved such an exquisite smile. I thought the car was gaudy, the colors were ugly, it was far too ornate, and the chauffeur was ridiculously dressed. As for the owner he seemed to me too fat, too dark-complexioned, too old, too indifferent as he stretched out on the chocolate cushions, too . . . But, heavens! I feel it is inopportune, and moreover I feel it is completely useless now to list the first impressions produced on me by César Leal, since the first impression produced on us by anyone we've not dealt with yet has no importance whatever and clinging to said first impression is not rational nor possible, except when it has to do with inanimate objects that one is going to buy, such as, for example, shoes, colored stockings, evening dresses, depending on their cut, and, above all, hats! To be sure, the first impression of a hat is faithful and extremely important, because it almost never, ever deceives us . . .

But on the other hand, our first impression when dealing with a person should never be taken into account and much less still if between us and the person in question a very delicate net of love has been stretched—a divine and luminous net in whose trap the unknown, the unforeseen, discoveries and surprises by the thousands are tangled.

Not a month had passed since the afternoon that I have just mentioned, when one morning, going from my room to the dining room to get a glass of water, I heard Grandmother's voice, very solemn, far away in her oasis there in the entrance hall, and she was talking about me. Then, immediately, on tiptoe, cutting through the rooms, I reached the door of the little sitting room that is next to the entrance hall and, once there, I realized that Grandmother was holding a family council attended by Aunt Clara,

Uncle Eduardo, and Uncle Pancho, and that I was the person under discussion. Although I know perfectly well that eavesdropping is a very ugly thing, and absolutely reprehensible as far as good manners are concerned, I always practice it whenever I have the chance because I consider it one of the very few ways that truth can ever show itself to us in all its gleaming splendor without circumlocutions or reticence of any kind, and above all without having that aspect of insult that it always acquires whenever it is heard face to face, whether as advice or in any other form.

Having settled the principle of eavesdropping, it is not then cynicism, nor have I any reason to be ashamed of confessing, that no sooner had I arrived at the little sitting room and heard the first snatches of the conference, instead of leaving, no, I quietly dragged one of the armchairs to a place next to the door so I could escape easily in case circumstances demanded it, and afterwards I sat down, leaning my head on the back of the chair, and dedicated myself to listening in a comfortable and relaxed posture.

For the moment, it was Grandmother who had the floor and in the midst of general silence she was saying, "No one, no one, in my opinion, is good enough for her! It's not because she's my granddaughter, but she's very superior, yes, far superior to all the rest! Of course, Eduardo, when I say that, I'm not referring to Cecilia Margarita, who is also a delightful young lady. I'm talking about the majority of those insipid and spoiled girls who, as you yourself say, are found everywhere nowadays." And she repeated, "It's not because she's my granddaughter, but she's far superior to all the rest."

"Well, I think exactly the same thing!" said Uncle Pancho's voice. "And because I firmly believe that, it seems crazy to me for María Eugenia to get married right now, without having seen anything of the world. First let her get out of these four walls! Yes, let her dance, laugh, have some diversion, and after she has had enough fun, then let her get married if she wants to!"

"What do you know! They're talking about a marriage for me!" I thought, preening myself and putting my feet up on a nearby chair in order to be more comfortable still. "And I'll bet Uncle Eduardo is the defense attorney for my matrimony."

"Women, Pancho, should take advantage of a chance when it is offered to them," I heard, and sure enough it was Uncle Eduardo's nasal voice, which, besides being nasal was also hoarse because of a cold. "Be aware that in Caracas there are few eligible bachelors, and it's quite probable that later on María Eugenia would not again find what she has found now."

"Well, then, it would be fine if she doesn't marry now or later! She doesn't need to get married at all!"

I recall that this solution of Uncle Pancho's sounded ominous to my ears, so much so that I heartily approved Grandmother's voice when it began to say, "No, Pancho, no, I don't think that way at all! María Eugenia is the soul and all the joy of this house; the day she goes away will leave a terrible and immense emptiness for us, but I'm not selfish and although I'm not one to push marriage, I feel as Eduardo does: María Eugenia needs a husband. She needs one because of her situation and she needs one because of her character. She's too pretty and at the same time too free in her ideas; alone, she might perhaps make a bad use of her liberty. Yes, that excessive independence, that impressionable character, that disdain for everything that represents authority are very, very dangerous things! It's true that lately she is much chastened, but even so, I think that it's indispensable for her to have a strong will to guide her, or, rather, to dominate her and to educate her for life. Oh, no! I couldn't die in peace if I were leaving María Eugenia alone without any support in the world!"

If Uncle Pancho's phrase had sounded bad to me, Grandmother's words filled me with indignation, and if I hadn't been hidden in the little sitting room, I would have responded very haughtily, saying that my education had ended more than three years ago, that I was quite well satisfied with it, that I judged the educational period the most disagreeable epoch in existence, and that if now I were to accept a husband, it was in no way so that he might continue insisting on the tedious theme of my education, but rather so that I might deal with matters I deemed much newer and more diverting. But fortunately, I wasn't visible, and this happy circumstance saved me a serious quarrel which would have ended in the well-known and lengthy rosary of advice that I now know by heart.

And while I was indignantly protesting to myself against Grandmother's words, Uncle Pancho, who was still locked in his antimatrimonial theme, didn't even dream of fighting that horrid project of future and eternal education, for he said, "Eugenia, frankly what seems selfish to me is for you, just for your own peace of mind, to perhaps sacrifice María Eugenia by marrying her off right now."

"And just where do you get the idea that I'm marrying her off?" said Grandmother then, a great deal more indignant than I, and with a voice that demonstrated the height of excitement. "To hear you talk, Pancho, anyone would say that I am a woman without a conscience who wants to get rid of her granddaughter at any cost and forces her to accept the first man who comes along! What an insult, Pancho! Quite the opposite. When

I know already and all too well that the day María Eugenia marries will be a day of sorrow, truly a day of mourning for me."

"Yes," for the first time Aunt Clara joined in, "Mother will miss María Eugenia immensely the day she leaves her side, and as for me, besides missing her, I'll be deprived of her assistance, because she helps me a lot in running the house. Why, for over a year she has taken care of the laundry by herself!"

"But Good Lord!" Uncle Eduardo whined again, "it's not a question of marriage yet! We don't know if they'll reach an understanding with each other when they become acquainted! We don't even know what María Eugenia thinks about the matter!"

"Oh! It's very hard, or rather, it's impossible for anyone to know what María Eugenia thinks," objected Aunt Clara's voice, "because she's so changeable that today she'll tell you green and tomorrow she'll tell you red. I think she has a hard time knowing herself what she wants. But just the same, it seems to me she likes César Leal. Yes, I'd swear she likes him!"

"Well, I don't think she likes him," said Uncle Pancho. "I'd bet anything she doesn't like him! What's happening is that, shut up in these four walls where you have her, she's lost her critical sense, she's disoriented, she doesn't possess any notion of better or worse, because she lacks points of comparison. María Eugenia's taste is in a state of anarchy. I greatly fear it might occur to her to marry César Leal, that she will repent afterwards, and end up being terribly unhappy."

"Well, I want you to know," Grandmother continued saying with the same degree of angry indignation, "I want you to know that, as for me, I haven't influenced nor will I ever influence her directly to accept this suitor, or even a king if one should appear. I still haven't told her one word about the matter, do you hear me, Pancho? Not one word! I want to leave her completely free to choose. But it's a far cry from this position to my being totally opposed and closing the doors of my house to an honorable young man, who has good qualities, who has acted properly, and who is madly in love with María Eugenia! Don't you agree, Eduardo?"

"Yes, a far cry!" answered Uncle Eduardo, his hoarse voice echoing, and given my distance from him, it seemed rather onomatopoeic, as if really a cry rising from the bottom of an abyss. But after a short pause during which he coughed obstreperously, he said in a much clearer voice, "If César Leal had presented himself as a suitor of my daughter, in the same proper manner that he has presented himself here, I would have received him with open arms. Naturally, I say 'in the same proper manner in which he has presented himself here' because it's true that basically Leal is one of those men who, though averse to marriage, likes to have a good time, and he has already jilted several girl friends, but on the other hand, never, ever, in any of his previous love affairs had he employed the respectful and correct manner that he has this time. As he himself assured me, this is the first time that he has fallen in love seriously, and as I have already said, I have come here, commissioned by him to announce 'that he is firmly resolved to marry María Eugenia whenever she accepts him, and whatever day and hour we may set.' I think that an honorable man cannot offer a better guarantee!"

"Ohhhhhhhh!" I breathed, swept away by emotion and with my mouth open upon listening to such unheard-of news.

"Naturally under any other circumstances I would not receive him!" exclaimed Grandmother at the same time, severe and very solemn, cutting off Uncle Eduardo's speech. "Oh, certainly! Otherwise I would never expose myself, nor would I expose María Eugenia, to allowing a man, no matter who, to enter my home just to walk out later, leaving me and her in the lurch!"

Aunt Clara, with a deep tinge of melancholy, as if some sad memory were surging in her voice, said, "Don't deceive yourself, Mama. Men who have been inconstant Don Juan Tenorios, no matter how good they may be, are never safe fiancés! But after all, Leal had to have some flaw, and inconstancy is his!"

"What?" asked Uncle Pancho, "the flaw of offering scant probability of getting married? Come now, Clara, in my opinion that flaw is his best quality, the most brilliant of all his characteristics, and the only guarantee of happiness that he can offer María Eugenia!"

But Uncle Eduardo, who was wrapped up in his role as head of the family, provider of news, and ambassador of such a great event, without heed to Uncle Pancho's final words, undertook anew his interrupted speech. "From all other points of view, there is no doubt that Leal is an unbeatable young man, and therefore in Caracas to what more could a father or a mother aspire? He has good manners, is very correct, very intelligent, highly cultivated, he has no vices, he is a Doctor of Jurisprudence, a Senator of the Republic, the head of a ministry, his financial position is very good, he belongs to a respected family, he has been a good son, he is a good brother. What fault can you find with him, Pancho?"

"Well, I find that besides being boastful, boring, and a bad writer, he has that horrible defect of 'qualities.' See here, Eduardo, if, instead of enumerating only a few, you had had the patience to enumerate all of César

Leal's qualities, you would unwittingly have composed a sort of grand litany like the one they chant during Holy Week."

Doubtless spurred by an association of ideas, Aunt Clara's voice instantly said, "He's very generous! A few weeks ago he gave a magnificent gift for laying the tiles in the Chapel of Christ in the cathedral. And I'm also almost, almost sure he was among the eight who were carrying the pallium in the Holy Thursday procession last year."

"Even without knowing him I've found him extremely appealing ever since I learned that he is a good son," Grandmother began to say quite calmly now. "And they've told me too that he takes very good care of his two sisters. He doesn't let them go out alone, he doesn't take them out to clubs, nor does he permit them to dance the terribly indecent dances that are the current rage. Oh! Men who are good sons and good brothers are always, always very good husbands!"

Uncle Pancho said, "I know both of César Leal's sisters. They are tall, skinny, dark-complexioned girls with pimply faces. It's quite possible that his not taking them to the club dances is because of how ugly they would look in evening dresses. Anyway, hiding unpresentable relatives is a quality like any other because it shows he is good-hearted and loves his family."

Grandmother, without listening to Uncle Pancho at all, had followed the thread of her own thoughts undisturbed and now she was saying, " . . . There's not much to choose from in Caracas, and every day it's harder to find a man without vices. What a shame that the Leals don't belong to our own circle, I mean . . . to our own social group!"

And here there was a very brief pause, during which Grandmother must have given one of her deep sighs, which under the circumstances didn't reach my ears, but which my imagination immediately supplied. After the pause, Grandmother's voice took on a sweet tone well suited to evoking memories and began to say slowly, "Leal . . . Leal . . . these Leals were not around in my day! It seems to me I've heard the name, but like . . . really second-rate . . . no, they're a long way from first-class . . . But it's true, too, that things have changed today!"

Here there was another pause that corresponded to another sigh and she added, "Oh, it's not because she's my granddaughter, but she deserves so much, so much!"

Since I'm so susceptible to praise, this opinion repeated now for the second time decidedly went to my head, and still lying back in the armchair, with my feet crossed on the chair opposite, I said to myself, mimicking the biblical expression, that, in truth, this César Leal was unworthy even to untie my shoelaces. And naturally, once I had expressed this judgment, I decided that during the conference, Uncle Pancho had shown himself a true wise man, except of course when he uttered that stupid opinion: "let her not marry now, or marry later, let her not get married!" I meditated a second on the aforementioned opinion, and suddenly, it annoyed me so much that I stopped paying attention to the conversation, and as if Uncle Pancho were present, and just in case the same words were repeated in front of me, to carefully prepare what I would answer, I rebuked him in my imagination saying, "'Let her not get married'! . . . sure . . . that's right! . . . 'let her not get married' . . . of course! . . . because it's not you, Uncle Pancho! I'd like to see you in my place to see if you'd say the same thing! . . . Do you think the life I'm living is a lot of fun? . . . hmm? . . . Do you think I'm going to renounce marriage just like that, just because you say so, when the idea of getting married is absolutely the only thing on my mind, and the only aim toward which all my acts are directed at the present? Tell me, do you think it would be pretty for me to spend my whole life as elegant and as happy as Aunt Clara is now, with Chispita, her ferns, and her rosary? . . . You think so? . . . Fine, I won't marry César Leal now, but it's because, as Grandmother says, he doesn't seem good enough for me, and because I have the certainty that I can find someone a great deal better later on! . . . Of course, if it weren't for that I'd get married right now. Yes, now, now, now, twenty thousand times over I'd marry César Leal!"

But in the hall, Uncle Eduardo's voice, which was now intoning a solo full of solemnity, because he was voicing the final consensus of the conference, came to tear me brusquely from my soliloquy as I heard him say with the peremptory precision of fact: "Then, Mama, I'll let him know that there is no objection and that you will receive him tonight at nine o'clock. As he himself has told me, he already knows Clara and María Eugenia because a friend introduced them the other evening while they were in the window. He is charmed by Clara, and mad, absolutely mad about María Eugenia. I believe if she accepts him she'll make a very good marriage. I hope she'll come to a decision and accept him!"

"I hope!" repeated Aunt Clara, and she again said: "But it's so hard to figure out what María Eugenia thinks! She's so capricious!"

"I am going to talk to her," said Grandmother. "But of course, I don't plan to influence her one whit either in favor of or against Leal."

"Well, as for me, since I think he's wrong for her, when I talk to her I'll influence her against him all I can," said Uncle Pancho's voice with perfect tranquillity.

"Very well, that's your affair, Pancho!" answered Grandmother angrily and as if reminding Uncle Pancho of the weight of responsibility he was taking on.

And as far as I can recall now, in that memorable conference, nothing else worthy of mention was said about the matter, for now, once the final agreement had been reached, the four members of the board began to talk of other affairs. But the last words exchanged about my coming decision left me behind the door, sunk in a sea of perplexity. Gazing at the tips of my shoes, which were no longer entwined on the seat, but were now on the back of the chair opposite, almost at the level of my head, I started thinking that the world was organized in a very stupid and very disagreeable way since a pretty woman could not smile from her window whenever and however she wished without there immediately following such a flurry of discussions, conferences, and introductions . . . Oh! above all, suddenly facing me with such a momentous and immediate decision, like that of the traveler to whom a thief says, "your money or your life," was what seemed to me the most horrible and vexing. But finally, after reflecting, to save myself from so great a perplexity, I resolved positively that even if Aunt Clara should repeat a thousand and one times that "today she says green and tomorrow she says red" I, in spite of having smiled daily at César Leal for twenty consecutive days, would under no circumstances marry him, among other reasons because I didn't like the way he sat in the automobile, because he wouldn't let me dance the foxtrot, and he wouldn't let me go out alone, and because those two ugly sisters Uncle Pancho had talked about wouldn't suit me either, since some future day, married to him, I might have a daughter, who instead of looking like me might look like her aunts, an irreversible disaster, which probably would leave me forever inconsolable. And having once made this firm resolve, I took a deep breath of satisfaction and, lowering my feet from the chair and getting up from the armchair, I disdainfully abandoned the sitting room and the banal conversation that droned on in the entrance hall.

An hour later, Grandmother, just as she had announced during the conference, called me and, in effect, brought me up to date on the visit and intentions of César Leal. Naturally, I listened to her as if it were all news to me, and just to give myself airs, I made up my mind to adopt the mysterious attitude of the sphinx. Thus, I listened to the news impassively and in complete silence. When Grandmother had finished talking, as my only answer I said laconically, "Very well."

And I left.

But it happened that during the afternoon, when I was in my room deeply engrossed in one of those English novels that are set in high society, suddenly, just as if it were an act of magic, María del Carmen, the maid, appeared at my half-opened door carrying an enormous bouquet made up of white roses and orchids.

"They brought it from Dr. César Leal!" said María del Carmen, delighted to announce such a great event to me. And my room was filled with an exquisite fragrance, quite in harmony with the atmosphere of the English novel.

The sight of the flowers surprised me deliciously, and filled me with the liveliest satisfaction and joy, but since behind the flowers, besides María del Carmen, Aunt Clara was coming in, too, melting with praise about the whiteness of the roses and the delicate tint of the orchids, I rose from my chair and, taking the bouquet in my hands, I chose to place it disdainfully in the big jug, saying at the same time with a certain severity, "They're very pretty, but I'll put them in vases later because now I'm very busy. I'm reading!"

"How rude you are, María Eugenia!" commented Aunt Clara, "such pretty flowers! Mama says she's never seen such a wide variety of orchids at this time of year!"

But as soon as Aunt Clara and María del Carmen left, I closed my bedroom doors and, gathering all the containers and vases I could find, I filled them with water and began to arrange the flowers in languid and dreamy attitudes. There were flowers for the desk, for the bedside table, for the window, for the dressing table, and for the bench. They stood out very delicately next to the snowy white of my embroidered curtain, they swooned gently from the high whatnots, and they were reflected and multiplied a thousand, thousand times, as I was, in the infinite repetitions of the three folding mirrors of my dresser. And gazing at my handiwork, and breathing the air, with my nose alive to the sweet scent, I was in ecstasy for a long time.

Oh! My room wasn't my room, but rather an enchanted dwelling from a novel where the most subtle and delicious perfume floated. I remembered the Oriental boudoir of Mercedes Galindo, always full of flowers, which had captivated me so in an earlier time, and to imitate her, I put on my cream lace *déshabillé*, I arranged the golden wisps of my hair in front of the mirror, I perfumed my neck and arms with Nirvana by Bichara, and, after polishing my nails, I again took up the English novel and stretched out on my bed to continue the interesting reading interrupted by the visit of such agreeable guests.

But I didn't manage to read at all. The book, my place marked and held half-open by the index finger of my right hand, lay indolently, immobile, and mute like my whole body on the sky blue satin of the eiderdown, while I admired the shades of the flowers and voluptuously breathed that tenuous and complicated perfume made up of roses, orchids, and Nirvana by Bichara, and I told myself that after all it must be very pleasant to have an enamored suitor who would send flowers almost every day. Gently intoxicated by such a subtle perfume, for a long time, I let myself fly on its wings down the delicious meanderings and pathless ways of a thousand delicate fantasies. And if I say nothing now of such sweet fantasies it's because they all dealt with very imprecise matters that it would be arduous and very difficult for me to try to manifest in words. But as I seem to remember, I believe they were influenced by the lords and ladies, parks and lakes, castles, dances, and hunts described in the English novel that, under the pressure of my hand, still lay inert on the sky blue silk of the eiderdown.

After having wandered at my will and pleasure in the labyrinths of such tranquil digressions I returned at last to reality and began to think about César Leal and about his visit tonight. I told myself that in spite of my firm resolution, within the bounds of a reserved and negative attitude, I should be agreeable, since he had offered me such lovely flowers, and since Uncle Eduardo said he was so enchanted by me, something that after all recommended him as a man of refinement and good taste. Then, I began to think also, that in general, it was nonsense to allow myself to be led too much by Uncle Pancho's criteria, for, as Grandmother rightly says, he has never shown either good judgment or common sense in directing his own life. Besides, it was very logical that from now on, I should distrust his opinion, considering that he found it perfectly natural to condemn me to never marrying and to vegetating eternally alone, poor, slighted, and dying of boredom, as Aunt Clara was vegetating.

Once these philosophical considerations were made, I went on to decide what dress I would wear tonight to receive my guest, and how to make a better impression than I had made up to then behind the crosses and balusters of the window grating, which may rather favor one, since they enclose the bust in a very Oriental and suggestive prison-like atmosphere. I decided first to dress in a dark color to emphasize as much as possible the general harmony of my figure, but then I thought that in the small space of a drawing room it's very difficult to call attention to your figure, and that it is a great deal more important to work out the color harmony in relation to your skin, eyes, and hair. Then unequivocally I resolved to put on my pink charmeuse dress, for in my opinion pink is my true color, even if Aunt Clara, who has no eye for color and who is obsessed by paintings of the Immaculate Virgin and the Virgin of Lourdes, is of the opinion that blue is my best color. Keeping in mind the matter of color harmony, I told myself that if I had dressed in black, without any doubt whatever, I would have worn two big "snow queen" roses at my waist, but since I was wearing the charmeuse outfit, instead of the two "snow queens," two orchids would look much more becoming . . . yes! definitely, two orchids pinned gracefully at the waist of my charmeuse outfit would look like two great butterflies opening their wings above a rose. And in anticipation I felt enthusiastic, already foreseeing the delightful effect that my Greek bust would make as it rose classically and airily amid such delicate tones.

But since I measure and reflect carefully on even the most insignificant of my acts, even though Grandmother may spend her life saying the contrary, I immediately thought that if I pinned two of the orchids sent that afternoon at my waist, this might appear to be proof of acceptance, something not on my program and absolutely at odds with my definitive resolution. And then, as an evident demonstration that I consider all my actions carefully, I made up my mind to wear my rose charmeuse, without pinning any kind of flowers at my waist.

&   &   &

When the clock struck nine-fifteen that historic night I was still in front of my mirror, gazing at my exquisite self, which, in accordance with my earlier plan, was enveloped in a simple and delicate pink charmeuse gown. Suddenly seeing myself up close in the mirror, I found something insipid about my image. I was pondering some way to paint slight circles under my eyes that would give me some character, without at the same time letting Grandmother notice them, when María del Carmen's head appeared in the open window, repeating this message for the second time, "Miss Clara sent me to say that the visitor arrived over fifteen minutes ago, and that it's ugly to make people wait for you so long."

I glanced at the clock on my desk, and, while with great concentration passing near my eyes the tip of a Faber number 2 pencil, which painted quite well because it was a little blunt, I said to myself, "It's strange how little sense of time Aunt Clara has! It's only been six and a half minutes since I heard César Leal come in and she calls that 'fifteen minutes'! Never mind, even if she and Grandmother send me two thousand more messages, I'll make him wait for me at least, at the very least, ten minutes. That is the indispensable minimum to pique the interest of the person waiting, and that way prepare for the success of the one who arrives!"

And now, the circles lightly penciled in, just to kill time, but only to kill time, I took from the imitation Sèvres vase in my window two May orchids, I brought them up and held them with my hand at the waistline of my charmeuse dress, and I looked in the mirror to better appreciate how the delicate tones matched and harmonized. For a few seconds I was absorbed contemplating the two orchids, which against my rosy bust stretched out their two butterfly wings, ethereal, trembling, capricious. And since they looked so fine, with such fine, delicate color, I reached my hand out to my dresser, I picked up a long corsage pin, and taking great care that the two flowers not move one bit from the position they had adopted, I pinned the stems with the long pin, and then I secured the leaves with several small pins, while I was saying to myself, "Come now! . . . why shouldn't I wear them? Oh! No, no, these obstacles that get in the way of color harmony or any other important detail of the *toilette* are very irritating and it seems best never to take them into consideration if I aspire to be well dressed. Anyway . . . does César Leal have a monopoly on May orchids, or are the flowers he gives marked with some initial or monogram? . . . Psss! I might very well have acquired these flowers on my own account, and in that case I would certainly have worn them, even if he, who is so boastful, as Uncle Pancho says, had sent me baskets, cars, and wagons full of orchids!"

And since once I'd pinned the two flowers to my waist, the three-and-a-half minutes needed for the prescribed ten-minute minimum had gone by, with an agile step, elastic and elegant, leaving in my wake a lovely scent of Nirvana by Bichara and exhibiting the attitude of importance and sternness that every distinguished woman should adopt when she plans to scorn a suitor, I headed for the drawing room.

But . . . oh! It's terrible, terrible, the amount of tense expectation that can develop among four people, in the small space of a living room and in the brief space of ten minutes! Never, ever would I have believed it. But it's true. It's terrible! There are psychological moments when the attention of people who are waiting begins to develop, and it grows, and grows, it becomes big, enormous, immense, until finally it is a monster that throws itself upon the one who arrives and devours him.

I found that out when, my face bright with a charming prepared smile, I appeared at the door of the living room. A single glance was enough for me to understand that the environment had already devoured me.

Oh! It was frightfully solemn.

Grandmother, sitting on the sofa, was wearing her black velvet dress with the Brussels lace collar, something that happens very rarely, and to indicate even greater respect for the occasion, she had taken from her jewelry box her tortoiseshell lorgnette, which, as she saw me arrive, immediately was lifted to her eyes and balanced on her nose like a comet escorted by its tail, which was the habitual gold chain, and she began to look at me, her eyes brilliant, luminous, and sparkling with critical spirit. In an armchair beside Grandmother, and facing the front door, imposing and imperial, in a tuxedo with ruby buttons on the shirt, a gardenia in his buttonhole, perfumed and with a beautiful solitaire on the little finger of his right hand, was César Leal. As he saw me enter, he automatically stood up, and I found him so arrogant and so formal that it seemed to me as if suddenly, by some magic art, a very luxuriant tree, loaded with branches, leaves, fruit, and everything, had sprung from the floor. As for Aunt Clara, she had decided to wear her navy blue dress, which like Grandmother's velvet doesn't come into play save on certain grand occasions, and her eyes, without a lorgnette, paid no attention to the whole of my appearance, but fixed themselves sharply and tenaciously on the orchids at my waist. Facing them, Uncle Eduardo, who, like César Leal, had leapt to his feet when he saw me, judged it very distinguished and fitting under the circumstances to come to meet me, and while he, full of paternal gallantry, was crossing the room, I remember that I, over his head, cast a glance through the open window and I saw, through the grating, the resplendent Packard, which, illuminated by the streetlight, was gleaming brightly with copper, glass, nickel, and varnish, gloriously exhibiting at the front end of the motor a bronze eagle, proud and haughty, with its two wings open.

I repeat that it was terrible, and since, besides being terrible, it was also unexpected, I felt that at that point all my elegant disdain, my elegant severity, and my elegant importance were dissolving in that atmosphere of solemnity as a lump of sugar dissolves in water. Overwhelmed, feeling that I was the center of such a great ceremony, led by Uncle Eduardo's hand, I advanced bashful and nervous, I said good evening, blushing furiously, and, with the humble docility of a prisoner, I sat down on the sofa next to Grandmother, not daring to cross my legs, my hands clasped like a school-girl, and indignant with myself for my cowardly and imbecilic attitude.

And so it was that at once, thanks to these mysteries that sometimes float in the atmosphere, I was changed from ruler to subject, from victor to conquered, and from jailer to prisoner. Properly speaking, I must say that in my inner being an absolute inversion of behavior took place, subconsciously and with the dazzling rapidity of lightning.

But since I want to paint even more clearly the psychic phenomenon whose cause intrigues me night and day, the above definition is certainly not sufficient, and following the Oriental system and the evangelical system, I am going to try to describe the abnormality of my case, using a parable or a metaphor.

I have sketched what happened here.

Let us suppose that we have been transferred to the fantastic world of Perrault, and that I, at the moment when I appear at the doors of the living room, understand the attitude of the people present, and I breathe the atmosphere of expectation that surrounds them, at that moment, I say, instead of being María Eugenia Alonso, I am not María Eugenia Alonso, but rather an enchanted princess, yes, the proud and pearly white daughter of a king, who, dressed in brocade, pearls, and ermine, comes to be installed on her ivory throne to witness the parade of princes from distant lands who aspire to the glory of winning her hand. But it happens that at the very instant that the blonde princess advances, noble and smiling, toward the steps to the throne, when she is already starting to feel the delightful gratification she will have in dismissing the adoring princes one by one, bestowing on each the same mocking laugh, suddenly, under the spell of an evil fairy, by means of the omnipotent touch of a magic wand, the throne, the ermine, the brocade, the pearls, the smile all disappear, and finally the blonde enchanted princess is not a princess at all, but a timid shepherd girl dressed in rags and sitting at the door of a hut, who is approached by a very powerful king escorted by a hundred pages and a hundred squires loaded with jewels and gifts, who says to her, "Poor little shepherdess who lives in this hut and who trudges all day after her sheep, do you want to marry me?"

Very well, this case, described in the style of Perrault or of Calleja, no matter how unlikely it may seem, was exactly my case. As to how and why such a great psychic reversal occurred, I cannot easily say, nor can I explain it in any way except by using the absurd and puerile simile of the princess turned into a shepherdess. However, I have observed that every time I reflect on the incident, to my great puzzlement, and in my absolute lack of analytical spirit, I can comment on the case only by spontaneously offering these philosophical considerations:

"Oh! How the infinitely small rules and imposes itself on the infinitely great! What a mystery love is, and what an influence, what an influence will be exercised on my whole life, and perhaps also on the mysterious combination of many future generations, by a Brussels lace collar, the two brilliant, luminous lenses of a tortoiseshell lorgnette; the disturbing perfume of a gardenia, the clear sparkle of a solitaire on a little finger; the step of a figure that advances ceremoniously across a drawing room, and the sight of a Packard that, beyond an open window, gleams brightly beneath the electric street light!"

But I see that, in accord with my deep-rooted habits, I have started rambling far from the theme that I had sworn to set forth in absolutely concise words and ideas. Therefore, I will cut short all comments and return to my tale.

Once seated on the sofa, next to Grandmother, I recall that I immediately made two observations. The first was to confirm, as completely obvious, the fact that César Leal was proud in the extreme of having made me blush, and that my shyness, which I was so indignant about, filled him with satisfaction and seemed to captivate him much more than my charmeuse dress, the golden waves of my hair, the Greek bust, and all my many charms.

My second observation was relative to Aunt Clara, and it consisted of noticing how her eyes busily followed my two orchids. But it was not that they stared fixedly at them, which would have lacked importance, but rather that they would gaze at them a second, afterwards they would wander through space, they would finally stop on a flower pattern in the rug or on a prism of the chandelier, while her mouth was smiling imperceptibly, and the general attitude of her face was exactly that of an exegete or a seer in the throes of interpretive intuition. And as I only too well understood that behind that vague gaze lay hidden at the very least the refrain that she repeated twice this morning: "I would swear she likes him . . . I would swear she likes him . . ." I got very nervous, and I felt a violent and real desire to rip the flowers off, throw them on the floor, and stamp on them exclaiming, "That is so you can see how false your oath would be, Aunt Clara, and how very ridiculous your interpretations seem to me!"

Fortunately my good manners, always alert and watchful, kept me from performing such an ugly act of violence. Even more, while the active cells of my brain were thinking and protesting against Aunt Clara sincerely and in the aforesaid way, my outer conduct, as always mannerly, shouted the opposite. It seemed as if my behavior had determined to betray me, allying itself with Aunt Clara, in the vilest manner. Yes. The majestic presence of Leal, his powerful voice, his very black gaze, dominated and possessed my outer self, as fever possesses the body and as a vigorous hand possesses the reins. It was proclaimed by the invincible timidity of my eyes, by the clumsiness of my movements, the flushed color in my cheeks, and there is no doubt, I must declare it—they represented the initial and most sincere manifestations of my love!

If that were so, a curious reader would now ask (given the absurd hypothesis that my writings might have readers)—if that were so, why such a contradiction and why then did the brain protest against Aunt Clara's wise suppositions?

Faced with such a logical question, I think I would feel a little confused at first, but I am certain that in the end I would recur to the apostrophe, and like a skillful syllogist I would very gracefully escape the quicksand by exclaiming, for example:

"Oh! shady, delightful groves of love, among whose branches, the infant Cupid, that divine and terrible ally of the shadows, leads us as he flies on his swanlike wings! Oh, unfathomable mysteries of life! Oh, delicate and discreet subterfuges of Destiny! I have felt you palpitate invisibly next to me, like a flight of doves in the night! And because I saw you very near, and because I opened my heart to you so that you might make your nest there, now I am able to speak of you with total certainty, and I say, 'In these affairs of love, the wise, vigilant, jealous, and alert brain is the one that always is the rear guard. Its telescopic eyes, like an eagle's eyes, fall asleep an instant, and when it tries to appreciate the sting of the arrow with which Cupid wounded us, all, all points of our body are sensitively aware, much more than the grave and meditative brain, which, as they say of deceived husbands, is always the last to know.'"

These apostrophes about the myopia or slowness of the brain to evaluate the phenomenon "love," besides being most elegant, are also absolutely right! And as generally I don't like to state any principle without setting forth an example, I shall prove what I said by telling this little incident, which clearly shows the conflicts that arise in matters of love between the orders dictated by our intellect and our audacious and disobedient behavior.

As I think I have already said, that night, during his visit, César Leal was majestically seated in an armchair, which to me, given my feeling of being a prisoner, in my ridiculous and inconceivable timidity, I imagined as being an imperial throne. His conversation was like his physical presence and was constantly pleasant and varied. He spoke very eloquently of his travels through Europe, about the delights of Paris, about the races at Longchamp, the beauty of Versailles, the Louvre, the Venus de Milo, Isadora Duncan, Sacha Guitry, and the Arc de Triomphe, among whose superb decorations Venezuela is gloriously represented by the immortal name of Miranda. He then spoke at length on this theme of the History of our Country, of the incommensurable wealth of our land, and of the genius of our Liberator. He then expressed himself concerning the Venezuelan woman in very carefully chosen terms and he said, full of patriotic gallantry, "Our women are the most beautiful, and above all they are very elegant! All of them, even the poorest, even our black girls, have excellent taste and dress like true Parisians!"

He also praised the wittiness of the people of Caracas, their creativity in inventing nicknames, and finally, as convention demands of every suitor making his first visit, he expounded his wholesome and well-founded theories about morals, whose foundation depends upon the absolute purity and irreproachable deportment of women. I found him very eloquent, and, as might be expected, Grandmother listened to him with great attentiveness, almost, I can almost say that she listened to him with religious fervor, so that, when he finished his exposition, making this brief synthesis and summary: "I believe, madam, that a man should always conduct himself like a man, and a woman, like a woman!" the memory of Monsieur de la Palisse flashed through my mind, while Grandmother said brimming over with approval, "I think exactly as you do!"

And at the same time Uncle Eduardo, a little further away, snuffled, "That is just what I preach to my children, every day!"

And more or less in the same vein Leal's pleasant chit-chat continued. It seems to me I can still hear him. I remember that while the words flowed to his lips with the same ease as drops of water flow from a fountain, his left hand lay inert and regal on one of the arms of the chair, while the right hand flew back and forth in space, generously spilling the bright rays from the solitaire on his little finger. To sum it up—César Leal on his first visit was distinguished, pleasant, and philosophical.

But at a given moment, doubtless remembering that I was the valley to which his river of eloquence was directed, and the axis around which his distinction turned, he suddenly halted the course of his varied conversation, considered my silence for a second, and then, fixing his eyes like Aunt Clara on the two pale orchids which opened on my bosom, with gracious gallantry and with an insinuating and mysterious smile that embarrassed me greatly, he said, "I see, Miss, that you like orchids, and since I also see that they look very pretty on you I shall permit myself the pleasure of sending you some from time to time."

Right away my brain, joining dignity, foresight, and invention, dictated this phrase to me: "Quite so, Doctor Leal: I love orchids! For this very reason, I order them from a florist every day. They brought me these two very early this morning from the Galipán gardens. When they arrived they looked beautiful and especially—so fresh!"

But my tongue and my lips, instead of obeying and repeating the whole text of my discreet and well-put-together phrase, began: "Quite so, Doctor Leal: I love orchids! For this very reason . . ."

And here my tongue hesitated a second. It had the absurd sensation that the material weight of the four people in the room lay upon it, and then, in the midst of great embarrassment that Leal again judged charming, it completely twisted the direction of the phrase as it finished it this way: "for this very reason, I greatly appreciate your flowers—they were beautiful!" And copying Grandmother's judgment, "I had never seen such a wide variety of orchids at this time of year!"

As Leal, who is very observant, has assured me since, when he heard me talk that way that night, he immediately understood that such a phrase together with such embarrassment, was the most ardent and rotund declaration of my love. I think so too since later events have now confirmed it. For this reason I consider the above anecdote or incident enough and more than enough to demonstrate my assertion, to wit: the slowness or myopia of our brain when we name it the judge or we call it as a witness in these complicated processes of love.

When Leal that night called an end to his visit it was past eleven o'clock, and as I usually go to bed at ten, I was very sleepy. Thus, on the way to my room, with great indifference I went by the window of the room where Grandmother and Aunt Clara were undressing and making their interminable comments. Nonetheless, in the brief space of a second, Aunt Clara's voice reached my ears like a gust of air through the half open shutter, " . . . it's very hard to figure out what she may decide, because today she'll say green and tomorrow she'll say red, but just the same, no matter how giddy she may be, when a girl wears the flowers a suitor gives her . . ."

I kept walking without staying to listen to any more because I was very sleepy, and I just longed vehemently to feel my head on the soft fluffiness of my pillow.

Two days later Leal sent me another lovely bouquet of orchids, and be-

sides the orchids he also sent a large lacquered Japanese chest full of Boissier candy. When the box arrived I opened it and, looking at the brand
of the candy, I recalled those long-ago afternoons, when Mercedes Galindo, submerged in the innumerable cushions of her Turkish divan, would
stretch out to me her Bohemia chocolate box saying, "Have one, *ma chérie*,
have one, they are Boissier. Oh! I know there are no bonbons in the world,
and particularly there are no fondants like those Boissier makes."

Therefore on this afternoon, once more reclining on my bed, wrapped
in my cream lace *déshabillé*, with the English novel in my hands, my throat
and arms perfumed with Nirvana by Bichara, besides contemplating the
shades of the flowers and besides breathing their delicious aroma, I could
also from time to time take from my crystal bonbon coffer a sweet and
tasty Boissier candy, which, as Mercedes rightly used to say, are the best
in the world!

Leal came back to see us two more times that same week. His visits,
always preceded by flowers, candy, or some other nice surprise, were
gradually becoming more frequent, and, as they no longer had the cere-
monious character of the first day, they were gradually becoming more
agreeable to me. But what I enjoyed most of all was to think that my
dresses, my hair, my eyes, and my Greek bust at last had a reason for
being, since there was someone who could see them and admire them as
is their just due. To further that purpose, I took great care that such admiration should grow instead of diminishing. Thus, on the day when Leal
would announce a visit, I would spend more than an hour-and-a-half,
among the scent of flowers and bonbons, dedicated to the pleasant and
fascinating task of dressing and embellishing myself. This care was always
well rewarded because when I appeared dressed and perfumed in the living
room, Leal, who was awaiting me with great impatience, would come
toward me, majestic, smiling, and while his hand squeezed mine firmly,
his enraptured eyes would look at me a second and his lips would murmur
softly, "You're prettier than ever today!"

An opinion that usually agreed exactly with my own. And because mu-
tually held opinions usually breed mutual ideals and also esteem and affection, I started to hold Leal in great esteem, and I considered the judgments
Uncle Panchito had expressed about him quite unfounded and erroneous,
and one day when the latter had the impertinence to make fun of Leal in
front of me, I answered very displeased, "Listen, Uncle, please keep your
opinions about Leal to yourself and don't tell them to me anymore. I consider him a very intelligent man and above all—very refined in his tastes!

Moreover he's a friend of mine and I don't want you to make fun of him in my presence."

And with no other events worthy of mention, several more weeks went by, until at last, one magnificent moonlit night, as I was going to bed, I opened the two shutters of my window wide, I gazed at the immensity of the sky, I penetrated for a moment into the sensation of the infinite, and smiling at the placid face of the moon, as if it could really hear my confidences, I began to tell it:

"And now, Moon, I have a sweetheart! . . . Yes, finally, love, this wonderful and transparent dragonfly, is held a prisoner fluttering between the rosy tips of my fingers. Do you remember with what eagerness I pursued it at one time? Do you remember that time when, weak from the joy of pursuing it, as I was about to close my fingers around its gossamer wings, it flew away and left me sad and abandoned? Well, now I tightly hold the divine dragonfly! I feel happy that I possess it and in the tiny filigree threads of its wings I like to decipher all the secrets the future has in store for me. Sometimes, Moon, when I look closely at it, very, very, close, looking at it seems to frighten me. Isn't it true that any radiant butterfly, no matter how heavenly it may be, when we look at it very close up, our eyes tell us then that all that splendor is a poor little worm dressed up in wings? Oh, the wings, it's the wings that I adore, white Moon . . . Yes, it is they, the two heavenly bits of filigree woven with the little threads of my dreams come true, they that will carry me flying like a beam of moonlight toward all the unknown peaks of life!"

❧   ❧   ❧

I believe I have set forth now, very exactly, the two points I had proposed when I started writing these pages, that is to say: first, why I decided to continue my diary of impressions that had been interrupted for more than two years; and second, about how and when there appeared in my life my sweetheart, César Leal, Doctor of Jurisprudence, Senator of the Republic, and present Director of the Ministry of Development.

As I believe I have already said, the beneficial influence of my sweetheart has transformed me advantageously in every way. I believe that is true, I feel that is true, and I am firmly convinced that it is true. But since I don't think it is right to praise myself, even though it is in private, I do not wish to speak on my own behalf about my improved behavior, and it seems better to yield the floor to others, transcribing the opinions which the people around me habitually utter concerning the matter. Grandmother, for example, frequently says, at the same time lifting her two hands in a pious gesture of thanks: "How much María Eugenia has changed, Lord! From an independent and bad-mannered child, in less than two months she has turned into a thoughtful woman, submissive and very moderate. Thank God she's making such a good marriage! I'm leaving her in good hands, and as old Simeon said, I too can now say that I can die in peace."

For her part Aunt Clara opines: "María Eugenia has changed. Yes, she's a completely different person! She has lost that bad habit of spending all day gobbling up books, and now she prefers to cook. I think she'll be a magnificent housewife, because she's smart about everything, but in the kitchen . . . Oh! . . . cooking is her specialty. I don't believe anyone in Caracas makes such perfect 'gateau d'Alsace' and 'ahogagatos' as María Eugenia does."

I heard Uncle Eduardo say in one of the almost daily conferences that he holds with Grandmother: "I always thought, Mama, that this child would stop her moods and bad behavior when she had a sweetheart. Antonio, her father, brought her up very badly. He gave her too much freedom! Fortunately, directed by Leal now, a man with so much talent and such high standards, María Eugenia will gradually lose these traces of independence that I feel are very dangerous in a woman!"

As for Uncle Pancho, like a black butterfly he has recently contracted a mania for announcing dismal things, and he has totally lost the fun and wit he used to have. Now he makes a habit of saying stupid things like this: "You've fallen into the trap, María Eugenia! You've surrendered! . . . Oh, oh, oh! . . . Now you'll find out what a woman's fate is! . . . Say goodbye to your *polissoir*, your low-cut dresses, the *dolce farniete*, and to literature. A year from now you'll spend your life in a cotton piqué housedress, you'll have the figure of a middle-aged matron, and you'll weigh . . . at least . . . one hundred fifty-five pounds."

Naturally I pay no attention to predictions as unfounded and trivial as these made by Uncle Pancho, who really knows nothing about morals and who doesn't understand a thing about practical living. Very logically, to guide my conduct, I only listen to my heart and to the solid opinions of Grandmother, Uncle Eduardo, and Aunt Clara, who foresee great happiness for me in the future.

The fact of the matter is I get along marvelously with my sweetheart. I do everything I can to please him, and he, feeling pleased, shows me his approval, continually sending me lovely perfumes, whimsical knick-knacks, and diminutive art objects, which always arrive with a river of flowers or a cascade of Boissier candy. Isn't this a charmingly cordial system? Oh! I still can't understand what reason there could be for arguments, anger, and disagreements. I am and I will eternally be the most faithful ally of peace. I can still understand how my bad nature can lead me into an argument sometimes with Grandmother or Aunt Clara, something that has few consequences, but . . . argue with my sweetheart? . . . get mad at my sweetheart? . . . no, no, no! Never that, or at least almost never, I mean, only and exclusively when there is no other way, and then, in that case, I always try to surround the spat with the greatest number of extenuating circumstances.

For example:

I have noticed that my sweetheart becomes indignant at the very idea that I might use makeup, and so, properly, so as to please him, I assure him daily, on my word of honor, that the blushing Guerlain liquid, and the *Rouge vif de Saint-Ange*, are the natural colors, most natural, of my lips and my cheeks. And as I have always believed that God has given us intelligence in order that we may prove the veracity of a lie, since the veracity of truth proves itself, by itself, without need of any intervention; with the purpose of wholly satisfying Leal's wishes by showing him clear evidence of the natural color of my lips, after asserting, "It's quite natural . . . ," I add, "The proof is . . . (here I press my lips tightly inward and together, as I quickly wipe the handkerchief across my mouth) . . . the proof is that the handkerchief isn't stained. There you see!" I have also noticed that it is profoundly displeasing to my sweetheart to see me wear my pink charmeuse dress, because he says I look too theatrical and with the two open windows I attract the attention of people going by on the street. Well then, to please him in this matter, too, I only wear my charmeuse, invoking some good excuse, every Tuesday night, which is precisely when, given the extraordinary number of people on the street because of "Tuesday Choices" celebrated at the nearby movie theater, I can reach the maximum number of admirers, while at the same time achieving a minimum of unpleasant consequences, since the following day, Wednesday, is not a good day for sending flowers, sweets, or knickknacks. I have also observed that my sweetheart likes to have people call him by his surname, and never, ever by his given name, a thing that really takes some of the edge off a man's importance. So, naturally I follow his wishes in this detail also and never commit the indiscretion of saying to him, for example, "Listen, César . . . ," but always, "Listen, Leal . . ."

To sum it up: no matter what Uncle Pancho says, my sweetheart and I agree on everything, we understand each other very well and I am certain that we will be extremely happy!

About our plans for the future, I can only say with certainty that our wedding will take place in two or three months, that is, just the indispensable length of time for finishing the house and furnishing it—an elegant house and furniture, sumptuous, very luxurious, that Leal describes every day to me in minute detail and with a torrent of truly fiery eloquence. My wedding then will be no later than two months from now. There is no doubt that it will be a very pretty wedding, there is no doubt that I will receive many congratulations and gifts, and, above all, there is no doubt that I will be most beautiful that day. Yes, I have already decided that my bridal gown will be all Chantilly, simple and classic with no other adornment than the lace except the orange blossom crown and the bouquet of slender, tremulous orchids that will spill languidly over my snow white right hand. I don't know yet if I'll order a veil of Chantilly too or if I'll order one of illusion, which although less exquisite is much filmier. Anyway, whether it's lace or whether it's illusion, when I enter the church it will cover my face, like a dreamy mantle, like a wisp of fog, like a wave of whitest foam. And incidentally, at the instant I enter the church, the orchestra will burst into the "Wedding March" by Mendelssohn, and I, step by step, lifted up by the music, with my white Chantilly train trailing across the dark carpet, resting my arm on Uncle Pancho's arm, who is the one who should give me away, because he's Papa's brother, walking step by step on Uncle Pancho's arm, I will look like a bride and, being a bride, at the same time I'll seem like a Queen . . . I can already hear the prolonged "Aaaaaaah!" of admiration that the people at the wedding will breathe on both sides of the church, and I can also almost hear the comments softly made and which I will perceive very well because in such cases I listen very hard and my hearing is very keen anyway. People will say: "What a beautiful bride! . . . She's a vision! . . . She looks like an angel! . . . She's like a flower! . . . Oh, what a lucky groom! . . ."

I think that, really, none of this will be an exaggeration, and that those comments will all be very just and very impartial comments.

As it happens I still have not done anything about the details relative to my wedding dress because it would be too soon, but on the other hand I have already ordered all the rest of my trousseau. It was only a few days ago that I sent my letter addressed to Mercedes Galindo, who will be in charge of choosing the dresses and sending them from Paris. I think in this particular I've been very fortunate, since I know with absolute certainty that my trousseau will be really beautiful. Yes, thanks to Grandmother's compliance and generosity everything will be lovely and exactly to my taste. I can still see the scene during which Grandmother announced the joyous news to me. I remember that it was one morning while she was engrossed in her mild vice of making drawnwork, sitting as usual in her big wicker chair, under the palm trees that stand before the entrance hall. I was going by at the opposite end, and she called me saying, "Come here, María Eugenia, sit down a minute here beside me, because I want to talk to you!"

I firmly believed that one of those daily lectures was going to take place, worded ordinarily in the following tenor: "You have to be careful when you sit down, María Eugenia. Yesterday night you had your dress held in such a way that you could see your legs up to your knees and that's no exaggeration whatever—up to your knees!"

Imagine my surprise, when instead of the expected lecture, no, there was no lecture, instead, using a tone at the same time serious and very affectionate, Grandmother said to me, "Doctor Leal wants to get married in about three months and I approve. Marriage shouldn't be put off! Well, I very much want you to have a pretty trousseau, and since I still have among my jewelry a pair of emerald earrings that belonged to my mother, and that I always planned to give you on your wedding day, I think in view of our circumstances, and seeing that the setting of the earrings is quite antique, it would be better, instead of spending money to have them reset in the current style, to sell the emeralds and to give you the money they bring so that you can have a pretty and elegant trousseau. They're offering me twenty thousand bolívares for the emeralds, but before I decide anything I want to consult you. What do you prefer?"

Since I didn't have the remotest idea that in the antediluvian mysteries of Grandmother's closet there existed emeralds reserved for me, the news produced such a magic effect that under its spell I suddenly saw two green and radiant stones that were growing, miraculously growing, until they turned into a torrent of white embroidery and into a sea of rose-colored silks. Seeing this vision, blind with joy, I leapt abruptly from my chair, and in order to show without delay my deep appreciation and my immense joy, I exclaimed, "Thank you, thank you, thank you, sweet Grandmother!"

I leapt forward to give her a hug, but so effusive and sincere that, before

I reached her, I bumped into the table, and then, as I was stumbling and hugging her at the same time, her glasses happened to fall off the bridge of her nose into her lap, the scissors fell on the floor, and a spool of thread went rolling away at top speed, until it was lost under the leaves of a growth of ferns.

And it was only after I'd shown all my gratitude in the way described, when on my knees, picking up all the fallen objects from the ground, I at last answered the question, "Oh! yes indeed, Grandmother, it seems much better to me for you to sell the emeralds and give me the money. What great happiness! That way I can order a trousseau from Paris that will be entirely of pink silk, but everything, all of it, down to the last thread, I want it all in pink silk, with hand-made drawnwork and white embroidery! . . . Oh, oh, oh! . . . What joy! . . . Just what I've wanted all my life—a silk trousseau! A silk trousseau!"

"You're always so eccentric, María Eugenia!" answered Grandmother, absorbed, searching at her side and on her skirt for the needle that because of my hug had also fallen along with the glasses, the scissors, and the thread, "A silk trousseau? . . . silk underwear? No, no, no! That is not decent, and it's not practical! Cotton clothes with lace and white embroidery are much better and prettier. Moreover in the laundry . . ."

"Oh, Grandmother, for Heaven's sake, if you're going against me in this too and you're going to force me to order cotton clothes decorated with bits of lace like they wore in the year one, then I prefer that you not sell the emeralds, . . . I prefer not to order anything at all from Paris . . . I prefer you not give me anything! I prefer not to get married! . . ."

And my voice as I made this reply, still humbly kneeling on the ground, took on such a highly pathetic intonation that Grandmother must have felt very moved, since she acceded to my wish for the first time in her life, responding, "Whenever you get a whim, María Eugenia, you are blinded by it and you don't know what you're saying. How stubborn you are! I thought you had mended your ways, but I see with sorrow that it was all an illusion. All right, I'll give you the money and you can do whatever you wish with it because I'm determined not to argue with you anymore. But you'll see, you'll see what the laundresses will do with your silk trousseau! Then you'll remember my words, but unfortunately then there'll be no help for it!"

And I don't need to add that it was that very afternoon when I wrote to Mercedes Galindo, begging her to choose a complete trousseau for me of pale pink silk with drawnwork and white embroidery 'just as if it were for herself.' "

Well now, I don't know why, it has displeased my sweetheart very much that I am ordering my trousseau from Paris. When, full of happy excitement, I gave him the news, he received it very coldly and his only comment was, "I hope the dresses will not be low-cut, because in that case you would lose them. I will never consent to my wife's wearing low-cut dresses!"

"Then," I asked very upset and about to burst into tears, "will I have to wear high-necked dresses at dances and the theater too?"

"Don't think so much about dances!" he replied very annoyed. And leaning a pensive head on the knuckles of his left hand, where the solitaire flashed more brightly than ever, he added, "What role does a married woman play at a dance? And above all, what role does a husband play who lets his wife dance in public?"

If it had been anyone else who was speaking, I would have answered then and there, "And who cares about roles? We're not a company of actors, to talk so much about 'roles' and to think so much about 'the public'! What interests me is to be happy and to have a good time, what the heck!"

But since I was dealing with Leal I took great care not to express such thoughts and, above all, not to express them in the disrespectful form of a pun or a play on words, since as I believe I have already said, I don't like in any way or under any pretext to oppose a sweetheart who loves me so much. Then, as I remained silent, in view of my approving silence, he continued showing me his interest in this way: "For the theater you can wear dresses a little open at the neck, decently cut, but cut low—never!" (And again) "What could be a more ridiculous role for a husband to play than to sit down in a theater in front of the public with his wife naked?"

Then I did risk answering by explaining very gently, "I don't mean naked, but after all . . . fashionably cut, a little bit low, like all the chic women."

"No, no, no! I will never consent to low-cut dresses on my wife . . . even though she isn't 'chic'!"

And when he said the word "chic" his voice assumed such a sharp and disagreeable pitch that, thanks to that, I instantly understood the profound and wise scorn that we should experience in the face of dangerous worldly frivolities.

In addition to having observed the great interest that Leal has in me in other cases as eloquent as the above, I have observed too that it displeases him greatly for me to take any initiative whatever that is not suggested by him, and I have especially observed that it displeases him deeply for me to grant myself any pleasure however insignificant that doesn't come from his hands. Grandmother, who has observed these details as I have, also appreciates them greatly, as I do, for she often says, "I like Leal better with every day that passes. What a loyal character, and how he takes care of María Eugenia! It's evident that he truly loves her. Oh! husbands who give total freedom to their wives, who don't watch over them, or tend to those little details that make up the fabric of life, it's because they don't love them!"

And Aunt Clara, who has observed the same thing, too, often says to me, "How lucky you are, María Eugenia; how Leal adores you! You should always try to please him, and most of all, you should give thanks to God continually for having provided you such a good fiancé. Don't think they're all like that. Oh! how lucky you are if you finally get Leal to marry you. He's jilted so many other girls!"

Like Aunt Clara, I too am humbled by the magnitude of my good fortune, I feel small, very small, and . . . a strange thing! . . . I who for two years or more anxiously awaited the coming of love, I who waited for it on bended knee as if for the archangel of the Annunciation, now that it has come to me, now that I behold it up close and face to face, its brilliancy has blinded my pupils and the majesty of its grandeur crushes me to the point that very, very often, when I seat myself to rest beside the abyss of my perplexities, I have heard a mysterious voice that has whispered very softly in my ear this absurdity, which makes no sense: "Oh, happy are the unlucky girls who do not have the great good fortune of possessing the perfect treasure of love, and who being pretty, still in their misfortune, can always, always dance at dances and wear low-cut dresses at the theater!"

CHAPTER II   *After sailing for three days in the caravel of her own experience, María Eugenia Alonso has just made a very important discovery.*

 I can no longer resist the absolute necessity that I feel of expressing the following aphorism, whose truth overflows from my soul: "Love does not exist."

Yes, unhappily, love, flowery love, exalted love is—nothing! Like so many other pious lies, its dazzling lustre is only the lustre of a mirage that glows from afar in this arid desert of our lives. Since I have discovered this cruel truth, I profoundly despise human existence, and I would prefer a thousand and one times over to have been born a rock, a lake, or a chasm—all things which, being eternal, immobile, and grandiose, have the advantage of never getting bored and of not having the ridiculous pretension of aspiring to love, which as I have already said, is no more than a utopia, an Eldorado, and a will-o'-the-wisp.

And since it is improbable that Grandmother or anyone else should come on tiptoe to read over my shoulder what I plan to write here, a thing that would fill me with the most horrible confusion, I am going to explain the reason why I have arrived at this very sad and depressing knowledge that love is nothing, or, more clearly still, that love is less than nothing, and much, much worse than nothing.

With no more beating around the bush and with no reticence of any kind, I shall speak with utter frankness. If I hold this knowledge and if I profess this axiom that love does not exist, it's because my sweetheart has kissed me; and because I have kissed him, not once, which would give me no basis for making a judgment nor sufficient experience, but he has kissed me about . . . twice . . . but no . . . no . . . the truth, let's tell the truth, I think it's . . . three times . . . yes . . . that's right! . . . a trio or a triptych of kisses, which for experience constitute a very respectable number on which to base a judgment and formulate an opinion on any matter.

And to think that poets have written poem after poem extolling the sweetness of a kiss! To think that Bécquer, for example, has written, with a delicious and perturbing emotion in which I was ingenuous enough to believe:

"For a kiss, I don't know what I would give you for a kiss!"

And to think that Rostand wrote wonders about the matter in that moving balcony scene between Roxanne, Christian, and poor Cyrano, who in my opinion was the luckiest of the three, since not having climbed up to receive Roxanne's kiss, he kept his illusions till the end and had no chance to experience this horrible disillusionment that I am experiencing today.

A kiss! Oh, I say now and I will repeat it all my life, a kiss, "that secret of love, in which the mouth is taken for the ear," is not at all, absolutely not the least bit interesting! The first kiss still holds the attraction of the unknown, the terror of the forbidden, and the remorse of the illicit, but once past that remorse, terror, and attraction, nothing is left for subsequent kisses . . . or rather, yes, something is left . . . something that becomes quite disagreeable . . . If at least the horrid vice of smoking did not exist in this world, and if at least men did not have a mania for cutting their mustaches in the American style, prickly and stiff like a horse brush, still. . . I would still be able to understand how some people might commit the oddity of praising kisses! . . . And that is nothing, if added to cigarette breath and horse brushes, is added this dreadful fear of having the *Rouge vif de Saint-Ange* discovered! . . . Because of that I here solemnly declare for the second time: I will never, ever praise kisses. I am totally certain that it is a very insipid invention, that besides exposing us to the danger of being seen by a third person, a circumstance whose least consequence would be to feel ridiculous, I believe that as an entertainment it is very monotonous, and as a habit it can be unhygienic.

Thanks to my natural slowness to judge, I only formulated this reasoning two days after having received the first kiss from my sweetheart's lips. But certainly after forming said reasoning, with my natural firmness, I also resolved without delay to put an end to a custom as disillusioning as it is unhygienic. That same evening, after dressing with more care than ever and after greeting my sweetheart, while I was settling down next to him as usual on the dark blue damask sofa, I told him full of austere and stately distinction, "Leal, I know very well that a virtuous woman should never kiss a man to whom she is not yet married. Well, for two nights now I have failed in my duty, and since my regret will not allow me to sleep, and since I want to prove to myself that I know and will always know how to resist temptation, I will not kiss you again—even if you beg me on bended knee!"

And it was useless for my sweetheart to employ the most gentle, insinuating, and seductive words in his lover's vocabulary, it was useless later, speaking to me very severely, for him to invoke his authority and to tell me that I had no right to make such judgments, since in matters of morals as in any other matters, my conduct should never be based on any criterion save his exclusively. But everything, gentleness and forcefulness, everything, everything was in vain. Disobeying him for the first time I answered him with theatrical dignity, "No, no, no! I want you to respect me! In the future I want you to have confidence in your wife! And now so you can see how final my resolution is and how solid and unbreakable my virtue is, between my kisses, between you and me, I shall immediately create an abyss."

And then, addressing Aunt Clara who, with her back discreetly turned to us, was knitting under the light of the chandelier, I said, "But Aunt, every night you sit in the middle of the room, in a draft, and you're going to catch cold, and maybe even pneumonia! I think you should sit there, in front of us, in Grandmother's armchair. By turning on the floor lamp you can knit under that light. The green lamp shade is excellent for better vision."

Aunt Clara, who for the past few nights, while Grandmother goes to bed, has been left with the job of keeping vigil and presiding over the drawing room during Leal's visits, no sooner had I spoken than she stood up saying, "That's true!"

She walked to Grandmother's empty chair, she turned on the floor lamp, she gave us an inquisitive glance, and after breathing a very long sigh she took up her two bone needles again and continued knitting.

And I, now, as then, am quite certain that in Aunt Clara's long sigh there were the invisible atoms of her thought that sprang from her mouth and flew for a second through the atmosphere of the room, a thought that would say more or less, "We used to sit there too on the blue damask sofa . . . and sometimes, too, in this corner facing it . . . there was no one!"

I say that Aunt Clara's thought must have been expressed that way, because as soon as her gnarled hands bathed in the green light from the lamp shade began to move the two bone needles deliberately, while the ball of wool yarn spun for a second on her skirt and fell to the dark rug, I, sitting beside Leal's indignant silence, without knowing why, began to sweetly evoke some far-off scenes, but so far away, that my memory barely managed to sketch them . . . In those scenes I felt I was very small again, sitting on the floor, with my back to the damask sofa, a white form just there, on the dark rug, a little larger than the white shape of the ball of wool yarn . . . and I saw myself there again, installed on the floor, very formally lining up beside my little shoes the white row of paper roosters that Aunt Clara's sweetheart had made for me . . . yes, Aunt Clara's sweetheart! that amiable and enigmatic person who, behind me, on the damask sofa, would converse with her hour after hour, in an undertone that was very mysterious and that was interspersed with pauses that were still more mysterious . . . Now after fifteen years, the ball of wool was where I had been and in place of Aunt Clara and her sweetheart, sat my sweetheart and I . . .

"Oh!" I thought filled with melancholy, "life is a tree that dresses and undresses continually, always putting out new leaves, over the same places, in rhythm with the age-old monotonous march of time!"

And since such gentle considerations inundated my heart with a wave of sentimentality, with the double objective of expressing my feelings and at the same time distracting Leal's bad mood, I spoke to him about the charms of lyric poetry and I proposed to recite that moving nocturne by Silva:

"One night, a night all full of murmurs, perfume, and the music of wings . . ."

But he, a great deal more displeased than before, when I reached the word "murmurs" brusquely broke into the nocturne to pronounce, himself, an extensive monologue, energetic and imperious, which, compressed into a few words, expressed more or less the following: that he hated romanticism; that he hated recitations; and that he hated still more women like me, who tried to be learned and academic; that in his opinion, a woman's head was a more or less decorative object, completely empty inside, made to gladden the eyes of men, and adorned with two ears whose only function should be receiving and collecting the orders that men might dictate to them; and that further and finally, it seemed indispensable to him that said decorative object should wear very long hair since the learned philosophy of Schopenhauer had thus disposed.

But this last bit about Schopenhauer was not expressed that way, naming Schopenhauer, but rather I deduced it from the following stern order with which the monologue concluded: " . . . and finally, I don't want you to keep wearing your hair short. Like makeup, short hair is not proper for decent women!"

These last, as much as the preceding forceful concepts, left me speechless with surprise and sorrow. The idea of sacrificing my two beloved short tufts of hair, the adornment of my temples and constant occupation of my hands, afflicted me greatly, but it afflicted me a great deal more still to think that I had worked ceaselessly reading and studying, to instruct myself, and thus acquire a pleasing accomplishment, which instead of being appreciated, suddenly turned out to be, as Leal had just emphatically declared, a detrimental condition, very ugly and jarring in a woman—"the pedantic woman."

"Oh! What a terrible conflict," I thought with desperation, as I sat humbly and submissively on my half of the sofa. And now, in order to please Leal: how to cleanse my head of this confusion of reading accumulated in more than two years, which, in nebulous forms, will float in my mind eternally?

Staring with wide-open eyes at the ball of yarn that, preceded by the thread pulled by Aunt Clara's fingers, was jumping imperceptibly on the dark rug, I began to consider that, after all, ignorance was much more liberal than wisdom, because an ignorant person can become a wise one, while a wise person can never become ignorant. Then, I felt for a minute a nostalgia for things lost beyond recall, and I said to myself sighing, "Oh! the infinite sadness of the definitive! and what wouldn't I give now to please Leal, by acquiring anew the lost treasure of my absolute ignorance?"

But finally I consoled myself thinking that even if it was true on the one hand that I had no possibility of acquiring said treasure, on the other hand I always had recourse to making people believe I possessed it. This solution satisfied me tremendously, not only because it smoothed out the conflict, but also because it reminded me that I have great aptitude for pretending, which, far from being a defect, as the masses suppose, is proof of genius, and an evident indication that I could have had an extremely brilliant career in the divine art of the theater, an art that, in my opinion, is the most sublime of all arts. And so, thinking about this talent of mine, which, abetted by my beauty, might have taken me perhaps, perhaps, to the level of a Sarah Bernhardt or of a Duse, I felt in an admirably good mood again; and then, given this joy, I lifted my eyes from the ball of yarn, I turned them to my sweetheart, and I gave him to understand by means of glances and funny gestures that Aunt Clara was horribly in our way, and that I was in the throes of a crisis of remorse, desperately sorry for having disobeyed him. This demonstration, far from calming his displeasure seemed to unnerve him more and more, so much that I believe that night Leal, sitting next to me on the damask sofa, really wanted to beat me since he couldn't kiss me. But since both, equally disagreeable, were also equally impossible, I thought my situation highly interesting, and I continued developing with more freedom all of my repertoire of winks, smiles, and gestures, and though unfortunately I couldn't see them in any mirror, I understood that all of them, absolutely all, were subtle, delicious, very charming, worthy of being exhibited not in a drawing room and before a single person, but in a great theater, where l would be wearing a wonderful evening dress, and standing in the center of a luxurious stage set and before the packed and sophisticated audience of some great city.

Since that night my sweetheart has not kissed me anymore. But instead he has advanced the date of our wedding and every day he rains upon me laws, prohibitions, and orders of every kind. I consider that these, like the kisses, also constitute a clear proof of his love, and therefore I receive them and always accept them with respect and affection. Aunt Clara who has well observed these mutual interchanges of our affection, with her natural good sense, understands them and comments on them saying, "If Leal loves María Eugenia, María Eugenia adores Leal. She sees everything through his eyes! I never imagined that she could fall so in love. But after all, it's no wonder. You understand, he has a kind of charm—a special mysterious ability to attract women, because all of them, all of them, adore him!"

In contrast, Uncle Pancho, with every day that passes, increases his continual lapses of tact, and is angered and irritated by these shows of compliance and affection that I give my sweetheart. He keeps on with his black butterfly system of prognosticating horrors, and every time he has the chance to create a conflict for me or put me in a difficult situation with Leal, he takes advantage of the opportunity. Besides, as I think I have already said, Uncle Pancho has totally lost the wit he used to have, now, he makes stupid jokes, but so very, very stupid, that they're not funny.

And to demonstrate how little wittiness Uncle Pancho now has, I am going to cite a few examples.

Day before yesterday, without going any further back, at about ten in the morning, I was standing in the dining room, about three feet from a chair, busy braiding silk threads, because I recently bought some matching lingerie made of Milanese silk for my trousseau, but they are a little loose at the neckline, and I have to draw them up with a ribbon or cord, so they will fit me better. Suddenly, when I was most absorbed in my work, Uncle Pancho comes in, sits down, and asks, "What are you doing here, María Eugenia, stretching threads on that chair as if you were a spider?"

"Well you see! . . . I'm making silk cords to tighten my bodices that are a little loose on me."

"They're loose on you? . . . are they? . . . Well look, if you want my advice, if I were in your place, I wouldn't try to draw them up, instead I'd try to stretch them as much as possible. In a very short time you won't be able to wear them any more, María Eugenia. I calculate that you'll gain about ten pounds a month, until you reach the standard one hundred seventy-five matronly pounds."

Faced with such an impertinence, which suddenly increased the usual weight gain he foretold by twenty pounds—total silence from María Eugenia! The threads kept spinning beneath my fingertips and the chair trembled slightly, pulled by my work and by my rage. A short while later he asked, "When is the wedding?"

"Very soon!! . . . When they finish decorating the house. They're making it look adorable."

"Yes? . . . I can already imagine those decorations. There will probably be some Cupids flying at top speed in your bedroom, and a huge green and blue landscape, probably sea and sky, painted from top to bottom on the patio wall . . ."

Again, as my only answer, nothing. Silence!

Then he spoke, "Look, now that you've finished with that cord, before you start another one, give me a few drops of brandy, please."

Since I don't hold a grudge, I bring him the brandy, but I bring him something else too! It's the newspaper, where Leal's latest article appears, published with high praise by the press. When Uncle Pancho has drunk his brandy, I extend the open paper to him, on the table, and I say with an air of challenge, "Look: read what they say here about this article and afterwards read the article! . . . See 'turn to page two' (I turned the page), 'turn to page three' (I turned the page) and 'turn to page five' (I turned the page) . . . Come on, Uncle Pancho, read, read!"

But Uncle Pancho, instead of putting on his glasses and starting to read, no, he is quiet awhile, then he looks up, and he asks me sweetly, gently, acting the role of a confessor, "Listen, tell me the truth, María Eugenia, did you read it just like that, turning to page two, and turning to three, and turning to five, and all?"

"No. I haven't read it at all, because you know perfectly well I'm very busy with the cords. I haven't had time to read it yet."

"All right, then, to please you I'll read the whole article, but on condition that first you drink down, in no more than four or five seconds! . . . that bottle of Rubinat water that is over there."

And he pointed to the very bitter purgative that Aunt Clara was going to take that very morning, so repugnant that the very sight of it gives me chills, nausea, and vertigo.

Now I ask, is that answer witty? . . . Is it clever? . . . Does it have *esprit*? . . . Well certainly not! And it's evidently right what Grandmother and everybody says: Uncle Pancho lacks any moral sense, he lacks common sense, and he can't discern what is respectable and good from what is contemptible and bad.

Another more recent example:

About two nights ago, Leal, during his visit, sitting next to me on the damask sofa, was not talking to me at that moment, but was addressing Uncle Eduardo and Uncle Pancho, because the themes their conversation touched on were absolutely not my concern. He had declared, speaking of the relationship between mysticism and the feminine mentality: "Religion, in a woman, is completely indispensable, and no woman has the right to say that she does not believe . . . because after all what do women understand about metaphysics, or about biology, or about the theories of Lamarck, or the cosmogonic system of Laplace, or the new ideas of Einstein, or anything? . . . I, for example, do not believe, I am completely materialistic, it is true, but why am I a materialist? . . . Why, because I have my reasons! . . . I think; I have studied in depth; I reflect; I have a certain mental capacity; I have my system; I have my special method; I have my, etc., etc."

But he had said all this some time before. Now he was talking about literature, about oratory, about politics and he had offered to read a bit from the speech he was soon to give in the Senate. At a given moment in the conversation Dante and his work were mentioned. Naturally, in accord with my program, instead of offering opinions about the matter, I was discreetly silent, thus giving to understand that that name "Dante" lacked all meaning for me. But Uncle Pancho, instead of minding his own business, no, he waited until there was a great silence, and then, with a stentorian voice he asked me, "Why don't you ever recite anything by Dante anymore, María Eugenia?"

"By Dante?" I asked very puzzled. "I don't know what you're talking about, Uncle Pancho."

"Oh! So, María Eugenia, you try to make us believe now that you've never read Dante, when last year you wore us out with your opinions and literary judgments about the *Divine Comedy*? I remember that you would recite it in an Old Italian that probably was very poorly pronounced, because you speak French and English like your native language, but in contrast you murder Italian."

"Well, really, Uncle," I answered him very miffed, "I'm not in the habit of lying. I've told you many times that I have a very bad memory, and just as I've almost forgotten my English, I'm now forgetting my French, and I've totally forgotten all of the verses of the *Divine Comedy*. It's as if I'd never read them. For that reason I say sincerely, I don't know who Dante is!"

And as if this were not enough, Uncle Pancho, instead of understanding and being quiet, went on the same way, harping on the same subject. "Oh! Well, it seems very strange to me that you are so alienated from literature, when you yourself are a writer. And don't deny it, don't deny it, because I know it for a fact! The other day I went in your room to look for a book and on your desk I saw a great stack of written and numbered sheets. You came racing in behind me and covered them with a magazine, but it was no use, because I had already seen them quite clearly . . ."

When I heard that iniquitous indiscretion, I instantly denied it without letting him conclude:

"A writer? . . . Me, a writer? . . . Me? . . . Really, what nonsense! . . . Oh! . . . Oh, yes . . . now I remember . . . you're referring no doubt to some recipes that I was copying the other day . . ."

"Quite . . . quite! . . . recipes, with question marks, exclamations, dialogues, and dashes. Well, unless in your recipes the ingredients carry on dialogues among themselves, like the characters in a fable, so while the cake is beaten, let's say, the sugar asks a question of the eggs, the milk replies to the butter, and the flour exclaims in the pan or the oven . . ."

"Oh! For Heaven's sake! How absurd . . . Remember for Goodness' sake, that you can't see anything without your glasses, and that's why you get everything mixed up."

Fortunately, Leal paid no attention whatever to the above conversation, busy as he was taking from his pocket, unfolding, and scanning some written sheets, on which he searched, absorbed, for the most eloquent passage of his speech. And finally, having found it, with the sheets held in his right hand, gesturing broadly with his left, he drowned out my discussion with Uncle Pancho, because he started to read, "The diverse incipient groupings of heterogeneous entities that, united in a single heroic creed, commune fruitfully, and unfadingly, in the ethnic and sociological palpitations of our Great War of Liberation, whose glorious annals are evident in the communities that give birth to epic legends, that rising to the fiery heights of the Andes, like an Epiphany of condors, had conceived the venerable concept of our patriotic individualism . . ."

When he reached here, while Leal went on reading, I cast an inquisitive glance at Uncle Pancho, who was listening seriously, motionless and absorbed, showing signs of profound attention. But since I know him all too well, seeing him so attentive, I could only exclaim to myself, "Oh, what new stupid remark, what new graceless joke are you ruminating here, Uncle Pancho?"

But Leal's voice continued, growing more and more vibrant, "Conjured by the thaumaturgic word that in a broad cosmogonic embrace had lighted with its faith that radiant torch, which lighted then in the intense plutonic energy of the epic heights, shone at last on the heroic heads, like a radiant rose of fire, redivivus in the triumphal Apotheosis of our most pure Glory!! . . ."

I didn't pay attention any more because I began to think that, really, my ignorance was much greater than what I had thought, since I had not managed yet to follow the thread of such an eloquent discussion, and let it be said in passing that it was a true success in the Senate. And I say that it was a success, because the newspaper that reproduced it, when it came to this last paragraph, wrote, in parentheses and in italics: (*the speaker is warmly applauded*).

I remember Uncle Pancho also has given me more than one bad moment because of his itch to talk, whether it is on the subject or not, about my close friendship with Mercedes Galindo, and about those times when I used to dine with her almost daily. It happens that Leal knows Mercedes only by sight and reputation, but it is certain that without having known her personally, he professes the most sincere and vehement antipathy toward her. Several times he has announced to me that if Mercedes should return to Caracas, I, as his wife, will never again set foot in her house. As Leal is not accustomed to explain to me the reason for his orders or prohibitions, I was ignorant of the cause of this latest one, just as I am ignorant of the cause of all the rest. But a few nights ago, sparked by something Uncle Pancho said, after the latter had left, the conversation among Grandmother, Aunt Clara, and Uncle Eduardo began to revolve around Mercedes. They were sitting apart, at a distance from us, there at the opposite end of the living room. But all at once Leal sat up very straight next to me on the damask sofa, he solemnly began to speak, and with that imposing and energetic tone that should be used when speaking of those people whose contact corrupts or scandalizes others, he said that Mercedes was and had always been a woman who was too free in her conduct, who attended dances literally naked, who treated men with too much intimacy, who had very improper conversations with them, and although in Caracas her name had not been linked with anyone in particular, he knew for a fact that in Paris she had had more than one lover.

I felt it was my duty to defend Mercedes from such charges, and with that objective, a very bitter argument instantly developed, because Grandmother as well as Uncle Eduardo and Aunt Clara, present at the scene, all three took Leal's side and were against me. It was all in vain as a defense of Mercedes that I described with the greatest eloquence possible her abnegation toward her husband Alberto, the merit of being so good although so unfortunate and so pretty; her generous sentiments and her warm heart. Everyone replied saying they didn't see any merit in it, since a well-born woman, once married, no matter how unhappy she might be, should suffer her misfortunes in silence, without ever failing in her duties, and without giving to society the grotesque and scandalous spectacle of divorce. In view of so much evidence mixed with so much unanimity, I judged Mercedes's cause definitively lost, and I opted for a discreet and docile silence.

After declaring myself defeated, I remember that on the damask sofa, Leal and I that night took up anew our interrupted private conversation, while at a distance, Grandmother, Aunt Clara, and Uncle Eduardo continued talking in low voices. Without failing to listen to what my sweetheart was saying, straining my ears, I realized that now, on the subject of Mercedes and divorce, the group was talking about Gabriel Olmedo. Grandmother was recalling that Mercedes had had the wretched idea of his marrying me, and Uncle Eduardo added that thanks to his interest and thanks to a miracle of Providence, I had been saved from such a great calamity. But Aunt Clara was certain that I would never have liked Gabriel Olmedo. Grandmother confirmed this opinion, and then Uncle Eduardo began to relate that Gabriel and his wife in fact were separated, because they had never managed to get along; that she really had a detestable character; that Gabriel was finding amusement elsewhere and that around Caracas it was rumored that they were going to be divorced. Then they went on talking in a still lower tone, which I didn't manage to hear, divided as my attention was between the two conversations; theirs finally was closed with these considerations by Grandmother, "Maybe! . . . since they have no respect for morals, and since they have no children either! . . . oh! children, how much children are needed! . . ."

Save this argument caused by Uncle Pancho on the delicate theme of Mercedes, as far as I can remember, I haven't argued anymore with my sweetheart. And in mutual and complete accord, on our damask sofa, time slips softly, softly by, while there, in the distance, the date for our wedding grows and races forward with the strides of a giant. Counting from today it's only twenty days. Our coming marriage has already been proclaimed and last Sunday at eight o'clock Mass, the priest of the Cathedral, after communion, read the first of the banns.

Because of urgent business affairs, Leal is preparing for a trip to the interior of the country, a trip that will last only a few days. It will take more or less the time between now and the wedding. During his trip I plan to dedicate myself body and soul to my wedding dress. I already have the dressmaker working on it. It will be all, all, veil, train, and dress, of a single cloud of snowy white Chantilly lace, with no decoration except the tiny orange blossoms that will bloom hidden in the cloud of lace . . . and speaking of clouds . . . I was forgetting my big news.

One of the reasons why I defended Mercedes Galindo so heatedly the other night was in gratitude for the great affection that she showed in the selection of my trousseau, because it arrived a few days ago—and my trousseau is a marvel! Everything, absolutely everything, is made of pink crêpe de Chine, with white drawnwork and embroidery just as I had dreamed. When I have it put away in my mirrored wardrobe, the sheer silk makes it so tiny that sometimes, just to look at it, I open the wardrobe door. Behind the door, first comes a smell of Paris silk that is glorious, and afterwards, after the smell, as if it were a rose garden, growing on a single shelf, the whole garden of roses that is my trousseau. I contemplate it for a long time, arranged in diminutive rows, until suddenly, for the pleasure of seeing it grow, for the pleasure of filling my room with its smell of Paris, for the pleasure of feeling it's mine, I take down the rows, and piece by piece, I spread it all out on my bed. And it grows and multiplies so much that, in order to receive it all, my bed seems to stretch with joy, it seems to move, to walk, and at last, my bed, covered with my trousseau, is a stream that has waves and eddies and cascades and whirlpools and pink silk foam. Sometimes, from looking at it so much, I want to bathe in the stream, and without further thought, since crêpe doesn't wrinkle, I whip off my kimono, I stretch out on the bed, and I take a bath in silk. But an instant later, I fear I'm going to ruin it, I hurriedly get up,

I sit cross-legged at the foot of the bed, I smooth it lovingly, and piece by piece I again fold my pretty bath of roses. While I am folding it, since everything is scrambled and heaped up, with the blue eiderdown showing through, and with fluffy pieces climbing to the tops of the white pillows, I look at it a long time, and there, at the head of the bed, beneath the illusion of my embroidered curtain, my trousseau mixed and disordered, it reminds me then of those edges of the sky when a sunset dresses them in frivolous and capricious wisps of fog, with wisps of white clouds, red clouds, and a red beauty spot that is the sun and lighter cloud scenery and many, many hazy spots of pink crêpe that become transparent and lose themselves in a sky as blue as the blue of my eiderdown.

But as much as I like to look at my trousseau laid out on my bed, I don't know why, I don't like my trousseau when I see it on myself. And it's not that it doesn't look good on me, no. It looks wonderful on me! It looks so good on me, the color is so becoming, and the cut is so becoming that one day when Aunt Clara insisted that I should try it on, when I put on the first chemise, which was a very short empire style, Aunt Clara was ecstatic, and she, who never tells me I'm pretty, clasped her hands, was quiet for an instant, and then exclaimed with much astonishment, "But what beauty! . . . Why you look just like a rosebud, María Eugenia!"

And also Gregoria, the laundress, came to see me in my rose chemise; her woolly head appeared behind the bars of my window and accompanying the words with those loud laughs of hers that say so many things that can't be said, she assured me that she had never seen anything so precious, and that she personally would always wash my silk clothes for me, so no other crass laundress could commit the crime of spoiling them.

But in spite of what Aunt Clara says and of what Gregoria says with words and with laughs, I don't want to try on my trousseau and I prefer to put it on the bed. Yes. I remember that on the same day it arrived, just after taking it out of the boxes, I decided to try it all on. Mad with curiosity I locked myself in my room and, trembling with joy, I began to slip on one after another of the perfumed crêpe de Chine dresses. But when I was at my happiest looking at myself from every angle in the mirror, looking like a "rosebud," as Aunt Clara says, suddenly, without exactly knowing why, it seemed to me that the fabric of the clothes was too transparent, I thought what Grandmother had said many times, "those silk clothes are neither decent nor practical" . . . and I, who am never afraid of nudity, beneath the sheer crêpe, suddenly saw myself nude, and I felt . . . I don't know what I felt . . . but I took off the dress I had on, I put on my everyday clothes, and instead I spread out the trousseau on my bed.

But now that I think about it . . . not trying on all the dresses was also because, besides remembering what Grandmother says, I remembered what Uncle Pancho says. While I was tying the ribbon of an empire chemise, I looked at myself in the mirror, but . . . staring, fixedly . . . and all of a sudden, it seemed to me that my back was getting broader, and then that my bosom was swelling, and then that my head was growing until it became square like María Antonia's head, and that finally, my hands, my pretty hands, with their well-polished nails, their charming dimples, and their pointed, slender fingers, were getting thick, and instead of polished nails the nails were opaque, and the fingers swollen, gnarled, and even twisted like Aunt Clara's fingers . . . Yes, yes, before the mirror, dressed just in my empire chemise of crêpe de Chine I suddenly felt that all Uncle Pancho's words besieged me. It seemed to me that they were moving around me . . . yes . . . it seemed to me that they had wings and that they were flying near me, like a flock of crows! . . . Or, no . . . no! . . . it was more like a swarm of black butterflies, that's right . . . it was a frightful swarm of black butterflies that in the mirror were flying and fluttering invisibly and persistently around a poor rosebud . . .

And of course, it must have been because of that that I suddenly stopped trying on my trousseau! . . .

Now, as I write, I can't stop remembering, and I can't stop wondering: why, but why, has Uncle Pancho taken up the very ugly habit of announcing lugubrious things? . . . It's not that I'm superstitious . . . but always . . . caramba! . . . always . . .

Iphigenia

In the early hours
of a Monday

 The clock has just struck two in the morning . . . And the two chimes that sounded as if they were two groans in the silence have echoed in my ears, calling me, and in my heart, they have awakened fear . . .

I am afraid . . . Yes . . . I am writing to forget my fear . . .

It was the old worn-out dining room clock that struck two. Can it really be two? Now the clock goes on as before: tick, tock . . . tick, tock . . . tick, tock . . .

Clocks striking in the night are the voices of silence that complains . . . and the ticktock of clocks in the night are the steps . . . the steps of death . . . No, no, no! . . . they are the steps of silence that walks . . . yes! . . . the steps of silence . . . And how slowly, how slowly and how long, My God, silence walks through the night! . . . Above all when the night is as black and as still as this night. It's so black and so still that barely an instant ago so I could see some light other than the light of this flame that dances and dances like a crazed ballerina on the narrow pedestal of the candle . . . an instant ago, so I could see some light other than this mad flame, I rose from my chair and I opened one of the window shutters; but since in this house, which is so old and so poor everything creaks, the shutter creaked as it opened, and since I was frightened by the sound, and since there isn't a single star in the sky, the shutter has remained half-open, and now, in the white frame of the window, there is a black, black hole through which enters a mystery so black and so cold that the flame on the narrow pedestal of the candle now twists and writhes as if it were in pain . . . And that mystery entering through the shutter is touching my face and touching my hands, while my hands move over the paper with my pen. It is a black mystery, and damp, and cold . . . yes! . . . It is like the mystery of dead eyes! . . . because there are times when in a frozen face, beneath white eyelids, black eyes are still half-open . . . like . . . like that shutter . . .

Oh! Death! . . . It's not silence that walks in the night, no, that's a lie! it is . . . it is death . . . yes! Death! . . . And only clocks have ears to hear its steps . . . That is why they always repeat them at all hours. But in the daytime they repeat them and no one hears, and they repeat them at night, and in the night, in the midst of the silence, the ears of those who watch over the sick can hear them . . .

Oh, the horrible hole opened by the shutter! . . . What a cold mystery, what a damp, black mystery!

I have gotten up from my chair and I have closed the shutter. I have opened the door to the dining room; and now the clock ticks harder than before: tick, tock, tick, tock, tick, tock . . . This door, too, the one to his room, is half-open and his breathing is in rhythm, like the ticktock of the clock . . . They seem to keep time with each other . . . or maybe not . . . the breathing is faster . . . no! . . . it is slower . . . no, no, it's faster . . . Oh! Old dining room clock, you're so old now that you don't know how to measure the urgent pace of death!

Now, I have gotten up from my chair again, and for the hundredth time I have softly pushed open the door to his room. Against the white pillow his head lies motionless and asleep while that anguished breathing goes on . . . and on . . . as if it did not come from his motionless head. He is like the winded horse of some traveler who, at the very moment when he is about to arrive, when he is most eager to arrive, and he runs . . . runs . . . runs . . . his strength exhausted.

Oh! Poor Uncle! How well I remember now when he would enter Grandmother's house, overcome by weakness, and so run down and so jaundiced and he would say to me as he sat down, "Bring me a few drops of brandy, María Eugenia, to see if I'll feel better . . ."

And I would bring him the drops of brandy; he would drink them, and soon his cold hands were warmer, his dull eyes brightened a little, and he would begin to joke with everyone, saying nothing of his fatigue and telling no one that he was sick. But I remember that when he would get up to leave, he was bent over; he dragged his feet as if he carried some terrible weight on his shoulders, and that way, with very slow steps, he would go walking to his house . . . his house! . . . Poor Uncle Pancho! His house was this little damp narrow house, where there is no electric light except in two rooms, and where the rooms, instead of wallpaper, have whitewash on the walls.

How poor, how poor your house was, poor Uncle Pancho! . . .

But what does it matter now? With the same speed with which he is now racing away, on that runaway fatigue, he would also go away if in place of this poor house he had a palace, and if instead of having whitewash on the walls, the walls still had those tapestries that, according to Grandmother, were a marvel in the splendid ancestral home of the Alonsos.

In his damp, poor, and cramped house, the same as if it were a palace, Uncle Pancho is dying irremissibly. Last night when the doctor was taking his leave he told me for the second time, "It's a matter of a few days. It may be two, five, ten, but there is no hope and there is no remedy. First a lethargy, a comatose state, and then death! We will try to see that he suffers as little as possible."

From the first moment when he had the attack, Grandmother wanted me to come stay in Uncle Pancho's house, and when she said goodbye she told me, "Make sure he has everything he needs, María Eugenia. I will be here to send anything needed. And you, nurse him with the tenderest care and with the greatest affection: remember that he is the last part of your father that you have left!"

In spite of Grandmother's offers, I haven't wanted her to send anything. Asking anything of her is to ask it of Uncle Eduardo, and I can't stand for Uncle Pancho to have anything that comes from Uncle Eduardo's hands. Looking through the drawers in his wardrobe, I've found a few articles of some value, some money, and with that, as well as the little that I have left from the emeralds, we will have enough for everything.

Together with me, Aunt Clara and Gregoria have come to Uncle Pancho's house. But Aunt Clara can't leave Grandmother alone all day, and so she comes and goes continually between the two houses. As Aunt Clara knows a lot about nursing, Uncle Pancho is very well cared for, and he lacks nothing. When she is gone, Gregoria, the nurse, and I are at the foot of his bed, and then I am all eyes and ears and I don't leave him alone with anyone. One night Aunt Clara stays up to watch him, the next night I do. This has been my first night to watch over him. It has seemed to me long, eternal, a black, silent, and humid eternity, like an eternity hidden in urns welded beneath the earth.

I believe, at last, it is starting to dawn now. In the door to the dining room a gray reflection is showing that still has no light. It is gray because it is a mixture of the black of night with the white of day . . . It is a murky reflection that still casts no light . . . It is like the turbid reflection of eyes when they have both the whiteness of life and the blackness of death, in these horrible hours when we await the death agony . . .

And how many nights of watching do I have left?

Oh, Uncle Pancho, Uncle Pancho! Looking back on your poor life I have suddenly peered into the future and I have seen my hopes pale with doubts, like the green cemetery there below the city that silently awaits you with its white tombs . . . It's just that tears are blinding my eyes and through the blurred film of tears everything looks indistinct . . . And how death takes delight in playing with life's plans! . . . Oh, now it won't be you, Uncle Pancho, who takes me on his arm on my wedding day, when dressed as a bride, I walk slowly, that long train trailing behind me stretched out on the dark rug . . . a long train . . . that is like a long cloud of Chantilly lace!

Early Tuesday morning

Tonight is Aunt Clara's night to stay up, and it was my night to sleep. But, instead of sleeping, I am awake and not feeling at all sleepy.

For, as if I were another seriously ill person, I have a terrible dread locked in my heart that is keeping me wide awake again tonight. A few hours ago, so great was my fear that, to see if I could relieve it a little, I got up from my bed, I opened the two big shutters on the window, I jumped up to sit on the sill, and this way, in my nightgown with my head leaning back, to see above the low wall that makes the patio look so much smaller, although it can't make the sky look smaller, I began to gaze at the heavens . . . And how fast the hours go by, when they are hours of contemplation, drunk from the fountain of such a clear night!

When I came to myself, still sitting on the windowsill, the old dining room clock was striking the early hours of the morning. And tonight is not a black night like yesterday. No, it is a serene and very clear night, with a tumult of stars, and the white edge of a half moon, and two bright stars in one corner of the sky, so bright, so very bright, that they have made me think of those two diamonds that Mercedes Galindo used to wear at night . . . then! . . . when at her table, joking, she would make signs to me, smile, wink, the light in her eyes like starlight, while a little below, the two diamonds in her *pendentif* twinkled happily, like two more bright stars, in the heaven at her neckline.

And with my head leaning back, looking at the stars, the night was slipping insensibly away.

Finally, after sitting so long on the windowsill, in my gown, I got very cold, and to warm up, I went back to bed. Now I'm writing in bed. I'm writing by the light of the candle that flickers and dances, and it sputters, and its sputtering is so soft it is like the soft music that accompanies the dance of a pretty ballerina.

Next to this room is the room where I watched last night, and where today Aunt Clara is watching . . . Under the door there is a little thread of light . . . Then comes the room where Uncle Pancho is dying . . . and finally, comes . . . the living room, the narrow little room where last night they put up a bed for . . . him! . . . But . . . is he sleeping? I imagine he is sleepless too . . . and that he too has opened his window and he too has looked out . . . Although there, in that little room, there is electric light . . . Maybe he has turned on the light and he is reading . . . but no, no! . . . he's not sleeping or reading . . . surely he has opened the window, he has leaned against the sill, and not looking at the street, he's looking at the sky. And over there, in the sky over the street, can he see, as I can see in the sky over the patio, Mercedes Galindo's two bright diamonds?

Ah! what a unique and strange day yesterday was! This night, like yesterday, all of it, absolutely all, seems to me like a dream or a nightmare . . . No, not a nightmare, just a dream—a long, nice dream that never ends, and that goes on . . . and on . . . and on . . . during the night and during the day.

Now that I remember, how silly, how terribly silly, dear Lord, I was yesterday, when, in my confusion, I dropped the spoonful of coffee with milk next to Uncle Pancho's pillow, and the sheet, and the pillow, and the blanket and the whole bed was spattered with coffee! . . . How ridiculous I must have looked at that instant, blushing and disheveled and not knowing what to do, with my kimono half-open at the top and the cup of coffee trembling in my right hand . . . But of course . . . it was the shock . . . it was the last thing I expected! . . .

Oh! In the monotonous rosary of my days, what a strange day yesterday will always seem! And how well I remember everything, everything, in its smallest details!

After my night of insomnia, breakfast, a bath, and then, while Aunt Clara stayed to take care of Uncle Pancho, exhausted emotionally and from lack of sleep, I came to sleep awhile in this same room where I am now. I slept deeply. When I got up I went as usual to see what was happening in Uncle Pancho's room. Aunt Clara had gone out for a few minutes, and Gregoria, who was on duty, told me, "A young man who understands medicine spent the morning here. He's so good-looking, and so refined, and he was so good with poor Don Pancho! He just this minute left with Miss Clara, and he said he was coming back."

Distracted as I was peering across the hall at the clock, and paying no attention to Gregoria, I cut her short telling her to go right away to get the coffee with milk, because it was past time to feed our patient. Gregoria was back shortly with the cup, and then I sat down on the bed, beside the pillow, and holding the poor gray head against my breast, slowly, I let the warm milk mixed with the infusion of coffee fall a drop at a time between the pale lips. Suddenly, someone knocked on the door and Gregoria answered, "Come in!"

But so great was the care I was taking in pouring the milk between the blanched lips that the door opened, closed, some steps were heard, and for an instant longer, without raising my eyes, I continued concentrating on those lifeless lips that can no longer speak. Finally I looked up, and then . . . oh! . . . it was then that I saw next to the bed, standing before me, so slender, so slim, such a trim physique, was he . . . yes . . . he . . . Gabriel Olmedo! And naturally, since I was rather disheveled, and since from holding Uncle Pancho's head, my kimono had fallen open a little at the top, I first moved my hand up to arrange my hair, but then it seemed better to first arrange my robe, and from my indecision between the two movements my hand struck the teaspoon that was in the cup, and the teaspoon flew like an arrow, sprinkling coffee with milk all over the bed, and fell on the floor with a terrible clattering of silver against cement, and I, looking at the spattered coffee, and looking at the spoon on the floor, and looking at my half-open kimono, and looking at him, began to tremble and blush scarlet red. He then took a few steps, picked up the teaspoon from the floor and with a smile that was rather mocking, and that was very bright and that showed very white teeth, and with a laughing look from very shining and very black eyes, and with the sound of his voice so . . . so . . . good! the same voice as *then*, he said, "It's easy to see this isn't the most experienced nurse!"

Fortunately, at that very instant Aunt Clara arrived and helped me in the battle of the coffee and milk. Then I got up from the bed, and while I was arranging my hair and straightening my kimono, Gabriel came up to me and said again in a low voice and with the same expression with which he had spoken before, "And me, don't you say hello to me now, María Eugenia?"

I smiled at last, stretching out my hand. He took it in his, and then I felt his in mine, so long, so fine, that looking at the two united in the air, my eyes instantaneously brought back Mercedes Galindo's table, when that same long vigorous hand, without hair and without diamond solitaires, lay sometimes on the tablecloth, next to my hand, and both were so alike and so perfect that, on the whiteness of the cloth and among the whiteness of the dishes, they were like a large lily beside a small lily on a field of lilies.

Aunt Clara, who was very grateful and very satisfied, came to look for me, took me to a corner of the room where Uncle Pancho couldn't hear, and then she told me that during the morning, while I was sleeping, Gabriel had come to visit. Talking and talking, she had related to him how, since Pancho was so gravely ill, the doctor had advised us to find an intern who would be always at the patient's side; how we had already called one and how at the present we were expecting him to come any moment. And Aunt Clara, touched, greatly exaggerating Gabriel's good heart and kindness, added that, when he heard her, he had answered right away saying that, given his great friendship with Uncle Pancho, it would not be anyone, absolutely no one other than himself, in person, who would serve as that practitioner. And more and more moved, Aunt Clara finished by saying, "I accepted his offer, María Eugenia, because it seemed to me that he made it with great sincerity and with great affection . . . Besides, though he doesn't practice, he does have his medical degree, and of course, a real doctor is always a lot better than a student . . . don't you think?"

Without understanding why, with Aunt Clara's news, I felt that in my whole being, together with a great fright, an immense joy also was shaking me, and wondering, "How can fear grow together with joy?" I answered Aunt Clara, unconscious of my words, "Well, that seems fine to me!"

And I went right away to thank Gabriel for his great affection and very great kindness. He listened attentively, with his eyes fixed on my mouth, pleased, as one listens to music, and he answered very kindly, "It is the least, and the last, thing I can do for him . . . and for you too, María Eugenia."

And then, as I had asked him, with the same anxiety, the same question that I have asked the other doctors so many times, he answered with sincere melancholy, shaking his head, "Hope . . . no! There's no hope!"

And while he was saying, "there's no hope" I don't know why it seemed to me that, as he spoke of Uncle Pancho's life, Gabriel was speaking of something else at the same time.

Then a long sorrowful silence ensued . . . I stood tremulous with tears looking at that head, sleeping and under sentence of death, which sank peacefully into the white softness of the pillow . . . But after gazing at him a long while, I aroused myself from my meditation, I looked at myself, I told myself that my kimono was very rumpled and it would be much better instead of my kimono to put on my white crêpe *déshabillé* with the lace. Then, leaving Uncle Pancho's room for a second, I came here to change my robe. And while I was combing my hair and dressing and fixing myself in the mirror, I thought that it was very foolish to have been frightened to have Gabriel stay in the house to attend Uncle Pancho, because . . . of course! . . . just as I thought then, and as I still think now, "After so long a time and after so many things . . . what can Gabriel Olmedo matter to me now?"

CHAPTER III

Wednesday noon

Now I'm writing in the morning, with sunlight, footsteps that pass on tiptoe, doors opening and closing gently, and the persistent buzzing of a fly that is driving me crazy.

It is eleven o'clock exactly. I came to be alone in this room under the pretext of sleeping. I came about ten minutes ago. It was when Aunt Clara returned to the house. No sooner had she come in than she began staring at me, and then, while she was taking off her veil and folding it and sticking the pins in it, she said to me twice, "Go rest awhile, María Eugenia, because I'm here now."

And I came knowing that I wasn't going to sleep. I'm so nervous that, just as I can't sleep at night, naturally! . . . much less still can I sleep during the day. Nevertheless, not sleepy or anything, after Aunt Clara spoke to me, I left the room and I came. I don't know why . . . why did I come? Doesn't it show indifference and selfishness and isn't it also absurd to settle down to write nonsense when a few steps away there is a sick man who is dying?

Oh, but I was longing so much to talk to someone! To someone capable of understanding these very subtle things that can't be said and that only a very few understanding people can understand. But Aunt Clara doesn't understand anything; and Gregoria, who understands everything, is always busy there in the kitchen or in the corral boiling water and washing clothes. Yes! I would like for someone to appear in me who can tell me the size of the immense anxiety that has opened such a great abyss here, inside my heart. This anxiety undoubtedly comes from lack of sleep. Of course! . . . since I don't sleep and I don't dream, and I'm always awake it's as if I were dreaming while awake, and as if awake, I'm sleeping, with no other tension in my heart, except this tension that lives always waiting and watching, alert and trembling, listening to the steps of death, that walks, and walks, and walks, always close, and always, always, not quite arriving.

As usual Aunt Clara left very early today to go take Communion for Uncle Pancho and to spend a little while with Grandmother. The nurse left too because of who knows what that happened to one of her children. When I saw that the nurse was going, I became quite upset, but Gabriel said to me, "Let her go, María Eugenia! And if she doesn't come back, then let her not come back! She isn't needed. I'm here to take care of everything."

And since seven o'clock this morning, taking care of Uncle Pancho, I have been alone with Gabriel.

Oh, how good Gabriel is! I didn't know he was so good. Taking care of Uncle Pancho he is as affectionate as a son, and he has the sure touch of good doctors, who, like mothers, always intuit all the nuances in the weakened spirit of the sick.

And moreover . . . how white Gabriel is! I didn't know that either . . . no . . . I had never noticed. Judging by his face I thought he was more a brunet, but no, he is white, white, very white. And as he is so clean, and as he is always so well groomed and so neat, he seems even whiter yet . . . yes . . . Gabriel has a bright and gleaming cleanliness. Do you suppose it's because of that, perhaps, that he never wears diamond rings, or a diamond tie pin, or diamond cuff links, or anything at all with diamonds? Gabriel adorns himself only with his shining cleanliness . . . Why do you suppose Gabriel's cleanliness shines so?

I remember that this morning very early, as he was preparing one of the injections that they are constantly giving Uncle Pancho, Gabriel began to roll up the sleeves of his silk shirt. Folding the sleeves back, he left his arms bare almost to the elbow, and they caught my attention because they are white, like my arms, and like Grandmother's arms, for she's very blonde too . . . And I remember that a second later, while he was giving Uncle Pancho the injection, I, who was standing right by him to help with the iodine in my right hand, and with the cotton and cologne in my left hand, observed that as he bent his head, his shirt collar stood a little away from his neck, and then I saw for the second time how, beneath the very black hair, and between the two transparent red ears, the back of his neck was opaque and extremely white like his arms. Certainly, looking at Gabriel's collar and his neck, a little accident happened to both of us, which almost turned out worse than my accident day before yesterday with the teaspoon and the cup of coffee with milk.

What happened was, after looking at the back of Gabriel's neck, and confirming that it was the same smooth white as his arms, I began to consider the fine weave of his silk shirt, and looking at it I thought, "You can see that Gabriel likes to feel silk next to his skin, just as I do." Then I started mentally to enumerate all the shirts Gabriel has worn in the two days he's been taking care of Uncle Pancho. I remembered that I'd seen: the raw silk, one; and the white silk with thin blue stripes, two; and the other one like it but with lavender stripes, three; and the green checked, four; and finally the white one today, five. And as in all that was five shirts in less than three days, I thought and said to myself, "Since Gabriel is so rich now, he probably has dozens and dozens of Japanese silk shirts and that is the finest silk made." And so when I was most absorbed in this idea of silk, he suddenly lifted his head, striking my right hand which was the one with the iodine, and a few drops spilled on my thumb, and as I moved my arm away very frightened, believing I had stained my white *déshabillé*, he very contritely said, "Oh! . . . pardon me! What disaster, dear Lord, has my head caused now?"

But since I immediately found that the so-called disaster only went as far as the end of my thumb, very happily and calmly, I answered holding up my stained thumb, "And very handsome, yes, very handsome he's going to look all day, with his cap of iodine, this young gentleman!"

Gabriel then looked at it, smiling, and said jokingly, "Well, this sick or wounded patient or whatever he is, must be treated too!"

And as soon as he finished with Uncle Pancho, he took a cotton ball, wet it with cologne, and started cleaning the nail, the tip and all of my poor thumb with great care.

After he quite finished that delicate treatment, we sat together on the upholstered settee that is in the room, and we sat there a long time, not saying a word, considering with mute melancholy the thin pale face that under the influence of the narcotic was sleeping peacefully now, with its eyes half-open, and its mouth half-open, and its pointed beard, and all its features elongated, white and pitiable, like the sorrowful features of a dying Christ . . . Until after a time, little by little, in a very low voice, Gabriel and I began to converse, and we went on talking, talking, until Aunt Clara arrived.

It's strange! . . . but when two people converse together in a room where there is a sick person, all, everything that is said seems to have a hidden or unknown meaning, and it's just that, naturally, no matter how sound asleep the sick person may be, when you talk near him, you have to talk in a very low voice . . . like this . . . softly, secretly . . . and when you talk softly, I don't know what happens, but each word that is spoken is a mystery . . . Yes . . . a deep mystery, and it almost seems that you speak with your eyes instead of your lips and it almost seems that you listen with your eyes instead of your ears, because ears and lips are made for the sound of a voice and eyes aren't . . . Eyes are made to hear and speak the dumb language of silence.

And in that way, almost whispering, sitting next to each other on the upholstered settee, Gabriel and I talked almost all morning.

It was I who initiated that long and singular conversation. Because it happened that once Gabriel had cleaned my thumb, while a faint scent of cologne floated in the air, I, sitting next to him, began to study Uncle Pancho, with a strong feeling of sorrow, and when I was most convinced that Gabriel was looking at him, too, I discovered that his eyes, instead of looking at Uncle Pancho, were looking at me, with a tenacious, profound, and disturbing expression that in the shadows and silence of the room scared me and inhibited me like the threat of something that may come and you don't know what it is . . . Then, to distract Gabriel's eyes from me, I asked him very quietly, indicating Uncle Pancho with my eyes, "Do you think he's suffering?"

In effect, his disquieting eyes left me, and Gabriel for a second contemplated the sorrowful Christ head and answered, "He's not suffering at all now. The narcotic has him in an unconscious state and he feels absolutely nothing."

"But when he wakes up he must suffer, because then he looks at us, and he knows us . . . poor Uncle Pancho! And in those lucid moments, Gabriel . . . do you suppose he understands that he is dying?"

"Maybe!" replied Gabriel. And the word escaped grazing his lips as if it were a sigh.

I said, "Perhaps he doesn't know anything, and he'll wake up in the beyond, just as we wake up in the morning after a night of sleep!"

"The beyond! . . ." repeated Gabriel like an echo. "The beyond! . . . And you, in your life now, do you confidently expect that beyond, the same way that at night you expect the morning, María Eugenia?"

And as the voice the two of us were using in the darkened room was the same muffled and whispered voice one uses in the confessional, I, with no effort, as one confesses a sin . . . yes, an enormous sin, which as it passes your lips brings your soul great relief and peace, for the first time in my life, I confessed to Gabriel this enormous sin that I had never confessed to anyone: "I firmly believe there is nothing beyond! . . . And it pains me . . . Oh, yes! . . . It hurts me to believe it to the point of weeping and with tears of blood, because this faith of believing in nothing, Gabriel, is an arid and horrible faith, which puts a complete end to hope, when hope is precisely the great, and the sublime, and the fitting, and the only object, yes, the only object of faith! . . . And it's so necessary, above all for us, poor women, who go through life, always, always, under a weight of resignation. You see: resignation to suffer boredom, resignation to forget ideals that cannot be, resignation to remain silent and to silence everything within ourselves always . . . oh! . . . so much, so much resignation that also needs to be hope, because naturally! without hope, everything becomes black and eternal desperation like the desperation of those condemned to Hell. If this isn't so, tell me, what would become, for example, of poor Aunt Clara, if, thanks to her faith, she were not living her life in hope? Look . . ., some mornings, when I see that Aunt Clara is leaving for church with her veil draped across her back, and there she stays for more than an hour on her knees, together with many others, who like her are called 'the pious old maids,' the 'beatas,' . . . well sometimes, when I see her leave in the morning, if I am in a sentimental mood, or 'daydreaming,' as Gregoria says, I imagine Aunt Clara's soul, and I imagine the souls of all the beatas at the moment they approach the fount of holy water, like this, as if they were a white row of biblical young girls . . . do you recall? . . . those whom they paint with a water jug on their shoulders, beside Jacob's well, coming to draw water to slake their thirst that day . . . The water of the beatas, Gabriel, is hope, and the beatas are thirsty people who have water to drink . . . For that reason . . . do you understand? . . . because of that I say that I am afraid of having a faith that has no hope."

I had spoken almost the whole time, with my eyes lowered, looking at my hands, in that quiet voice used for confession. When I stopped I timidly lifted my gaze and I met Gabriel's eyes, which were looking at me with an intense expression. They were kind eyes, which no longer frightened me as before, but, on the contrary, had an effect on me like a pure caress, a caress like kissing a child on the cheek, and a caress like kissing the hand of a saint. And it was in this way, looking at me with his curious and kind eyes, that Gabriel said to me, "And what need do you have for that chimerical hope that the beatas go to drink beside the fount of holy water in the mornings? Why, you have all the divine realities of life, María Eugenia! Life gave you everything in abundance and with open hands! . . . and see, you have beauty, you have youth, you have love."

I said, "It's true, I can't complain yet! I have youth and . . . I also have . . . love . . ."

"And by the way," said Gabriel then with mysterious insinuation, "I already know . . . I know . . . that very soon you're getting married, María Eugenia! I haven't congratulated you yet because . . . since you haven't wanted to tell me about it! . . . Oh! apparently, in moments of happiness old friends from the past are quickly forgotten!"

And it was then that I, putting a lot of cruel intention in my words, and hiding in them all the resentment from those dark days in San Nicolás, responded, "Well, after all, you have no reason to feel slighted, Gabriel! . . . Remember . . . remember that two years ago now, you didn't tell me either about your engagement that was so . . . grand! and your marriage that was so . . . grand! . . . to María Monasterios."

I don't know how I sounded, nor how Gabriel took it, but the fact is that he drank in all the cruel intent of my words as if by surprise he had drunk a very bitter medicine. Impatient, nervous, and very red, he cut me short and said very excitedly, talking almost, almost, in his full natural voice, "Oh! for God's sake, María Eugenia, for the sake of what you care for most in this world don't ever talk to me about my marriage, above all, never mention my wife to me! Oh, my wife! Imagine the most stupid, the most vain, the most ignorant person; put her in an atmosphere of absolute vulgarity and then you'll be able to form an idea of what my wife is and of what sort of life I lead. She always speaks out of turn, she hovers over me when she shouldn't, she talks to me when she shouldn't, and she even embraces and kisses me when she shouldn't . . . Oh! . . . You can't imagine what that is like! . . . And to make it even worse she's a woman who is wicked without being dissolute, that is to say, she's a woman I'll never be able to divorce, because the law is so idiotic that it doesn't consider it grounds for divorce if a person is as foolish, as irritating, and as disagreeable as my wife is! . . . Oh! what imbecilic acts we commit in life! and what a frightful torture it is to make a mistake in this way and forever! . . . Fortunately, in this horrible mismatch, I am the man and, therefore, instead of staying home facing a perennial scene, I leave the house and stay away all day! But if, by misfortune, it were the opposite, that is to say, if being the victim as I am, I were also the woman, instead of being the man . . . oh! . . . I would already have died of desperation and disgust!"

Gabriel was talking with passionate excitement. Hearing him, I recalled Mercedes Galindo, when in the dim light of her boudoir, she too related to me, sincerely, all the failure and hidden desperation of her existence . . .

And thinking these things, and looking at the horrible truth of what Gabriel was saying, I felt a breath of fear race through my heart, because I seemed to see all the hidden tragedies that life inflicts aching in the bosom of its tranquil appearance. But besides hearing him talk, I felt I don't know what . . . a kind of perverse joy, because I told myself that now, at last, I was seeing reparation and vengeance for that crushing grief that, first in San Nicolás and later in Caracas, tore my heart with sharp and silent suffering that no one near me ever came to suspect.

And because I was thinking about these things, and because I considered how very difficult it was to give opinions on the delicate matter Gabriel was discussing, I chose to say nothing. He too remained silent a few seconds. Then he drew very close to me and resuming his low voice, he said, "After all, María Eugenia, what do these . . . trivial . . . things in my poor life matter to you? . . . Let's talk about you and your happiness, yes, let's talk about you. I'll confess something to you . . . will you allow me to confess it? . . . Well . . . I had planned to go to the church the day you get married, to watch you go by at a distance, dressed as a bride, at a distance! . . . which is the only way I could see you . . . but now that I have seen you personally, I will not go to see you, no, never, never will I go to see you as a bride."

"And why not?" I asked, opening my eyes wide and lowering my voice, very low.

"Well, just because," and Gabriel said no more.

I smiled and started to tell him, "Yes, . . . my wedding was supposed to be next week, but with Uncle Pancho, it will have to be postponed . . . a short time, because both Grandmother and Leal say that marriage, no matter what happens, should never be postponed. Everything is ready, the house and all, but Leal . . ."

And abruptly, interrupting me, for the second time, Gabriel again said impatiently, "Oh! María Eugenia, please, don't talk to me so much about your marriage, and above all, have the kindness not to ever mention your fiancé to me!"

"Why, how nervous you are today, Gabriel! Remember . . . think carefully and tell me, who was the first to talk about my marriage? . . . wasn't it you?"

"Well, that means, then, that I committed an act of stupidity. And if I said something stupid it's no reason to prolong that stupidity eternally all morning long!"

"Well . . . then, it seems to me best for us to be quiet . . . yes . . .

the best thing will be not to talk about anything. I'll start being quiet right now!"

And I sat a moment smiling with my index finger across my lips.

Gabriel, getting excited again, said this which began by making my hands turn cold, and colder, and colder, until at last it left my whole body chilled and trembling, "Yes! María Eugenia, let's talk, let's talk, but let's talk about the time when I didn't have a wife, and you didn't have a fiancé . . . do you remember? Do you remember, when poor Pancho, and you and I, used to go to eat every night, there at Alberto and Mercedes's house? . . . Do you remember how they cared for us, and they would seat us together at the table, and drive us crazy with their teasing? Do you remember that before sitting down, I would always steal some flower from the centerpiece and give it to you? Do you remember that Mercedes was the one who always looked for a pin for the flower and as she handed it to me she would say, 'put the pin through the flower first so I won't have to fuss at you.' And then I would take your hand, and mad to kiss your hand with my lips, I would only hand you the pin. And do you remember, later in the drawing room? . . . Sometimes you would go sit at the piano, and there, in the shadow of the piano, very close to me, you would start to play, and your hands, on the white and black keys, would run through the arpeggios, flutter over the trills, and when suddenly they would pause to gently touch a chord, I looked at them and kissed them with my eyes thinking, 'They have the melody, the whiteness, and the uneven fluttering of dying swans . . .' And then, besides your hands, your lovely arms, and the pure line of your neck, and your pretty head, and your glorious smile, and all the harmony you have together with the harmony and the sound of the piano, which was like the voice of my heart that was dying of happiness . . . And suddenly, one day, you went away, I don't know where, and you never came back to Mercedes's house again! . . . Why did you go away, María Eugenia? . . . And why didn't I set out to find you, desperately, as you look for water when dying of thirst? . . ."

And in the grip of great emotion, Gabriel's eyes were enormous and glittering, as the eyes of madmen glitter and as the eyes of criminals must glitter. And staring at him and hearing him I was petrified with shock; while he, with his crazed eyes, went on saying, "Yes! How could I lose you? . . . I don't understand it . . . What horrible crime have I committed, my God, to have to live now, eternally, faced with the frightful torture of knowing that I have lost you forever, forever, without hope! Oh! no, no, no, you don't know, María Eugenia. Listen to me because I need to tell you about it now that chance at last permits it. When you least suspected it, and least believed it, many months ago now, I thought of nothing but you, always you, María Eugenia! . . . and crazy to see you, I walked down your street every day, but every day, and when I reached your house I would see the windows closed, and see the door to the entrance hall ajar, and I would console myself by walking past the door, and by telling myself: 'she is here' . . . And a year later, a few months ago, when I returned from my last trip to Europe, they told me, 'María Eugenia Alonso has a fiancé and is getting married' and then, like those poor sick people who are past recovery, who are not in bed, and who drag their desperation everywhere, loaded down with my desperation, like a thief and like a spy, I continually went past your house, and seeing that the windows were open now, I would walk slowly hugging the wall, slowly, to see if I could see you, and I almost never saw you; but one day I did see you and you seemed like a fairy, a vision, something impossible . . . I remember you were crossing the room wearing rose . . . don't you have a rose-colored dress? . . ."

"Yes . . . I have my rose charmeuse . . ."

"Well, I saw you dressed in pink, and for days my eyes saw nothing else! . . . Oh, María Eugenia! Do you want me to confess the truth, here where no one can hear us? . . . Well, listen . . . you and you alone are the cause of my misfortune . . . yes, it's your fault that I hate that hateful creature who is my wife, because every day when I wake up, I think, and I say to myself with the most horrible desperation, how could I have lost her? What crime have I committed to find myself married to María Monasterios, when I could have been married to 'her,' yes, to you, María Eugenia!"

And as he said this, Gabriel was weeping, almost, with desperation, and I . . . my hands were icy and I didn't know where I was, nor what was happening to me, while he, his wild eyes flooded with tears, went on talking and talking, and among a torrent of things I can't remember now he told me, "Because . . . don't deny it! . . ." and he repeated, "Now that we are alone where no one can hear us, don't deny it! . . . You loved me too with all the divine passion of your exquisite and loving temperament . . . You told me so! And the way you told me! You told me in time, but nevertheless, you told me too late . . . yes, I found out about it too late! At times I wonder, María Eugenia, if that could have been a terribly cruel vengeance of your keen spirit, so refined and so wise in matters of the emotions. But no! impossible . . . it was true, yes, it was true! . . ."

"What? . . . What was true, Gabriel?" I asked trembling with emotion, already knowing what he was going to respond. "What?"

And moving closer to me until he was close enough to kiss me, he told me with a smile—as gently and lovingly as a human voice could speak, "Well, that little blonde beautiful head, and those pretty white hands, know how to write ardent love sonnets, and leave them hidden between the pages of love stories, like pressed flowers, the memories of love."

I was tremulously awaiting it, and nonetheless, as my ears heard the sweet music of what Gabriel was saying, I instantly remembered all that mad passion and all that mad daring of my love sonnet, and seeing it shine bright and clear-cut in the mirror of memory, all the blood in my body suddenly rose to my cheeks, and blushing furiously, for several seconds I wanted to die of shame. But Gabriel, growing more and more and always more impassioned, was little by little assuming a voice that was weak, the doleful and heart-rending voice of poor people who beg because they're dying of hunger, and so, with his heartbreaking voice like a starving beggar he asked and said to me, "Isn't it true, María Eugenia, that it was I? . . . Isn't it true that it was I and no one else, that dying Romeo, that sad Romeo, that you, looking out from your balcony, awaited the entire night, carrying on a dialogue with the moon?"

And since Gabriel's voice was so heart-breaking, and since that tale of the balcony is such an old story now, and so lost in the past, I let myself be led gently by the force of truth, a gentle force like a breeze, and I said, just as if exhaling a sigh, "Yes! . . ."

Then, unconscious of speaking, as softly as a breeze, I also added as I blushed, "And certainly, there on my balcony you left me waiting forever! . . ."

Gabriel now, with his grief-stricken voice choked with tears, again implored and said to me, "María Eugenia, for God's sake, don't be so cruel and don't tell me that! It wasn't I, it wasn't I! . . . It was chance, it was my destiny, and my bad luck, which is very bad indeed . . . I don't know how it happened! . . . Mercedes was always talking to me about you, and I had planned to go see you there at the hacienda, where you were . . . To be more exact, I was supposed to go with Pancho, because he had offered to introduce me to your family, but I don't know, dedicated body and soul to business affairs, busy every hour of the day and night, when I least expected it, I had to travel to the interior of the Republic on an urgent matter; there I met María, who was also passing through with her family, they were all very hospitable to me, and . . . I fell, I don't know how I fell for it! Maybe, speaking honestly, I can't deny it, it's very probable that I was pushed into this marriage by my insatiable ambition to reach the top . . . to become somebody . . . these things in life are so complex, and they're so obscure! And it's true that through the influence of my father-in-law, I finally achieved the concessions I wanted, with those I made successful speculations, and I have grown rich . . . so rich, even richer than I longed to be, but, oh! if you knew how I've been punished, María Eugenia! If you knew to what extent I regret and loathe this money that I can never share with you, this useless stupid money that never, never can give me the only, the only thing I long for and covet: you, María Eugenia, you! Oh!"

And holding his head in his hands, Gabriel was quiet a moment because he couldn't find the words to show the fury of his desperation. Then, more calmly and with his eyes fixed on the floor, he began to search the past, and he went on saying, "But look . . . the more I think about it, the more I'm convinced that it was all the accursed workings of fate! . . . Once . . . wait, let me recall . . . no . . . it happened twice, with my coach at the door I was on the point of leaving to pick up Pancho so the two of us could go together or I would go alone to the hacienda where you were at that time . . . San Nicolás, it's called, isn't it? Well before leaving for San Nicolás, as I had already arranged with Mercedes, and as was natural, I telephoned first, to see if they were at home, and if they could receive me. Both times they told me you had gone out horseback riding; and naturally! as that happened twice, and as they always answered me in such a dry and disagreeable tone, and since besides I don't know your family, even though Mercedes would say to me, 'Look, she's expecting you, Gabriel,' I, frankly, was afraid of not being welcome. I still remember very well, both times a woman's voice spoke to me on the phone, but so sour and so unpleasant . . ."

And now it was I who suddenly broke into Gabriel's speech, and I did so with a kind of strangled cry, but so profound, and so full of surprise and hatred that until today I never knew a human voice could utter. Yes; it was a cry so unexpected and so grating that Uncle Pancho's head, asleep on the pillow, moved abruptly with the nervous jerk of a scare during deep sleep. And so in my cry of hate, which I felt arise more from my heart than from my throat, I explained, "Oh, María Antonia!! . . . That was María Antonia while I was out horseback riding with Perucho! . . . And she never told me anything!"

When Gabriel heard me cry out like this, he looked at my face and since I too must have had the light of madness in my eyes, he was very frightened, and suddenly grasping my two hands, he held them passionately in his own, and he said with a soothing voice, "Calm yourself . . . calm yourself, María Eugenia . . . calm yourself."

I, lowering my eyelids to hide my tears, answered, "Yes . . . yes . . . All of that, Gabriel, is over!"

And Gabriel, with a very sweet and soothing voice and with my two hands held in the nest of his hands, said again, talking to my hands, "Poor cold little hands that waited frozen in the night, under the moonlight, and which are cold and damp now too, just like blocks of ice!"

And since Gabriel's hands were burning like two burning embers, for a second I felt the infinite pleasure of warmth on my cold hands, and unconsciously I remained still and yielding. But all at once, some steps were heard, terrible steps approaching . . . coming closer . . . and, with the hammer-like blows of the heels, it seemed to me the whole house was shaking, because the sound of those steps was the sound of the steps . . . the steps . . . the footsteps . . . Leal's footsteps! . . . and shaking with terror I pulled my hands away from Gabriel's hands, I jumped to my feet, and I said trembling with fear, "He's coming, Gabriel, he's coming!"

And the door started opening little by little, and when it was wide open I understood that they were not the loud footsteps of Leal, who is far away, but the soft steps of Aunt Clara, who, as usual, was returning now from taking communion for Uncle Pancho and spending a few hours with Grandmother.

It was then that Aunt Clara stared at me fixedly, and said to me as she was taking off her veil and as she was folding it, "Go rest awhile, María Eugenia, because I'm here now."

And not sleepy or anything I came to lock myself alone in the most isolated room in the house.

But . . . oh! this immense anxiety that nothing relieves! . . . oh! what an immense abyss has opened here in my soul! . . .

This immense anxiety doesn't come from my conversation with Gabriel, no, no, it can't be, I had this anxiety long before, because my relationship, our relationship, that relationship of mine with Gabriel, is no longer anything in my life now, nor will it be anything in my future life; no, it's an old and sad story that, together, for a moment, the two of us have looked at this morning, as one looks at all sad, old tales of love that happened in other times, many centuries ago, and that are still seen written in books and in the translucent stained glass of Gothic windows, and painted in antique pictures where the color is fading now, and embroidered in the tapestries of the Gobelins of France, and rhyming in the verses of all the poets . . . Yes . . . I said it very clearly this morning for Gabriel to hear, "That, Gabriel, is over now!" Yes . . . it's true, that story of mine and of Gabriel is over now. It's an old and sad story, where the lovers died, as lovers always die in the sad, old tales of love . . . as Leander and Hero died; and Ophelia and Hamlet; and Tristan and Iseult; and the lovers of Teruel; and pale Werther; and as the persecuted and tormented Romeo and Juliet died . . .

That story and that earlier life are over now, and now this life is a different one . . . yes, it's as if Gabriel and I had been born anew . . . Gabriel says his present life is a very sad life and a very wretched life and he weeps when he says it . . . but not I . . . I don't cry, because my life is good and I have my sweetheart who loves me, and I'm going to be married soon . . . and I will be happy . . . and I will live peacefully . . . and happily . . .

But, oh! this immense anxiety, where does it come from, dear Lord? . . . It must without a doubt come from lack of sleep and from the dreadful tension that dwells in my alert and trembling heart, as it listens to the footsteps of death, which walks, always near, and always, always, without arriving! . . .

CHAPTER IV

*From Wednesday night
to Thursday*

I'm afraid of Gabriel now.

I'm so afraid of him! Today, in the early afternoon, while we were in Uncle Pancho's room, his eyes did nothing except follow me, obstinately returning to me with the dizzying, black obsession with which bats flutter, and with which crime hovers over the plot of classical tragedies.

For the whole afternoon I have done nothing except avoid Gabriel and hide my eyes from those mad eyes that call aloud to mine—I'm not quite sure for what reason. Whenever Aunt Clara left the room, I would follow her in order not to be alone with Gabriel. Until finally, he became so nervous that, while Aunt Clara was standing near the window with her back to us as she carefully measured out a sedative, letting drops fall slowly into an empty glass, he walked up to me and said in a low voice, very hurriedly and very anxiously, "María Eugenia, please, listen to me. I must have a few words with you!"

I answered, "We have nothing to say, Gabriel, that can't be said in front of Aunt Clara."

And he implored me again hastily, "It's about what we were discussing this morning!"

"What we talked about this morning," I told him very seriously, "those things we talked about this morning and the sonnet, and all the rest, is finished now! It's as if it had happened many centuries ago. Those friends of the past, Gabriel, have died!"

But he said with his desperate, rapid voice, "No, no, no. I haven't died. No, I'm alive, more alive than ever because now is precisely when I love life most and you must listen to me. I beg you, for the sake of what you love most in this world, María Eugenia, listen to me!"

Aunt Clara, who had finished measuring the drops now, left the window, and when Gabriel saw her coming toward us, he stood as still and quiet as if he were at mass.

If Gabriel's lips say nothing in Aunt Clara's presence, Gabriel's eyes say terrible things that his lips cannot speak. They follow me all the time with an obstinacy so deep and so black that it is like the obstinacy of death running after life. Yes, Gabriel's eyes frighten me. I feel in their sparkling blackness the great attraction that I have felt sometimes near the void, when, on my excursions through the mountains, vertigo has shouted at me from the bottom of an abyss.

In order not to see the luminous obsession in Gabriel's eyes, beside the hazy obsession in Uncle Pancho's eyes, at twilight I left the room to rest a moment. But since this morning, Gabriel's eyes, Gabriel's voice, Gabriel's words, and Gabriel's presence have entered my thoughts, and they pursue me, tenaciously, wherever I go. And since the Gabriel that is in my mind frightens me much more than the Gabriel that is in Uncle Pancho's room, in order to run away from him twice, I ran away from my solitude, and I came to seek relief in the outdoor peace of the corral, which is the only generous space in this poor, cramped house.

There, facing the sunset, and facing her tub overflowing with suds, was Gregoria, soaping some very white sheets and pillowcases that had just been boiled. I sat down next to her on the rickety ironing table, and looking at the varied hues of the clouds and at the black tumbling of her hands in the whiteness of the foam, as I used to do in other times, I began to talk to Gregoria to see if it would distract my thoughts.

And there, too, in the corral, while Gregoria's hands swam in the foam, Gabriel's name suddenly appeared on Gregoria's lips in her colorful vocabulary, and it began to echo again and again in my ears.

That name, however, in the country atmosphere of the corral, no longer frightened nor inhibited me, nor did it seem like black crime nor a dizzying abyss. Gabriel's name, rose-tinted in the sunset, fell naturally from Gregoria's lips, and sounded in my ears, and fluttered over the grasses and under the sky with such graceful flourishes of its wings that my eyes, gazing at the distant tree branches, began to ponder the sweet love of little birds that hide their nests among the leaves, and, without knowing that men inhabit the earth, spend their lives swinging in space with their wings spread.

When I settled down on the broken table, Gregoria first spoke of the clothes she was washing. Then she spoke, with many sighs and great sorrow, of the inconsolable pain that Uncle Pancho's death caused. She spoke of what good care we were taking of him, and it was while she was praising Gabriel's help that she began to talk about him, asking me, "And that boy, I mean, the doctor, Don Gabrielito. What a good boy! He's married, isn't he?"

When I heard his name, I shivered with emotion, and I think I smiled and answered, "Yes, Gregoria, he's married. And why do you say he's so good?"

"Why do I say he's so good?" And Gregoria straightened up from her little pool of suds, and addressing me as *tú*, as she did when I was a child and as she did in our times of greatest closeness, she said with amazement, "María Eugenia, do you think that nowadays you can find doctors who will take care of sick people for free the way this boy is taking care of Don Pancho? He says he has affection for him . . . well . . . it must be because of his affection for Don Pancho, but just the same, he's showing a lot of kindness! And besides, he's a very handsome man, and he's so refined."

"And isn't he very light skinned and very well groomed, and very good-looking, Gregoria?"

"I should say so! And the way he laughs! I've never seen anybody else who laughs like he does! And you tell me whether I've seen high-born men and handsome young men, here, in your people's house and other places too. But the way he laughs, I've never seen before. Just him. What nice teeth! It makes you want to kiss him on the mouth when he starts laughing!"

"Kiss him, Gregoria? Kiss him on the mouth? Do you know what I think, and what I've always thought? Well, that you like men very much, and that in your youth, Gregoria, you must have been really wild!"

Gregoria's only comment was great Wagnerian laughter, in whose notes I heard a troupe of all the happy storms of her youth pass in review. And after bending over the tub again, and after scattering her judicious dabs of soap here and there, she took a pillowcase heaped with bubbles in her hands, straightened up again, and lighting the phrases with her laughs as she rubbed the soapy cloth on her knuckles, she added, "Yes, I may be really black, and really ugly, and everything else, but I always had someone interested in me. That's the honest truth! And if I never got married it was because I didn't want to get mixed up with marriage, because I've always believed that marriage was only made for high class people. Oh, yes. Black women who are married put on airs, and they're ashamed of their color, and they have to put up with insults and even beatings from their husbands. They have to keep quiet and go where they're told and suffer a lot to keep their respectability. (Here she gave a sustained laugh, full of little pauses, in honor of respectability.) If you don't marry, you can love someone today and if that someone doesn't act right, or turns out to be a no-good, well, you leave him and love someone else, and they're all as considerate and loving as can be. Yes, María Eugenia, when men feel secure, they're impossible to put up with. That's because, Ave María, they only care about what is doubtful and very difficult, and what may slip through their fingers!"

"Really, Gregoria, you're saying the most immoral things! What if Aunt Clara heard you!"

And Gregoria's only answer was another Wagnerian laugh. Then she bent over and pulled a cigar from who knows what mysterious hiding place at the base of the tub. She had no doubt hidden it when she heard me coming, because I know this habit of hiding her tobacco when she hears high heels is an indispensable part of her protocol. Revealing the cigar, she first blew on it and then gave it several drags. With her skillful tactics, the cigar glowed again. Gregoria happily created a great halo of smoke, and surrounded by the gray, voluptuous little clouds that were drifting apart and fading into the gray night, she set the cigar aside and, taking up her work, she said very gravely and philosophically, "Every color and condition has to have its own morals, María Eugenia. Miss Clara can't say anything to me, because I'm a good Christian, and I'd die before I'd fail to light a candle to the Virgin of Carmen every Saturday night, or before I'd forget to go to church on Palm Sunday and get my palm leaves, blessed by the priest, and before I'd miss communion on Ash Wednesday at the very altar where the Nazarene stands, and before I'd fail to hear the sermon of the seven stations of the cross and kneel while they're preaching the seventh, which is the very time the Lord died. Yes, I'm a good Christian, and no one can say a word of reproach to me about it. But everything has its place, and they can't fool me! God sent us to this world, and commanded us to adore Him and bless Him every day, but He never said who we ought to love nor how many we ought to love on this earth. Let them say what they wish, in these questions of love He observes, but He doesn't intrude. And so you'll know what I'm telling you is true, all you have to do is think about this: if God disliked certain things, He'd have made some difference between married people and unmarried people. But you see, He doesn't, because He sends them all the punishment of children. Without ever getting married even once, I had four children. And do you want me to tell you the truth, María Eugenia? I've always been glad I was born black and poor, first, because that was God's will, and then, because black and poor I could love whomever I pleased. There are great and powerful people who seem very happy, but they hurt inside, María Eugenia! Look. Think, and tell me if it isn't so. Do you believe Don Gabrielito, for example, loves the lady he's married to? Are you thinking he loves her? As for Gregoria, an ignorant black woman, a common old woman, who isn't good for anything but bending over a tub scrubbing rags and burning her hands on hot irons, she doesn't let anything get past her. In spite of being black and common, she has a keen sense of smell!"

"How do you know . . . how do you know he doesn't love her?" I asked, very intrigued.

Then Gregoria, with a mysterious smile, bringing back to me all the surprise and shock and all of the upsetting scene of this morning, repeated, "Why, you ask? Oh, my Lord, all his curiosity! Why! Well, I say he doesn't love her, because if he loved her, he wouldn't be driving me crazy asking me questions about someone else when he has the chance and he's by himself with me taking care of Don Pancho. Then, as soon as he knows we're alone, the questions begin, and the questions never end. When she was little was she as pretty as she is now? Does she spend her time reading, or does she spend her time embroidering? Does she play the piano much? Is she very much in love with the sweetheart she has? Is she excited about her marriage? Was she sad before she got engaged? And it's all sweet words and presents for the old woman so she'll loosen her tongue and talk freely. But do you want to know what I said to him? Well, I warned him, 'See, Don Gabriel, she's as good and sweet as a skein of silk, but if you make her mad, you'll hear from her, because then, then she's fierce, really fierce. All the fierceness comes out that she inherited from her people here, the Aguirres!' "

But without knowing why, when I heard this last bit, my pleasure and surprise turned abruptly into a lively disgust with Gregoria. I shivered nervously and interrupted her, annoyed.

"What a string of nonsense you're saying, Gregoria! It seems as if you're so old and senile now that you've completely lost the little sense you used to have!"

"Nonsense? Nonsense?"

Gregoria fixed me with such a long, intense stare that I found it impossible to face her despite the dim light. When she had finished this language of the eyes, she renewed the battle with words.

"Sure! It must be senility and old age! Look here, María Eugenia, do you want the truth? Because, except for your age and color, you might have been my daughter. Well, listen, María Eugenia, that boy is dying for you! And he's the one, don't deny it, he's the very one. It was on account of him they sent you off to the hacienda two years ago when we spent three straight months there, and I got a sunstroke that nearly killed me. Well, he's the same one. And when you heard he was marrying someone else, you were so, so sad that I wanted to cry whenever I saw you, and what I felt like doing was holding you in my arms and saying, 'Come here where you can cry on the bosom of your old black friend who loves you truly and is the only one who knows the bitterness you're suffering!' But, Gregoria observes, and keeps quiet, and swallows it all so they won't call her a busybody or uppity or disrespectful. That's why I never said anything to you. But now I warn you, María Eugenia, because I can see you're in danger. You're climbing slippery stairs. Listen, that boy is married, and you're married, too, in a manner of speaking. And you're not Gregoria, María Eugenia, because you were born very high and very lofty, and you have to walk the straight and narrow path of decency. And if he loves you, you love him too, the very same way, don't deny it! He'd be the one you'd marry if you could always do whatever you please, and follow your heart! Sure, sure, and today he'd be capable of even killing people just to have you, because that's the way men are. They despise what they have and when it escapes them, then comes the crying and the desperation. But that's not the scary part, María Eugenia. The scary thing is that now you're more attracted than ever to that past love, because once you love, that love lingers. These old eyes have seen so many things in life, and from what they've seen they know that love is reborn and reborn over and over, the same way weeds sprout again. Don't you think I can see the happiness on your face every time I mention his name to you? Don't you think I noticed that day when he appeared all of a sudden, and you were so rattled that you came within an inch of spilling a cup of coffee and milk on poor Don Pancho? And do you think I didn't notice just now when I mentioned his laugh and kissing him on the mouth? I just did it to see your face when I said it, just offhand!"

I had hopped off the table and, beside myself with fury, stamping my foot on the ground, I started shouting with a strangled voice, "You be quiet! Caramba! When you start talking nonsense, you lose touch with everything, as if you'd gone crazy! The only true thing you've said is that you're stupid! Yes, you're very stupid, very stupid! And you're very presumptuous too and very interfering, and you don't understand anything, and you get everything backwards, and you arrange it any way you want. Yes, go on saying stupid things, and shout them at the top of your lungs so everyone will hear, and you'll wreck my life with jealousy on account of your gossip!"

"That's right, María Eugenia, that's right! Insult me and kick me and throw me out on the street if you think it's a good idea, but even insulted and kicked and all, I don't take anything back, just because. And because I think I'm here to tell you the truth, María Eugenia. Why, I raised your own mother, and I was the first to hold you in my arms when you were born. Go on, insult me! Insult me more; Gregoria was born to hear insults, just a worthless black woman! And don't think, don't be thinking that this is the first time you've mistreated me, or the first time I've let myself be mistreated by you. When you were a tiny thing, no bigger than the size of one of these wet pillowcases, well, whenever they took you to spend the day at the house down there, it was Gregoria who spent the whole day carrying you around. And do you know what you liked to do and what amused you the most? Well, you liked to grab my hair and you died laughing, hanging on to my braids, so hard that I don't know how your little fingers didn't break squeezing my wool. Hearing you laugh, I laughed too, saying, 'Those blessed braids, finally, are good for something.' If people tried to butt in to keep you from pulling so hard, I'd tell them, 'Leave her alone so she won't cry, because this isn't hurting any of you!' Well, child, just as I used to say then, I say now, if insulting Gregoria relieves you of your pain, insult her all you want and unburden yourself to her, for the day will come when you understand how wrong these insults are! And for the moment, although it may seem rude to leave you like this, with words in your mouth, I'm going to hang up these clothes so the night air will dry them, to see if by morning they're dry."

Gregoria, who had already rinsed and wrung out the sheets and pillowcases, put them in an empty bucket and slowly went off toward the clothesline, at the back of the corral. There the white pieces fluttered gaily and snapped as they were shaken out, until finally, pinned to the clothesline, like a row of birds ready to go to sleep, they became silent and still. Then I could see the black head that had melted into the semidarkness, standing out against the wall of cloth. From the distance, while my eyes saw her appear against the white background, I thought sweetly of the days of unconscious childhood, when I had so much fun pulling at those braids of tight wool. And staring at the black head coming and going against the sheets, I envied my lost childhood; I envied her humble hair; I thought of the insurmountable distances that separate lives. And once more, there at the back of the corral, above the woolly head, I saw, in a fiery black and red spiral, all the tragic happiness of my thoughts that had turned again to Gabriel.

CHAPTER V

Thursday night

to Friday

Today two unpleasant things have happened to me. One was unintentionally caused by Grandmother. The other was caused by Gabriel, very much on purpose. He says it wasn't. He swears that it was an accident. I don't believe it. No, I don't believe it! But . . . suppose Gabriel is right? These things . . . can they really happen that way . . . suddenly . . . accidentally? Because then, well . . . It wouldn't be his fault, poor Gabriel!

How true it is, as Gregoria says, when she sets forth her fatalistic doctrines and explains, "What is going to come, starts walking and walking, and its steps are counted, and it arrives when you least expect it, even if you try to dodge." It's true. Gregoria is right!

This morning Gabriel and I haven't been alone as we were yesterday, and as I so feared might happen today. No, Gabriel and I haven't been alone for an instant all morning, because the nurse returned very early. After giving one excuse after another for having left yesterday, she stayed with us every second in Aunt Clara's absence. I remember that Gabriel glared at the nurse furiously while she was making her excuses, and without letting her finish explaining, he turned his back on her and muttered to me, "For what this devil is worth! She's the clumsiest and most useless I've ever seen! And so disagreeable!"

I, too, think she's very clumsy, very useless, and I really think we could do without her. Besides, she has the flaw of talking when she shouldn't. Decidedly, this poor nurse is what you might call a very tiresome person. But after all, this morning she came at the right time because I didn't want to be alone with Gabriel under any circumstance.

As if it were a presentiment, Gabriel was very dejected. In my opinion, he must not have slept all night. So, sad and with circles under his eyes, in front of the nurse, he softly said a few phrases to me about his hopeless life. He spoke so humbly and with such grief that frankly it broke my heart and, little by little, I began losing the fear I felt yesterday. Finally, I began to feel, not very afraid of him, but very sorry for him.

For example, I remember that, looking at Uncle Pancho, he said several times with his eyes bright, swimming with tears, "I wish I were he!"

After he repeated that the second or third time, I asked him, "Why, Gabriel?"

"Well, because I have no goal in life anymore, and now the only thing I passionately desire is death!"

"Death?" I said, astonished and shocked, "You want to die! Really! When you have so many means for being happy! There are others, many others, who are more unfortunate, Gabriel, and they don't complain."

But he replied, "No one is as unfortunate as I."

Then he remained silent and listless, with a sad face, until Aunt Clara arrived.

But, oh! It was Aunt Clara who was to bring the greatest portion of sorrow today. When she walked into the room, pale and shaking, without taking off her veil or anything, Aunt Clara sank down on the sofa next to me and, pressing her handkerchief to her eyes, while her voice emerged muted, and her poor, thin, knotted fingers trembled with grief, she told me between sobs, "Oh! María Eugenia, María Eugenia! How true it is that troubles never come singly! You don't know what has happened at home! You don't know! Do you remember the dizzy spells Mama was having? Do you remember that I told you that she had a long spell yesterday that had alarmed me so much, and here, in front of you, I spoke with the doctor and asked him to go examine her today? Well, he went and he listened to her heart carefully and he told me she has heart trouble, that her heart beat is irregular. Naturally, I was very scared and I asked him if it was something to be concerned about. And he . . . oh! Do you know what he told me? Well, he said, 'Yes, it's serious, but it's not an immediate emergency. She could live like this up to two or three months.' Imagine, María Eugenia, how I felt! Two or three months, María Eugenia, two or three months! And afterwards? Afterwards! Oh, my Lord, Lord, how alone I'll be! Give me resignation! And how true it is, God, that in Your wisdom, You never send troubles singly!"

Sitting on the sofa, with her veil fallen over her back, and the handkerchief pressed tight against her eyes, Aunt Clara wept bitterly for a long time. Seeing her like that, I started crying, pulling out my handkerchief too. Gabriel tried to calm the two of us as well as he could, while he sighed deeply from time to time. But of course he wasn't sighing for Grandmother's heart problems, but rather because of the sadness and the immense hopelessness of his own life that has him so afflicted and clamoring for death.

Naturally, since sorrow is such an intimate tie, this morning, Gabriel, Aunt Clara, and I, sitting in a row on the sofa, were like a single soul in three bodies, united by grief. And since that time, Gabriel has been sweeter, gentler, and more diligent than ever in taking care of Uncle Pancho. Because of that, trusting and relaxed, I thought all the time, "How good Gabriel is!" With all the comings and goings of the nurse and Aunt Clara, I found myself alone with Gabriel, the two of us quite close, silent except for our continual sighing, first one and then the other, which in the quiet room was like the reading and response of some rosary of grief, when, instead of praying Ave Marías, we were praying with two sighs for each bead.

When we felt so close and so sad, and he was so respectful and reserved, how could I have imagined what happened then? No! It was impossible; I wouldn't have dreamed of such a thing!

It was around six o'clock in the evening. Was it six o'clock? I don't think it was six, because it was already getting dark. It must have happened about six-thirty—somewhere between six and six-thirty. But what does it matter! The time is not important.

It happened this way:

I was in Uncle Pancho's room with Gabriel and Aunt Clara, and since it was very hot, I said, "I'm going out to get a little fresh air and drink a glass of water. I'm terribly thirsty."

I calmly left and walked toward the dining room. Once there, I began pouring a tall glass of cool water from the pitcher, and while I stood there with the pitcher in my right hand and the glass in my left, I heard someone walk up behind me. It was Gabriel, who came in the dining room saying, "I'm thirsty too."

Since absolutely everything Gabriel had said today, he had said with such great humility, when he said, "I'm thirsty" to me, it reminded me of the dreadful thirst Christ suffered on the cross, and to distract him and somewhat relieve his grief, without speaking of Christ's tragic thirst, I spoke of another more pleasant, and I said with a smile, "That's right! Imitating me, you came to get a drink too. Well, then, like Rebekah, in the patriarchal tradition, I'll give you my water to drink."

And I handed him the glass that was so full that it was splashing and spilling. But Gabriel rejected it gently and moving it toward my lips, he said, "No, no! I accept the water, but I can't accept it in a patriarchal way. No, you drink first, and I'll drink whatever you may leave for me, and maybe I'll find some secret in the bottom of the glass."

"Secrets?" I said with such a deep sigh that it no longer seemed like an Ave María, but more like an Our Father with glory, mystery, and all. "Secrets! I don't have secrets any more! But in case I may perchance have one, and I don't remember it, I think it will be safer not to let anyone drink from my glass. You take this water, Gabriel, and I'll pour myself another glass from the pitcher."

But Gabriel didn't take the glass and he looked at me smiling and with his very sad voice like a sad caress, and with his sad eyes like a black caress, where a dawning of happiness barely glimmered, he began to say, "Not that way! For I won't drink except after you and from the same glass! Yes, María Eugenia. Then, while I'm drinking, for the short space of a few seconds, I'll be happier than all the patriarchs and all the prophets of the Old Testament, because as my lips drink, my eyes will see eyes that they never looked upon."

Since it delighted me to see that Gabriel was finally losing his lugubrious tone, I said, smiling and contented, "I'm sure it was no great loss to the Old Testament! But, anyway! Thanks to water and thirst, and thanks to God, I can finally stop weeping for Don Jeremiah."

He seemed not to hear me, as if he were deaf or as if he were in a trance, and he went on talking while I was talking.

"Because like this—tired and pale and with circles under your eyes, dressed in pink—you're prettier, more like a rose, and more like Juliet than ever. This is the way, just like this, I always saw you in my dreams, so romantic and so delicate, writing my sonnet!"

Now, when I heard him mention Juliet, and talk about the sonnet, I became very serious again, and with a grave and severe voice I replied, "Not Juliet! Juliet died, Gabriel. I told you that yesterday, don't forget. Don't talk about that anymore! And take your glass of water because I'm getting tired of holding it."

As Gabriel is so insistent and so stubborn, he wouldn't take the glass. Instead, he insisted on talking about Juliet, and with a voice . . . with the same divine and troubling voice he used yesterday when he said, "For that pretty little blonde head, and those pretty white hands know how to write ardent love sonnets," he now said, "Well, if Juliet has died, María Eugenia,

I'll make Juliet come back to life, the way one revives people who have died of cold."

Out of sheer curiosity and without even suspecting what Gabriel was insinuating, I asked, "How is that?"

It was then that Gabriel, swiftly and gently, enfolded me in his arms and, holding me close, he answered, "This way!"

I don't know how he managed to kiss me exactly on my lips for a moment while I couldn't move or push him away. But I think Gabriel managed this not just because he was quick, but also because of the circumstances, since I was wedged between the sideboard and the dining table and holding a glass of water in my left hand, and couldn't run or defend myself out of fear of breaking the glass or spilling the water. No, with just one hand free, and squeezed between two pieces of furniture, how could I defend myself from Gabriel, who is so agile and so strong? I couldn't keep him from kissing me! There was no way to avoid it!

But then . . . Good Lord, what that poor Gabriel heard then, as punishment for his treachery! It isn't fit to write here, nor do I think anyone in the world can ever write it, because it wasn't words, it was a river of indignation, a cataract of insults, a torrent of reproof. Oh, yes, Gregoria was right, after all! What Gabriel heard from me today, between six and six-thirty, I'm sure his ears had never heard before. The first thing I did, in my rage and with all the strength that indignation lends, was to stamp my feet and to throw the glass on the cement, forming a great puddle and making such a fearful crash of broken glass that I still can't understand why Aunt Clara didn't come in a panic to investigate. And then, in the midst of the shattered glass and the water that was soaking our feet, after having splashed on our clothes, I told him he was no gentleman, and to leave Uncle Pancho's house immediately because here I made the rules. I called him a hypocrite, a fraud, despicable, a traitor, and I told him that I hated him with all my heart. I stopped when I couldn't find any more epithets in my vocabulary or any more tones of indignation in the gamut of my voice, while the miserable Gabriel, insulted, pained, and splattered with water, kept repeating, "Forgive me, María Eugenia! I didn't mean to! It's not my fault . . . it's not my fault."

I abruptly turned my back to him, sat down in a chair, buried my head in my arms on the table and bitterly burst into tears, with deep, muffled sobs.

Gabriel edged nearer and nearer to me until he stood beside me and his voice, in rhythm with my sobbing, told me in secret, with a tone so gentle, so melodious, and so soft, so very soft that it was like a barely audible song beside the cradle of a sleeping child, "Forgive me, María Eugenia! Forgive me, it wasn't like me! It was my love, the madness that is killing me, it was this blazing fire inside me, the unavoidable cry of nature. It was the kiss of the sonnet! But I won't do it anymore, I swear I won't, never again, never again!"

And I went on crying and crying inconsolably, because now that I was silent and my face hidden and my arms drenched in tears, was when I really felt Gabriel's burning kiss like a hot ember pressed upon my ignorant lips. And close to my ear his caressing voice was saying with the sincere contrition of a repentant man, "Never again! Never again!"

I thought of the terrible anathema of the raven repeating "Nevermore, nevermore," and tears poured from my eyes like an endless torrent.

I don't know how long I sat there shedding tears on my arms and on the dining room table. Sometimes I think I cried for an eternity, and other times I think it was only a very brief second that stretched out and seemed long due to that miraculous mystery of feeling Gabriel's lips fixed tenaciously on mine, while I could barely feel the close contact of his voice grazing my ear, kissing me, kissing my soul as he softly repeated with the sad consolation of farewell, "Never again, never again!"

Until finally, I don't know if it was because I heard footsteps or for some other reason, I abruptly got up, and embarrassed because of the kiss I'd received and embarrassed because of the insults I'd hurled, covering my face with my handkerchief, unwilling to look Gabriel in the face, I precipitously left the dining room and came to this room. I lay down on the bed, and hid my face again in the folds of the pillow. Little by little I stopped crying and there, alone, I began to smile. I smiled until finally I was laughing out loud, laughing at myself. At myself, because one day, not so long ago, shortly before Uncle Pancho got sick, I had philosophically written the most absurd and ridiculous opinions about kisses.

Kisses . . . kisses! Thinking and dreaming about kisses, I gradually began to think about Gabriel's mouth, and I realized that, away from him, I couldn't call to mind the exact shape of his lips in the silence of my imagination. I could remember his teeth, and I could remember his laugh, but I couldn't remember at all the shape of his mouth when he is quite serious. My curiosity was so great, and so great was the anger I felt against my insufficient memory and imagination that I suddenly said, "I'll go to Uncle Pancho's room to ask something, and that way, casually, without letting Gabriel realize it, I'll study him carefully!"

Getting out of bed, I washed my eyes, combed my hair, put on some powder and lipstick, and when almost no traces remained of my tears, very seriously, prepared to stand on my dignity, and utterly determined not ever to speak to the treacherous Gabriel again, I went off to make my observation. But, the chance happenings in life! Without thinking, I quite absentmindedly pushed the door that leads from the dining room to the first patio. Since the door is old and sticks, I had to open it as I always do, with a forceful shove, and what happened? Well, as fate would have it, Gabriel was not in Uncle Pancho's room, as I believed. Instead, he was walking toward the dining room, going in the opposite direction from me, and as I pushed the door, he arrived at the exact same instant as I. As the door suddenly yielded, it hit Gabriel such a hard blow on the head that the whole door shuddered with the violence of the impact and, like the door, I shook too and gave a sharp cry of surprise. But Gabriel didn't. Gabriel said nothing. For a few moments he stood in front of me, stock-still and wordless, not even lifting a hand to his battered head. Impassive, like a statue of stoicism or of holy patience, he complained at last with great resignation, "First with words! Now with actions!"

His joke, and the chance accident, and my surprise and Gabriel's face— all seemed so funny to me that, without saying a word, covering my mouth with my hand so that he wouldn't see that I was overcome with an attack of laughter, I hurried toward Uncle Pancho's room. Instead of following his original path toward the dining room, as I naturally thought he would do, Gabriel imitated the behavior of a lap dog that turns to go with its master whenever their paths chance to cross. He walked behind me to Uncle Pancho's room, although I didn't hear his footsteps nor realize at all that he was following me.

Once there, to complicate matters, this is what occurred:

Since I had left Gabriel battered and immobile beside the door, I had been making superhuman efforts not to laugh. When I walked in, thinking that now I was quite serious, and just to say something, I asked Aunt Clara with my face convulsed with laughter, "Is there no change, Aunt Clara?"

And foolish Aunt Clara, instead of answering my question, glared at me and observed with disgust, "You look like you're at a party, María Eugenia, as if you were asking something very funny. Really, I don't think we have anything to laugh about today!"

Naturally, such a reprimand made me want to laugh even more. To hide my reaction, I turned my back to Aunt Clara, and then for the second time I unexpectedly came face to face with Gabriel. He was standing behind me, hidden from Aunt Clara, and he was dying laughing in silence, with that laugh of his that so charms Gregoria. Seeing his laugh, just as if it were my own laugh reflected in his mouth, hardly knowing what I was doing, I silently laughed with him for a few seconds. I laughed with him from pleasure and surprise, with all the great surprise in my soul, which in the joy of our laughter had just shouted out to me that I, too, like Gregoria, just like Gregoria, and much more than Gregoria—Gabriel's laugh . . . delighted me too! Oh, yes, I like Gabriel's laugh, I like it so much, my God, I like it so much, and it delights me so, and it dazzles my mind so that my mind's mirror is fogged, all the light of memory is extinguished in it, and it doesn't allow me to reproduce the shape of his lips alone, when his lips are serious and still.

With Gabriel's laugh fixed in my mind, I left the room, came here, and locked my door. I began to write, and I haven't heard anything else from him. I don't want to, either. No . . . no! I want nothing further to do with him!

Now, too, the same as this afternoon, and the same as always, away from him, in the silence of the night and in the cold silence of this solitary room, with my eyes closed and my pen held between my fingers and the smooth paper under my hand, I've stopped writing several times to try to call up in my mind how Gabriel's mouth looks when he is serious. But before, and now, and always, it eludes me. It only appears with his divine laugh. Oh! What does his mouth look like? What do his lips look like when he is not speaking and he is serious?

If I can never see Gabriel's lips in the silence of my closed eyes, for several hours I have felt his lips constantly, constantly, on mine, just as I felt them for a moment in the dining room around six or six-thirty. Gabriel's lips can't appear in my mind because they have remained on my mouth, and I feel them there, clinging and burning, as if I were feeling a wound, the kind burning embers leave on your skin! In vain, for more than two hours as I've been writing, I've brushed my mouth with the back of my cold hand. I've tried to tear Gabriel's burning lips from mine. They horrify and frighten me, but no matter what I do, I can't get them off my mouth. They are stuck, stuck tight, like scars made by hot coals, scars that will be there eternally!

CHAPTER VI   *Early Saturday*

morning

 What had to happen has happened. Uncle Pancho
has died.

His poor, exhausted, pain-racked body is still,
and they have already enclosed it in the black coffin that has slowly been covered with flowers, in
the light of the candles, like some lugubrious springtime.

A few minutes ago when I saw them close the coffin and when I heard
the horrible sputtering of that macabre fire as they melted the lead that
would solder shut the zinc cover of his casket, I could bear no more, and
for a happy moment I was lost in the sweet unconsciousness of a faint.
They gave me a sedative then and they brought me here to rest and sleep.
But I'm not sleeping. I'm writing, because writing, like crying, soothes
me more than sleep and much more than any sedative.

I fainted a while ago because the sputtering of the fire next to the still
body awoke in the depths of my soul an ancient terror of fanatical sacrifices, and because as I watched the flaring of the macabre flame, my eyes,
my ears, and my whole body evoked the dreadful torture of burned
flesh—burned flesh in which the faith of all beliefs has lit its torches, the
pious light of all pious religions. That was why . . . that was why, seeing
the flame dancing near the defenseless corpse, watching them about to
cover it with the mirror of laminated zinc—with that zinc mirror that,
alone and in the dark, witnesses worms feasting on the flesh . . . When I
saw that they were about to put on the zinc cover, I jumped up quickly
from my chair, and, looking for the last time at the profile of his cold face,

I asked . . . I don't know who! I asked the mystery of the universe in a desperate cry that choked me with fear, "My God! Suppose he's alive!"

That was when I fainted dead away as I leaned against an armchair. It was because of the faint that they brought me here to rest.

I remember now. I also fainted because, thinking about ancient and fanatical tortures, for an instant I feared that Uncle Pancho's motionless body might still be alive. But when I felt with my hands that he was dead, thoroughly dead, I envied his real death and I don't know why. I don't know why I told myself that next to the horrible torture of the flame and black urn, I was not dead, but alive! Alive! Like those who suffered torture in ancient times.

I don't know why I thought that about myself, when I am a person in good health, with a will of my own, energy to overcome all obstacles and to choose the right path in life, as all the others who walk with me down this narrow path of life.

I'm a little weak . . . rather worn-out, torn by emotions. That's all! It will pass. This great quantity of emotions will slowly diminish. I'll weep for Uncle Pancho; I won't see him anymore; I'll become accustomed to his absence, and I'll return . . . of course, I'll tranquilly return to my tranquil everyday life.

Tranquil life . . . tranquil life! I don't know why I say "tranquil life" and I think about the white tranquillity of cemeteries, and I think about the horrible tranquillity of closed coffins beneath the earth.

Everything now seems to me like the blackness of a coffin, and the desperation of being enclosed in a sealed space where no air can enter. This narrow room feels to me like the tight enclosure of a funeral prison. In vain I open my mouth, breathe in great gulps of air, and fill my lungs to capacity. The air here inside doesn't seem like air and I would like to open the door to cry out, "You, air in the patio, come in, come in!" But I can't open the door, because next to the door, against the door is he! Yes. Right here, a yard away, is Gabriel. At this moment, I am like the dead locked in a tomb, and he is like desperate living people who weep outside the tomb and try to resuscitate the dead, with the infinite strength of desperation, as if the desperation of the living at the doors of a tomb had ever revived the dead body that sleeps within.

Gabriel thinks I'm asleep, and he stands guard by my door, watching over my sleep with the horrid desperation with which one watches over the sleep of a loved one who has died. I hear his steps outside my door and I distinguish them from everyone else's. I would recognize them among a thousand others or among thousands of millions. To the faithful affection of my ears his footsteps are the same as his voice, and like his voice, they, too, speak words of love to me, as they ring anxiously on the floor, beside my closed door. Here, near here, sitting in the black row of chairs that have been set out in the patio, are many friends of Uncle Pancho, who, when they heard of his death, came to keep me company on this last night that he will sleep in his home. I hear them whispering, I hear the muffled sound of their footsteps. But Gabriel's exasperated footsteps cannot be confused with the others. He believes I'm asleep and he watches over me, desperate and tragic, very close to my door. But for many hours, closed away here, I'll pretend to sleep, and I'll remain asleep for all eternity to him, because I'll wait until he's gone and then, quietly, like a criminal, I'll slip away from this house and go away where he'll never see me again.

Yes, Gabriel! You're here, right here, a few steps from me, and you, who cannot see me because the thick wood of that rickety door hides me from your eyes, and I, who cannot talk to you because my voice has fallen silent for you, I, who cannot speak to you, am now writing to you on this square white page, the size and color of those poor marble headstones that are humbly lost under the grass in a graveyard. Yes, I'm writing this and it's like writing my own epitaph.

"Your eyes that I adore will never see me again, and your ears that I adore will never hear me again, Gabriel. Not after what happened yesterday as Uncle Pancho lay dying. Gabriel! It's impossible for you to see María Eugenia Alonso again, because although you shout it in your kisses, and although my soul has answered your cry in a kiss, saying yes a thousand times, María Eugenia Alonso is not yours, nor can she be yours, and you, hungry for love, must respect her, as starving men who are honorable respect treasures and respect wealth that would satisfy their hunger, but that doesn't belong to them!"

Yes! Yes! When Uncle Pancho has gone, in the luxurious coach with its glittering glass, pulled by great horses with black plumes, I will also leave, hidden, and I'll slip away to Grandmother's house without letting Gabriel see me. I don't want my eyes to see him either, close or from a distance, because my mouth and my eyes are no longer mine; they follow him. When they perceive him they go, they go after him, as submissive and happy as dogs freed from ropes and chains. He urges them on from afar, and since the sound of his voice excites and rules them, this mouth and these eyes that no longer belong to me break every chain, and when they hear him call, like unleashed dogs, they run to him, paying no attention to me.

Oh! Yesterday morning! What happened yesterday was such a revelation of joy, and such a revelation of horror! How could both exist in the single lightning flash of a kiss? Yesterday, yesterday! What a violent spark of life to forever light up this eternal darkness of death!

At eight in the morning, when I was sunk in a deep, peaceful sleep, Aunt Clara, who had not gone to mass, came to the room where I was sleeping, knocked on the door, and woke me, saying, "Get up now, María Eugenia, because Pancho has taken a turn for the worse!"

A moment later, dressed, pale and upset, I entered Uncle Pancho's room, and when I looked anxiously toward the bed, I saw with horror that death, crushing the pillows, now lay on Uncle Pancho's body, where he was stretched out, still and white, under the sheets.

Gabriel was alone in the room, standing at the head of the bed. He had taken Uncle Pancho's pulse, and was gazing sadly at the kind but tormented head that looked like a dying Christ, a death rattle vibrating in his throat.

When I saw him looking so distressed and nervous, I went to the bed near Gabriel, I took one of the poor hands that lay inert on the blanket in mine, and I felt that it was icy . . . icy and damp and hard, his hands already dead. Shivering with fear, without thinking of my displeasure of the previous afternoon, I spoke to Gabriel again, asking him anxiously more with my fright than my lips, "This, what do you suppose this is, Gabriel?"

Very sadly and very softly, he answered saying what I knew all too well, "This is because now . . . he's going!"

It was a strange thing! I who had known this perfectly well, I who, for a week, convinced and certain, had been resigned and waiting for this death, I, who had just seen it with my own eyes face to face, I who had just felt its icy touch on my anxious hands, when I heard Gabriel announcing it with his voice, I felt an immense terror that chilled my whole body. Then, shaking, with a question in which the pain of eternal separations writhed, and in which, with extreme bitterness, all of my secret loneliness was sincerely exposed, not knowing what I was saying, I asked, "And now, Gabriel, now, my God, now without him who loved me so, what is going to become of this horrible life of mine, so alone and so forsaken?"

Since my voice, full of desolation and sincerity, was just like a voice that begs for protection, Gabriel, gently and sympathetically, even as Uncle Pancho was struggling with death, sheltered me in his merciful arms and said with the most convinced and passionate tone, "You won't be left alone, María Eugenia, and you won't be forsaken, because you'll stay with me. I adore you as no one has ever adored anyone on earth!"

In my deep despair, Gabriel managed to put so much consolation and unity, and so much energetic love, and so much tender protection in his words that I forgot the sacred distances that separate lives and yielding to my feeling of weakness and helplessness, I rested my head on his affectionate shoulder. Then . . . an instant later, when, for the second time, like last night in the dining room, I felt the divine touch of his lips on mine . . . when for the second time in my life, I had the delight of Gabriel's lips on mine . . . Oh! What I felt! I felt a wave of consolation that progressively swept over me, encompassing me, until finally it stopped at my mouth, which was passionately kissing Gabriel's benevolent mouth.

It was then . . . I think it must have been then, in the brief time that my kiss lasted, when I saw with the violent speed of a bolt of lightning the infinite happiness, now impossible for me, which is true love on earth. As I glimpsed it so close and so impossible, its dazzling light, like the fatal brightness of lightning, lit up everything, all of the blackness of these shadows that surround me now and which will surround me forever . . . forever! It was that bright light that also, tragically, revealed me to myself, when in a very clear flash, I saw with sudden horror the horror of what my mouth was doing next to Uncle Pancho's dying body. Propelled by the very force of my horror, I tore myself from Gabriel's consoling arms, which held me and which hold me still with the infinite and sweet communion of love.

When I was completely free of his arms, my frightened eyes met the glassy, staring eyes of Uncle Pancho, who was facing us. It seemed to me that in his grave, still eyes all the impossibility of our love was reflected, as the sky is reflected on muddy swamps where death bathes. My horror growing more and more as I looked at his fixed and glassy eyes, I came to my senses at last and with my right hand, very trembling and uncontrolled, I nervously pushed Gabriel away from me. Indicating with my eyes the body like a dying Christ I said, choking on my words, sobbing in terror, "Gabriel, for God's sake! We're profaning death . . . we're profaning Christ!"

For the second time, like last night in the dining room, falling on my knees at the foot of the deathbed, I rested my folded arms on the bedcover and buried my head in them, horrified, and I began to sob.

Like a man in a frenzy of madness, Gabriel, kneeling beside me, talked to me for a long time without stopping, in a rapid and very low voice with infinite frenzy. In that frenzy of madness and love, as he begged me for God's sake not to cry, I remember that he told me, "Because you're mine, María Eugenia, my darling, and you'll be mine forever, because I adore you and you love me, yes, you do love me! You love me! You just told me so in the eloquence of your kiss! Because only this way, María Eugenia, only in the language of kisses are the most noble loves revealed. They can't be told with words, because the world, in its criminal stupidity, doesn't allow it. But we two, we two who adore each other above all, will scorn the world, and we'll scorn convention, and we'll scorn the laws, and we'll scorn everything, everything that crosses us, because our love is greater, and stronger, and more respectable than they. Yes, María Eugenia, look, right here with the two of us so close, on our knees, like couples who are married in a church, we are being married, witnessing our own marriage, beside this body of Christ in agony who blesses our immense love and who, while an image of Christ in agony, is also the body in agony of Pancho, who like a father, has united us to bless us together at the supreme moment of his death!"

Through my shuddering sobs, horrified to hear so much impossible happiness offered in such great profanation, I tried to stop him, saying, "Gabriel! That is an impossible sacrilege! We're profaning death! We're profaning Christ!"

Without hearing me, Gabriel, desperate and loving, went on talking to me, addressing me intimately and passionately in a way that intoxicated me and burned my ears with love, as his kisses had burned my lips. My lips! My lips forever burning and silenced by kisses! Now hiding against the bed my lips could only repeat between sobs, "It can never be! It can never be!"

Finally, tired of so much arguing in my ears, and seeing that my tongue denied him everything, Gabriel, surrendering to love and weariness, began to implore me humbly, his pleas as persevering as a litany. There, at my side, on his knees, as if he were praying for Uncle Pancho, repeating the litany for the dying, he repeated ceaselessly and without pause, "Tell me you'll be mine, María Eugenia, my dearest! Tell me you'll be mine! Tell me you'll be mine! Tell me you'll be mine! Tell me you'll be mine!"

When Gabriel and I found ourselves most united in desperation—he in the voluble desperation of his words, and I in the silent desperation of my tears—slowly, one after another, ceremoniously and sadly, the others began to enter the room. First came Aunt Clara, then the nurse, and last, Gregoria, who was weeping, walking very slowly, shielding herself from the air, and bearing in her pious black hands the white candle for the soul, already lighted and flickering, like the faint palpitation of Uncle Pancho's life that was being extinguished as it slowly escaped through his pale lips.

Like Gabriel and me, they also were piously kneeling around the bed, and then Aunt Clara, who had knelt near the head, close to the pillow, holding the mystic candle for the soul in her left hand, and holding in her right an open prayer book as worn as her own hands, with the same fervent voice, monotonous and insistent, that Gabriel had used to implore my love, began to repeat, and to make us repeat in chorus, the mournful and sad imploration of the Seven Words.

With my face hidden and bathed in tears, to the melodic and funereal rhythm that Aunt Clara marked, for a long time in the darkness of my closed eyes, I repeated and repeated intensely, with words and with every fiber of my body, the sweet, slow music of the Seven Words.

Then, tired of weeping, I gradually lifted my head from my arms and, staring ahead, my eyes clouded with tears, I again studied the dying light in the glassy eyes, and with the lively light of mine I desperately began to question if they, in the mystery of their vision had shown to Uncle Pancho's departing soul that profane kiss that I had just lavishly given in the presence of his death. Staring and staring at them, still and cold, through the mysterious gaze, I began to talk to the fleeing soul, and I said goodbye to it, telling it with only my tearful gaze, "Uncle Pancho, Papa, when he died, left me an inheritance of poverty and servitude. And you, Uncle Pancho, Uncle Pancho! What tragic and terrible inheritance are you going to leave me?"

Since my voice now, in the monotonous grief of the chorus, was repeating together with the twin voice of Gabriel "I thirst, my Lord, to die in your love! I thirst, my Lord, to die in your love!" I fused hopeless death and my hopeless, infinite love into a single burning thirst. Overcome, in the grip of bitterness, longing only to taste the water that is drunk beyond the tomb, beside Gabriel, to whom I could never speak again, I went on repeating, "I thirst, my Lord, to die in your love! I thirst, my Lord . . ."

The thirst for love that made me long for the water of death, the thirst for love beside Gabriel and beside Uncle Pancho's deathbed, was not the thirst for God on the dry lips of the dying, no, no, no, it isn't true! It was only my thirst for love, my mortal thirst for love, which my voice was proclaiming, as ever since then, for more than twenty hours, next to the icy corpse of Uncle Pancho, my whole body has been loudly proclaiming.

But my body will die of thirst, because my eyes, yes, my living eyes . . . I swear it before this door, behind which his footsteps of love are saying words of love to me! My living eyes will never, nevermore see my adored Gabriel!

No! They can't see him anymore, because these eyes that are no longer mine, when they feel his presence, go to meet him, like unleashed dogs, and I am afraid, yes, I'm very afraid that, seeing him anew, my eyes that obey him and follow him, so happy and submissive, will carry away my whole body on the wings of their joy! Yes, my whole body that burns and is consumed in its great thirst for love.

I felt a fear that my body might follow after Gabriel on the wings of submission and joy. I felt it yesterday during the delicious and infinite second that my kiss lasted. Most of all, it was later, several hours afterwards, when I understood it better.

It must have been about mid-afternoon. Uncle Pancho had fallen asleep forever, beneath the white sheets and beneath the white handkerchief that sketched the purity of his face in snow. Since the idyllic kiss in the drama of death, I had not spoken to Gabriel, nor had I dared to look at him again, neither close nor from a distance. The last care given the dead and then the arrival of the first friends who came to keep us company were circumstances that necessarily kept me away from him. When things were back to normal, there were slow, silent hours. I was dressed in black, sitting at the head of the deathbed, dazzled by the light of two candles that stood in front of the bed on an improvised altar. The candles watched over the body and they illuminated a wooden Christ suffering on His cross. I felt drunk with the mournful perfume of the tuberoses that had gradually covered the funeral wreaths with white. I was presiding over the wake, close to Aunt Clara, silent, unaware of everything and everybody. Thoughtful, grieving, I sat motionless near the cold white body. It seemed to me that, like Uncle Pancho, my soul also had been left dead, and that it too now lay stretched out and blanched in my quiet body as if in its mortuary chapel.

Suddenly someone came to rouse me from my sphinx-like immobility, announcing that a telegram had come for me that required my signature. I rose, left the room, and went to the dining room, and there I met Gabriel who wordlessly was holding out to me the sealed envelope of a telegram addressed to me. First I signed the receipt, then I tore open the envelope with trembling hands, and while I was doing this, Gabriel, whose eyes, like the eyes of an eagle, see and follow everything from a great distance, Gabriel, who is a triumphant eagle with open wings that pursues and watches me from the heights of heaven, Gabriel, this Gabriel whom I bear within myself, and who at this very moment as I write, calls me over and over with the voice of his footsteps, right here, behind my closed door, just as, in the grip of exhaustion and love, the weary and beloved Bridegroom of the Song of Songs called in the night, Gabriel, this Gabriel of mine, this Gabriel who is now a piece cut from the most sensitive part of my bloody and mutilated soul, Gabriel, while I was signing and tearing open the envelope, came close to me and so that no one present could hear anything, he spoke to me in a very low voice, his face full of love and authority, "María Eugenia, that telegram is from that man, whom you do not love, whom you have never loved, and to whom you can never belong now, because you love and belong to me—to me! And because you love me and you are mine—mine! Understand this well, because you're mine, I'll defend you against him and against the whole world, desperately, to the death, as any real man defends and fights for what is his! You mustn't be afraid of him. Have faith in me! María Eugenia, María Eugenia, my dearest, listen to me! You must know that at this moment the two of us are gambling on the happiness of our entire lives!"

While he was saying this with apparent calm, Gabriel's whole being radiated such forceful attraction and authority that I, like a poor dove fascinated by death, felt nothing save a vehement and mysterious desire for the eagle's claws to bear me away from this desert where I live, to carry me off to dizzy heights, through the air, through the clouds, up to inaccessible mountain peaks—I don't know where! Even though it were only to then rip me apart and torment me, and cruelly devour me in a bloody banquet.

Since I could not hide my feelings, and since I couldn't hide the great fascination that drew me so strongly, I replied, with gentle surrender, my eyes lowered, totally defeated, "Yes, Gabriel, yes. We have to talk alone tonight. Later. When Uncle Pancho is in his coffin. But not now, Gabriel! Not yet!"

Gabriel, who instantly saw mirrored in my face and mirrored in my voice all of the pleasure of weakness and yielding, took my hesitant words as acceptance of who knows what fearful and divine plan that he wants to propose to me, and to which he is already dedicated body and soul. Without even knowing it or having heard it yet, it makes me tremble as I am trembling now—from fear and happiness! That's the reason, that's the reason—it's because he wants to tell me about it that he besieges me now like a madman here, very close, barely two yards away. And because I don't want to hear about it, and I don't want him ever to tell me, I'll pretend to be asleep for a long time, I'll leave my door closed like the Bride's closed door in the Song of Songs, and I won't open it until I can silently and quickly slip away from this house . . . Yes, I'll escape in the daylight with all the hurry and fear of a criminal escaping from the scene of his crime.

But the dead person, the victim of this nefarious crime, I'll carry forever in the mysterious sphinx of my body, which must be its tomb and its bleached mausoleum!

As I was saying, when Gabriel spoke to me, I answered him with emotion, folding the telegram shakily, and he, without listening to me carefully, in his great conviction, took everything for granted beforehand.

Granted! "Granted." Good God! What a delightful and terrible word. Just writing it scares me. "Granted!" Well, Gabriel, who immediately took for granted that plan I don't know about and that I'll never hear about from him, said to me in the sweetest tone, "Thank you, my beloved! I thank you twice; thanks for my immense happiness, and thanks for your happiness, which is much dearer and more sacred than my own!"

When I finally opened the telegram, despite the dancing of the words on the trembling paper held before my eyes and between my hands, I read:

"I have just heard about the serious condition of your uncle. I'll be with you day after tomorrow in the afternoon.
LEAL."

Reading the telegram, and reading the name signed to it, clouded my eyes. I felt a voluptuous flash of sadistic punishments pass through me, something like a whip cracking in the air, near a back bared for the lash, and its spell in my subconscious awoke, stronger than ever, my great terror of Gabriel.

Then tearing myself away from his commanding eyes which were looking at me, and from his commanding lips which were questioning me with imperious love, without looking at him, without listening to him, answering haphazardly, not knowing what I was saying, I murmured, terrified, "Later, Gabriel. Later, later, tonight, yes, we'll talk later!"

I left the dining room, I nervously crossed the patio, I went into the death room, I sat again at the head of the bed in the light of the candles, and with the crumpled telegram in my hands, for many hours I resumed my sphinx-like attitude, motionless, thoughtful, grieving. The crumpled telegram in my fingers breathed terror, which traveled up my arms and, like ripples on the surface of a lake, ran shivering across the skin of my whole body. It was then, as I shivered beside the white bed, wrapped in the fragrance of tuberoses, and hearing the candles sputter, that I understood all of the attraction and dominance that Gabriel's magnetic body exercises on my body. As I again contemplated the great attraction of the abyss, I spent a long, long time, shaken by fear and pleasure, until slowly

I came back to reality. I felt this infinite heaven of my forbidden love dissolve in the most inaccessible distances. Looking at the still face beneath the white handkerchief, my eyes shedding tears like blood, with the black desperation of prisoners condemned for life, like the martyr who voluntarily, out of respect for an idea, gives up his body to torture, I solemnly swore that my eyes would never again look upon my adored Gabriel.

That is why now, near here, next to my closed door, while I write with my own blood, I hear the footsteps of his love, which call to me. They call, and they will call me in vain all night, as in the voluptuous, lost night, beside the closed door, the honeyed voice of the Bridegroom called wearily in the sublime love of the Song of Songs.

CHAPTER VII

The same Saturday

at midnight

Finally! Finally! I've grown wings to fly! I'm going to fly with them to you, Love, Sun of my
life! I'll fly to you! I'll go, I'll go! Wait for me
confidently, because I'll go!

Yes, now I can go in peace, because here, in
Grandmother's respectable house, in the familiar
seclusion of my room, sitting by my wide-open window, my elbows
propped on the table and my triumphant head leaning on my ten ivory
fingers, which are piously entwined, looking out at the pomp of the sky
presided over by the Moon, my Royal Bridesmaid, beneath the nuptial
incense provided by the orange trees with their thousand innocent orange
blossoms, in the solemnity of this quiet night, and in the presence of the
bejeweled crowd of stars, I have celebrated my betrothal. Now, like Egyptian virgins in the temple of Isis, I, too, in the temple of this august silence,
trembling with anxiety, will keep watch all night, awaiting the glorious
dawn, which will be the first day of my festival of love.

At last, at last, my wings have grown!

They are both fluttering, impatient and open on my impatient body,
triumphant with beauty, triumphant with love, and triumphant with
pride, under my proud open wings.

I've dressed in white for my wedding party, but my wings, transparent
and glorious, are dressed in all the transparent and glorious colors of light.
Thanks to them, thanks to their tissue of dreams, at dawn tomorrow, like
lyrical little butterflies that happily leave the warmth of their chrysalis and
the rich treasure of their skein of silk, I, too, tomorrow, like the lyrical
little butterflies, at dawn, will leave the warmth of this good, old house.

I'll leave the treasure of my good name, I'll leave the pure silk of my social reputation and because my wings have grown, on the miracle of wings spread in the air, in the faint white light of dawn, I'll fly away with a single flap of my wings, toward the Sun, toward the Light, toward Mother Nature, who waits for me in her closed garden, where she has painted the bright, fragrant flowers of all joys for me.

I'm free! The dreadful chains that bound me to earth, and that forced me to walk slowly, dragging myself on the ground like a poor worm that can never become a butterfly, have mysteriously broken in a thousand pieces, as my wings began to sprout. Now I'm free!

I'm free now and I'm going! All guests and all who officiate at my Wedding, I'm going! Generous companions of my captivity, I'm going!

I'm going, my protector Sky, you who attentively guarded me from afar, above the square sadness of this patio, in my moments of anguish. You always maternally gave me the blue love of your lap, all embroidered with jewels. I'm going, Moon, my confidante Moon, my white Maid of Honor, my generous Queen, who in the frosts of misery and disillusionment always wrapped me in your royal cloak made of ermine and silver fabric. I'm going, Stars of the night, twinkling little ballerina stars who gaily, in the joy of your happy winks, taught me to laugh at myself and to laugh at the dark nights of my boredom. I'm going, Bars of my open window, guardian Bars, compassionate and redeeming jailers, who in the blackest days of my imprisonment, through the mercy of your eternally crucified bars, let me always see the infinite hope of heaven. I'm going, Doll lamp on my desk, luminous companion, intimate friend, pink and green professor of flirtation, who, with your fluffy skirt and your make-believe swoon and your mysterious light, daily recounted to me the frivolous delights hidden in love and luxury. I'm going, Orange Trees, gallant and enamored swains, who, day and night, forever green with hope, always stood beside my window. I'm going, Blossoms on my orange trees, little foster brothers, kind and wise, who so many times relieved the sting of my wounds with the salve of your perfume and the cotton of your white petals. Innocent, virginal orange blossoms, little perfume censers, who in the temple of silence are still perfuming my nuptial ceremony, I'm going! Sweet companions of my captivity, officials and guests at my Wedding, thick crowds of stars, goodbye all, because I'm leaving, at last I'm going tomorrow to rule eternally over the great splendor of my festival of joy!

Yes, all my friends, I'm going, because Love, sweeping away mountains and hills, has miraculously come to me. It has awakened me from my sleep by kissing my eyes, it has affixed these two wings of light on my shoulders, and it wants me for its Queen, there, in its exalted and glorious kingdom. I have now celebrated my wedding and while I watch in the mysterious night, I begin to foresee the tumultuous Festival when I arrive at my mighty kingdom. I can already hear it; I hear it all! A great crescendo of harmony!

I hear the tinkling bells of the harnesses that the lackeys polish; I hear the venerable voice of the great bells; I hear the thousand infant voices of the carillons wildly repeating choruses; I hear the chords and thunder of a rain of stars from the fireworks; I hear the impatient stamping of the horses with their white trappings; I hear the majestic gliding of my mother-of-pearl carriage; and above it all, I hear the terrible cry of the frenetic multitude seeing the unheard-of cortege which, without touching the earth, passes by, free, on the wings of its royal pomp and splendor.

If my eyes shed no tears of farewell, it is because they have dried all the torrent of tears they wept and wept for death in the wasteland of hope. If my eyes shed no tears of farewell, it is because the shining eyes of the Wise Virgins, afraid their flames may die before their night of love, weep only for their lost home and weep only for their lost virginity, with orange blossom tears, and with tremulous sobs under their transparent veils.

Brilliant gathering at my Nuptials, kind companions of my captivity, and you, dear little foster brothers, all weep for me, for I do not wish to dull my eyes with the water of weeping, because they are the two lamps with which tomorrow I shall light the Beloved with the light of joy, in the mystic night of my Festival of Love.

Brilliant attendants at my Nuptials, while I watch, weep, weep, weep for me!

Just now, with its religious voice like a muezzin, my old friend the cathedral tower has called out one o'clock.

I have now spent one hour in the ritual of my vigil. I have now lived an hour in this sacrosanct day of my resurrection. Now, as my vigil continues, I want to meditate on all the steps that I have taken on the bloodless road to redemption.

It seems to me that here, in my ears, I can still hear that soft murmur that early yesterday morning began to move and stir there in the poor, sad house, full of flowers and black chairs. It was Uncle Pancho's funeral that was quietly setting out. I sensed its agitation, closed in the tomb of that narrow room. Little by little the black fluttering was growing in muffled excitement. It grew and grew in soft whispers, and finally, carrying its load, it left mercifully on the way to the cemetery.

Gabriel also left to follow the funeral procession.

I listened to the loving goodbye made by his footsteps on the floor beside my door. When all the footsteps died out, and the distant sound of cars rolling down the street faded away, my very skin, with terrible pain, felt the newly opened tombs of my two dead. Now orphaned and free, wrapped in a cape, stealthily, I opened the door, left the closed room, and without saying anything to Aunt Clara or saying goodbye to anyone, I took a cab that was going down the street and, hiding my flight, I came to the jail of this virtuous house.

When I entered, I found Grandmother sitting in her wicker chair, facing the door, next to the lines of palm trees and ferns.

Seeing me appear so unexpectedly, she was surprised, and I, too, seeing her, felt a shock of surprise. In the mortal fatigue painted on her face, that fatal weariness that had made Aunt Clara weep copiously two days ago, I seemed to see the same agony that was killing me reflected as if in a mirror. And it was Grandmother's own words that expressed my thought when, in her surprise, trying to describe her impression, she described herself, "How run down you are, María Eugenia, my dear, how run down you are! You're hardly a shadow of yourself, you poor thing! How much sleep you must have lost and how much you must have suffered to exhaust yourself so! But now that everything is over, go rest, dear, go rest peacefully."

While she was saying this, Grandmother was hugging me and crying over Uncle Pancho's death. I hugged her, too, in silence, but without shedding a tear. Then, following her advice, I automatically came here to my room. Automatically I opened the door—oh! When I opened the door, all the familiar objects here, all these close friends that truly love me, when they saw me return so pale, and so poor, raising their arms, together shouted at me, "Having held the entire universe in your hands, you come to us with nothing, María Eugenia!"

I was horrified, and in order not to see them cry out my enormous crime of love, I closed the shutter to the light, I closed my eyes, I lay down on the bed, and I cried the bitterest, deepest tears of desperation that human eyes have ever wept in the paroxysms of sacrifice.

Lying awake, in my desperation, I spent many hours crying and crying.

First came Aunt Clara's arrival. When I heard her voice in the distance talking to Grandmother, I ran to her. Seeing me, she cut short her comments and reproached me.

"How badly you behaved, María Eugenia! I'm ashamed of you. You didn't tell me you were coming here, or say goodbye to anyone, not even to Gabriel Olmedo, to whom we owe so many favors. When he came back from the cemetery and asked about you, frankly, I didn't know what to say to him. Why, you didn't even thank him, María Eugenia! You didn't even say thank you!"

And resuming her interrupted comments, Aunt Clara began to praise Gabriel's behavior. But I was in a state of mortal anxiety, and with my demoralized voice, I asked her weakly, "What did he say to you, Aunt Clara?"

Since Aunt Clara paid no attention to me, and continued with her litany of praise, I repeated in a disagreeable and commanding tone, very excited, "I want you to tell me what he said, Aunt Clara!"

Amazed, she looked at me for an instant without speaking. Then she reproached me again, "Heavens, what a way to talk! Either it's your nerves or very bad manners, but what a way to act, what a way to act! Well, he didn't say anything, what could he say? I was the one who read in his face how very hurt he was by your rudeness. I think you should phone him today or tomorrow to beg his pardon, and to thank him!"

I went back to my room again and, again, stretched out in bed, I wept for the frightful wretchedness of having done my duty. But while I was crying, through my tears, full of faith, I was waiting . . . waiting . . . I don't know what I was waiting for! Since perfect faith can move mountains, what I was waiting for miraculously came at last at twilight.

Yes, at twilight, in my darkened room, the closed door opened a crack and on a little ribbon of light, María del Carmen's voice solemnly vibrated like the voice of a sorceress announcing a marvel.

"Miss María Eugenia, a servant has just come to give you a personal message."

When I heard the news, I shook off all of my suffering, and now, sure of myself and sure of what was going to happen, triumphant, daring and luminous, I rose gloriously from the bed just as someone resuscitated would rise from the dead. A moment later, at the entrance door, some hands held out an envelope sealed with wax, while a voice said to me, "From Don Gabriel Olmedo."

I felt dazzled by the light I myself was radiating, because that still-unopened letter was this very letter that I have here on my table, beneath the passionate love of my hands! Yes, it was this adored letter, this redeeming letter, the one my eyes had waited for in vain for more than two years. It was the one I watched for at San Nicolás; the one with the little fly's feet;

the one that one day, generously, in my great illusion of love, I read thousands of times to the fraternal countryside; the prodigal and ungrateful daughter that now begs the charity of my forgiveness at the indulgent door of my soul; the healing letter; the late one, which finally comes to my thirsty spirit, like beneficent rains long delayed come to the thirsty land cracked by drought; the audacious conqueror, the one that invited me to follow it when life had placed impassable abysses and mountains on my path of love, the wise letter; the merciful teacher, which to span the abysses came to teach my helplessness the sublime delight of flying through the air; the letter that has crowned me queen; the letter whose sheets, zigzagged in black and sprinkled with light, are the triumphant wings on which I'll fly tomorrow, and I'll fly forever, forever, above the cringing impotence of human precepts; the letter I opened with a bouquet of kisses; the one I read with that garland of kisses that bit by bit my eyes wove on the burning love of each word. Yes, yes! That envelope addressed to me, which at twilight next to the street door some hands held out to me, was my letter . . . my letter . . . my redeeming letter from Gabriel! It stunned me with its light, it threw me to my knees on the path of my prejudices, converting me suddenly to its new religion, like the blinding light that felled Saint Paul on the road to Damascus; it held me gently to its loving bosom; it has converted me to its gospel, and that is why now, like a neophyte, or a youthful convert wearing the white dress of baptism, I have solemnly taken my vows before the beauty of this nocturnal nature, bejeweled black Queen that reigns majestically over all the enjoyable mysteries of my new religion of love.

Now, with my luminous sheets of paper, which are my wings, beside my window wide open to the infinite, like the Egyptian virgins in the temple of Isis, I, too, in this temple of august silence, await the dawn of love at the dawning of day!

CHAPTER VIII   *Gabriel's letter*

"María Eugenia, so dear to my heart,

"Yesterday, after Pancho passed away, as you stood in the dining room of his house with that accursed telegram in your hands, you formally promised me that you would talk to me that night. But you didn't keep your word, María Eugenia. You hid from me, you closed your door to me, you heartlessly made me spend the cruelest hours of my life there, and, finally, this morning, you took advantage of my absence and, abandoning me, you tried to escape me forever. But this letter, which is my voice, fulfilling my promise, will seek you out wherever you may hide, and you, María Eugenia, in your hiding place, must listen to it and obey it, because my letter is the cry of life, calling to life, and I feel that you are waiting for it, half dead of anxiety.

"When you tried to deceive me, María Eugenia, my own, you betrayed yourself. By the way it frightens you, you have let me see how greatly the immensity of our forbidden love draws you. I know that, hidden as you are, you are only waiting, poor little coward, for a few hours to go by to kill our love, turning it over, yourself, with your own hands, into the coarse hands of that cruel man who will arrive tomorrow. But you won't do it. You can't commit such an iniquity, María Eugenia. You thought of doing it in a moment of cowardice because of your great weakness, but now, when you read this letter and it tells you how, from a distance, mad with love, I am near you, ready to save you from that horrible ignominy, you won't do it, no, you can't possibly do it. I know that after you listen to me, you will become strong. I know that you will immediately conquer your visible contender, and I know that you will conquer all those spiritual and invisible scourges that are struggling so terribly in you. Yes, María Eugenia, together we will conquer them all, because you are my ally against them, because our love is inevitably much stronger than they, and because united against them, you and I are truth, we are life, and we are the corporeal world fighting against shadows and chimeras.

"My letter comes to beg you, for the sake of your life, for the sake of mine, and for the holy sake of love, to come with me, now, tomorrow. I expect you confidently and without the shadow of a doubt. I feel that now at last you are going to come, and I have everything minutely planned for our happiness and never-ending joy; I'll explain the details to you later. But don't hesitate as you read, for God's sake, don't hesitate, even if my words sound immodest and scandalous, don't let them deter you, for time is pressing and it's the only real enemy that can betray us. But there is no reason for me to tell you this, for you will not hesitate for an instant! No, you won't renounce the glory of living eternally in a delirium of love and joy for the passing sensation that the conventional sound of the word 'scandal' might awake in your ears. No, there is no reason for me to recommend anything to you! I say there is no reason because as my hand writes, my heart is shouting to me that your eyes that I adore, your eyes full of fire and passion, your eyes that have betrayed you to me so many times, when they read these lines and see in them how I'm waiting for you, longing for you, and half dead with impatience, when your adored eyes that belong to me scan these lines that tell you my dignity as a man is ready to defend you, to the last drop of my blood, burning with love, you, like your eyes, mine a thousand times over, will not hesitate to run to me.

"But if you should hesitate? No, it is impossible, for yesterday, without knowing it yourself, beside the bed of Pancho as he lay dying, you desperately begged the help of my love in its strength against your weakness. Remember that's what your lips asked me for, and remember they didn't ask me with words. Because your lips' intense plea was the most positive of all affirmations, I know that you are mine. That's why I call you now, and at the same time that I implore you, I imperiously demand that you come. It's my right as a man to command you to come, María Eugenia, because you are my wife, and if you don't come to me, now, immediately, tomorrow you will be trapped in the ignominy of that marriage that threatens you. You will fall forever into the claws of a kind of slow, resigned prostitution, which makes you cry with impotence, and makes every fiber of my body rebel.

"You can't belong to that man, María Eugenia, because you are mine, and you are mine, just because. You belong to me by the law of nature; you belong to me for the very simple reason, mysterious and undebatable, that my life belongs to my living body. You and I are joined intrinsically and we belong to each other because that is what nature decreed when it conceded us the very rare privilege of being united in true love. It is the most sacred and respectable of all privileges and treasures ever granted. Remember, María Eugenia, that we had this treasure within our reach once, and I profaned it by neglect, spending myself on small, vile business advantages. Today I weep for that with tears of blood, and with those tears I beg you not to profane it again and beyond all hope. Don't deny it out of cowardice, María Eugenia, no, no, don't deny it! Just think, it will redeem and save you from an ignoble slavery, and think, too, that besides saving you, it is the invaluable and divine gift that Nature has showered on us as her favorite children, and Nature is our eternal Mother, our eternal goddess, our eternal benefactress, the only one that has the holy power to distribute love as she distributes life and she distributes death.

"It is then in the name of a sacred right that I call you and I wait for you. Our union, soon to be realized, blessed not only by the supreme will of nature, despite the unanimous reprobation of society, and in spite of the indignation of those close to us, will be a legitimate and wholesome union, while that marriage of yours is only a lifelong prostitution, which, recognized by laws and accepted by everyone, blindly and unconsciously, you, like many other women around us, are going to contract soon, unless I defend and shield you with my love. But my love, which is immense, shields and defends you, cost what it may, since it is the only one that has any legitimate claim on you.

"Consider well what I write to you here, María Eugenia, and consider and weigh my reasons, because they are not blindly formulated; rather, I have formed them after long and careful analysis, made with complete knowledge of cause.

"In the first place, for your peace of mind, I must declare that I am morally free and completely disengaged from this marriage of mine, which, as you well know, at present is no more than a social appearance, a sort of absurd comedy, sustained at the cost of my happiness, and behind which is daily played out the hateful and immoral drama of a mismatched union. Therefore, as far as I am concerned, I have a perfect right to dispose of my life as I please. As for your case, which I am as familiar with as my own, that right is even more legitimate and much greater.

"María Eugenia, crazy as I am for you, for some time, first with Pancho, and then later with Gregoria, the old laundress at your house, I have made all kinds of inquiries about your sad life, about the progress of your engagement, and about your fiancé, that vulgar, grotesque man whom you do not love, and whom I abhor to the death. Very well, because I know Leal personally, because I also know him thanks to information and facts I have collected, and because, although you may not believe it, I know you even in the slightest details of your exalted and loving temperament, I know that in your thirst for life, you have called love all of the latent and repressed anxieties of youth. From them, in your imagination, more alive to you than reality, you have created an imaginary feeling, and in spite of the evidence of the very vulgar Leal, you, as idealistic and vehement as you are, have loved in the name of your longings, and you have loved him, above all, in the name of the one you wished to love. But since such conditions and such sentiments never existed except in your fantasy, if you consummate that marriage, when you wake up and become conscious of reality, you will understand your mistake and the horror of a wretched and hopeless life. Think about what that eternal secret tragedy would be, your resignation, your respect, and your obedience, feigning love, and always, always hiding, in words and actions, your aversion and your scorn for that despotic master, who would impose everything on you, from his convictions to his grotesque personality, which would become your own, even to the very life of your children, in whom you would see a copy of his features, his character, and perhaps the very traits that in your silence and resignation you hate most. You, María Eugenia, are so intuitive, so intelligent, so sensitive, and so unconscious, all at the same time. I don't know up to what point you have recognized for yourself what I am telling you, and I don't know up to what point, if you haven't recognized it by yourself, you may wish to acknowledge it now that I am declaring it loudly and showing you, as if, by casting a light, to save you from a dangerous situation. But anyway, no matter how blind you may wish to be, it's impossible for you not to see now when I tell you and when circumstances make action imperative, as if they too wanted to save you from misfortune. Before your eyes circumstances have patently brought together the two culminating points where all the history of human existence begins and ends—the splendor of life in me, who represent its origin in love, and the darkness of death in Pancho, who showed you the intense final drama, so imminent and so inevitable. Thanks to these two violent extremes, you still hold the fatal vision of our brief journey on earth. You have just felt intimately the inexorable laws that Nature imposes on us. In your philosophic concept of existence, and in your mystical outlook, you don't expect anything beyond this life. I know, because the other day you sincerely confessed that to me, with words that let me see how penetrating your intelligence is when you objectively observe the world. Then, if you expect everything of this life, and you expect it precisely for the very reason that it has heaped all its gifts on you to make you love life; if you only expect the happiness of your present life, now that my hand frees you of eternal servitude, and breaking your chains, opens wide all its doors, and calls you and invites you to celebrate the festival of your youth, what can stop you? What? What can stop you on the road to glory and happiness that I lay out for you today with the strength of my passion, and in a supremé moment on which your whole existence will depend?

"Don't invoke your family, and don't invoke your scruples about dishonoring, with our love, the home where you live, which is not really yours, and which from decay and from age will soon be extinguished, after having been the cause of our despair and the accomplice of the ignominious marriage that pursues and threatens you imminently. That home cannot impose its principles on you, because it has no moral right to do so. In the first place, I know that your uncle Eduardo Aguirre, head and real power in your house, taking advantage of circumstances and hypocrisy and of your weakness, signed over to himself all of the inheritance left to you by your father. When he took everything away from you, he bound you with a thousand moral and material chains of absolute dependence. In such a situation, like any poor and pretty woman, you have had no other recourse than to try to sell the beauty of your body. You were going to sell it forever to only one man, and you were going to sell it with the approval of the laws, of the Church, of society, and of your family, as if those circumstances of eternal submission and general approbation did not make the sale a thousand times more hateful than those that are made clandestinely, without legal or religious approval. But, honorable and pure and unconscious of yourself as you are, you gave the name of love to this joining of financial and spiritual needs that propelled you to make that sale, that makes me rebel, and that I will in no way allow. Yes, understand, no matter how paradoxical it may seem, today I have the right to defend you against your family, with even greater reason when I know perfectly that it was they who, because of their extreme intransigence, forbade Mercedes's house to you, isolated you at the hacienda, and, out of spite, or envy, or I don't know why, treacherously cut off all communication between us. They, even those who really love you, like your Grandmother and your Aunt Clara, love you before society and within ideas and points of view that neither you nor I share. For that reason they do not see the repulsive iniquity of that marriage, where you go blindly without any inclination, pushed by circumstances only. Nonetheless, tomorrow they will look with horror on the great happiness of our union, merely because it is in conflict with respect to social precepts. They passionately desire the good name of your outward appearance and they completely disdain your personal well-being. How, then, when you must organize your whole life, this life, the true one, the real one, the immediate one, the only one you believe in and for which you were born, how can you possibly stop to take into account moral values that are so absurd from the point of view that you and I have?

"I understand, María Eugenia, my own, because I know you very well, I understand that stronger than all these arguments is the unreasoning reason of affection and of compassion. I know that when you think about the happiness of our triumphant love, you will be troubled about the pain that your happy life will inflict on your Grandmother, now at the end of her days and at the very doors of the tomb. I respect the compassion of your tender heart, and I love you all the more for it. But don't let such compassion dominate you to the point of sacrificing to it the well-being of your whole life, since then you would commit a monstrous deed and a crime against yourself. Love, which is the patrimony of youth, and the holy fountain of future life, places itself above all other affection, because Nature has willed it so, and Nature is cruel and inexorable against all that is old and decrepit. You must not sacrifice to the two months of life that remain for your Grandmother the many years of happiness and joy I'm going to give you. Weep filially for leaving her, weep for her pain, weep for her death, but, good as you are, grieving and compassionate, be strong, conquer compassion with duty, and come away with me, for I, because I am true love, am the supreme duty of your young and triumphant life.

"And now, so your ears won't be scandalized by the words your lips might pronounce, read, read intensely, and in silence, with only the adored light of your faithful eyes, what I dictate and what you must do to realize, we two together and in agreement, the most perfect and delightful idyll of love. Hear me, and obey me, and follow me in everything I tell you, life of my life, for I, in payment for these hours of obedience, swear to carry you with me to the highest peaks that happiness can reach on earth, and I swear too that there, submissive, devoted, and mad with love, I will always be at your feet like a slave.

"When you have read my letter, my bride, and you have decided to come down this flowery path that I sketch and sow for you, lock yourself up in silence, alone with my letter, and don't speak to or see anyone. I send you all of the strength of my spirit on these sheets of paper, and I know it will sustain you and give you courage if you keep it carefully, inside yourself. My letter will reach your hands today at nightfall. I feel that you expect it, I feel that you will read it anxiously, and I feel that when you finish reading it, inevitably you will be mine. Therefore I beg that when you finish reading it you stay alone in your room. If you haven't eaten yet, call a servant, and have her bring dinner to your room, and notify her you're going to sleep, and you don't want to be awakened early tomorrow. With these very plausible precautions, no one will notice your absence until we are beyond their reach. Because very early tomorrow, from five o'clock exactly, I'll wait for you in a car that will be parked at the west corner of your house. For this undertaking that will assure the happiness of our entire lives, you need to perform only one act of moral courage, and that is to make up your mind to walk, without alerting anyone, those few steps that separate your house from the corner where I'll be waiting for you, consumed with impatience. But once you reach me, you have nothing to fear, nothing to think about, nothing to do, because, being mine as you are, I'll take charge of protecting you against all your enemies, visible and invisible. At present I want to defend you from them by the surest and most efficient means, and they are isolation and flight. At noon, a steamship that is now anchored in the port will leave La Guaira, going straight to Colón and New York. We will stay hidden discreetly, like two newlyweds, but we'll be on board when the ship sails. I have already reserved passage, we have permission to embark, and if you are resolute tonight, as I know you will be, in five or six days, free of the chains of this atmosphere, in full freedom and love, like true children of Nature who from now on will be our mother and our goddess and in whose cult we'll have the whole world as our home where we will love each other.

"How wonderful it will be then, María Eugenia! You, beautiful, refined, harmonious, exquisite, an artist who has created yourself, passionate, sensual, ideal of womanhood, endowed with all gifts, think of the power you will achieve, raised to the high throne my love erects for you, and think, my ruler and my queen, of the infinite delights that await us in our future life. Close your eyes awhile, forget everything around you, set your spirit free, and for a few hours, unbound, think . . . think with me.

"First, tomorrow will come, and with dawn the victorious moment of flight. Trembling with fright and emotion you will come to me, and when I see you at last, pale, mine, I'll be mad with gratitude, I'll chase away your fear as I gather you into the protective asylum of my two arms. Anxiously, together, while we hastily escape, like two legendary lovers, I'll soothe your divine eyes with my softest kisses, until my arms and lips win you over and turn your shivers of fear into the sweet shivers of love that brides feel on the eve of their honeymoon.

"Then, my dearest, will come the long voyage, with the broad sky and the wide sea. Think! We'll have nights aglow with the full moon. You may hide away during the day, fearful of the passengers who know and comment on our lyrical idyll of love, but when night comes, silently clinging to me, as if you were my white moon shadow, leaning on my arm, you will climb with me to the highest bridge on the ship. There, very close and quite alone, gazing in each other's eyes, kissing each other's lips, we will bathe in the serenity of celestial Nature and with our kisses we will praise and bless the white majesty of the moon, our pale, symbolic and sweet honey-moon. And then if you should still weep with fear and weep with compassion as you evoke what must be happening in your abandoned, old house in Caracas, I, leaning on the rail, with your precious blonde head resting on my shoulder, will point out to you in the distance the white wake the boat is leaving on the waters, glistening under the moon, and I'll console you saying, 'We, too, my darling, like the ship, are life that bravely advances. See how it moves forward, and it moves without stopping to examine that white, deep wound in the waters, which is only foam and which finally heals and fades, and is diluted and disappears, while the boat, marching on calmly, feeling neither fear nor compassion for the sea, advances and advances proudly to its destination.' With your gaze lost in the distance, you will answer me with tears, 'That's true!' I will love you a thousand times more because of the pain of that wound that with our departure we will have inflicted far away in your old home in Caracas. Then will come the arrival, and with our arrival quiet love, idyllic, deep, serene. Think . . . think! Like all lovers hungry for voluptuous pleasures, we will weave our first nest under some eave in the shadow of a tree, in that Parisian springtime, always rosy and blooming with flowers. But, if in the quiet nest you should still feel the sting of remorse, and an atavistic longing for the routine of bourgeois life, eager to convince you and to show you how legitimate our love is, I will take you on an apostolic pilgrimage of faith through the whole world. We two, lighted by our passion, will read together from that true book of human history which lies open everywhere. In that book you will see the great variety of religious laws that over different centuries and in different climes have struggled, always in vain, to channel the overflowing torrent of life, when life wells and spills out and imposes itself in the case of a love as noble and omnipotent as ours.

"We will carry our idyllic joy with us everywhere on that glorious pilgrimage from which you would return completely convinced and converted to our holy love.

"Think . . . before leaving, we will clothe our souls in the simple spirit of art, and thus, equals, pilgrims, we will go to find the secrets of beauty in all the corners of forgetfulness and shadows, where past life still dreams . . . And what a delight, and what joy, to always make new discoveries stemming from the very conflict of our forbidden love, eternally tormented and eternally triumphant!

"Think!

"When we set out on our long journey of absolution and faith, like good, dutiful children, first of all we'll go to greet the austere soul of Spain. We'll leave our nest in Paris, we'll cross the Pyrenees, and we'll filially go to greet our motherland at the Escorial, and in Toledo, and in Salamanca, and in Burgos, and in Granada, and in Córdoba, and in Seville. There we'll hear its voice in dark, winding streets, where balconies, abloom with pots of flowers, tell old tales of love cruelly persecuted, full of racial or religious hatreds, always glorified by smiles of flashing white teeth, and the whisper of kisses, strumming of guitars, poetry and silken ladders, and nocturnal knifings, and lighted statues of Christ, and processions and autos-da-fé . . . Then, when you have seen that picturesque triumph of love, perpetuated in racial vestiges and characteristics, which, in spite of all prohibitions and of all fanaticism, were victoriously founded in the heat of the same fire that burns in us, then, when we have seen everything, with the faith of our love burning brighter than ever, we will leave Spain and, sailing down the Mediterranean, we will lose ourselves in placid forests on green temperate islands where in winter swallows nest and romantic consumptives dwell. Then sailing along the old Latin sea, we will go ashore on the beaches of Naples and enjoy the sweet charms of Italy.

"Think!

"Like two migrating birds, enamored of the ambience, we will perhaps halt our flight, behind some gentle cove on the bay, in a little white house set among rosebushes and lime trees. . .

"Then, at last, along the Adriatic, toward the South, we will undertake the real pilgrimage of faith, toward the Orient, toward the lands of our origin, toward the lands where primitive life first was born. We'll see Athens and Constantinople, and Baghdad and Alexandria and Jerusalem, and view the splendors of yore . . . Think! . . . Oh! The charm of our idyll, sailing lakes and rivers, bordered by the remains of long-dead cities! Our two silhouettes together, on the lonely desert, riding camels, in the melancholy solitude of palm trees and pyramids, and the brown cities, and all the holy grandeur of the Orient woven by ancient races with venerable religions and venerable prejudices! . . . And it will be there, at last, my dearest, in the lonely heat of Asia, when you are tired of traveling about the world, with our oasis of love always fresh and always green, that you will someday tell me, 'Now I believe, Gabriel, now I believe!' I will be mad with the joy of possessing all of your heart, and I will return with you, my treasure, and my life, to live, drunk with happiness, youth, and love, in our adorable nest in Paris. There our lives will be brilliant. What pride and what glory it will be for my eyes to see you, my precious doll, in your perfection, molded by virtue of that ambience into an exquisite Parisian, graced with luxury, and elegance, and refined exoticism, and worldly charm and faith—mystical faith, convinced and exalted, dedicated to the holy divinity of our own love!

"This is the plan for happiness that I place in your hands, my bride. You may vary it at will and weave into it all the whims of your imagination. Wanting you to be mine, I want you to be very demanding, so then I can make you pay for all your caprices with a fortune in love and kisses.

"I must say 'Until tomorrow,' for the darkness of this night is falling, the triumphant night of our wedding. Remember that I'm waiting for you starting now, and that at dawn, at the meeting place, longing for you desperately, I will await you as the only possible salvation for my soul, which is dying for you.

"Come, then, compassionate to yourself, to save your existence, at the same time slaking this thirst that is killing me. When you arrive, a living fountain, command, be a tyrant, and rule in our kingdom of love, for this is the way, my goddess, my queen, and my despot, I always want to adore you,

GABRIEL"

CHAPTER IX   *The following Monday*
            at nightfall

After a very long sleep, deep and dark, which has lasted almost twenty-four hours, I have just opened my eyes to the sad, sad light of this horrible afternoon, which beyond my window is blending and dissolving into night.

In the dying light, I've come to record here, on this white sheet spread out and waiting on my confiding desk, the goodbye that my soul left in my hands as it died.

Because only my body came back from the long, deep sleep I awoke from just now. When my soul fell asleep it was mortally wounded, and it remains asleep forever, still and in peace. Why didn't my eyes, the living windows of the soul, also remain eternally closed, granting peaceful sleep to a poor martyr? Why keep lighting this suffering flesh, an errant relic, condemned to walk without direction, a corpse, a perpetual sacrificial offering?

Oh! The silent conformity of those who live when their souls are dead! Oh! The silence of those who are resigned, who walk in the great caravan, and walk, carrying a burden of mystery on their shoulders, never asking how long they must walk, nor where they are going, nor for what reason. Life, the cruel and bloodthirsty captain of the great caravan, lashes us with her whip of hours to force us to carry the burden down the road, and to leave it wherever she says, "here"!

Why, why, Life, cruel Captain, have you just awakened me from my sleep? Why in the dying light of this horrible, sad afternoon, as I bear my burden on my shoulders, and trudge on like an icy sacrificial corpse, do you begin to beat me, cracking your whip of hours and shouting implacably, "on, on"!

On? Go on? Oh, Life! Destiny! Death! What do I know of myself or what does anyone know of anything? Walk, walk, walk, docilely, in the caravan, as Life wishes, some day to be left still and cold beside the road, and that is all, sad body that goes on walking. That is all, eyes recently opened to the dying light of this afternoon, poor dreamy eyes that on a starry night saw in the distance the glowing fascination of a mirage. No! That glorious brightness was a lie, poor deceived eyes. In the distance, the length of the long route, we have nothing save sand, and we must walk and walk across the sand while the evil and bloodthirsty captain scourges us!

Oh! The divine fascination of my mirage two nights ago, here beside this very desk, in front of this same window open to the infinite heaven! Oh! Blessed night, two nights ago! Saturday night, fantastic night, a witches' Sabbath, a night of enchantments, which dressed me in splendor, and like a poetic Cinderella, let me reign for a few hours at the dance of my dream Prince! How you have disintegrated in your chariot of stars, glorious night! How far away, how far, I see your thousand little lights fading, little fireflies of love, mystic lamps, a legion of twinkling, distant stars that, like an impossible sky, will always shine above the profound darkness of my resignation and my chains!

Do you remember, little table of mine, white and confidential desk? Here, my elbows propped on your polished whiteness, with his miraculous letter in my hands, I read and reread the fertile, unknown delights which, as they dazzled my eyes with love, intoned a concert of hosannas and glorias in the astounded glory of my soul. Do you remember, open window? Here, facing your redeeming crosses, with my hands piously folded, I celebrated my white betrothal, and it was through the mercy of your bars that the Moon and Stars gave me gifts and dressed me in a wealth of ermine and silver. Today, confiding desk and open window, I return, a humble, disenchanted Cinderella, to weep for the last time for my rags and unshod foot, which will never find its lost slipper.

And I come to weep here, and I come to write here, beside you, where I wrote so many dark pages of my poor life; here where I celebrated my marriage of love on Saturday night; here where I felt my ephemeral butterfly wings grow; here where finally on that same Saturday night, after reading, and singing, and writing to soothe my impatience as I waited, when I heard the cathedral clock striking the long hours of dawn, I halted on my dizzy spiritual race, I smiled ecstatically, and I told myself with ceremonial solemnity, "It's time now!" and I stood up.

I remember that at that august moment, to fortify myself with the infinite, and to find greater intimacy with the Moon and the Stars, I turned off the light, silencing you, frivolous little doll lamp that frivolously lounges on my table. Truly, with the light off, my room emptied of material objects, I was filled entirely by the spirit of moon and stars. Then, standing beside the barred window, looking at the heights, I stood very quietly, and since I was dressed all in white, and since inside too I was full of white happiness, in the silent room, the soul of night that surrounded me melted into me so that for a moment, my silhouette and my bright soul were a single brightness fused with the bright moonlight, which, from the ground to the heavens, seemed to be vaguely floating on a celestial and distant journey.

Turning from the Moon, still feeling the mystery of its astral influence, I stared at Gabriel's letter, which lay loose in open sheets or half-folded ones on the desk, in the dim light, looking to me like a flock of carrier pigeons. With the same ultra-terrestrial eyes with which I had gazed at the heavens, I looked at the table, at the fluttering chaos of the sheets of paper. Seeing them that way, so winged and so alive, I felt a childish fear that they might fly away through the open window. To keep them from leaving, I turned away from my thoughts, hurriedly gathered them together, imprisoned them in the nest of their envelope, and I maternally sheltered them beneath the two warm wings of my breasts!

Now, with my meditation broken, ready for action, the envelope holding its letter was the first provision I made for my journey of love.

Still standing, as I mentally arranged my departure, I decided before anything else to groom and dress myself with great care, and I told myself I must begin with my hands. To study them better, I lifted my two bare arms toward the light and, in the distance, in fantastic brightness, I saw my hands looking so fragile and tired that I felt a kind of pity for them, and, gratefully, while I observed them open under the moon, I told them in my thoughts something more or less like this:

"Pretty hands that belong to him, hands bejeweled with rhymes, good, hard-working hands that labor to the rhythm of the syllables, one night you wrote that sonnet, and now the love sown in those fourteen furrows has grown and yielded a huge crop. But now, for the victorious harvest, I must make you beautiful and polish you, my gardeners."

Happy, as I always am at moments of great enthusiasm, and so I could feel well dressed and very pretty, I ran to my dressing table, I took my mother-of-pearl *nécessaire*, I hopped up to sit on the sill of the open window, I leaned my head against a shutter, and, half-reclining, still glimpsing bits of sky from time to time, I busily and quickly began to file and polish my nails. I polished and polished them until I could see the reflection of the moon in the ten little pink mirrors with their pointed tips. I remember that the cold night air was coming through the window, and it invaded my body in a strange, pleasant shiver. Because of that, my brisk and happy activity increased. When my *polissoir* struck the charms hanging from my bracelet, they clanged together near my ears and their silvery tinkling sounded sharp in the deathly stillness of the early morning hours, broken only once in awhile by the distant crowing of a cock. The continual ringing of the charms by my ears seemed the voice of a paschal serenade of bells to brighten my spirits, saying, "Hallelujah! Hallelujah, love is about to be born!"

When my hands were finally ready, I got down from the window.

I felt very happy, with the fresh happiness of early morning departures, foreseeing the way the road winds and trees pass by swiftly and the delicious vertigo of very deep gorges and the clear sound of water on the rocks, and the mystery—the great, wonderful mystery of Gabriel near me. In the half-dark and silent room, where a wise presentiment made me prefer to avoid the glare of artificial light, I undressed completely and, carefully, almost groping and blind in the dark, always expecting dawn, I began to bathe, to perfume and to dress myself afresh. So I would leave dressed in light, ethereal attire, as brides leave the church on the groom's arm, I put on my white organdy dress that I hadn't worn yet. In my ruffled outfit, which made me look so slim in its misty, trailing fullness, I looked in the mirror activated only by moon and starlight. It pictured me as hazy and transparent as if I were the vision of some poem. Proud of my idealized image, I began to move around the room like a fantastic ghost, sometimes imitating the poses classical ballerinas take, moving right or left to better see myself in different effects of half-light in the full-length mirror of my wardrobe. Enchanted by my own vision, I came and went in the mysterious room. Suddenly, I don't know why, the echoing click of my heels as I walked across the floor seemed like something that was pursuing me. The conscious fear of being afraid made me take off the shoes I was wearing, and I put on my white chamois slippers with rubber heels that make no noise when I walk.

And without the sound of footsteps, I pranced a moment more in front of the mirror.

But now, fear had caught me in its claws.

It had caught me, because now, seeing myself come and go, framed by the mirror, white and immaterial, I was so greatly impressed by my own lack of substance that I felt a kind of sharp cold that was slowly overpowering my whole body. No longer in the mood to lift my arms or stand on my toes, or take another step, frozen in front of my own paralyzed image, I clearly recalled, with vibrant faith, all the suggestive spiritualist beliefs, stories of the dead who come to warn the living. The principle of tortured souls always wandering, invisible, near us. The desperate pleas of people who have recently died, calling us from the dreadful torments of purgatory. Thinking all of this with my eyes wide open, staring into the mirror, I suddenly seemed to see that there, in the changing outline of one of my organdy sleeves, was the shape of Uncle Pancho's head, tragic, cold and stiff, lying beneath the white handkerchief, just as I had seen it during so many hours just two days ago. Looking at this hallucination, as if some ghastly insect were crawling up my sleeve, I shook my arm wildly, I moved away from the mirror and, shaking and full of remorse, I told myself that my incomprehensible fear must be a punishment for my selfish happiness, for my absolute indifference, and for abandoning my mourning.

To placate Uncle Pancho's offended soul that perhaps was hovering near me, my hands trembling, I felt for my long cloak of black velvet, and I felt for my floppy black velvet hat, and I hurriedly put them on, saying, "This way he can't object, for I'm wearing black!"

As I fastened the cloak I felt the delightful contact of the letter hidden in my bosom, and I felt strong again. Again I evoked the joy that my arrival would bring to Gabriel's anxious wait and, recovering from my fright, I added with a smile, "This way, too, mysterious and cloaked in black over my white bridal dress, I'll be, in appearance, as one should be, when one goes to a rendezvous of forbidden love, as Gabriel says."

To accentuate the mystery, I turned up my collar, tilted the brim of my hat down, and, thinking about the eyes that were soon to see me like this, I tried to see myself, and I peered into the mirror again.

Since the moon was almost completely covered by clouds and since there was still no hope of sunshine, there on the white surface, I could only see my black silhouette, melting into the surrounding blackness. And once more, without knowing why, I shivered from head to foot, from that same intense and superstitious cold.

The intense cold of fear, in bodies exhausted by lack of sleep and by the horrible vision of death! How it paralyzes our movements in the dark, how it allies itself with darkness, and how it makes us crave light, to dissipate strange and magical influences!

Before the mirror, dressed in black, my silhouette almost lost in the shadows, I felt again the icy blast of air, and this time it grew so strong that finally, despairing of having the sun decide to come up, with an abrupt and thoughtless gesture, I could stand it no longer and, blundering with quick, uncertain steps, I reached the head of the bed and turned on the overhead light, which flooded the room with brightness. Once the light was on, my fear evaporated, but I instantly understood that now, under the artificial light, a new, well-defined influence, much more terrible than fear, was clutching me with a great force of attraction. Nonetheless, paying no attention to it, to pull myself free of it with the sound of words, I told myself out loud that I must fix a little travel case with the things most indispensable to me. Moving left and right, all around the room, naming things one by one while I looked for them, I began to gather them in a pile on the bed.

Familiar objects, seen in full light, at moments of great crisis have a living soul that talks to us, gestures to us, wriggles under our touch, and sometimes even bites us, and scratches our fingers as we pick them up. The toothbrush, with its scent of toothpaste half vanished, is a voice that calls out and admonishes. The closed vanity case with the puff that moves inside like a prisoner is a very delicate conscience that formulates its protest in a soft voice. The teeth of the comb grab on to anything, not wanting to leave. The pins slip through the cracks in the pin case to prick the fingers that try to pick them up. The dozens of spying eyes on the thimble open in shock, recalling sewing sessions that we have shared here. The hairbrush bristles aggressively, like the unending bristles of regret. The cologne bottle has a cold silver cap. Oh! The cold metal of a bottle in one's hands at the moment of flight! How it protests and how it shouts of cold daggers, and cold revolvers, and of another distant and horrible cold—the cold of illness and poverty in the mortal cold of abandonment!

But still determined and tenacious, racing, paying no attention to the importunate voices of things, I went on collecting my travel articles on the bed, which was still made up and intact, through my sleepless night. When all the objects were together and ready, incapable of concentrating enough to mentally review what might be missing, I stood still a moment, looked around at the furniture, and murmured again aloud to inspire myself. "That's all. Now I need to add a few clothes. Yes, from my trousseau!"

For a second, all other feelings fled and I smiled with pleasure thinking of the delicious effect that the outfits of pink silk made as they clung softly to my white, silky skin. After evoking the image of myself in that glorious second of happiness, I went to the wardrobe to choose the clothes that I should take with me. Before opening the mirrored door, out of a feeling of irresistible curiosity, I tried to look at myself just as Gabriel was going to see me, that is, very close and under the direct rays of a bright light.

I stood in front of the mirror. Looking into my eyes like that, so close, made me feel I was in the presence of a very familiar and very loved person who was not me and who anathematized my behavior by the expression on her face, so pale, so grave, and so severe. And again, for the third time, standing before my own image, regretting my curiosity, I shivered violently from head to toe.

However, wanting to be strong, I made up my mind to chase away all my negative thoughts with the sheer power of my beauty, and I stood stock-still before myself. But at that cruel instant, between the black velvet of my cloak and the black velvet of my hat, my frightened face, pale and worn out, looked completely faded, with the hollow-eyed fatigue of sick people and the funerary marble of withered roses. Before the mirror's hateful lie, offended, indignant, I furiously answered no, that it was a lie that that pale, white image could be my own, my slender, perfect image of undisputed beauty, the same, the very same triumphant and glorious image that Gabriel adored and that Gabriel waited for with longing, dying of thirst. And defying the mirror, after thus exalting my own image, I tried to smile at it. But I couldn't smile. In my eager effort, I saw only how my white lips trembled imperceptibly, with a continual and nervous tremor. Then I told myself it was just because I wasn't wearing lipstick, and immediately, to give life to that tremulous and discolored mouth and to make my smile stand out and show off the whiteness of my teeth, I went to look for my lipstick among the things piled on the bed, and I painted my lips carmine. But the bright mouth remained mute and went on trembling obstinately in the mirror. Since that tremulous red lie reminded me suddenly of the painted lips that prostitutes wear on their weary faces, I quickly rubbed off the carmine with a white handkerchief.

Then I opened the wardrobe.

My pink, sweet-scented trousseau was lying as usual in orderly piles on its shelf. Hungry for happy and voluptuous impressions that would lift my spirits, I eagerly picked up one of the rosy stacks and, to see what the caress of silk on my face would say to me, as other times, with my two hands full, cupped together, as if some ideal lotion were overflowing them, slowly, I plunged my face into the perfumed softness. But this time, the touch of the silk as it caressed my cheeks did not speak to me of its suggestive origin in Paris, nor did it speak to me of love, nor of my beauty, but, instead, by a strange association of ideas, it reminded me vividly, with infinite cruelty, of its original and previous origin—that of two antique emeralds that were set in a very complex gold filigree and placed close together in a little green satin box that smelled of cedar and vetiver. Simultaneously, precisely and clearly in my ears, it brought back the voice of Grandmother, who, here in my own room, had said to me one day as she held out the emeralds in their open box, "They belonged to my mother, María Eugenia, and I've always set them aside to give to you as a gift on your wedding day. They were my only article of value . . ."

To chase away such a painful thought, I moved the silk garments away from my face and dropped them brusquely on the bed, I examined the pink clothes stretched across the wardrobe shelf and, energetically defying my memories, I spoke out loud again while I continued my preparations.

"Well, almost . . . I could almost carry all of it. If you fold silk right, it doesn't take up much room!"

And without further debate, in a few armfuls, I moved the garden of roses that was sown along the shelf. Then I went to look for my *nécessaire*, I opened it on a chair and I stood there perplexed, realizing that it was quite impossible to fit all the things on the bed into the hand luggage.

Then I remembered that near the laundry area, in the room where Aunt Clara neatly stores old furniture, including the big buffet with linens, the other big cabinet with the good china and baskets and steamer trunks, there was a small black leather suitcase in good condition, less bulky perhaps than the *nécessaire*, and in which, given its long, flat shape, all of my limited belongings could be squeezed.

I still stood perplexed between the chair and the bed, thinking over the plan.

Yes! Decidedly, I must give up the *nécessaire* and go get the suitcase. Go get the suitcase! And how could I cross the patio, go down the corridor, go through the kitchen, and open the corral door, and take down the chain to the laundry, and then cross, to the right, and finally enter the room where the trunks and old furniture are kept, feeling my way the whole distance, without turning on lights that could give me away, with the overwhelming fear that the dark now caused me?

To test the darkness, I came to this door that opens onto the patio, I opened it, I stuck my head out, and it seemed to me that out there, beyond the patio, the whole corridor was buried in deep shadows that were frightfully lugubrious and impenetrable. Then I lifted my eyes, and I saw that in the sky only a few very dim, dull stars were shining. Because it was cloudy. Maybe it was going to rain. Anxiously, in that enclosure where fear and darkness were holding me prisoner, I murmured in a low voice, my eyes imploring, and fixed on a star that was fading away, "Lord! When will it be daylight? When will it be daylight?"

Considering my inspection ended, I closed the door, and again studied the open *nécessaire* and the objects gathered on the bed. Finally I resolved, "It would be best to avoid complications, to take only a few items of clothing, to put the most indispensable things in the *nécessaire*, to leave the rest where it goes, and to wait for time to leave, forgoing the suitcase and the trousseau."

I looked sadly at my trousseau, which, docile and gentle, stretched out on the bed, was resigned to everything. My trousseau! So pretty, and so longed for, and so becoming to me!

But I reacted immediately. Oh, no, no, no! I could never leave my trousseau! It would be preferable to wait patiently for dawn and then go get the suitcase, in the light, and therefore unafraid. But suppose at dawn the maids were awake, and even up, and even moving around the corral and the kitchen? No, I couldn't wait, I had to take my trousseau, I had to get the suitcase, and I had to go now. I couldn't wait any longer, now while the servants were asleep. Just so, in the dark and all, without a light, feeling my way, and scared to death. Yes, right away, right away . . . now!

For the second time I walked to this door that leads to the patio, I opened it, walked out, and, unable to make up my mind, I stood in the luminous strip that fell on the patio from the half-open door of my lighted room.

At last, shakily, holding my breath, listening to the violent beating of my heart at every step, finding my way by the two strips of light thrown on the patio from the door and the open window of this room, I walked ahead until I reached the bend that the kitchen makes to the right of the corridor. When I reached there, I turned my head around to see how far I had come, and I stopped. The light from my room didn't reach to the kitchen. Therefore, to my dazzled eyes, and to the great excitement of my imagination, the darkened kitchen became a cavern of mysteries and horrors. Still, I found the courage to advance in the darkness with my eyes closed. I had to walk blindly and feel for the door that led to the laundry and the corral. I told myself that a box of matches would have saved me from this bad situation, but since I didn't have one or know where to find one, I went on fighting against the occult power that palpitates in the shadows, and with my hands open and trembling, I began to feel along the greasy wall of the kitchen. I suddenly thought about the cockroaches that sometimes walk on those walls at night and, horrified, I pulled my hands away, I backed up a few steps, and, increasing my fear with my horror of cockroaches, I stood frozen in the dark, fear sharpening my physical senses, which seemed to be concentrated entirely in my violently beating heart. Then I heard the cathedral clock striking in the distance. I listened, my hearing more acute in the dark, and I counted two quarter-hours. It was four-thirty! No matter how cloudy it might be, it would be dawn soon. Encouraged by this hope, I overcame my horror of cockroaches, returned to the wall, and felt for the door, and then for the bolt, I drew the bolt, and swung the door open. The fresh air in the corral blew on my face and, simultaneously, in the hazy light that barely filtered through the clouds, there appeared in view the chicken coop, the trees, clotheslines flowering with occasional pieces of clothing, the walls topped with tiles, and the big stones stained by soap, as if it all moved in a dance of capricious and fantastic forms. At that very moment, as I was going down the step at the doorway, a black shape went by me like lightning, near my feet, and was lost ahead under the dark tangle of plants. It was a cat that had come in over the rooftops to sniff around the kitchen. Unable to reason at all, as soon as I felt it brush past me, I was shaken by something like an electric shock, and I stepped back. As I did so, my head struck the feather duster, which, as usual, was hanging near the door. The unexpected contact with the feathers and the unexpected vision of the fleeing cat gave me a spasm of terror. Leaping away from the wall after the spine-tingling brush with the feathers, I stood in the laundry, my eyes wide, staring at the ground and paralyzed with shock. I wanted to run back to my room, but as if in a nightmare, I was in the implacable grip of fear and, worse, in my excited imagination I made an absurd tragedy of childish and macabre fears. Motionless, my eyes drawn as if by a magnet to the dark tangle of plants, I observed my thoughts.

"That black, sinister cat that was hidden out there! How could I be sure it wouldn't come back from its hiding place to treacherously jump on me and scratch out my eyes as they do, or sink its claws in my neck and cling and squeeze, until it chokes me, without having time to defend myself or even scream? Black cats with phosphorescent eyes that shine in the night like will-o'-the-wisps! I had always heard they were in league with the devil, and with witches, and with ghosts, and with all invisible and occult powers! Oh, the occult! Oh, disembodied spirits! It was all true! Many wise men had seen and believed in them firmly. Therefore, in the body of that black cat, might not some dreadful spirit have taken shape, wanting to stop me at all costs from leaving with Gabriel? Maybe it was some very powerful spirit that could read the future. Maybe it was someone who cared a great deal for me. Someone. Someone. Who could it be? Oh, no doubt it was 'he' who had led me, against my will, had made me leave my room, had brought me, helpless, to the corral, and held me there now, as if chained, solely to prevent my flight. Heaven knows by what fearful and sinister means . . . to prevent my flight . . . to prevent . . ."

Reacting again with that strange nervous energy that the memory of Gabriel's letter gave me from time to time, I exclaimed to myself defiantly, "Well, I'm going! In spite of 'him' and in spite of the others! Yes, I'm going with Gabriel, who is alive, and strong, and young, and rich and who loves me madly and will make me happy and will love me always. Yes! He'll love me always! He'll love me always!"

"Oh! Will he love me always?"

And feeling now as if a dagger of doubt had been painfully thrust into me much deeper than my fear, to escape it, unconsciously, I began to walk headlong into the room with the old furniture, and as I had done awhile before back in my lighted room, now in the total dark of this room full of old furniture, I accompanied the movement of my hands with the sonorous rhythm of words in whose noise the evil voices of my thoughts were drowned out to some extent.

My eyes closed tight and my arms outstretched in the darkness while I was feeling the furniture, I was saying, "Here, to the right, is the buffet with the linens. All right. This is the big mahogany table with the broken leg. Here is the dresser. Good. The china cabinet. The back wall. A trunk. Fine. Another trunk. Here . . . here's the suitcase!"

And grabbing the handles I lifted it in the dark. But I had forgotten that on top of it there was a chipped flower vase, which fell to the floor and shattered with a noisy shower of broken glass. Startled by the crash, I jumped nervously as I had before at sight of the cat. Then I remembered the vase on the suitcase, I understood what had happened and, coming back to the world of real dangers, I reflected, "Oh, my God! Suppose this infernal noise woke up the servants!"

Assaulted by a rational and probable fear, I stood still, watching for the slightest sign of alarm while I readied a plausible explanation for my very strange excursion. There wasn't a sound. No one had awakened. The silence was absolute. You could tell that everyone in the house was still sleeping deeply. Feeling that a great weight had been lifted from me, suitcase in hand, I decided to return to my room, passing quickly through the laundry and kitchen. I took a few steps toward the door. Before I reached it, some strange fascination stopped me, and from the center of the room I began to look again at the dark place where the cat had hidden.

It seemed to be getting light. Everything was quiet, very quiet. The corral was the same as always, with the clothesline festooned with white articles, with its soft country sweetness. Why, then, was I afraid of it?

Suddenly I shivered. Oh, there, right there, in the tangle of plants where the cat had hidden, there was a flash of light. Oh, how awful! Could it come from the very eyes of the cat? Suppose it was the pale reflection that announces ghosts, announcing to me the terrible vision of that spirit that had taken over the cat's body? The light grew, and grew, and grew. It was no illusion. It didn't seem to come from the underbrush now. Now the light was dancing. Good heavens, how it danced around the whole corral! And to the left I could hear something. It was something that seemed to be dragging itself lugubriously across the ground. Something that was getting closer, and closer, and closer as the light grew. Now it stumbled against the kitchen door. Now it stumped down the step. It kept coming with its stream of moveable light, it crossed to the right, and it was coming . . . it was coming toward the room, toward the room . . . toward me!

"Oh!!"

As if the specter of some singular Chinese hallucination, wearing a kimono and bedroom slippers, with a thin braid falling down the back, a lighted candlestick, and a face working with a flood of questions, in front of the room of old furniture, tragically appeared the grotesque and frightened figure of Aunt Clara.

When I recognized her beyond the nimbus of light the candle radiated, and thus realized that I was only dealing with the world of the living, I felt a tremendous relief, and meanwhile, still invisible in the shadows, I was reasoning and deducing,

"Why, it was only Aunt Clara's slippers and candle! Why didn't that occur to me before?"

Instinctively I hid the hand that was holding the suitcase behind my back and I waited quietly in the middle of the room. Aunt Clara, with her eyes dazed and vague, as if they were half opening still amid the fog of a dream, stared for a moment into the dark with her candle held high, and thus discovered me in the shadows, and as if she, too, were relieved of some great fear, she asked me very gently and wonderingly, "Whatever are you doing here, María Eugenia? At this time of the morning! You're wearing a hat? And your new velvet cloak!"

Keeping the suitcase hidden, my face well protected in the dark for my boldfaced lie, without the least logical sense, I began to mechanically stutter the most absurd and contradictory explanations.

"It was . . . Aunt Clara, because I couldn't sleep, you know? Not at all, not even one minute all night! I haven't slept for so long! And then, thinking about Uncle Pancho, I wanted to hear a mass for his soul, and so I wouldn't have to go to a later mass, you understand? I got up early and since I was cold I put on my wrap and at the same time, I put on my hat. But then, when I walked out, I saw it was too early . . . and since I felt . . . I don't know. . . . very restless, very hot, I came here to the corral to wait for dawn . . . But outside, you know, it's so damp, and that's why I came in this room . . . to wait here instead . . ."

I believe now that apparently Aunt Clara must have been greatly moved by the deep feeling of religious piety that induced me to go out so early after a night of insomnia. Thanks to her great emotion she paid no attention to anything else and she didn't catch on to the stuttering and vacillation of my stream of contradictory lies. That was why, without letting me finish, still wearing the halo of her flickering light, she exclaimed tenderly, vehemently, and very affectionately, "You see? Don't you see, my dear? I sent María del Carmen last night to tell you not to drink that cup of espresso coffee! But since you didn't want to eat at the table, but instead in your room, you didn't listen to me and you drank the coffee. I could just see it! Why didn't you let me know you couldn't sleep? I would have given you some drops of essence of orange blossoms, or it wouldn't have taken me a minute to make an infusion of lettuce leaves, which is wonderful for sleeping. And then later, we would have gone to mass together. Later. Of course. There's no need to go so early just because you're in mourning. That's going too far!"

I stood still, as if stunned, not answering a word, surprised by that touching and absurd credulity that solved everything.

With her poor, sleepy, exhausted face, which now looked doubly foolish because she was so ridiculously easy to deceive, and because of the Chinese air given her by the kimono and the thin braid in the grotesque flickering of the candle, she went on explaining, "Imagine the scare I had when I went to your room and didn't find you there, and looked for you all over the house and you weren't anywhere! Since it's so dark out here, I didn't dream you could have come to the corral like this. And the mess in your room!"

She smiled a smile of gentle reproach, which seemed frightfully dramatic to me, and she added tenderly, shaking her head, "Even with insomnia, María Eugenia, even at night, my Lord, you have your obsession of folding and unfolding your trousseau on the bed!"

I remained impassive, without moving, squeezing the handles of the suitcase hidden behind my back, while she, immobilized no doubt by my own immobility, and also excited by the fears that assault us at night, loquaciously continued that absurd dialogue, staged as we stood in the dark room full of old furniture, she in kimono, I wearing my hat, and between the two of us, to give the scene greater eccentric intensity, the dancing and intermittent light of the candle.

"I got up because Mama started feeling bad, fatigued, bad, really bad. Oh! She gets worse every day!"

She sighed and the candlelight trembled in the grief of the sigh.

"To give her drops to her, I went to the dining room to get some water, and I noticed the light was on in your room. After I did what I could for Mama, I went to see if you were all right, and imagine my surprise when I didn't find you in your room, or anywhere else. I felt like . . . oh, I don't know why I felt like something was wrong with you. I don't know why. Some terrible misfortune! And then, after awhile, I heard a noise out here."

A few words would have sufficed to calm any suspicion that still lurked in Aunt Clara's mind, in this way continuing the deceit, and then, half an hour later I could carry out my plan. However, those easy words, those brief, clear words, already framed in my mind, were not spoken by my lips.

Since then, today as yesterday, at night as in the day, awake or asleep, I never stop delving into my mind with these penetrating questions, "Why? Why did it happen? Why was it? What sincere and prescient ghost was it that finally arose in the true, mysterious night of myself?"

Yes, the ghost arose like a specter in the shadows, and commanding, powerful, terrible, spoke through my own mouth. It took my destiny in its claws and destroyed it cruelly. Imperiously and tyrannically it set my destiny rolling on these harsh rails, these two rails with no return that climb steeply toward my arid future, toward the burning sand of the desert through which, without rest, I must now walk forever. Forever!

What ghost could it have been?

I don't know. No! I don't know, nor have I found out, nor will I ever know anything about the profound occultism that stirs in the subterranean deeps of my soul. In these last hours of depression and resignation I have suffered greatly, sharpening my memory to analyze the causes that determined my behavior. It's useless. There is a void in my memory. About the end of that scene and about what happened afterwards, I have only vague impressions. Now I only remember faintly that while Aunt Clara was talking to me in her Chinese kimono with her candle burning, I started to lose consciousness of my own personality, I felt that something very oppressive was swelling in my chest, and it swelled more and more, until finally, when she said, "I don't know why it seemed to me that you were suffering some very great misfortune," without listening to anything else, unconsciously and swiftly, with a terrible cry like someone who begs for mercy, and like the cry that death no doubt chokes off on the tortured lips of a suicide, I, too, forsaken and suicidal, dropped the suitcase that slammed on the floor, I ran toward the door, and with my arms stretched out, and a voice that did not seem to be made of my own voice, I implored desperately, "Oh! Aunt Clara! Aunt Clara!"

And I clasped my hands about her neck, while my whole body, shaking with sobs and bathed in tears, suffered a terrible spasm of nervous crisis.

I can still hear Aunt Clara's voice, alarmed, sympathetic and gentle, as she maternally asked before the great drama of my two desperate hands around her neck and my head buried in her bosom, "What's wrong, my dear? What's wrong? What is it? What is it?"

I repeated mechanically through my intermittent sobs and all the muffled tones of terror, "I'm afraid, Aunt Clara! I'm afraid! Afraid! Afraid! Afraid!"

After that?

I don't know what happened after that. I think Aunt Clara talked to me again about the coffee that had kept me awake, she talked to me about nervous excitement, about my nights of insomnia, about the shock of Uncle Pancho's death, while, step by step, holding me tightly in her embrace, despite my torrent of tears and sobs, she led me through the laundry, the kitchen, the corridor, she led me past the bleeding wound of my room where the light streamed from it onto the patio, and she finally left me tucked in Grandmother's own bed.

Very close to Grandmother, who listened with emotion to Aunt Clara's account, my body, stretched out under the absolute renunciation of my will, had the horrible immobility of bodies chained for torture.

Very slowly, with the voluptuous cruelty of prolonged martyrdom, a crowd of conflicting feelings passed in review, a blood-drenched inner crowd that I can't recognize now, because its destructive passage left my memory almost blind.

Nevertheless, I remember something. Yes, I remember vaguely.

In the physical vision of my eyes, facing me, on the wall, were the big roses drooping at intervals on the tapestry, Grandfather Aguirre's picture in his hero's uniform, the big antique wardrobe in whose labyrinth of carvings my painful vision was lost at times, in the corner the wicker chair, next to the chair the altar, on the altar the venerable old Nazarene, black with age, carrying his cross under his glass dome, and suddenly, beside my mouth, the sedative Aunt Clara was holding out to me, in a glass that was one of the set of glasses we three drink out of every day.

But there, there, inside, in the inner vision of my mind, was the desperate attraction of the letter. The letter glowing with love and ignominy that shouted at me, clinging like a flame to my breast, in my imagination showing me clearly the door to the street, the few steps I would have to walk to the corner, around the corner, the automobile, and in the automobile, he, consumed by love, full of anxiety, watching everyone passing by, devouring the street with his eyes, and waiting, waiting, waiting, always waiting!

Oh! The horrible pain of Grandmother's face, emaciated and condemned to death, her hands caressing my forehead and her voice in my ears, the torture of temptation still burning, killing me slowly. And the minutes were passing! And day had dawned at last! A sunbeam was stretching across the floor. And fixed in my mind was the idea of making some excuse to leave the room, the short distance to reach the corner, on the corner the great black tip of the closed car, and in the car lifelong happiness for one condemned to death, already dead, awaiting my pardon.

Oh, no, no, the horrible torture of that morning, whose light my eyes never should have seen. That cruel torture, even though my memory retained many of its details, I wouldn't be able to describe it now with words. Words can't say! Words don't know!

🙣   🙣   🙣

After the hours of torment, when the time elapsed had completely resolved my dilemma, tired of crying, exhausted,

I fell little by little under the influence of the sedatives, and finally I fell asleep lying close to Grandmother, whose gentle voice caressed my ears, skillfully soothing like a cradle song.

I had an agitated dream full of subconscious conflicts, although the dream was very short. When I opened my eyes, I fixed them upon the carved labyrinths of the wardrobe. Still palpitating with memories of the struggle, I drew this conclusion, "Because now, after what I know, I can't marry Leal!"

Recalling the telegram Gabriel had given me at Uncle Pancho's house, I thought of the arrival of the train, I saw the late hour marked by the clock, and, without a word, I got up, went to the telephone, and called Leal. He answered it himself and after listening indifferently to his words of sympathy, I asked him to come to see me, as soon as possible, because I had something very urgent and very interesting to tell him.

When they came to let me know that Leal had arrived, I was ready to see him, and rising from the chair where I happened to be sitting, I started for the drawing room. When Aunt Clara saw that I was going immediately, just as I was, with no primping, she was amazed and asked me, "Are you going to see him like that, María Eugenia? By yourself, wearing that old dress, without even powdering your nose?"

To prepare her for the sensational news I planned to tell her a little later, I stopped and answered resolutely, "If Leal has come here at this time of day, Aunt Clara, it's because I called him myself to talk to him alone. I called him urgently, and when you call someone urgently you don't make him wait. Besides, I'm not in any mood to put on airs!"

And I walked out.

When I entered the drawing room where Leal was waiting for me, I came in resolutely, firmly, sure of myself, and I felt an immense aversion to him. I remember that I had prepared how I would break off with him, and that on the way I had been rehearsing mentally, "Leal, while you have been absent, I have discovered that I don't love you enough to marry you, and therefore, since it involves the happiness of our whole lives . . ." But as I appeared at the door, he, who had apparently heard my footsteps, when he saw me, rose, very surprised, came to meet me, greeted me by taking my hands in his, looked at me with amazement, and finally said more or less what Grandmother had said early this morning, "Oh! How emaciated you are! How pale and thin you look, María Eugenia! How ever could you have gotten so run down in just a few days?"

Instinctively I turned my head to look in the mirror, and really, as carelessly as I was dressed, I looked pale, lifeless, hollow-eyed, almost ugly, and above all, I saw a striking resemblance to Aunt Clara's faded features. Given my state of nervous depression, that likeness struck a spark in my mind like a horrible revelation. I remembered the scene in the early hours of the morning in front of my wardrobe mirror, and I also recalled the expression I had heard so many times about Aunt Clara, "She was a flower that lasted only a day. She was precious when she was fifteen; at twenty-five she wasn't even a shadow of what she had been."

I felt that was what they would be saying about me, and I imagined my beauty in total eclipse. In the face of such a catastrophe, a horde of cowardly feelings rose up in my soul. Watching them spring forth so abruptly, I stood there feeling inhibited, disoriented, in suspense. Then, slowly, I pulled my hands away from Leal, I invited him to sit down, and when we were both seated on the damask sofa, I began to say hesitantly, "I've spent some bad nights, you know? They've left me very run down. I'll feel better after I've rested for a few days. Because, I slept very poorly last night too!"

And hastily, as I said this, I straightened my hair and smoothed my skirt with my open hands.

While I was talking, for his part, following his established custom, he had leaned so far against the sofa that the sofa back made a creaking noise. To change positions, he leaned his head on his closed hand, he looked at me with a penetrating and fixed gaze, and with his eyes pinned on me, and with the solitaire, which was like another terrible eye embedded beside his temple, he asked me, lighting his question with the sparkling of the diamond, "Well, come, come, what is this thing that is so interesting and so urgent that you need to tell me?"

With his free hand he pulled the tip of the silk handkerchief that was tucked in one of his pockets, he wiped his face, waiting indulgently for my answer, and a penetrating smell of fine tobacco mixed with Origan by Coty, "Leal's scent," so familiar to me, spread, suggestively, through the room.

I was still perplexed, applying to myself the pain of those opinions I had heard about Aunt Clara's fleeting beauty. I had lost all unity of thought, and I had muddled the firm and precise form of my speech to tell Leal it was all over. Feeling that I was on the witness stand because of that imperious question circled by lights from the diamond solitaire, and perfumed by Coty's Origan, I looked, cornered, for any momentary interchange, and I spoke stammering and timid, "I just . . . I wanted to talk to you about our wedding . . . I think . . . that is to say, I think it would be better not to get married yet . . . let's wait . . . at least until a few months have gone by . . ."

With his energetic and booming voice, he, who always knows what he wants and who always says exactly what he requires, lifted his head from his hand, sat up regally on the sofa, and interrupted me instantly.

"Absolutely not; under no circumstances! I don't believe a wedding already planned should ever be postponed because of mourning. Ten days after the death, and that's enough! Not one day longer! We'll have a private wedding, just the family. Otherwise . . ."

And to show me the inconveniences of postponing the wedding, and the advantages of having it at the time agreed upon, Leal's voice, resolute, virile, overflowing with words, with logic and common sense, began to set forth arguments and enumerate circumstances. A complete change of plans would cause many possible upsets in his business affairs; Grandmother's condition, which he had just heard about, and which could worsen; the house, which was completely ready now; the other house in the country had been rented for the honeymoon; his family had made plans to attend; and a hundred thousand other things of a pressing and urgent nature, which I can't remember now.

Not wanting to admit defeat and trying to reply, I was beginning, "It's just that . . . It's . . ."

But he wouldn't let me talk, and since he went on explaining so loquaciously, I didn't speak another syllable, but dedicated myself to observing him, as I sat mute, perplexed and absent.

Really, of all his powerful arguments, and all his eloquent enumeration, I had only given consideration to the complications that Grandmother's present illness could bring us. When I heard her mentioned by that concise voice, I caught a clear glimpse of the almost certain catastrophe of my life if I lost this opportunity now to get married. If Grandmother died, there would be years of mourning and after the mourning . . . oh! After the mourning, in case I had also lost the great power of my beauty, my only guarantee and my only reason for being, the only thing left for me would be the same existence that Aunt Clara led, forever humiliated and dependent on Uncle Eduardo and his family.

No doubt it was due to these rapid visions of the future that, a few seconds later, when the same concise voice continuing its enumeration, mentioned the house that "was now completely ready and waiting for us," I saw it open in my mind like an asylum to save me, and I said to myself with huge satisfaction, "My house!!"

Now, surrendering completely, I don't know whether defeated by the force of my destiny, or by the absolute negation of my will, annulled by Leal's powerful will, without attempting the slightest reply, I fell silent definitively, with the resigned silence that gives consent.

Leal's eloquence, encouraged by my silence, kept growing. He adduced reasons, he cited cases, and to spin them out fully he acted and argued freely and logically for a long while.

I looked at his face, pretending to pay close attention, but in reality I was no longer listening to him. Absorbed in myself, alone with my drama and my defeat, I watched his flow of speech and I considered the great triumphant vulgarity of that firm, concise spirit, symmetrically squared like a fortress, powerful and guarded like one, omnipotent to always offer to my weakness every kind of material support, and incapable of even suspecting a single one of the subtle refinements of my soul.

The powerful timbre of his voice, the sensitiveness of my hearing, made me foresee all of the protective and hateful weight of his impending despotism, deforming the fragile beauty of my body, unconsciously and cruelly trampling on the infinite longings of my spirit, irremediably my master, and irremediably my executioner. That's what I felt and foresaw in the liveliest fashion as I stared at Leal with my lying, attentive face, not even blinking. But mentally, because of an irresistible feeling of vengeance for what was going to be my eternal servitude, I compared his grotesque inferiority with Gabriel's great superiority, and I imagined almost with fear and with much perverse delight, how ridiculous he would have looked if what nearly happened, had happened.

When a little later Leal ended his visit and rose to say goodbye, he again took my hands in his. Then, with a sort of very commanding affection, as if those hands he held, and my face and my whole body were something inanimate, acquired by him and that belonged to him in some absolute way, he said, "Now, you must take care of yourself! Eat more and above all, rest. Lots of rest!" Then he added, "And there's nothing else to say about the wedding. It's settled. A week from tomorrow!"

I responded like an echo, "Yes, yes. A week from tomorrow!"

While his echoing steps moved away through the small parlor, the corridor, the entrance hall, and were finally lost on the sidewalk outside, I sat still on the sofa, my arms limp, my eyes staring at the floor, thinking and thinking.

Summing up all that violent and momentous process, I now felt my soul hardening into a profound disgust with myself. The duplicity, the cowardice, the humble renunciation, the absurd discord between my convictions and my behavior! My behavior, my cowardly behavior, criminal to myself, was at the same time horribly disloyal to the man who in one week was going to give me a luxuriously appointed home, filled with everything I needed, and his name and his support, and a position in society, and a secure future sheltered from want and humiliating dependency.

Perhaps it was a strong need to define and rehabilitate my behavior for myself that finally gave me an idea.

Before carrying it out I looked at the clock. It was three-thirty in the afternoon. I thought that by then Gabriel must be at his house, still waiting for some answer from me. Without considering it further or wasting a minute, I came to my room, closed the door, and here on this very desk, mute witness to my hours of infinite love and infinite dreams of happiness, right here, on this smooth white surface, I spread out a sheet of paper that I had chosen, stamped, perfumed, clean, and not understanding how I could write such a thing, I wrote:

"Señor Gabriel Olmedo:

"Last night I read the letter that you had the insolence to send me. I'm not returning it to you in this very envelope, torn to shreds, as your audacity deserves, and as I would like to do, because last night, as soon as I read it, I ripped it to pieces and burned it in my first reaction of disgust. I don't know who you take me for. I think the day before Uncle Pancho died, there in the dining room of his house, I told you very frankly what I thought about you. I don't wish to repeat it now because I don't like to be insulting. The only reason I am writing is to warn you that if you continue to harass me with degrading propositions, come what may, I will inform César Leal."

The name "César Leal" sounded too pompous to me because of its double meaning and it seemed to me it could sound ridiculous. I erased the two words, I decided to discard the letter, I carefully chose another sheet of paper, I copied what I had written and continued.

"I will inform my fiancé. I want you to know that I am not alone. I have someone to protect me, and incidentally I wish to tell you that the man who will know how to defend me against you will be my husband one week from now, because I esteem him greatly, I love him with all my heart, and moreover I consider him vastly superior to you from every point of view."

And I signed:

María Eugenia Alonso.

Then with a kind of deeply voluptuous cruelty I reread what I had written, I folded the sheet, put it in an envelope, and wrote "Señor Gabriel Olmedo" on it, and rushed to find Aunt Clara to explain to her, "Aunt Clara, I have written to Gabriel Olmedo, as you told me to do yesterday. Here's the letter. It would be best to send it right away because he should be home now, and later it might be hard to find him. I think I heard him say he has a trip planned, I don't know where."

Aunt Clara was very satisfied with the success of her advice and with my feeling of gratitude and she answered, "Naturally, naturally! You couldn't fail to do it. Remember all he did and all his affection."

And she went in search of Gregoria to have her take the letter to Gabriel immediately.

Just before Gregoria left, with her black shawl already over her head and the letter gleaming white in her hands, she came up to me and with her back to Aunt Clara, asked me softly, less with her voice than with her astute, all-seeing and all-knowing eyes, "Shall I wait for an answer?"

I replied in the same tone, "Yes, Gregoria, wait."

I still remember the sound of her footsteps fading in the distance as she left with my cruel denunciation. To further crush my spirit, the sound of her footsteps was like the tragic and solemn sound made by a funeral procession.

But Gregoria, who apparently had some business of her own to take care of, left in the early afternoon, and came back only when night had fallen.

Exhausted by depression and grief, I was waiting for her, lying in bed under the sheets, in a kind of nervous frenzy. That is why when I heard her returning at last, her steps like the sound of mourners returning to the home of the dead after leaving the body in the grave, when I heard and recognized her footsteps, I leapt from my bed and, barefoot and in my nightgown, looked through the patio door, calling secretly, "Gregoria! Gregoria!"

Then I went back to bed.

At my call, she came in the room, her black shawl that covered her head casting shadows across her face and falling over her chest, just as if she were some doleful sorceress. She stood quietly beside the bed waiting for me to speak. The half-light in the room was sufficient to give the scene the great spiritual intensity of confidences where the participants don't look each other in the eye. So I waited a moment also; I withdrew into myself and I asked in a low voice, putting my whole soul in the simple question, "Did you hand the letter to him personally as I asked you to do, Gregoria?"

Invisible and mysterious under the black shawl she answered sadly, "I put it in his hands myself."

She was quiet a second before adding more sadly, "The poor man read it in front of me."

My voice intense with anxiety, I asked again, "How did he look while he was reading it, Gregoria? And afterwards? He must have said something. What did he say to you after he finished reading?"

Gregoria hesitated when she heard the mortal anxiety of those two questions, but finally, touched, she decided on the truth and she related, "How he looked while he was reading, María Eugenia, I couldn't see because the letter was hiding his face. Well, I can say, after he read it he was, how can I explain it? He looked pale and shaky, just like someone who has had a great shock! And then he told me with a kind of laugh that was sadder than if he were crying, 'Well, what can I do! But tell María Eugenia for me that all this she has written here is a lie! And tell her too that since I can't embark today because the ship has already left, by mid-week, alone, completely alone, do you understand? I'm leaving Venezuela never to return.'"

Gregoria commented, "I say that by that he wanted me to tell you, María Eugenia, that he's separating from his wife forever."

That simple tale that I had waited for echoed in the darkness of the room with the dread solemnity of a death sentence ringing in the ears of a criminal.

When her pained voice fell silent, my only reply was to grab a great fistful of the sheets with my nervous hands. With the sheets stuffed in my mouth, I choked back a terrible sob that wrenched my chest, then I hid my head under the pillow and thus submerged deeply in myself, I was no longer aware of Gregoria.

I didn't even hear her walk away discreetly and compassionately.

In my overwhelming grief and in the intensity of my renunciation, that merciful phrase, "Tell María Eugenia that all this that she had written me is a lie," shone blindingly in my mind like a light made up of both desperation and joy. Very clearly, in the soft, black darkness under the pillow, I heard the phrase repeated by Gregoria. I heard it vibrate in my ears spoken by the unforgettable voice of Gabriel, and I ceaselessly blessed him. Oh, how good, yes, how immensely generous and good Gabriel was, not wanting to believe the infamous lie of my letter! He tore my love from its grave to carry it with him and adore it, always martyred and bloody in his memory! How we two would have fulfilled our lives, and how happy we would have been! Oh! How wildly happy we would have been together!

Seeing with my own eyes and touching with my own hands this great, odious lie which society decorates with artificial flowers, giving it the appearance of morality, no matter that it goes against nature, I compared the joyous kingdom that would have been my future with Gabriel with what is to be the dark slavery that awaits me. I thought about the iniquitous injustice with which our shares are distributed in the great fair of life. All the happiness for some, all the pain for others. I thought too about the invisible force that fatally guides our destinies, and with my face always hidden under the tear-drenched pillow, I condensed that complex absurdity into a single word, and I murmured many times, desperate and defeated, "Oh! Life! Life!"

It was then, worn out by the exhaustion of so many emotions, that I slowly fell into this long, deep, and dark sleep that has lasted almost twenty-four hours.

🙠   🙠   🙠

Today, in order to tell my story to the end, I have written my poor, sad adventure for a long time.

I have just halted my pen, and I observe that it is midnight—a midnight all white with moonlight.

It is like Saturday's midnight, except that this one is brighter and naturally it has fewer stars. Everything else is the same—the same blue in the sky, the same twinkling stars, the same orange trees on the patio, the same orange blossoms on the trees, and here near me, the same wrought-iron bars.

However, to keep me company in my sorrow, today everything is in mourning, just as two nights ago everything was festive to keep me company in my mad happiness.

Oh! Good and maternal nature rejoices and grieves with us, without ever changing her dress. Like her silent, sentimental children, she too carries her joy or sorrow hidden in the deepest part of her heart.

On the other hand, here in this room it's a different matter. The doll lamp has changed its place on my desk, and behind me, under her insinuating light my little personal armchair is not empty. My wedding dress lies on it in a languid faint. Aunt Clara, thinking she would please me greatly, brought it into my room at nightfall, when I had just gotten out of bed and started writing. They had just brought it from the dressmaker's. Aunt Clara herself took it and, hurrying, came to knock on my door shouting phrases of happy excitement.

"Open the door, María Eugenia! Open up! Open! Look what I'm bringing you!"

I hid my papers, I opened the door, and it was the wedding dress which, in Aunt Clara's arms, was spilling its lacy foam from its wooden box. She put the box on the bed, lifted the dress by the shoulders and said, smiling brightly, perhaps to distract me from this gloomy melancholy that, as I can see, has marked my face with its stigma.

"Try it on! Yes, try it on right now; let's see how it looks on you!"

I was still standing near the door, stern and somewhat out of sorts because of the sudden interruption. I looked the dress up and down with a rapid glance and I remember that I instantly observed, "Oh! They didn't fix the veil completely loose as I wanted! It wasn't supposed to be this way; not this way."

Then remembering that all of that blatant lie of the dress was going to forever cover my terrible silent truth, I added nervously, "I won't try it on today. It would look awful on me with these circles under my eyes and as run down as I look!"

Then, ceremoniously and taking care not to crush it, Aunt Clara slowly rested it on the chair, saying, "This isn't like you, María Eugenia! To get the dress and not try it on! And I so wanted to see you in your bridal gown."

"You'll see me, Aunt Clara, you'll see me, don't worry. But not today. You see how my face is today, and with this exhaustion, I'd be an ugly, sad bride."

"You could never be ugly," objected Aunt Clara with conviction.

Without insisting any more, after studying the dress from different perspectives, she left the room. I closed the door after her, I was absorbed in the stream of my memories, and from that moment, behind my back, my chair has been carefully watching over my pretty, snowy guest.

During these long, feverish hours of the night, full of the pain of memory, and full of the obsessive enigma of myself, I had totally forgotten its majestic white presence. Now, though, sitting before my table, I stop writing from time to time, I slightly turn my head, and my eyes wander to the dream of foamy lace.

At this pious and reverent hour, how the black chair silently speaks, and how the limp whiteness screams in its black arms! The chair seems like a sadistic lover embracing a dead woman. The disjointed dress is a corpse, with its two empty sleeves open to form a cross and drooping almost to the floor. It looks like the ravished, incorporeal body of a young girl. Now, under the fantastic light of my little green lamp, the filmy, empty dress is a cadaver without a soul. One of those bodies that are buried alive in some cruel sacrifice!

No doubt that is why my whole being, from head to toe, feels a living part of this tableau of perverted love.

My eyes are fused with it, I stare, and stare at length, and, as usual, I see much, I feel even more, and I understand imperfectly.

Oh! The mystery of that dress, swooning in death in the chair's embrace. Is it the symbol of my soul without a body in the arms of Gabriel? Or can it be the symbol of my body without a soul in the arms of Leal?

My body without a soul!

Oh! Highest gratification of souls that intangibly yield themselves, having never felt the impure touch of the body! Oh! Perverse voluptuousness, profound voluptuousness of bodies destined to writhe with pretense in the repugnance of kisses that do not touch the soul! Oh! The sublime lie of silent suffering! Sacrifice! Object of my affection! Ruler that desires my whole life for yourself! At this august hour of acute awareness, with my eyes fixed on the dead pristine dress lying on my little chair, I have tried to decipher the mysteries that rule my destiny, and I only see your name arise, floating in the symbolic foam of lace. Your name! Your name is Sacrifice! Oh, but wait, wait, for now, in ecstacy, enlightened by your name, on the symbolic froth of lace, at last I am reading the beauty of my destiny.

As in the ancient tragedy, I am Iphigenia. We are sailing against adverse winds, and in order to save this ship of the world that, manned by I know not whom, races to sate its hatreds I know not where, it is necessary for me, branded by centuries of servitude, to yield up my docile, enslaved body as a burnt offering. He alone can extinguish the ire of the god of all men, in whom I do not believe and from whom I expect nothing. Dread ancestral deity, Sacred Monster with seven heads that are called society, family, honor, religion, morality, duty, conventions, and principles. Omnipotent divinity whose body is the ferocious self-love of men. Insatiable Moloch, thirsty for virgin blood, on whose barbarous altar thousands of young girls are immolated! And docile and white and beautiful like Iphigenia, here I am ready for my martyrdom! But before giving myself up to my executioners, as I sit before this candid whiteness which is to clothe my body, I want to shout aloud, so that my whole conscious being will hear.

It is not to the bloody cult of the ancestral God of seven heads that I meekly offer myself for the holocaust. It is to another much-higher deity that I feel alive in myself. It is to this great anxiety, much more powerful than love, that moves within me, rules me, governs me, and leads me to high, mysterious purposes that I accept without understanding them. Spirit of Sacrifice, my only Lover, more perfect Husband than love, you and you alone are the God of my holocaust, and the immense anxiety that rules and governs me for life. In my mad race as an enamored handmaiden, it was you I pursued without knowing who you were. Now thanks to the revelations of this greatest of nights, I have just seen your face, I have recognized you and for the first time I look at you and I adore you. You are the Husband of all sublime spirits, you shower on them continually the gifts of voluptuous suffering and you make them flower daily with the open roses of abnegation and mercy. Oh! Lover, Lord, and God of mine, I too have sought you without rest, and now that I have seen you, I desire and implore the beauty of your cruel body, which embraces and kisses with torture. I too long to feel your deep and burning kiss, which, lips pressed together, will kiss me eternally on my silent mouth. I too long for you to take me in your thorny arms, to delight in me and to make me for once and always intensely yours, because as love engenders all bodies in pleasure, you, a thousand times more fertile, with your kiss of pain, engender the infinite beauty that surrounds us with light and redeems the world from all iniquity!